The
Merchants
of
Souls

The
Merchants
of
Souls

John Barnes

A Tom Doherty Associates Book  New York

THE MERCHANTS OF SOULS

Copyright © 2001 by John Barnes

Edited by Patrick Nielsen Hayden

A Tor Book
Published by Tom Doherty Associates, LLC
175 Fifth Avenue
New York, NY 10010

www.tor.com

Tor® is a registered trademark of Tom Doherty Associates, LLC.

Library of Congress Cataloging-in-Publication Data

Barnes, John.
        The merchants of souls / John Barnes.
            p. cm.
        "A Tom Doherty Associates book."
        ISBN 0-312-89076-1
        1. Leones, Giraut (Fictitious character)—Fiction. 2. Life on other planets—Fiction. I. Title.

    PS3552.A677 M46 2001
    813'.54—dc21

                                                        2001042323

First Edition: November 2001

Printed in the United States of America

0 9 8 7 6 5 4 3 2 1

For Dad, and it's way overdue.

I will make one song out of the utter void—
Not about me or anyone,
Not about love or youth,
Made of nothing else at all.
Merely found while sleeping on my horse.

Could I have been born at a good time?
Not happy, or angry,
Not foreign, or native,
Unable to be anything else at all.
Transformed by her, the power who lives in the high mountains.

People have to tell me
Whether I am asleep or awake.
My heart is so mauled by grief,
I'm not ready to face a mouse,
I swear by St. Martial.

I am sick and I feel death coming.
Or so I am told. I know what doctor I need.
Sometime I will seek Doctor I-don't-know-who-that-is,
You will know which doctor I found, the right one if I heal,
The wrong, if I sicken.

I have a friend named I-don't-know-who-that-is,
I swear oaths that I've never seen her,
She has never healed me nor sickened me,
She has never given me any reason to care.
Thus no Frenchman or Norman has had to come and see me.

I have never seen her. I love her with all my strength.
I deny that she has ever healed or sickened me.
But when I see her, I am healed,
And, sick at heart, I say to my friends, "I don't know who that is.
I know a prettier, kinder, worthier one."

I don't know where she lives,
The mountains? The plains?
I fear to speak of any pain from her,
And the fear itself hurts.
I knew the pain I would feel if I stayed,
So I rode this way.

I have made this song. Really, I don't care.
I will send my song to someone—
Who will send it to other someones—
I don't know who that is, that my song will reach, in Anjou,
Who will have, in her sweet secret treasure-box,
The key.

—GUILHEM IX, COUNT OF POITOU, DUKE OF AQUITANE

Part One

So
I
Rode
This
Way

1

On Söderblom, there is almost never a still puddle, however small, because waves form so easily in the low gravity. That, and the never-ceasing winds, make the sea restless beyond any other in human space.

The waves are big and slow. It makes some people ill to watch. Me, I thought the waves were soothing.

The bright light of two of Söderblom's moons, both high overhead, and the scattered light from the warm sea, erased all but the brightest stars. I could have read by that light, easily. I could have sat there all night, comfortably—sand, air, and water were all at room temperature, and in low gravity, buttocks don't tire from sitting in the sand. I could have undressed and walked into the sea for a swim, unashamedly. In Hedonia, nobody would have cared, or noticed. I could do almost anything here.

I sat on the low rise, looking across the silver-gray beach at the big black waves. They marched onto the shore like a slow procession of idiotic monsters.

Self-pity is an unattractive emotion that leads to unfortunate behavior. It can cause me to drink heavily, pick quarrels, go to bed with the first willing partner, or sit on a beach feeling sorry for myself.

It was the night after the afternoon of my divorce. Like most divorces, it had been overdue, and had involved betrayals of trust, not all of them by the married people. Shan—my friend, boss, nearly a second father—had not only known of Margaret's affair; he had ordered her to continue it, because the Office of Special Projects had been gathering intelligence on her lover.

And it had all been for nothing. Despite dozens of OSP operations, Briand had been the first world ever totally lost to the rest of humanity. If anyone was still alive there, it would be decades before we could contact them.

Set against the total loss of a planet, Shan's failure as a friend didn't look so big.

Well. I wouldn't be seeing Shan for a while, anyway. I was on a stanyear's paid leave. Margaret and I had come to Hedonia, here on Söderblom in the Eta Cassiopeia system, to try to heal our marriage. We had struggled along for about forty unpleasant days, some promising, most not, until the day just past, when, still sullen and angry at breakfast, we had talked idly about what we might do that day, taken a walk on the beach, stopped for lunch . . . and at lunchtime, Margaret had said, emphatically, that she was now sure nothing could be worked out. "It's just time, high time, so let's get it over with, Giraut."

We agreed that I would stay on in the house we were renting, and arranged a room in a hotel for Margaret. After tonight, she'd be springing back to Caledony to visit her family for a while.

We hired an adjudicator to divide the common property, which took him something like ten minutes—like any people who value convenience, Hedons take care of their bureaucrats and reward efficiency. The adjudicator's settlement gave the common property to whoever bid the highest for it and the cross-compensations came out about even. We hooked up to a brain reader to prove we weren't crazy or lying. Then we signed the papers and shook hands. One hour after lunch, it was all done.

If I didn't go near Margaret's hotel till sometime tomorrow afternoon, I could avoid running into her. It was cowardly, but at the moment I wasn't worrying about fine points of *gratz* and *enseingnamen*.

With two nearly-full moons overhead, and the other one close to new, the tide was unusually high. Each wave seemed to lay up onto the beach, then drag itself down, in a swirl of rasping white noise.

This might be a good place to bring a woman for a long conversation about life and art and meaning, perhaps with a bottle of Hedon Gore, the local deep-red wine. I was slightly, distantly pleased that I was thinking of bringing a woman here. Perhaps my first sign of life?

I watched more waves. The two moons sailed farther down the slate night sky, toward the sea in the west, leaving a belt of blackness, jeweled by the few visible stars, along the tops of the trees that lined the eastern horizon behind me.

My com chimed. I pulled it out of my pocket. "Yes."

"Giraut, this is Paxa Prytanis. Piranesi and I ran into Margaret, and she told us the news. We were wondering how you're feeling and if you'd like to come by our place in the next few days for a Service of Consolation."

The Service of Consolation is the Hedon tradition of marking the end of a relationship with a quiet evening in which the friends of the grieving person feed him a good meal and fuck him silly. I had heard that, normally, Hedons only did a Service of Consolation for a close friend, and we'd really only known each other since the Briand mission. But maybe because Piranesi Alcott and Paxa Prytanis were married OSP agents, they understood and wanted to help. Or maybe the Hedon definition of close friends was as elastic as their concept of marriage, which specifically disavowed monogamy.

I had been not-answering for a long time. "Uh, it's just that it's terribly soon for me to think about it, but it's a very kind offer, and I'll call you back in a day or two."

"Don't fret about it too much. Just accept. There's no sense being primitive and feeling bad for one second more than you need to."

"Primitive" is a dirty word to Hedons. They sometimes say it where I'd say "moral," sometimes where I'd say "self-defeating." To them, all three concepts are the same.

"Well, then, I accept. I think I might like it very much."

"We'll do our best to make *sure* you like it very much." She didn't purr it seductively, as a woman might anywhere else. Being Hedon, she used the same tone she'd have used to assure me that she had a good recipe for duck à l'orange, or that the guest room bed was comfortable.

"I'll keep that in mind," I said, "really. And it made me feel much better that you called. We'll get together for something or other within a few days. *Que merce, que gratz.*"

She laughed merrily. "I already invited you to a Service of Consolation," she said. "You don't need to seduce us with your sensual language. Though I suppose any Occitan is incorrigible, about his language and about seduction."

"That's what makes us Occitan," I agreed. "Thank you, again, for calling."

Then Piranesi got on the com, and I had much the same conversation with him that I'd had with his wife, perhaps with somewhat less sexual undertone. After I hung up I noticed I really was feeling better. I walked along the beach in the double moonlight—so bright I could see colors—casually looking for mimic-seals, the Hedon contribution to engineered wild species. They're highly intelligent perpetual pups, bright as chimps, madly playful, and genetically wired to be very affectionate to people. I thought I might enjoy throwing a stick for one, but none turned up.

Not long before dawn, I climbed a dune and sat looking out over the deep-green salt marsh to the east, with the sea at my back, to watch Eta Cassiopeia rise.

If I wanted, I could stay in Hedonia forever, drifting from one meaningless amusement to another. I was a wealthy man, even for our wealthy age. In addition to the ordinary standard living allowance from my home culture, I had two ample pensions: I had put in something more than twelve stanyears' service with the Council of Humanity, as an artistic affairs diplomatic specialist, which had been my normal cover, and exactly the same amount of time with the office of Special Projects, my covert job for Shan.

Since the Briand disaster, the existence of the OSP was now public, and there was talk of abolishing it, publishing its records, and perhaps inflicting various punishments on its past agents, but I doubted that I had done anything that would merit more than a few minutes of neuroduced pain or fifty standays in the dullhouse. Even if the Council repudiated all of the OSP's former obligations, my Council pension alone would still be more than I could spend.

Aside from my three regular checks, I had royalties from my music. As part of my cover in artistic affairs, I had performed and composed all over the Thousand Cultures. My composing and performing careers were still reaping the benefits of all that free travel and publicity. Many recordings and songs were still earning very nice piles of money, and if I wanted to return to it, I could probably restart my musical career, get back to composing regularly, and—after enough practice—back to performing. Even though my last few releases had sold mainly to completists and eccentrics, every new release pulled the early, popular recordings back into vogue. I might pick up a concert booking or two, or even a small tour, on my own.

I could have a perfectly nice life drifting back and forth between Hedonia and Nou Occitan, composing and touring if I wanted to, or pursuing little affairs with Hedons (who had a wonderfully rational ability to know the difference between fun and love), or just getting drunk every night.

Or I could try to collect on the promise that I had extracted from Shan, and go back to work for Shan's organization, one of six sections of the OSP. So far as I knew, the OSP did the only interesting work in all the Thousand Cultures: by whatever means available, they held humanity together, all 1228 cultures on thirty-three extrasolar planets, minus the 102 on Addams that had yet to build a springer.

Now also minus two cultures on Briand. Two cultures out of touch with humanity for decades to come. Given the precariousness of their artificial ecology, and the deadliness of the quarrel, probably no one was alive on Briand now, but we couldn't know for thirty stanyears, till a starship carrying a springer could reach them.

Probably half of the OSP's field personnel had been involved in that hideous mess, and the OSP had—not without justice—ended up holding the bag for it. So perhaps the OSP would not survive the Briand scandal, or if it did, it might not survive in at all the same form.

But surely, even if the OSP were abolished, its function would still be necessary. Though the Second Renaissance had begun seventy stanyears ago in the Inner Sphere, with the springer doing what gunpowder, the printing press, and celestial navigation had done before, those of us from the outer systems had learned of it barely twenty stanyears ago, and the adjustment was still bewildering.

Seven hundred stanyears of basic research, some of it not applied in five centuries and some of it never applied at all, was pouring out of the libraries and databases, and every sort of technology was being allowed, in a continuous uproar of change unlike anything since the Industrial Age. The number and variety of new things, and things done better, by machines, aintellects, geneware, and nanos, was exploding. Humans could have more of what they wanted for less effort than ever before.

The one thing a machine couldn't do better than a human

being was to reconcile differences between human beings and bring them together—not that people were *good* at it, but we could *sometimes* do it. In promoting human unity behind the scenes, the OSP negotiated, cajoled, bribed, and threatened, as needed—defusing centuries-old ethnic hatreds, removing trade frictions, teaching tolerance through dozens of artistic and religious front groups. When we needed to, we overthrew a local tyranny, launched an artistic movement, fomented a new religion, crippled a popular movement with a scandal, or introduced a new trade good to disrupt markets, all supposedly to promote tolerance, flexibility, and xenophilia. Often we won; sometimes, we lost. On Briand, we'd had our first total loss.

Forty years of success on the average, though, was not a bad record, considering our inexhaustible, always-in-motion, and relentlessly inventive opponent: the mixture of affluence with simple human bloody-mindedness. In the twenty-ninth century, most humans had far more capability than judgement or ideas. The OSP tried to make sure that they didn't hit on war, glorinatalism, totalitarianism, jihad, *discommodi*, genocide, neopredation, or any of the other social evils that make life impossible to keep it from being boring.

No question, I did love being in the OSP. But after that betrayal of Shan's, it might never be the same. Assuming Shan wriggled off the hook of blame for the Briand catastrophe, did I *want* to work for him again? And could my decision even be rational at all? By the end of a stanyear of doing nothing—an experience I had never had as an adult—I might be too bored to stay out.

M'es vis, all things in time. There were still 331 standays until that promise came due, if he kept it, if he were in any position to keep it. The only thing I was sure of was that sometime in the next few days I would com Piranesi and Paxa, who were both physically gorgeous, and accept the offer of a Service of Consolation.

Meanwhile, I only wanted to sit and look east into the salt marsh in front of me. Eta Cassiopeia, refracted and smeared by Söderblom's dense air into a dim, friendly blur, was about to come up. Maybe, after watching the dawn, I'd walk somewhere and have a quiet breakfast. Then I might spring to somewhere to wander around for the day. Söderblom had fourteen cultures scattered through its temperate zones, but so far I'd stayed entirely in Hedonia. Maybe I'd skip over to Texaustralia for some whooping, brawling, and excessive drinking—an approach to a broken heart very like my own Occitan tradition. Or perhaps I'd spend a few days in Hubbard City and let them try to clear me, or sit on the rocks among the Diné, sharing my story if anyone asked, listening to anyone who came by. There was Freiporto, the next most famous place on Söderblom after Hedonia, but the combination of crassness and wildness there offended me esthetically even if the freedom was remarkable.

Really, I had nothing but options.

Something moved in the corner of my eye. A man was coming up the beach toward me. He wore a baggy black jumpsuit, and he walked like he was in a hurry to get somewhere, which was un-Hedon-like. Maybe another tourist?

He was tall and thin, older, but not old. His vigorous stride hitched slightly, suggesting some chronic pain in a leg or hip. His head was up and alert, with a practiced way of looking for a threat. That was a habit he couldn't have gotten here—the western shores of Hedonia are safe as a nursery. And the neighboring cultures along the coast—Thetanshaven to the north and Bremen Beyond the Sky to the south— were both about as peaceful and safe as you could hope for.

He pulled off his black watch cap and used it to wipe his

face. A shock of white hair emerged, crosslit by the rising Eta Cassiopeia and the last sinking moon. I knew him.

"Shan, I told you to give me a stanyear."

Shan stopped as if I'd pointed out a poisonous snake at his feet. No matter where you go, everyone in the Thousand Cultures seems to think that we Occitans are flighty and violent. *Ver, Senher Deu*, it makes me feel like breaking heads.

"I would give you a stanyear if I had a stanyear to give you," he said, quietly, his face expressionless as it so often was. "If you like, though it wastes time, I shall begin with as many apologies as you feel you deserve."

"There's not enough time till the end of the universe."

"True. No doubt. I will rely on your curiosity about what would cause me to come here on this fool's errand and annoy you."

"I'm not going to ask but I'll listen if you tell me."

He held still for exactly three big slow whooshes of the waves down by the shore. The precision suggested to me that he was timing himself by the waves—a trick to make himself wait longer than he thought I could be comfortable. I suppose it must have worked on many people in the past. Me, I just stood there, hated him, listened to the waves, and thought about how typical it all was: with a big favor to ask, first he had to play games.

At last, on the trough of the third wave, he spoke. "I have a job for you if you want it. Possibly vital to human unity, and it has to do with the survival of all the smaller, more isolated cultures out in the outer parts of human space."

"Now you're going to tell me that I'm the only person who could possibly do it," I said, bitterly. I knew how Shan thought, and what he thought of me.

"I was," Shan admitted. "Telling you that often works. The truth is there are about ten or twelve of the OSP's agents who could also be helpful. I am contacting them too. But I do think your particular style of operations might be very helpful, and I will feel more optimistic with you involved than I would with you sitting here recovering.

"This new situation is related to Briand, and to the current political troubles of the OSP, only because our present weakness has made it possible for a truly stupid idea to gain momentum in the Council of Humanity. If this particular pack of fools is not thwarted, you can forget whatever most attracts you about Wilson, or Nansen, or Söderblom, or any of the other outer worlds except Addams or poor wrecked Briand. I'm not exaggerating at all."

A big wave rolled in with a squashing sigh. Eta Cassiopeia had crept higher. Through the high, thick atmosphere, its amber light gave the whole beach a glow that would have been ridiculously sentimental if any lighting designer had done it.

Shan took a step closer to me, the way you might with a big dog you didn't trust. "I will give the full details to you, and to several other agents who are temporarily on leave on Söderblom, tonight at hour ten, in the Crucified Whore, which is a tavern in Freiporto, on Walpurgisnacht Street. Go in and say you're one of my friends and they'll guide you to the right room."

"What if I have other plans?"

"You don't, or at least none that you've discussed on any communications link up till the last fifteen minutes or so. But if you come up with some, well, then don't come, and there's an end to it—I'll see you when the stanyear is up. Otherwise, I trust your curiosity to bring you my way; that's part of why I came to see you in person."

"What's the other part?"

"I thought you might need to express some anger before you could think about accepting the offer."

I nodded; he knew me. "Then you know I'm apt to be there."

"I do. And thank you." He hesitated a moment, but clearly there was nothing more for either of us to say, so he merely reiterated, "Crucified Whore. Walpurgisnacht Street. The tenth hour. Ask for me. They'll show you where. Try not to be late."

He turned and walked away without bothering to say good-bye.

Too empty and sad, I had nothing to say, either. Once, I might have chased him down the beach trying for a hint about what the mission would be.

I still loathed boredom and uselessness and inactivity, but now my only hope of more interesting times was coming from the man that, out of the fifty billion or so alive, I most detested.

The irony was enough to make a scrap of a song start in my head. I willed myself to remember it.

Shan was a good hundred meters down the shoreline. The daylight had changed completely from dawn to early morning. I shouted after him, "I guess I'll be there."

He turned around and shouted back, "Don't worry about meeting Margaret. She's coming to the meeting in Utilitopia, two days from now."

Not knowing what else to say, I shouted "Thank you," but I don't know if he heard it over the big, slow wave that hissed up the beach then. Whether he did or not, he waved before turning and walking away as briskly as he had arrived.

I watched until he disappeared around a tall rock pile, then pulled out my computer, unfolded it and smoothed out the creases in the piano keys, plugged in the earphones, and sat down and worked out the first two verses of "Never Again Till the Next Time." Much later, it was going to make me even more ridiculously well off. At the time, though, it was a pleasant thing to think about on a sunny beach in early morning, a catchy melody with a lyric that seemed to come very naturally, in a paradise that I was already looking forward to leaving. *Que seretz, seratz*, as we used to say when I was a *jovent* back in Nou Occitan.

■ 2 ▮▮▮▮▮▮▮▮▮▮▮▮▮▮▮▮

Freiportese say that everything comes with ten stories, eleven of which are true. That didn't make much sense to the rest of us, but neither did Freiporto, whose economy depended completely on Freiporto's being a perfect place to lose track of an illegal shipment, irregular funds transfer, or inconvenient identity.

It was one of fewer than a dozen cultures that wasn't of the three major types. Most cultures were founded as "ethnic"—their living space had been purchased by some group of people who did not wish to be blurred off into oblivion in the Great Assimilation that began the Inward Turn, almost six hundred years ago. Ethnic cultures were places like St. Michael, New Buganda, Trois-Orléans, New Connaught, Nieuw Antwerp, and Texaustralia, which took to the Connect—the whole process of rejoining with humanity via springer—without much social stress. As long as you traded freely and refrained from violence, after all, the Interstellar metaculture only cared about your taste for gumbo, icons, or scarification insofar as it could sell them.

The next most common type were the esthetic cultures, the ones founded by rich eccentrics to create some imaginary place they might have wanted to live—the lost Tamil Mandalam and Yaxkintulum of Briand had been such, as was my home culture of Nou Occitan, as were Nova Roma and Starhattan. Most of them were collapsing fast under the impact of Connect, but a few of the least assimilated cultures—such as my own—were esthetic.

Least abundant, and most annoying to the OSP, were the utopias, the cultures created to fulfill some theorist's idea of the good state—Margaret's home culture of Caledony was one of those, as were Hedonia and Thetanshaven on this world, and most of the nastier dictatorships like Thorburg, Fort Liberty, Novy Leningrad, Pure, and Égalité.

Regardless of their charter and design, all cultures, whether ethnics, esthetics, or utopias, had started out the same. In the 23rd or 24th centuries, during the Great Assimilation, a starship, crawling out to one of the thirty-three habitable worlds within the distance that could be reached with half of light speed and unreliable suspended animation, had set down its cargo of ninety-six adults fresh from suspended animation (minus five to twelve deaths en route). They had moved into a town constructed in advance by robots somewhere within the territory that the Council assigned to them—by law, a contiguous patch of 650,000 square kilometers of more-or-less comfortable and temperate land. As soon as the nurseries and schools were set up, the ninety or so adults began decanting the million frozen embryos they had brought with them, raising the resulting infants into the culture.

In Freiporto things had gone very differently. You could have looked on Freiporto as a market-anarchist utopia, or as an esthetic culture that idealized the untrammeled rule of the strong as the highest purpose of society, or as an ethnic culture whose purpose was to preserve twenty or so different persecuted minorities known for their mercantile acumen and individualist aggression. All of that had been implied in their charter, but anyone who had looked carefully at that charter should have smelled a rat, or ninety-six rats to be precise; it defined Freiporto as an absolute democracy, so when the ninety-six thawed out, they voted the charter void and made "do what you want if you can" the only permissible law of the culture. In the early twenty-fifth century, when it took nineteen years for a radio message to reach Earth and would have taken about fifty years for a punitive expedition to come out and compel obedience to the original charter, there was nothing to stop them.

The ninety-six had concealed their traces well, but despite their many different backgrounds—Straits Chinese, Russian Jews, Texas Viets, Thai, Igbo, Jamaican, Bangala, and Corsican being only the most prominent—they all were younger sons and daughters of families that had amassed great wealth in the gray area between legitimate business and organized crime. Freiporto was the perfect place for their old family businesses, a place where everything and anything could connect *sub rosa*.

Originally the million frozen embryos had been decanted into hereditary slavery. After a brief war with the other thirteen cultures on Söderblom, two centuries ago, back in the pre-springer days, Freiporto had been forced to emancipate its slaves. Most of the old slave population moved out, but a few stayed on in the wide variety of criminal enterprises, regulation-free businesses, and no-tax operations that kept Freiporto going as merely a nasty corner of a remote, underpopulated planet.

Then Connect made Freiporto one of the trade hubs for all of humanity. The descendants of the original adult group, and the more vicious and clever former slaves, were now tightly intermarried, probably the wealthiest extended family in human space. Anything or anybody who needed to disappear went to Freiporto.

All this was why, before going, I strapped on a neural dart gun, a neuroducer epée, and a couple of belt knives, and put on a lightweight helmet. I could still be shot, and anyone with a weapon-grade laser could cut me in half, but at least I would be too much work for the average petty robber.

The Crucified Whore didn't have a springer. A bar where people meet to discuss criminal matters would be a poor place for people to pop in and out of instantaneously. The nearest public springer on Walpurgisnacht Street was about four hundred meters from it.

I checked my gear once more. I was surprised to be feeling so good. The man in the mirror was smiling, bald spot hidden under the helmet, no gray in the shoulder-length hair that hung below it or in the mustache and goatee. I'd stayed in shape. Only a certain caution in the eyes—and the fine spray of spidery crow's-feet around them, my memento of Briand's blazing sun—indicated my real age.

I was still more than a match for any *toszet* I'd ever faced in a duel. I wasn't relying on the quick reflexes of youth any more, I was taking care of myself, and I was used to fighting with real weapons and doing real harm, a distinct advantage against those who had fought only with neuroducers set for hallucinatory damage.

Deu, I was looking forward to this.

Enseingnamen? Romance? An end to ennui? An extra-fast recovery? I could be happy about any of those.

I checked the clock. Ten minutes till fifth hour here—coming up on sunset in Söderblom's eighteen-hour-forty-minute day. Freiporto was five time zones east, so it was time. I told the springer controller the number, took a last glance at the thick yellow sunlight pouring in through my window, and stepped through the pitch black of the springer into midnight on Walpurgisnacht Street.

Immediately somebody bumped me and felt for a pocket. I drove an elbow back, didn't connect, pivoted, threw my left arm out in a clothesline block, and barely grazed the back of the brat's head. He looked like he was about ten, but it's hard to judge age from a back that's moving away from you that fast.

In the brief contact, he had checked the tops of two pockets in my tunic and two in my breeches, and found all

of them sealed, besides briefly touching the hilt of my epée
and thus realizing I was armed. If I'd been a split second
later, my arm would have swung through empty air, and the
street would have been entirely empty. The local talent was
remarkable.

I walked past taverns, whorehouses, drug parlors, armor-
ers, and neural mod shops, with the occasional warehouse—
those looked like prisons, with high walls, barbed wire, and
usually a guard or two. Since the coming of the springer,
many of them had had their doors and gates walled up.

The street wasn't crowded, but the places along it were
mostly open, mostly crowded, and mostly noisy. You were
safer under the protection of the landlord than out in the
street, so people moved from one place to another quickly. I
walked fast myself. People avoided me by three meters or so,
looking away. Locally that was the polite thing.

The Crucified Whore's sign has to be the single most vul-
gar vu in human space. Against two moons and a few very
bright stars twinkling in the purple sky, it dared me to see
how ugly it really was. I passed under the leering, wriggling
figure, into the tavern itself.

No one drank at the bar—after all, no one came here to
be seen—but robots rushed back and forth between the enclosed booths and the taps. Five humaniform robots, naked,
with lifelike skin and hair—legal in Freiporto—stood in a
display case along the back, switched off and immobile, beneath a price list that began with "Robot and bedroom,
compliant with orders" for a merely ridiculous price and
worked its way up to "Robot, your scenario, terminate with
murder" for an outrageous one.

I was disgusted but not for the reasons most people are
when they see a humaniform. Most people think sex robots
are creepy. For me, robots in general are creepy, since one of
our main strengths against the aintellects has always been

that we can be mobile while unhooked from the system. The ability to go offline and attack the computer an aintellect was running on saved us in 2749, and although people say that nothing like the Rising could ever happen again, and it hasn't in eighty years, I say it wouldn't have to be like the Rising to be pretty bad, and humaniform robots provide far too many opportunities to the aintellects.

I had been staring at that case of robots for a full minute or more. I shook off my disgust and turned to the bar.

"Help you?" the bartender asked. She was at least human, a petite ash-blonde, wearing not much. By the way she carried herself and watched the room, I guessed she was armed, with backup under the bar.

"I'm here for Shan's—"

"Oh, another one," she said, grinning. I don't think I'd ever seen implanted teeth that were quite that long, or that sharp, before, and I wondered why she had chosen that mottled yellow color. "Back that way—" she gestured with her thumb "—door on the left, go ahead and walk in. Shan commed to say he'd be half an hour late. We have a a drink and sandwich special tonight. Or maybe you'd care for some fellatio? There's a combo special if you want all three."

I bought a special, but not the combo special, and took my Reuben and stout back to the room she had specified; there were about a dozen people there, chattering about old war stories. One way you could tell it was an OSP gathering, or a gathering in Freiporto, was that they were all sitting with their backs to a wall, so that the room had the curious effect of being a place where an in-the-round performance was about to happen.

"Giraut!"

I turned and saw Piranesi, by himself, sitting at a table for four. "Paxa will be along in minute or two—she had something to grab first," he said. "You look good for a fellow who must be miserable. There's a seat open here."

I sat down in the corner with him, peeling off my helmet and dropping my epée into it. "Well, this helps. Isn't it perfectly Shan to have the meeting in a place like this, right at midnight?"

Piranesi shrugged. "Our sky is virtually never dark, and we say 'the tenth hour' anyway, so 'midnight' doesn't have the connotations it would elsewhere."

"For the real romantic, the facts either cooperate with the story, or they get out of the frame," I said. We clinked glasses. "Another round for humanity."

"And one more for the good guys," Piranesi said, amiably. He had steel-gray hair that might have turned that color when he was twenty or when he was sixty, a deep lined tan, eyes so blue that they tended toward violet, and the dimpled chin that Industrial Age actors favored. We drank. "No Hedon will ever make much of a romantic. 'Facts are the stepping stones in the ford to pleasure.' "

"Who said that?"

"Me, just now. But I've said it many times before, so it probably sounds like I'm quoting it. Every so often, whenever I'm back in Hedonia for enough time between missions, I teach FFM class in the schools."

"FFM class is—?"

He smiled. "I thought it was in all the guidebooks that cover Hedonia—usually with a long discussion of how deplorable it is."

"I never read guidebooks. I prefer to know my way around."

"Ah. Well, it stands for Freedom From Morality. We don't think healthy amorality happens naturally."

"But you're not amoral," I pointed out. "I would trust you

to keep your word any time. You don't steal. I've never known you to harm anyone except enemy soldiers in time of war."

He laughed. "I didn't say 'immoral,' I said amoral. You *really* didn't read your guidebook. A person who has a compulsive need to break moral commandments is as much a prisoner as the person who feels bound to obey them. And the human brain is hardwired to produce moral commandments. That's why we think you have to train young people to keep them from developing morality and blocking their pursuit of pleasure. I teach it because—"

"It gives you an outlet for your sadistic urge to confuse children," Paxa said, coming in behind him and sitting down. She leaned across our small table, grabbed me, and kissed me on the mouth, somewhere in intensity between friendship and a proposition. "How are you feeling?"

"Better than I might have expected, worse than I could have hoped. Anyway, *mos companho*, on this particular evening, I am gladder to be with you, and here, than I would have been to be with anyone else, anywhere else."

Paxa raised her glass, and we had another toast. Conversation had died completely, and we had settled into eating our sandwiches, when Shan came in.

He was wearing something that seemed to have descended from Asian peasant dress—loose black tunic and pants like a martial-arts gi and a baggy coat over them. His expression was serious. He went directly to the podium. "I've walked through springers onto nine different planets today," Shan said, "and if that's not a record, I don't know that I want to meet the person who holds it. I am sorry that I was so late; too many questions to answer at the last meeting. I imagine there will be plenty at this one. Let me catch you up with our current situation.

"Despite all our current difficulties, it looks as if the OSP will probably survive, though we'll be an above-ground office with more public supervision, under a different name. It was probably high time to go public. So that will be all right, ultimately, and is only peripherally related to what I'm going to tell you about.

"Unfortunately, a truly ridiculous issue has come bubbling up from the depths of the Cultural Legacy Management Committee of the Council of Humanity. The committee, by the way, is commonly abbreviated CLMC, commonly pronounced 'Clumsy,' though I suggest you avoid that around the committee or staff.

"Until the Briand affair, we had two OSP agents—one of whom, Caron Czesckonatividad, was chair—on CLMC. The Briand affair led to a purge of known OSP agents from the Council of Humanity and its subcommittees.

"We'd always managed to keep a number of things that would be trouble for the Thousand Cultures bottled up in the committees. Now something has gotten loose, and it's *big* trouble. Technologies that would make possible the commercial exploitation of psypyx recordings, for entertainment, are coming on line, and CLMC is seriously considering licensing the psypyx archives for that purpose."

The twenty OSP agents in the room made enough noise for a hundred, and within a second or so most of us were crowded around Shan, shouting at him. He held his hands up as if we were going to beat him, and when we had calmed, he said, "It is going to take a major effort to stop this completely stupid idea. I am sure most of you are painfully aware that the idea would be unpopular—"

"I can promise that if the Council of Humanity even starts to move toward using the Hall of Memories in Noupeitau that way," I said, "we Occitans will destroy our springers and secede."

"The same goes for Chaka Home," a tall, thin dark-skinned man said, "and without asking I know that every other culture on Quidde would join us."

"Same for Trois-Orléans," a short, middle-aged woman added. "You might finally achieve genuine unity and peace on Roosevelt; all hundred and eleven cultures would declare *jihad* on Earth, and we'd be right in there with them."

The psypyx was the nearest thing to immortality yet achieved; it was a whole-brain recording. If you died, your personality could be coaxed out of the psypyx and into contact with another brain, usually a friend or relative who could wear your psypyx for a couple of years. While you were re-acquiring the skill of functioning as a consciousness in a living brain, a clone of you could be tank-grown to the age of four, with the brain blank, so that you could be transferred from your friend's brain to your clone, and over a period of decades, you would then migrate completely out of the psypyx and into the clone brain—at which point, the result had your DNA and your memories (up to the point where the recording was taken) and was effectively you.

Some cultures banned the psypyx, some encouraged it, some were indifferent to it—but you could be pretty sure that no one of the billion or so people who had had a psypyx recording made, in any culture, had ever done it to be used as an artwork, simulation, or game.

Research into a certain, effective re-graft method had only really begun in the Second Renaissance. For centuries humanity had lived with only about a five percent chance of successful restoration. Even now, with success rates over ninety-five percent and rising fast, the procedure could fail while you were being grafted onto your friend, or while you were being re-grafted into your child-clone body, or even later as the body aged. And if you had been recorded two hundred years ago, you usually had no friend or relative to wear your psypyx and start the process. Most of those billion recordings were stranded in storage. In most cultures, their storage and maintenance was in care of the public—and apparently, what the public had care of, the public might decide to sell.

When people had quieted, Shan said, "The Sol system has fifty percent of all human population, and the Inner Sphere, which is more and more like Sol as time goes on, and tends to vote with Earth and the other solar worlds more and more, is seventy percent of the remainder. The outer cultures may be on a majority of human planets, and take up nearly all of human space by volume, but they're only about fifteen percent of the total human population. Furthermore a quarter of the outer culture population is on Addams, which still hasn't built a springer or begun Connect.

"Nearly all people in the Sol system work for the minimum seven years of their lives, and then spend the better part of a century continuously running direct-to-brain simulations. Much of the Inner Sphere is moving rapidly toward the same system for coping with endemic boredom. A new source of entertainment would make the entertainment sector—two-thirds of the economy all by itself—much more profitable, increasing tax revenues *and* the value of everyone's trust fund. The books would balance better and the Sol system, and the eight planets in the six Inner Sphere systems, could expand services and do more maintenance on everything.

"So, essentially, we're talking about an improvement in the lives of about forty-two billion people, at the negligible price of converting copies of about a billion temporarily stored dead people into entertainment. Chances are the Council will vote for this every bit as easily as the Romans decided to impose Caesar-worship in Judea, as easily as the

British decided to tax tea, as easily as the Southern Hemi-sphere Organization decided that silly old temple in Kyoto could be replaced with something more practical.

"At least this stupid idea is a badly timed stupid idea. The Inner Sphere is going down the same road as Earth and the other five Solar worlds, but it's still not there yet—there's still not even one Inner Sphere world with much more than three billion people. They still have elbow room and some real work, and they aren't living their whole lives in the box yet.

"And no one's equipped for a big war. Any secession will be peaceful, and Earth would be left with only the Alpha Centauri and Epsilon Eridani systems, for a grand total of three extrasolar planets staying with Earth, twenty-eight breaking away, and Briand and Addams doing whatever it is they'll do, since both planets are beyond anyone's influence. That's 330 cultures sticking with Earth, 104 who knows, and 794 breaking away, if you prefer to count cultures."

No one said anything. If the situation was as he described, the whole mission of the OSP—to which we'd given most of our lives—was doomed.

"There is hope." His tone was mild but firm. "If we can cause the Council to decide not to allow this, and at least to *believe* that their reason was respect for minority rights . . . well, then maybe the precedent will be set and the next time will be easier. So this is one we have to win, right out in the open on its merits—novel as the experience is for most of us."

He paused, I think for a chuckle from the crowd, but only a dense, heavy silence filled the pause. I was not the only person he'd hurt with all his double and triple dealing during the Briand crisis.

Shan licked his lips, looked down, looked up, and gestured at someone behind us. A moment later, a robot brought in a big tray of sandwiches, coffee, tea, and snacks. "Anything you ordered earlier is on the expense account. Most of you will shortly receive orders to go to your home culture for a period of at least six months. Your job there is to stir up as much opposition to the plan as you can. Unofficially, I wouldn't mind a few 'unfortunate incidents' that 'got out of hand,' especially in front of any sympathetic people from Earth, the other Sol System worlds, Dunant, Passy, or Ducommon."

I was thinking how I'd enjoy half a stanyear back in Nou Occitan when Shan added, "All right, then, everyone except Piranesi, Paxa, and Giraut is free to go. You three, we'll take a table in the other room and have a caucus. Don't worry, it won't run long, I'm due on Cremer in three hours, and I hope to squeeze a nap in before that." He smiled at me, and for a moment it was almost like the old days. I looked at him and smiled back. *You are a liar and I can't trust you,* I thought, making sure I remembered that.

■ 3 ████████████████████████

We took a bathroom break. Piranesi and I settled into the enclosed booth with fresh cups of "dragon punch," the local stimulant-relaxant mix, warm thick purple wine thinned with something like black tea, plus dashes of some synthetics on both the up and the down side. It had a wallop to match its aftertaste, which would have been unacceptable in a cough syrup.

They served it with cups of hot strong cinnamon water. My first sip of dragon punch, before I knew that the cinnamon water was a palate-clearer, was brutal. "Yargggh. Has to be native to Freiporto."

"Yep. Definitely an acquired taste," Piranesi said. "If you get the cinnamon water to your mouth fast enough, you'll barely taste it, so it will be almost all right. As for enjoying the taste, start at birth, and you can fully enjoy it by the time you've got a long gray beard. But it's great when you need to be awake and uninhibited, and after a while the cinnamon will numb your mouth. No good for sex because it has you constantly peeing, unless that's your idea of a good time. They call it 'dragon punch' on the menu to avoid its real name, 'slavewater.' In the bad old days there was a physiological specific in it to make it addictive—a different one for every household—so that running away would make you sick." Piranesi shuddered and took a sip himself. "But if you have work to do . . . especially creative work . . . it'll help you do it." He knocked back the cup in a hard gulp, opened the little door within the door of the booth, and set it outside to be refilled; a moment later, having rinsed his mouth with the last of his cinnamon water, he set that cup outside, and closed the small door behind it. "Oh, good, I've burned my tongue. The slavewater will taste *much* better now. You know, there aren't many military families among the Hedons, but mine is one of them. It leads to an odd appreciation for some things that most people find nasty. Slavewater, violence with style, and the pleasures of being tired and freshly clean after a day in the field."

"You'd like Nou Occitan. You have to come and visit."

"I've told Paxa that any number of times. She's got a dislike for a culture where women are treated as trophies—or that's how she describes it."

I sighed, took another sip of slavewater, and immediately grabbed the cinnamon water again. "That's not totally fair, but it's not totally unfair, either."

"Like most generalizations," he said. "I'll get her there sooner or later. She loves the music, and the language, and the art. But she's, not, uh, the type to tolerate being . . ."

"The almost-victim of a would-be rapist," Paxa said, opening the door and sliding in. "At least that's what someone had in mind for me to tolerate. Stupid bastard kicked in the front door of the stall in the women's, while I was on the toilet."

Piranesi knew his partner too well to ask, so I did. "You're okay? He didn't hurt you?"

"He made it about one step closer before I had the neuroducer pulled, and he was reaching for my head. He was already not wearing pants. I would call that overconfidence. So I set the neuroducer to third degree burn, and applied it to the obvious. He'll hallucinate that I burned *that* off with a torch. While he was rolling around screaming, I imprinted him with loss of his tongue, vocal cords, legs, arms, eyes, and ears, in that order, very much one at a time, and I took a while about the eyes. Kept the ears on till the last so he could hear everything I had to say to him. Dragged him into the men's room and tied him to the sink with his butt waving in the air. In this town he'll be a public convenience for two days before the management of the Crucified Whore gets tired of it and calls an ambulance."

Shan came in, closed the door behind himself, sat down, and said, "There's a refill waiting on the door." Piranesi opened the small door and brought it in. "Paxa, the man you tied to the sink looked very uncomfortable. I know you, and I'm sure he had it coming, but may I remind you that we don't want to call a great deal of attention to ourselves?"

"Is that why you picked this nasty little den?" I asked.

"Well, it avoids having media send anyone who has enough reputation to make a good hostage, and since those are exactly the people that big stories are reserved for, it will slow them down. Now, as I said, I've got a specific project for the three of you. And a good reason to use you for it. Before you accept I should add that there may be some danger—there's enough prestige and power at stake for someone to play rough. The subject does stir up some strong passions."

"Surely most of the passion is on our side," I said.

Shan shook his head, his expression bitter. "Many Earth people desperately want something more exciting for their entertainment, and most of them believe in an unalienable right to try everything. 250 years ago the 'right to consume' groups got permission to go rampaging through the archived cultures, producing a great quantity of schlocky fake art, with exactly such arguments. And nowadays half of the Earth voters will tell any polltaker that the right to consume is *the* fundamental human right. You have to keep reminding yourself, when you're dealing with them, that many of your ideas and values are as archaic and dead on Earth as, oh, *gravitas*, or chivalry, and try not to appeal to feelings they regard as quaint." He shrugged, seeming to say, *What can we do?* After a moment, he went on. "You will go to Earth and testify at the Council of Humanity. You'll also be doing contact work with many different groups, trying to create a climate that's as favorable as possible for the reception of what you're going to say.

"Now, it's clear that my organization is never going to be fully acceptable to the Council again, at least not while I still am in charge of it. So although I have much the most experience at politicking with the Council of Humanity, the operation will have to run out of another OSP group. The Board fell into quite an argument about which of the other five groups should take it on—everyone agreed the job was important but no one could make themselves want to take it.

"Eventually it settled on Dji's group. So, Giraut, Piranesi, and Paxa, you will be working for Dji, on loan indefinitely, on a political campaign trying to stop the commercialization of psypyxes from gaining the support of the Council. You've all had enough experience to be able to help Dji and his people out, and you're all very much assets—I'd be using you if I were running the campaign. Now, you haven't escaped me completely, because Dji wants me to nod in frequently. All the same, no matter how involved I am behind the scenes, you answer to Dji, and you take your orders from him—clear?

"Good, then. The reasons for choosing you all should be immediately clear. Piranesi and Paxa are the only two Hedons who are regular OSP agents, which is to say, who have a solid knowledge of what is going on. There are probably more petitions to commercialize Hedon psypyxes than for the psypyxes of all the other cultures combined. I'm afraid your culture's image is overpowering its reality, at least in the market."

"But won't experiencing all their pleasures through the mask of a Hedon attitude spoil all the fun?" Paxa asked, brushing the blonde hair away from her cheeks and taking a sip of slavewater.

"It would if that were how they were going to commercialize. The process that creates salable psypyxes produces a copy of the personality with reactions and memories, but no will of its own. As to whether or not that is a conscious being, well, we'll be arguing that it *is*, in the Council courts and in dozens of cultural courts. The neuroscientists' best guess is that the psypyxed personality being used in a game, or as entertainment, must feel as if it were in a dream controlled by somebody else, experiencing everything, unable to wake up, unable even to say 'Stop' or 'That hurts.' "

"Deu aja merce," I muttered.

"Exactly," Shan said, nodding vigorously. "The kind consideration of God is about the only hope available to the personality trapped in that situation. This whole technology stinks of the ground it grew in. They misused psypyx copies from people who donated a copy to science. We know those people thought 'for research' would mean 'to improve recovery technique,' not 'to enrich merchants.' In their development process, the commercial interests have *already* sent a few tens of thousands of personalities into all sorts of madness."

"This only gets more horrible," Paxa said, shuddering.

"Right. As a matter of fact, we're seeking a sympathetic jurisdiction in which to bring criminal charges against the researchers; it's another angle of attack.

"But back to your part of the job. Dji's group, including you, is charged with trying to explain, as clearly as possible, to CLMC, to the Council, to the media, ultimately to all people of Earth, how it would feel to live your life according to a demanding cultural norm, like the Hedon or the Occitan one, and then have to dream it over and over again forever—reduced to pornography. Paxa and Piranesi, your testimony will strike against the exploitation of Hedon archives, which is exactly what these companies would most like to exploit. Clear enough?"

They nodded.

"Giraut, your task is easier and harder. As a creative artist, from a whole culture of creative artists, you will tell them that fundamentally the experience of creating art is not available to passengers, and that you won't be able to work if you have somebody always mentally looking over your shoulder."

"Ver, tropa vera." I said. Always, when a situation began to make me tense, I slid back into Occitan.

"But there's testimony you'll be giving that is even more powerful. You are aware, no doubt, that recovery technique has improved tremendously in the last few years? They've been able to reach older and older psypyxes, including some that didn't recover successfully when it was first tried. So we are going to present testimony from someone who was recorded, and died, long before this proposal came foward. Since we don't have nearly enough time to grow a clone body, the recovered personality will have to testify through a wearer—in this case, you."

"Raimbaut," I said. "You think he can recover this time."

"We do. It's perfect, Giraut. Thanks to your achievements as a musician and composer, you're a minor celebrity. So you'll be newsworthy, as a public voice for the cause. I assume you don't object to fame?"

"It sells recordings." I tossed down the last of my slavewater before noticing that I had already had the last of my cinnamon water. Paxa slid hers over to my hand, and I took a quick, mouth-clearing sip. "You're right, Raimbaut will be perfect. A *bo toszet*, a good human being, a loyal friend—but *not* a special talent, just a private, shy ordinary fellow. He couldn't possibly have intended to permit bored Earth people to pretend to be him." That thought crystallized. "Why isn't this whole business an easy win? Nobody in the psypyxes could even remotely have intended themselves to be turned into commercial resources."

"For the same reason we're filing suit against the people who did the original research." Shan sighed. "The other side is arguing that what is in a psypyx is not a person, and legally speaking, only people can have intentions."

"How can they say a personality stored in a psypyx is not a person?" Paxa asked. "What else could it be?"

"Well, remember, the psypyx is uncommon on Earth," Shan said. "Practically all Earth people spend practically all their lives in the box, consuming direct-to-brain entertainment. Why would they want to do it all over again? So they don't imagine the life of a *person* being stored in the psypyx. That's hard to imagine when you haven't had much of a life, directly. To them, what's in that psypyx is *data*. And songs and film and holo and poetry are all nothing more than data, true? And don't we exploit data all the time? Psypyx files are even recorded in exactly the same format as the experiences generated by professional experiencers. And we don't have hosts enough to revive everybody, anyway. That data will just sit there for centuries, inert. Why not make some money from it?

"That's why we have to persuade at least some of the people of Earth to stop thinking of our dead friends as 'data,' and our stored friends as 'dead.' We want those poor souls, dreaming in their concrete boxes, to see the people in the psypyxes as dead stored *people*, not so different from themselves. Hence, the plan is, we introduce lots of Earth people to a few articulate, concerned dead people, and formerly dead people, and dead-people-to-be."

"It's a better plan than I could have thought of," I admitted. "What are the chances that it will work?"

"On our side, we have one strength: we're right. The other side has people's self-interest, ignorance, and boredom, plus our weakness due to the scandals."

"Don't we also have their discomfort about sending human souls into eternal screaming nightmares for the sake of casual amusement?" Piranesi asked.

Shan shook his head sadly. "Wait till you spend some time with Earth people."

Supposedly it's healthiest to run at a speed at which you can hold a conversation; I know of no evidence for this, but like never going in the water for an hour after eating, never throwing a hat on the bed, and never wearing high heels in a vacuum dome, it seems to be ineradicable as a belief. So as Piranesi and I ran on the beach and the sun crept up toward noon, he kept a pace at which I could talk to him comfortably, and he could run figure-eights around me comfortably.

"So who *is* this Raimbaut you'll be wearing?"

"Hmm. Well, as I said, a *bo toszet*. One of my best friends when we were jovents together, in Noupeitau, fifteen or sixteen years ago."

"Jovent is like teenager, adolescent?"

"Either a young man or the time of first manhood." We turned up a slope toward the low ridge, and I concentrated on breathing for about twenty paces. As we leveled off to run along the ridge, I explained, "In Nou Occitan, Youth is personified, a being who becomes the *companhon* of a boy for a few years before turning him into a man. Or the boy is Youth's avatar. Not, mind you, that you can safely *call* him a boy. The jovent is also the age at which you can carry weapons outside the practice rooms; it's the age of consent for sex, and for drugs and alcohol without parental permission; it's when most of us fight most of the duels we'll ever fight."

"So you become a jovent at fourteen, fifteen . . . ?" He turned back down toward the water; if he'd been running by himself, he'd have zigzagged the whole way. I was in better shape than nine-tenths of people my age, but that is no consolation when your running partner is from the top one percent.

"There's not really an age for it. It's a set of standards for physical and neurological maturity. Growth plates, bone mass, corpus callosum, things like that. Some boys become jovents at ten stanyears, some not till sixteen. And then they stay as long as they want. So in a jovent tavern, you might see a ten-year-old draw his epée on a thirty-year-old, fighting over the favors of a seventeen-year-old."

"Sounds like a fun way to be an adolescent."

"It's a fun way to be a *male* adolescent," I said. "Paxa has a point about Occitan culture. But, yes, if you're a glib male athlete, your jovent is a great time to be alive. Trying to do everything, be everything, fight everything, and fuck everything you can. Brawls, wild nights, daring escapades, and the most powerful and astonishing sorts of adventures—or it looks that way during your jovent. Actually the average jovent is pretty stupid."

"You mean that the time of being a jovent is stupid, or do you mean that individual jovents are stupid?"

I shrugged. "That's why the concepts can't be disentangled." Now we were splashing through the shallow water's edge, and again, I was running out of breath. We trotted on in silence for a while, as Eta Cassiopeia climbed up above the land to our left, and the sea retreated from our feet, to the right.

Raimbaut had died—really died, not merely hallucinated himself into a coma, as he had done so many times before—in a dueling accident. Duels in Nou Occitan are fought with the neuroducer epée—a light touch on the eye makes you think you have been blinded, a hard slap on the arm makes you think it has been severed, and a firm thrust to the heart convinces you that you're dead and sends you into a coma.

Police everywhere use neuroducers as riot weapons, because in small, infrequent doses, the risk of permanent injury is small. It was the weapon Paxa Prytanis had used on her would-be rapist, and unless the Crucified Whore had finally sent him to the hospital, he was no doubt still tied to that sink by arms that he thought he no longer had, hysterically unable to see or hear, believing that his legs and genitals were also gone.

Getting the use of your "wounded" parts back, or getting rid of the pain, required a long time under re-hypnosis in the hospital, and it didn't always work fully. By the time he was twenty-one, Raimbaut had lost many duels, with many thrusts to the heart, including one to me when we were both fifteen. One evening, backing me up in a group quarrel, he had died of "hysterical distortion of the heart"—too many strips of cardiac muscle fiber refused ever to relax again, so they couldn't restart him.

I still felt bad about that brawl. It had been stupid to allow Raimbaut to be involved in it at all—hysterical distortion of the heart is produced by the same process in muscle fiber that produces "duelist's eyebrow" and "loser's grin," both of which Raimbaut had had, prominently, for a couple of stanyears before the accident. We should have known it wouldn't be safe for him. Now what was left of Raimbaut was a recording of his personality made eight days before his death.

Raimbaut had been the first real death among our circle of *companho*. Next had been Marcabru—a *tostemz-toszet*, a bully, a lunatic, a drunk, so careless of his life and himself that he had had no fresh recordings for six years before the day he fell out of a tavern window and fractured his skull on the pavement below. His old psypyx presumably still sat in the Hall of Memories, stuck about two stanyears after Raimbaut had died and shortly after my return to Noupeitau (and a very ugly fight that I would as soon forget had ever happened).

As for the rest of us, Aimeric had returned to his home culture of Caldeony, on Nansen, where he was Prime Minister at the moment, like his father before him. Rufeu had continued as a jovent for a very long time, verging on a *tostemz-toszet* (what other cultures called a boy-man, a Peter Pan, or a *puer aeturnus*—the literal meaning might be put into Terstad as "always just a guy" or "forever a fella"). At the age of twenty-six, he had fallen while rock climbing (I've always wondered how much of an accident that was—he had had a recording made only that morning) and was now in a six-year-old body, legally an adult, absolutely the most decadent, saturnine prepubescent it had ever been my pleasure to encounter. Once he was fully installed in his new body, had some reach, and had practiced his combat skills back into existence, he'd move back to the Quartier des Jovents, I felt sure.

Johan had become a respected professor of Romance Languages at the University in Noupeitau. He had always been the scholar among us, by disposition as much as by his small size and slowness with the epée. He and I had no contact with each other; he believed that my clash with Marcabru was what had sent my one-time best friend down the dark tunnel of depression to his death, and regarded me as little better than a murderer. What I knew of him, I heard through Rufeu. I heard nothing at all about Johan's younger brother, David, who had hung around the *companho*, except that he was also a professor.

Bieris was a farmer's wife in Caledony, known for her paintings, and about as happy a person as anyone I had ever known. Happiness had always been as much a part of her as her keen eye and her dexterity with the brush.

"I wonder which ones of the old *companho* Raimbaut will want to get in touch with." I had slowed to a brisk walk, and Piranesi was trotting all around me, doing the cool-down for his run. I had been explaining about the Occitan tradition of the *companho*, the group of lifelong best friends that formed in school and was in many ways more important than family.

"No doubt he'll be unhappy about what happened to Marcabru, and he may want to talk to Johan, which might be awkward, and otherwise the people he'd want to see are all your friends too. So it seems to me that you have two awkward issues: what happenened to Marcabru and that Johan still holds that grudge. Do *you* feel responsible for Marcabru's death?"

"Well, possibly my humiliation of Marcabru did turn him toward his death," I admitted. "Nevertheless he *chose* to become a drunk, stop renewing his psypyx recordings, and fight everything that moved. I was brutal and unkind to him, out of spite and anger. I'm ashamed of it. But he's the one that decided to ruin himself as a human being, and put himself where he was bound to die in some foolish accident."

Piranesi said, "If Raimbaut's not too judgmental, you should be all right—it would probably be a waste of time to worry about it."

"You know, Hedons are among the happier and more rational people I've ever met. Nearly everything here makes sense."

"*Sai-lo, companhon,*" he said. It was one of his ten or so phrases of Occitan. As always, his vowels were too pinched and he pronounced "nh" and "n" alike, sort of a bastardized nasal hum. "A quote from the Hedon philosophy: 'he who says an obvious thing to people who already know it will be revered as a sage.' " He put on his final kick, accelerating up toward his house.

I gave up, settling into an easy walk, and muttered, "Well, your accent sounds funny."

We had agreed that we'd do the Service of Consolation that afternoon. I was becoming steadily more nervous about the whole thing; when you come down to it, as the saying goes, you can take people out of their home culture, but you can't take the home culture out of the people. In Nou Occitan, sex with another man's *entendendora* is the sure way to humiliate him into fighting you, and sex between one *companhon* and another is what you do while you're hoping some day to be old enough to have an *entendora*. And having sex with a couple is . . . well, there really wasn't any expression for it, at least not among *mos companho*. The Terstad word "perversion," though, might have captured it nicely.

I showered, and afterward, as I was toweling off, Paxa came in, wearing nothing but a thin, short robe. She handed me a small glass of some warm, sweet juice that I hadn't had before, and said, "This one you drink before the service. You won't need clothes for it, so don't dress. Now, drink it all down and follow me."

That at least settled the question about whether dressing would have been bad form. I drank the juice in two long swigs. Still naked, I followed her up the open wooden stair to the loving room—almost all Hedon houses have one, separate from but adjoining the sleeping room, with a cleaning room and an excreting room connecting both of them. The Hedon idiom for "none of your business" is "upstairs." I had been to this house several times—Piranesi and Paxa were the kind of natural hosts who have you over every day if you let them—but this was my first time upstairs.

All the surfaces in the loving room were warm to the touch, but the air temperature was comfortably cool. Light came from piped-skylight floor sconces with mirror rotors, so that sunlight flowed up the wall and spread across the domed reflective ceiling in flickering swirls. In this room, if you normally looked good naked, you would look *great* naked.

The center of the room was an enormous bed in three sections, each as big as a double bed: one knee-high, one waist high, and one that sloped gently upward between them, all covered with taut, soft tan fabric.

"Stretch out on the middle section, on your stomach, head upwards," Paxa said. I did.

Piranesi came in with a bowl of warm oil; looking back, I saw that he was naked too. "Eyes front," he said. "You don't want to miss the show."

The music started. It was slow, random-tone, faux-Oriental, like most Hedon music is. Art in Hedonia tends more toward pleasant amusement than clear statement. It isn't a place where anyone throws paint, shouts poetry, or smashes guitars.

Paxa knelt on the upper section, in front of me, swaying slowly to the beat, not quite dancing. "We, your friends, have gathered here because you, our friend, are in need of consolation. Share the pleasures of melancholy and anticipation; melancholy for what will not be again, anticipation for renewal and regrowth." She reached under her gold-blonde hair, slipped the robe from her shoulders, and let it drift to the floor. "We remind you that you are desireable. We remind you of pleasure."

She had small, firm breasts with delicate pink nipples and almost no areolae. Her flat hard stomach barely swelled below the navel, and her runner's thighs indicated that she would have two balls of hard muscle instead of buttocks.

She had been born with, or chosen, evenly gold-brown skin, absolutely hairless below the neck and perfectly smooth. In Hedonia, where youth was so central to the culture, that sort of look was fashionable. I tried not to feel like I was being invited to molest a child.

The tension or the little shudder must have been noticeable, because at once Piranesi was pouring the warm oil over my back and massaging it into my skin, his big strong hands working the muscles loose. I could no more have remained tense than I could have flapped my arms and flown away.

"We ask that you release your discomfort," Paxa said. Piranesi's hands moved down, concentrating on my low back, thighs, and buttocks. This was getting more and more pleasant.

Paxa knelt closer to me, her knees far apart. "Reach forward," Piranesi said.

I did. Paxa took my hands and began guiding them over her body. She had neither the sort of body I had been raised to like, nor the sort I had grown to like, but it was a very fine one of the sort it was.

With my arms extended, my shoulders and upper back were forced to relax more, and Piranesi added more warm oil and kneaded more firmly. "Let me guide," Paxa said. "Let me position your hands and move them for you."

It was interesting, and nice, but nothing special. Piranesi's hands moved down. He pressed my buttocks apart, and a moment later his thumb slipped gently into me and began pressing against my prostate. His free hand massaged the tight spot in the muscles around my tailbone.

He was good at it; it would have stiffened a rag doll. In a minute or so, I was about as ready as I'd ever been. Gently, the two of them turned me over, and Paxa straddled me. My type or not, she was beautiful, and highly skilled, and it didn't take long before I came.

Then they oiled me on the front, and said more vague and meaningless things about recovering and renewing and healing. With all the nice physical attention, they made me excited again, and this time Paxa took a turn on the bottom.

After that second time, there was another rubdown, and a sponge bath to remove the oil. They spoke and chanted an endless plethora of sentences that used "relationship," "growth," "renewal," and "pleasure," over and over, some of it in time with that random set of odd noises that they used for music. The oiled touch, the gentle sounds, and the indirect light, quickly put me to sleep. My last thoughts were about Raimbaut, whom I would be wearing; and then that to understand Raimbaut, you had to understand all of us *companho*; and from that thought, I slipped so seamlessly into the memory of how the *companho* formed, that I could not, afterwards, have said which parts I recalled, and which parts I dreamed.

For a long time I believed, contrary to evidence, that had it not been for Marcabru, I would never have had any friends at all. In many ways this belief was foolish, for Marcabru probably cost me as many friends in the long run as he caused me in the short run. But when I was a small boy I was sure of it.

The Occitan culture is not as single-minded and devoted to pleasure as that of Hedonia, but Nou Occitan is still very much a culture of pleasure, and within such a culture children are often loved, and cared for with great affection, if for no other reason than that many people do enjoy caring for children, and children enjoy being well-cared for. But children are never abundant because to care for them well requires the efforts of a very large part of the people who genuinely like children, plus the assent of many who don't.

So Nou Occitan had a low birth rate, abundant care to the

point of spoiling available for the few children who were born, and (because after a few years of raising a small child, most parents wanted substantial time off) an extensive tradition of boarding schools for ages eight and up.

I went to St. Baudelaire's in Noupeitau, where both my parents had gone, and three of my grandparents too. As schools went, it had a middling reputation, good but not great.

Like most Occitan children, I had been thoroughly pampered and coddled. My parents had encouraged me in nearly everything. This was part of the Occitan system for producing creative artists; first the person must feel special and entitled, and associate that with creative work. The next step would be to make us feel lonely, isolated, and misunderstood, and would not be nearly as much fun, but through the centuries, in many different civilizations, creative artists have been drawn from people who are hurled from a loving Eden into a cold, bleak, savage Looking-Glass Land. The process is brutal but it creates the drive that leads people to find and train their talents.

Of course, for people who have little talent to train, the process creates only extreme, deep, lasting unhappiness. Occitans talk about our artists with pride, and we ignore our suicide rate with cultivated disinterest.

At eight stanyears old, all I knew was that my mother was being what my father called "ridiculously sentimental," my father was choking with some mysterious respiratory problem, and both of them were trying to get rid of me forever. I clung to them, cried, and was sternly told by my father that no one in the family had ever gone to a day school—that was for weaklings and mama's boys. Within minutes my mother asked if I'd rather go to day school. I manfully-but-blubberingly refused it.

My small trunk containing all of my personal possessions

was placed at the foot of my bed, the shirts, short pants, and jackets of my school uniforms were hung neatly in the closet, and the dresser drawers were stuffed with clean, neat socks and underwear. It was time for my parents to go. We went back down to the broad cobblestone courtyard. I clung to my mother, then to my father, then to my mother, like every child there (except a few bold ones who were running in circles, shouting and whooping).

After the parents left, the teachers came out, shouting directions, calling each of us by name, assembling us into groups. They then marched us to the dining hall and gave us bread, soup, sausages, fried potatoes, and pudding in quantity—the only meal at all to a child's taste we had all term.

From the dining hall we were then taken to the exercise field, where they had us all run a few short distances and a couple of middle ones, recording our times but not telling us much of what any of it meant. They showed us different pieces of sporting equipment, asked us to demonstrate simple moves, and took more notes. They asked us to do odd little tests like standing on one foot with a dumbbell held in front of us. Last, they took us to the swimming pool, where they made each of us swim a couple of laps, to see who knew how to swim and who did not, and probably also to get us all at least slightly clean.

They marched us back, gave us a snack, and let us all brush our teeth and comb our hair. At last they put us to bed as early and as tired as possible. (Homesickness tends to strike after dark, so they weren't going to let us see too much night for the first few weeks.)

At dawn the next morning, the housekeepers in the hall shouted us awake. I dressed hastily and ran into the hall to follow the mob to the dining hall. They put us in a long line for food, and told us that we could sit as we wished and talk or move as we wished but that in one hour there would be no more food, so we had best eat.

"They try so hard to sound mean," the boy behind me said.

I looked back. He had jet black hair and pale blue eyes. His skin was almost pallid. He had a big, merry grin.

"Sounds enough to me like they mean it," I said.

"Then I guess you better do what you're told."

"I don't know if it sounds *that* much like they mean it."

"Well," he said, "if we're *both* smart enough to keep our heads down, then I guess we won't know how serious the threats are until the first poor idiot breaks the rules."

That took no time at all. A boy at the front of the line demanded to have his eggs prepared in some special way that, probably, only the boy's mother knew. Told he could not have that, he shouted at the cook.

A tall, thin man with a narrow, rodentish face, wearing a bright red traditional costume, appeared from a side door and strode rapidly through the crowd. He grabbed the boy by the collar, and dragged him into the open area in the middle of the room. The boy seemed to be too startled to resist. With one hand still gripping the boy's collar, the man pushed him down so that he was kneeling on the floor.

"This boy is *ne gens*," he said.

I certainly knew the term. My mother used it for anything she didn't want me to do that wasn't actually criminal or dangerous—but here, apparently, it was criminal. "It is *ne gens* to insist upon special treatment from the staff of this school," proclaimed the tall, thin man. "I am *Donz* Peire Sanha Johan," he said, "And I am the headmaster here." He looked around at all the new children. "You will call me *Donz* Sanha Johan, or you will call me *donz*. You will use one expression or the other in every sentence that you speak to me.

I am the only, the final, the ultimate judge of what is *gens* and what is *ne gens*.

"There is no reward for doing what is *gens*. That is expected from anyone with even a trace of *merce*, *qratz*, or *enseingnamen*. Therefore there is no need to reward it. *But!*—" I seemed to hear an organ chord crash with a mixture of sorrow and mounting horror as he looked around the room—"there are some here, I deeply regret to say, who do not have the *merce*, or the *gratz*, or the *enseingnamen*, which they should have. And there are those who have it only *sporadically*." He spoke the last word with deeper, nastier sarcasm than I had ever heard before; even worse than to be *ne gens*, was to be *gens* only now and then, or without full volition.

The boy was crying now. "It is also *ne gens* to cry when you are punished," the headmaster said, firmly, without rancor, but in a tone that suggested that he was explaining something to someone unusually stupid. "It shows a lack of *enseingnamen*, for you should not fear physical pain. It shows a lack of *gratz*, for you do not appreciate the correction which your superiors are taking the trouble to provide for you. And it shows a deep lack of *merce*, for when you have so offended everyone around you, your atonement is needed to make them feel better after the offense. Everyone here—" He looked around, obviously daring any of us to disagree—"was disgusted by your behavior toward our assistant cook. That is not the way to treat someone who waits upon you. Now." He grabbed the miserable boy by the back of his head, sinking his fingers into the long, curly red hair. "This is what happens to those who are *ne gens*."

Donz Sanha Johan nodded to one of the older boys, who rushed off with a cheery smile, and came back a moment later carrying a small stool. The headmaster bent the boy over the stool, then drew a thin rod, not bigger than a pencil, from his pocket. He clicked it, and with a loud pop, a thin, translucent line extended about half a meter from it, ending in a flickering red tip.

It was a neuroducer epée.

"Hold the stool by its rungs. Put your chest down on the seat," the headmaster barked at the boy.

Though sobbing, the boy gripped the stool to his chest, bent almost double.

With the tip of the epée, slowly, seeming to take forever about it, the headmaster drew a large X on the boy's buttocks. The boy clenched his teeth, and though tears poured from his face, he managed not to open his mouth to shout. But the whine that did escape was probably more horrifying to the rest of us than a scream would have been.

By the end of the term, all of us would discover personally that the neuroducer on the headmaster's epée was a special one for the purpose—set not to simulate a razor sharp blade in its sensations, but merely to induce a tingle like sunburn. Objectively it may not have been much, but the majority of us had never really been punished for anything before. Witnessing the punishments probably changed us as much as real pain could; we lived in terror, felt powerless in the face of authority, learned to hate it for its arbitrary cruelty, and felt all the more alone for our hate and fear. Some of us were on our way to the sense of spiritual isolation needed for the arts; most would merely feel alone and unwanted for the rest of their lives.

The boy, now sniveling and keening, was sent to the back of the line and told that he could have breakfast—if any were left—after everyone else.

Donz Sanha Johan looked around and said, firmly, "Now, there is one other rule concerning punishments, and it is the most important of all. Anyone who teases this *toszet*, anyone who makes him feel any shame, anyone who causes him the slightest discomfort in addition to what he has already received, anyone who mentions it when it would hurt his feelings—will receive double whatever punishment the offender received. This rule applies to every punishment. If you are confined to the school grounds for two days, and someone makes fun of you for it, he will be confined for four days. If you poke fun at someone who received five stripes on the back, your back will receive ten. There are no exceptions at all to this rule. It is even applied to your teachers. So, remember that although we are strict, here, and our punishments harsh—once they are over, they are absolutely over. Is that clear?"

We all nodded, dumbly, afraid to be noticed.

He looked around and said, "A room full of bobbing heads. Now, this is *ne gens*."

For a moment we all froze, thinking that he might punish us all. But he shook his head and said, "I can see that much correction will be needed. For the moment, we'll be merciful in this matter. Let us try again. The correct answer is *Oc, Donz Sanha Johan*. Is this clear?"

"*Oc, Donz Sanha Johan!*" we all said, in loud unison.

"Let me stress that. '*Ja*' is a vulgarity, however common it may be. '*Oc*' is the proper word when speaking to your superiors. Is that clear?"

"*Oc, Donz Sanha Johan!*"

"There is hope yet," he said, looking around the room. "You may now talk among yourselves again."

The boy behind me said, "Well, I think you win the argument. That didn't look like pretending to me."

Realizing that this might be one of those mysterious *companho* that my father had assured me I would acquire soon, I said, "My name is Giraut."

"I'm Marcabru."

"I'm from Elinorien," I said. It was a little town on the

west coast, where, right now, I desperately wished to be, but I didn't say that.

"And I'm from Noupeitau," Marcabru said, "but my parents are on a long fall vacation in Terrbori, so that I won't have anywhere to run home to, they say. They say I won't have the proper experience unless I'm all by myself."

"Letting you find your own *enseingnamen*," I said, making the standard remark about a standard practice. *"Que merce."*

"Ja." He nodded vigorously. I thought there might have been tears in his eyes, so I immediately followed the rules my mother had taught me for polite conversation—always ask about the other person, and start with what they like to do, then what their favorite school subject is, then what their favorite anything is, then where they stand on any controversy.

"What do you like to do?" I said.

"At the moment," Marcabru said, smiling, "I would like to eat breakfast."

"Ja," I agreed. "The line looks long, doesn't it?"

He'd obviously been given some rules for having a conversation, too, because the next thing Marcabru said was a complete non sequitur. "Last year my father started me with epée."

"My father started me with it too. I don't think I like epée as much as I like ki hara do."

"Oh, my art is nisabo. But I've only been doing it for a little while. I don't even have a rank yet."

"Ki hara do has all kinds of belts," I said. "I'm an orange belt. They said they'd have ki hara do here and I'm signed up to keep studying it. Will they have nisabo here for you?"

"Ja," but it's still the epée that I really love."

It all seemed like the first few pages of a language book, as if we might suddenly give each other directions to the post office or talk about whether this was the line for tickets, but at least we were managing to talk, and I didn't feel nearly as alone. After a long, awkward pause, he revealed that our mothers must have taught us the same rule book—he asked, "What subjects do you like?"

"Poetry and music. Those are the only two I really like."

"You're going to be a *trobador*," Marcabru said, grinning. "This will be perfect!"

"Why?"

"Because I intend to be a great brawler, and there will be someone to chronicle my deeds."

I laughed. "Well, if you supply the deeds, I'll supply the songs."

We both laughed. Long before we reached the head of the line, we had established that although we didn't rank everything the same, we liked many of the same things in games, entertainment, and food. We could each make the other laugh. For two small, lonely boys, that was more than enough to start a friendship.

Marcabru and I were best friends within two days, and for the rest of the term we were inseparable. We ate together in the dining hall every meal. We watched each other's backs against bullies. We lied to protect each other from authority. We chose each other whenever we were team captains. We chose desks next to each other in the study room. In short, we did everything that *vers companho* do.

■ 4 ████████████████

I awoke in Piranesi and Paxa's guest room, slightly over a full day later.

My freshly laundered and folded clothes were in a pile on a side table; I dressed quickly, wondering how I could have slept twenty hours. Experimentally, wondering if the Service of Consolation had worked, I tried thinking about Margaret. I missed her, I wished I were going to see her again soon, but I wasn't miserable and it seemed like a problem I could ignore for the moment. So, maybe.

I emerged from the guest room to a wonderful smell, so unexpected that I had to think for a moment. *"Pescaroz!"*

"Well, as near as we can manage," Piranesi said. "That's the problem with surprising someone with his native dish—you can't ask him what's authentic. But we think it's impressive, and you can always have the fun of correcting us."

I approached the stove and looked at the dish cooking there. "Not a problem at all, I can tell," I said. "You're going to poach the fish in the same mix you used for stir-frying the cabbage and peppers?"

"That's what your mother said when we commed her," Paxa said. "But we didn't ask her and the instructions in all the cookbooks we can dial up are ambiguous; when does the lemon go in, and how?"

"Quarter it, squeeze it over the fish, and stir fry the peels with the vegetables," I said. "Looks like you're nearly done."

"Now that we know what to do, yes." She handed the vegetable pan to Piranesi and said, "Stir, love." He kept it swirling around as she plopped the fish into the white wine and broth, squeezed the lemon over it, covered the fish pan, and tossed the peels into the vegetable pan, which she took back from Piranesi without missing a beat.

"Now, go sit down at the table while I throw all this together—Piranesi, pick up the salad and shake up the dressing, Giraut, carry in those three bottles of wine if you would—there we go."

The meal was everything needed for an excuse to get pleasantly drunk and gorged. The *pescaroz* was accompanied by heavy brown bread, tomato salad, and Hedon Glass— their thin sparkling white wine that tastes faintly of flowers and honey, and hits like aquavit.

As she finished dinner, Paxa said, "And this completes the ceremony."

"*Deu*, I hadn't realized we were still in it."

"That's part of the point," Piranesi said seriously, dipping a piece of bread in the juice still on his plate. "People don't know they're still recovering, either, and the time of recovery can include some of the best times of your life."

"Lovely way to make the point."

"We think so. That's why we wrote it that way."

My head was warmly, pleasantly fuzzy, but I managed to say . . . "What did you . . . I mean . . . who, no why—what?"

The question must have been clear from context. "The Service of Consolation *is* a Hedon tradition," Piranesi said, grinning at me. "That much is perfectly true. And yours was completely traditional. The tradition is, we make up whatever we think would be good for the person. Usually sex is good for broken hearts, which is how the ceremony earned its reputation. But the actual mandate is that your friends do whatever they think might break up your personal grieving cycle, before it gets all stuffed full of guilt and morality and turns into addictive depression."

I stretched out, took a sip of the icy clear wine and let it sting my tongue, and then brought a bite of fish to my mouth, letting it melt until I had to swallow. I followed that with a chewy bite of dark bread, and another sip of wine. "Well," I said, "thanks for sharing . . . and I think your idea of what to share is *lovely*."

I felt my mouth forming the words, "I think he's beginning to wake up."

I had been dreaming of Raimbaut sitting across the table from me at Pertz's table, laughing. I became aware that I could see Paxa and Piranesi in front of me, and that I was sitting up.

My cotton-dry mouth was forming words differently, but I had enough control to slur "I'm here."

"I've been awake for about half an hour. Paxa and Piranesi have explained what has been happening to me," my mouth said, perfectly clearly. That time I clearly had a sensation of Raimbaut controlling it, like a streak of cool metal running painlessly behind my eyes.

"That's good," I said, my mouth still far behind my mind. As they had told me it would, the anesthesia was hitting me, in my brain, but not Raimbaut where he lived, in the psypyx at the base of my skull.

•Can you hear me if I just think in words?• he asked, without speaking.

•Yes,• I thought back. •For right now, I'd rather that you'd tell them what I say, than try to say it myself. I don't seem to have much fine motor control.•

"Giraut will talk through me until he gets fine motor control back," Raimbaut said. My mouth still felt far away.

"The aintellect that supervised the operating room said it was going to be at least three hours before you were all the way back, Giraut," Paxa said.

"Meanwhile," Raimbaut said, "while your neuroblok wears off, I've been practicing, and I think, if your kind friends will

help us, I can walk us back to your apartment, if you wish."
•It might give us some privacy for working out how to share
the body.•

•Good idea. I'm terribly tired. Am I allowed to fall asleep?
I can't remember.•

Raimbaut looked up at the ceiling—to me, it looked as if
the ceiling swung down toward me—and said, "Giraut wants
to know whether he's allowed to fall asleep."

A flat voice from the ceiling said, "Certainly. As long as the
pyspyx, emblok, and geeblok are not disconnected at any
time, he can do whatever he wants, although he is strongly
advised against the consumption of alcohol or any central
nervous system depressant."

Raimbaut snorted, a sound I rarely made anymore. It felt
very odd in my nose. "Well, Giraut," he said, aloud so that
Paxa and Piranesi could hear him, "I hope that *you've*
changed, because I will be a little disappointed not to be
able to have wine for two years."

•*Ja, ver, tropa vera,*• I thought at him. I fell asleep, and
perhaps because he was probing in my memory, or perhaps
because the past was on my mind more than usually, I
dreamed I was back at school, again.

One day, in poetry class, we were working on complex
scansions and the difficulty of sustaining emotional
force across them. It was not a very sophisticated discussion—how could it be, when eight-year-olds were conduct-
ing it?—but *Donz* Maines, a nice older man whose hair was
always in a mess, was being very serious about it. He was
drawing pictures on the board and trying to coax us to say,
for ourselves and in our own words, exactly what the problems were with complex scansion. We were not getting very
far, but it wasn't for Maines's lack of effort.

Tentatively, a very small boy in the front row said, "The

more of your brain is counting the scansion to make sure it is perfect, the less of your brain there is to feel with."

"I feel with my fingers," said a large boy in the back, very loudly. I cannot remember his name anymore. He was a bully who would go home halfway through the term, due to homesickness. "What a stupid answer, you raw piece of shit."

The small boy turned very red.

Donz Maines drew his epée, set it with a bang that reverberated in the suddenly silent room, walked up the aisle, put an *X* on the chest of the bully, doubled it, and closed the epée with another echoing bang.

The bully stared at him stoically—most successful bullies tolerate physical pain well.

As the teacher returned to his desk, the bully hissed at the small boy, "You got me notched, you raw piece of shit. I'll get even with you. We're going to fight tonight after dinner."

I don't know what got into me. Maybe the thought that if people could be harassed in poetry class, one of the parts of the day that I lived for would lose most of its savor. Maybe I liked the little *toszet* better than I liked the bully. Or maybe I liked the idea of beating up this particular bully—for some reason I was sure I could.

"You can fight me first," I whispered to the bully.

He blew me a kiss.

In Occitan, I told him that when he was born, his mother called the proctologist.

Donz Maines's hand landed on the back of my neck. He paraded me to the front of the room and gave me four *X*'s on my chest.

The tiny boy in the front row gazed at me in awe. The bully never came around to collect on the fight, the faint pink cross on my chest faded within a few days, and, by bearing with an unfair punishment to protect the smaller boy, I had achieved some reputation among my classmates for *gratz* and *merce*; Marcabru seemed to be proud of me.

The next day, at breakfast, I was there earlier than Marcabru, and the small boy I had intervened for the day before shyly approached the table. I invited him to sit down. Making use of Mother's all-purpose questions again, I learned that his name was Johan, and I was his first friend. A few minutes later Marcabru came along and became his second.

Johan was quiet and shy, but his loyalty ran deep, and there are advantages to having a friend who is smarter than both of you put together. I think he was amazed, all his life, that anyone ever even wanted to be his friend. Certainly, of all of us, he was always much the most loyal.

Three is a small *companho*; four or five *companho* are thought to form the ideal sized unit. So I suppose we were all of us looking for another *companhon*.

Rufeu was added to the group when we needed a fourth for the pairs dueling tournament. Given Marcabru's ambitions and predilections, it was simply impossible that we would not be entering it, even though normally students waited until they were nine or even ten. We needed two pairs to enter, and though Johan and I together would be fodder for the older, bigger boys, Marcabru was well-drilled enough and fast enough to have a chance—with the right partner—to beat any other eight-year-olds we came up against, and stand a chance against weaker teams of older boys.

Marcabru had noticed that, although Rufeu was so shy that he was still eating by himself at the end of the first term, he was a strong, fast, agile fighter—an odd combination in an Occitan, since the instrument we tend to be best at is our own horn, but there are deviants in every culture.

After some discussion, the three of us decided to ask him

to sit with us at dinner to discuss the possibility of his being our fourth. As children, we thought that if you invited someone to join you in one thing, you were inviting him to be a *companhon*, and so we took it much more seriously than older boys might.

We approached him after gym class. Marcabru explained that we needed a fourth to enter the competition. Perhaps Rufeu would be willing to eat with us tonight to talk about it?

Rufeu burst into tears. At first we thought that was because he didn't want to, and all three of us apologized frantically. After he became calm enough to speak again, it emerged, between sobs, that Rufeu had been terribly lonely all through the first term. Within minutes, we were discovering that he was that not-so-rare phenomenon—a shy person who loved to talk—and he didn't stop till bedtime. The *companho* was up to a respectable four, and we thought we'd probably close it to further admissions, then and there.

With Rufeu partnered with Marcabru, and me with Johan, we finished thirty-first in a field of thirty-seven in the St. Baudelaire's Second Term Tournament, beating out the other four teams of eight-year-olds, and two exceptionally slow and sluggish teams of nine-year-olds. Honor was served, I suppose, and at least a few older boys began to admit that Marcabru and the boys of our *companho* were recognizable.

When I woke up again, we were back at the rented house. Raimbaut was idly shuffling through my recordings. •I'm so glad you kept up with this and did well at it, Giraut. We all thought you were the genius in our crowd. Well, I guess Marcabru didn't think so. He thought he was. But for the rest of us, looking at all this makes me think that maybe we were right. You've played concerts on what, seventeen worlds?•

•Well, yes, but two of those were Wilson and Nansen, where I had to be there for other reasons, and I did a tour of the Sol system, which added six worlds right there. Still, yes, I have played a lot of places, and I think done pretty well in all of them.• It seemed pointless to try to hide my pride from anyone who could feel my emotions. •Partly it was just a matter of having my day job with the Council of Humanity.•

•Well, I remain impressed. Would you like to try walking across the room together?•

•*Oc, ja.*•

•Then let's try it.•

At first we clumped like a robot in an Industrial Age movie, but after our third trip around the room, we were walking more or less normally.

•Shall I let you have your body back for a second, while we're moving?• Raimbaut asked. •They say that's one of the hard parts.•

•Sure.• I stumbled on the first step but then walked well enough after that, so much so that I wondered if he'd accidently disconnected. •Raimbaut, are you still there?•

•Very much.•

•Could you hear my thinking?•

•Not as well as I can when we're sharing motor function, Giraut, but yes.•

I felt strangely reluctant about something—no, Raimbaut felt something. I thought, •There's something you want to talk about but you're not sure how to begin.•

Unhappy surrender passed through my mind in an instant, something like a sigh. Raimbaut thought, •Giraut, I am told that one of the things that drives hosts mad when they carry a psypyx is that sooner or later, the person in the psypyx begins to look through their memories—or else if their privacy is respected, the person inside the psypyx must spend hours every day reading things and viewing recordings that the host is already familiar with.•

•Well, that's what they told me, too. I suggest that you feel free to start going through my memory. You may not approve, but it will save me a lot of explaining. At least if you look through my memories you will know not only what I did but how it felt.•

A sweet smile crept across my face, an imitation of the Raimbaut-smile I remembered so well. •Oh, I think it will be all right,• he thought. •I'm just glad to be back. I'm told I can access your memories while you're asleep, but they won't always be coherent and the process may give you extraordinarily vivid dreams from your past.•

•Most of my past, I won't mind dreaming about,• I thought. •And I'm afraid I'm exhausted again. They say it will be four to six days of this, and right now I'm so tired—•

•Then sleep.•

I did, plunging swiftly toward sleep. He walked my body into the kitchen to order a meal. Barely, I thought •remember no wine—•

•Yes, Dad.• The gentle, sardonic thought came from far away. I fell deeply into dreams.

I had only been a jovent, really, for about twenty more standays after Raimbaut's death, because I had gotten caught up almost immediately in the affair that had led to my moving to Caledony, meeting Shan and Margaret, and eventually joining the OSP. Raimbaut also went through some other memories; I could hardly blame him for those, either. Who, given a chance to know exactly what his best friend thought of him, day by day for years, would be able to resist that temptation?

Where his mind touched my memories, dreams sprang up like soldiers from dragon's teeth.

The *companho* might have stayed at four—that was a usual size for such a group—but for three coincidences. We gained two "auxiliary" members, and through them, we gained our fifth full member. At the time I thought it weird and was sometimes embarrassed by the strange circumstances surrounding *mos companho*, but looking back I think that I was very fortunate; probably it had something to do with my adapting as well as I did, to the wider Interstellar world, later on.

Perhaps the most embarrassing fact was that both the "friends of the *companho*," as Johan dubbed them, were gained via me, and worse yet, the first one was *really* unthinkable—a girl.

Bieris went to the female side of St. Baudelaire's and she was a daughter of two very old friends of my parents. We had played together constantly as small children in Elinorien. I never did learn how, but in her first term over on the other side of the school, she had somehow become unpopular. Even if I had somehow learned how Bieris fell from social grace, I'm not sure I could have understood it, and I'm very sure I couldn't have explained it. The social system for girls was elaborate and baroque far beyond that for boys.

Boys were allowed to make friends any old how; girls had to officially register their best friends. Boys determined prestige unofficially, and although we did all know who ranked who, friendships between high- and low-status boys were encouraged—where else would leaders acquire their most loyal followers?

Girls had a formalized system that was intended to make the creatively talented ones flighty, excitable, and demanding, and all the rest mad, so far as I can tell, now, looking back. Over on the female side of the school, they had weekly contests for beauty, poise, popularity, and *merce*, with the results posted for everyone to see, and friendships were only permissible within a narrow range of your own position. It is possible, though I don't know, that Bieris may have been unpopular only because she didn't get along with the half dozen girls whose overall scores were close to hers.

Even to my eight-year-old self, the job of becoming a proper *donzelha* seemed to be far more demanding than becoming a proper jovent.

For whatever reasons, although Bieris had lost out in all the contests of popularity and the normal solution would have been to transfer her to a more hospitable school and try again, her parents refused to move her to any more congenial school. Again, if I ever heard why, it was all in grown-up conversation that went completely over my head. Bieris might have fit in fine at some schools that catered more to athletes, or to serious students, or the *toszeta* type, but they wouldn't hear of anything other than her staying where she had started.

Eventually it did come out all right for her at St. Baudelaire. By the end of her school days, she was fully accepted, for reasons no more clear than the ones for which she had been rejected. But for her first three terms or so, Bieris had no friends on the girls' side, and therefore no one to pal around with every fifth day, when we had a free day. Normally that was a day for taking your pocket money and exploring around Noupeitau, but that isn't much fun by yourself. Sometime in Second Term, during a parental visit spent staring at each other across a table while our parents chattered, I offered to let her tag along with me, and to my horror, she accepted.

My other *companho* were surprisingly tolerant about it; I think perhaps Rufeu had a crush on her, and Johan thought she was great company, probably because like him she was a more serious student than the rest of us. She was funny and cheerful whenever the five of us were out together, clever and resourceful whenever we were finding trouble to get into, and calm and silent whenever we got caught. After a while, she was more or less automatically accepted, and now and then we even addressed her as *companhona*—a word that normally disappeared from the vocabulary when you went away to school, though it was what I had called her, always, when we had both been at home.

I first met Aimeric when he was still named Ambrose, during the break between Second Term and Third Term at St. Baudelaire's, in my first year.

I had known about the starship from Nansen arriving, of course—no one in Nou Occitan could miss that. Starships arrived perhaps once in twenty stanyears, and if I lived a long time I might be lucky enough to see five of them. In our isolated corner of human space, they came mainly from our one close neighbor, Nansen, in the Mufrid system, a "mere" six and a half light years away. Perhaps one ship out of four was from the other systems within starship range, Mu Hercules and 70 Ophiuchi, and supposedly the next starship, scheduled to arrive when I would be thirty-four, would be from Mu Hercules. But even this "routine" one was more than exciting enough, and the adults made sure we knew it would be exciting. In those long-ago days (it's hard to remember that I didn't see a springer till I was sixteen) a starship arrival was something you didn't want to miss.

For several nights, it was the biggest free show anyone had ever seen. Normally the sooty skies of Wilson, redarkened with fresh ash and soot every six stanyears when a polar forest burned down, allowed only the brightest stars to shine through. The occasional clear spots that appeared over Terrbori or Terraust in midwinter or midsummer were greeted by a rush of tourists, anxious to see what the "starry sky," familiar from so many poems and songs, actually was.

The soot that dyed our sun blood red affected everything from our sense of color and texture in art to our own soft, fair skin, but usually it meant that there was no good reason to look up.

The arrival of a starship into orbit, even seen through a veil of dirty air, is an awesome business. Satellite telescopes had been tracking it for more than a stanyear, as it rode down on the immense light-parachute that was its primary brake. Many pictures of it had been distributed. But the starship hadn't been bright enough for naked-eye observation until it was almost upon us. It had made a relatively close pass almost half a stanyear before, glowing like a barely-visible red moon as it took a deep turn toward Arcturus as part of its deceleration maneuvers. Then it had retreated to invisibility, almost an astronomical unit beyond Wilson's orbit before at last dropping in for capture. My father had taken me out on the beach north of Elinorien, on a couple of dark nights, to show me the little disk in the sky, its dim glow tinted orange by the upper atmosphere, and had said that I would be at school before we saw it again.

During the past few weeks, *Donz* Bisbat, who taught science and mathematics, had frequently shown us some of the pictures from his own telescope, and programmed the holographic orrery to illustrate the process of bringing in the starship. The only part that had held my attention had been his promise that when the time came, we would stay up late to see it.

That night, Noupeitau scheduled a two-hour blackout so that everyone could see, and by sheer good luck there were no clouds, and the soot was thinner than usual.

As the starship arrived, still traveling at something considerably above escape velocity, the planetary power ring would give it an assist in slowing down into orbit. "Far up above us, in Wilsonsynchronous orbit," *Donz* Bisbat explained, while we all danced around him, shivering from excitement at least as much as from the evening chill, "the VNPs—the power satellites—are always gathering energy, much more than we need, and sending us what we need via the ground stations. When a power satellite goes into the dark shadow of the planet, the other satellites relay power to it, so that its ground station doesn't go down. Now, the starship is coming down during one of those rare times when almost all the power satellites are in sunlight, and they are beaming all their power to a special satellite much farther out from us, made out of a whole asteroid to serve as ballast—because that satellite has the biggest laser you can imagine, and it needs a big mass attached to it so that the reaction from firing it won't move it too far or too fast. The special satellite will send out a laser beam, through a magnetic disperser that will spread the beam out, so that it hits the whole light-parachute and doesn't cut or burn anything. It will still be about two million watts per square meter, and if it weren't for the near-perfect reflection and heat dissipation, the whole thing would vaporize. The light-parachute will be very, very bright when it reflects all that light, and since it's about four thousand kilometers across, it will be like suddenly having a new star in the sky."

"Four thousand kilometers is forty percent as wide as Wilson itself," Johan said.

Donz Bisbat nodded at him. "Exactly right. And the ship will go from being a dot to being a disk to filling the sky, all within three days, as it decelerates down to orbit us."

"How do they get rid of the parachute?" Rufeu asked. "And what if the ship gets tangled in it?"

"The whole sail doesn't weigh as much as one large building—it's practically a wisp of nothing. And the ship hangs many thousand kilometers below it. When the time comes, and they cut it loose, the sunlight will blow it away, out into the galaxy. And even if a ship did run into it, it's so thin that they'd probably never know it happened—it would be like breaking through a wall of tissue paper in a trakcar—unless you look right at it, you'll never know it happens."

We all stood looking up, not wanting to miss the first moment. They rang a bell, and suddenly a star, almost too bright to look at, appeared directly overhead. It was brighter than a rainy day, with sharp shadows everywhere on the pavement, and the light was a harsh blue-white unlike anything we had ever seen from the sky before. The crowd gasped and oh'd.

"Why can't we see the beam going out to it?" I asked.

"Nothing to scatter or reflect it," Johan said.

By the end of the two-hour blackout, that first evening, the star had become a tiny dot, no bigger than a period in fine print.

Two days later, when we watched cast-off, the circle in the sky was gigantic, stretching across a fifth of the distance from horizon to horizon, the light was more than bright enough to read by, and it made the evening uncomfortably warm. Then the great round shape suddenly shuddered and began to distort, as the ship cast off lines; in minutes, it looked like a misshapen cookie with a couple of bites out of it. The laser turned off, and it was dark; as our eyes adjusted, we could barely see the faint silvery-red glow of the collapsing sail, now far above Arcturus's escape velocity and on its way to drift around galactic central point for the next hundred thousand years or so, until light pressure pushed it out of the galaxy or it fell into a star or black hole.

"There's the ship!" *Donz* Bisbat said, and pointed. There was an actinic flare as the ship's thrusters redirected it, and then a high, shimmering light overhead, like the biggest meteor you ever saw. "It's aerobraking," he said. "They'll skip against the atmosphere a few more times to get into the orbit they want."

This all happened right at the end of Second Term, and, while exciting, as a focus of my attention it ran a poor second to the adventures of we four *companho* as a pairs dueling team. I knew, in an abstract way, because of what they told us in class, that Nou Occitan was getting about seventy immigrants from Caledony and about thirty from St. Michael, but they were like the King or the more popular *trobadors*—people who existed, people who I might sometime see on the street or meet at a formal party, but not people I expected to have intruding on my life.

When I arrived home for break, a burly young man with a bad complexion had moved into my house. My father had had a new room grown onto the house, and it was occupied by Ambrose Carruthers, newly arrived economist from the culture of Caledony, on Nansen. Carruthers had been in suspended animation for about thirteen years. Mother said that a close friend of his had failed to revive—that was common on the old starships, which lost 5-10% of all passengers—and so this mysterious Ambrose Carruthers was depressed, which was why he mainly sat in the new room, reading and sleeping, except when we dragged him along on family outings, where he would sit quietly by himself until it was time to go home again.

"What kind of a name is Ambrose Carruthers?" I asked.

"It's a Caledon name," father said, very softly. "Keep your voice down. He's an economist, specializing in free market economics, which is an obscure branch of the subject that our culture happened to need, something about the deregulation of some areas—I'm not sure I understand it myself." My father had held many responsible positions in the government, including some that involved the Manjadorita d'Oecon, which served some of the functions of a treasury, a central bank, an interior ministry, and a wage-price bureau, or at least as much of such functions as Occitans were willing to tolerate, so whatever Carruthers was an expert in, it must be obscure indeed. "He'll be teaching and doing research for a while, here, at the University; then after some time he's to go to work at the Manjadorita d'Oecon. He's had a terrible shock—waking up here with his friend dead beside him. They revive them several times on the trip, it's very rare for someone to die late in the journey, and from what I understand his friend had made it all the way until the very last time. He's gotten some bad news from home, too. So whatever he's normally like, right now he's severely depressed. I'm sure he'll be more sociable when you're back for Long Break, but for right now please be quiet and polite around him."

"Oh," I said, having received far more information than I had really meant to request. "Why is he living with us?"

Father shrugged. "He was going to stay with the de Argenez family, but they have a new baby coming over there. So he'll be here until it's time for him to move to Noupeitau. Look at it this way—if you get on well with him here, you may have an adult friend in the city, when you go back for your next stanyear. And adult friends can be useful, you'll find."

I shrugged. "I can't make friends with him when he's so quiet and withdrawn—especially not if I'm not supposed to bother him."

Mother nodded. "We understand that, Giraut, *donz de mon cor*. Perhaps when you're back for Long Break, things will be different. Meanwhile, if you're going to play any noisy game, you might want to play it elsewhere."

I said I would, and that gave me a perfect excuse to run all over Elinorien with Bieris, terrorizing smaller children and annoying shopkeepers and parents. I think my own parents thought it was my best behaved break ever—a tribute to the blissfulness of ignorance. I saw Ambrose Carruthers only at meals; he was always polite, and smiled shyly at me when I said something impertinent, but that was as much contact as we had.

By the time I came home for Long Break, Ambrose was much easier to talk to. He had brown hair, washed out blue eyes, and a blotchy complexion. He looked no more than twenty-five stanyears old, but due to suspended animation, in real time he was past thirty-five. The pot belly, tired eyes, and grayish skin he'd had when I first saw him were disappearing as he recovered from the lingering effects of suspended animation and depression, and he was willing enough to talk to me, though he was awkward, as most young, childless men are around children.

He seemed to be happy to hear me talk about school and what happened there, and he was reservedly polite when *mos companho* would come over on a trakcar from their home towns. He didn't seem to want to talk much about where he'd come from, except to explain briefly that he was a Caledon, and that Caledony was very cold and wet. "I've never gone so many Lights before without putting on a coat, in my whole life," he said.

"What's a light?"

"Caledony has a very short day," he said. "Only about fourteen hours. So we count two Lights and two Darks in a day, and live on a twenty-eight hour schedule. Your twenty hour day is glorious! I always feel like it's so much extra time awake *and* so much extra sleep."

Then Bieris yelled for me to come out in the street, that there was a chance to go skimming with her family, so I made my apologies to my parents—very quickly, since both of them were academics and often failed to look up when I spoke to them—and ran out to join her. Beings from another planet were interesting, but skimming—the Occitan combination of surfing and sailing—was *fun*.

During the early part of the long break, they kept Ambrose busy over at the University—getting an office, getting a schedule, observing classes, and so forth. So I saw very little of him. Meanwhile, my old friends in Elinorien and I reveled in being big enough (and supposedly responsible enough) to be turned loose every day. We were pretty much at large, and ready to tackle the world around us, and we had more adventures and amusements than ever before. We climbed rock faces we shouldn't have been on at all, swam too far out in water that was too rough, became lost in the woods so many times that my father threatened to have my transponder embedded surgically, and did our share of petty thievery, lying, and cheating.

Occitan children grow up in an environment that actively encourages rule-breaking and danger during puberty. Nou Occitan has one of the higher death rates for children and adolescents, but the survivors have had a great time. In *Redsleeves*, probably his best novel, Cercamon Raimon says that because of our upbringing, Occitans are slaves to custom but very badly broken to law. He has a point.

Perhaps in a desperate attempt to have us not in mortal danger all the time, my father and Bieris's father came up with the idea of joint family camping trips. We did many of these and we took Ambrose along. I could tell he was mildly embarrassed by the fact that I had to teach him how to do very basic things, but he covered it well, calling me the "Olde Woodes Hande" and disciplining himself to listen and get things right the first time. For a grown-up, he wasn't a bad sort, and I began to think that maybe I could stand having dinner with him on fifth days.

At the end of the Long Break, Ambrose and I took the same trakcar back to Noupeitau, sharing facing seats and reading, comfortable in each other's company. "Your father is sending me money on the promise that I will either cook for you myself or take you to dinner every now and then. Why don't you pick the day that has the most dreadful food in the dining hall, and we'll make that the regular day for it? And I'd be happy to have you bring along *vos companho* if you like."

That seemed like a wonderful idea, so I kept my voice and face expressionless, and tonelessly said, "Sure, that would be fine."

The meals were great. Ambrose was always polite, even to children, which, if you are a child, is such a surprise (a person who doesn't feel free to hurt your feelings as most adults do) that you tend to think there must be some wonderful secret behind it. He took me and *mos companho* to dinner every time they had Tartine With Tomato Sauce in the dining hall, and Bieris often came along. Sometimes Johan's younger brother David came too.

We had a fine little group of friends for a lifetime, absolutely self-contained and perfectly balanced.

If we had thought about the question, we would have been very sure that we didn't need a friend like Raimbaut, a washout from Rimbaud Academy—our archrival school, which was a bad enough thing, but worse because it saddled him with being "Raimbaut from Rimbaud" for the rest of his time at St. Baudelaire's.

He had failed to make any friends at all there, become homesick and depressed, and spent his Second and Third terms of his first year at home, going to some awful day school, in a state of absolute disgrace. His parents decided to see whether a change of school might pull him out of it, and so he was doing his second year with us. It did not look promising.

He was taller than most of us nine-year-olds, and much thinner. He might have had a passable face if he had ever smiled. The hormones were hitting early, so he had body hair and acne already. At academics, athletics, and art alike, he was about average. He spent almost all of his time alone, because no one was looking for new *companho* now.

Yet he wasn't the sort of accepted natural loner that had a role in the social ecology of the school, for his time by himself didn't seem to be spent on any personal projects. He had a talent for mathematics, or so we were told, and took all the voluntary math classes he could, so that I suppose a thousand years ago he might have been a mathematician or physicist, but in our age all the real math and physical science were done by aintellects; for humans, these were trivial hobbies.

Raimbaut's one talent was to arrive—after an hour—at the same solution the aintellect found in a microsecond. Human mathematicians were about as common as human starship pilots or human terraformers, for the same reasons—it was simply something at which machines were absolutely better. Now and then it might occur to us, and make us shudder, that a generation before, the aintellects had tried to lever their various superiorities into full equality with humans, from which it would have been a short step to domination and control. People like Raimbaut were living proof of how far ahead of us the aintellects were.

His most noticeable personal quality was an awkward shyness, suggesting that not only would he often be *ne gens*, but he might never have the *enseingnamen* to outface the people who mocked him. To the extent that I thought about him at all, I thought how glad I was not to be him.

Because Raimbaut had come to us with a poor record from another school, during his first term he was on probation at St. Baudelaire, which meant, among many other humiliations, that he was required to wear the school's formal uniform every day, not just for special assemblies. Our uniform was bright yellow hose, a deep red tunic with gold belt, and a gold and black high-collared *tapi* that came down to the backs of our knees, all topped off with an absurd falling-over-the-side liripipe. Marcarbru's summary of the uniform was all too accurate: "it makes you look like a fireplug a dog would be ashamed to pee on."

Until Raimbaut was off probation, he would be stuck as the most visually conspicuous person in every classroom. It led to a great deal of bullying and harassment, despite school rules. Worse, some bullies resented Raimbaut because they had been caught being cruel to him and been punished for it; and in his uniform he could be seen from a long way off. So by the end of the First Term of our second year, he seemed to live permanently on the fighting ground behind the school, meeting boys there almost every day to fight with fists and feet, pugil sticks, or the "tickler" epées that we were allowed. Some days he might fight three or four of them *seriatim*.

He had *valors*, though, you had to give him that—I once saw him lose three fights, back to back, but he was trying every bit as hard on the last one as he had in the first. His best hope of acceptance, in some ways, was that the teachers who drew after-class referee duty uniformly praised his *espiritu* (despite the way they shook their heads at his ability).

It was Tartine with Tomato Sauce day, so Ambrose had taken me, Marcabru, Rufeu, Johan, and Bieris to a café, where we were eating the chopped olive and fish paste after the big bowls of spicy soup with noodles, and quietly hoping that he'd feel inspired to buy dessert.

There was great reason for hope, because Ambrose was doing his best to make the evening entertaining. Trying to hold up his end of the conversation, he was quizzing us about school life. He seemed envious that we were all spending so much time on athletics and the arts. We talked about my rankings as a fighter and musician, and Rufeu's evolving

fine style of manners, and the way in which Johan and Marcabru were beginning to develop the sharp, biting wit that
would be so essential to reputation in a stanyear or so.

Children aren't usually very interested in what things
were like when adults were children—that being lumped in
with the Stone Age, the Renaissance, and the Inward Turn as
events that obviously had happened but had nothing to do
with today. And Ambrose was so obviously uncomfortable
talking about his family back in Caledony that we had given
up even the hypocrisy of polite interest. We knew in a general way that it was dull where he came from, that he had
had a few close friends, and that one of them had died and
given the six-and-a-half-year reply time he wasn't expecting
letters from anyone at home ever again. That was about all
we knew of him. It was good that he was glad to listen to
us—every child likes to be listened to—and it didn't cross
our minds, much, that he seemed uninterested in being listened to.

Marcabru was recounting, blow by blow, his latest fight,
when Ambrose looked up from his post-dinner salad, and
asked, "Isn't that the uniform for your school?"

We all turned to stare out the cafe window. With Raimbaut's typical luck, he had been cornered by five of what we
later realized were the leading bullies from Rimbaud.

Those merry *companho* were playing the always popular
game of surrounding and pushing the weaker, younger boy,
trying to provoke him into charging so that one of them
could then hit him and claim to have been attacked.

We all looked at each other. Ambrose said, very quietly, "I
don't understand the rules, but that boy doesn't look happy.
And it seems to me that if you owe loyalty to your
school. . . ."

Marcabru shrugged. "He's not one of our *companho*. I
don't know that *enseingnamen* demands it . . ."

Johan was looking at me fixedly, and I was remembering how we became *companho*. "Well," I said, "*M'es vis*, whether or not *enseingnamen* demands saving that poor fool, we have a perfect excuse for brawling with Rimbaud, and I feel like a brawl."

The strange twinkle in Ambrose's eye told me a warm, happy account of this would be going to my father; I liked the way Bieris grinned at me, too. Now I was in it, for good and for all.

I got up, so Johan got up with me. Neither of the others was about to let us look more eager for a fight than they did, so now we were all in it. We went out the door in a solid little formation with Rufeu and me leading, followed by Johan, with Marcabru as rearguard.

"Raimbaut," I shouted, using a very old and corny callout that was the best I could think of at the moment, "that's our school uniform. Don't let shit touch it. Especially not shit from Rimbaud Academy. You'll never get the smell off."

Their heads snapped around. Five to four, and they were all bigger than any of us. Maybe five to five, since doubtless Raimbaut would kick a few buttocks when the Rimbaud boys turned to face us. Good odds for honor. Also good odds for getting ourselves a solid thrashing, so I tried to concentrate on the honor.

The tallest of them sneered, making sure we saw it was a sneer. "How nice. And how appropriate. St. Baudelaire's is now dressing up their boys as court jesters. We all know that Saint Bawdy-boys, however they dress, are simply the boys who didn't have what it takes for the Rimbaud Academy."

Rufeu growled, "You're talking to me so much, I'm starting to wonder if you're going to fight me, or if you're trying to work up the nerve to ask me if you can suck my dick."

At nine, dick-sucking was a new concept for me, but I immediately saw its usefulness in insult. Johan giggled, which was an even better effect. The other side, in unison, stood up straighter, doubled their fists, and turned an interesting shade of purple, so it had been a fine calling out.

Schools varied widely with regard to how much unarmed combat they taught, and how they taught it. I learned, later, that Rimbaud Academy trained its boys to fight with pure direct force, not finesse. Right now I was about to learn that if your whole side is bigger and stronger, pure direct force is a great thing to use.

Raimbaut jumped onto the back of the tallest one, wrapped his legs around the boy's waist, and beat on the back of his head with his fists, not an elegant fighting technique, but a first-rate diversion. The four of us rushed to get the all-important first blows in.

Those were very nearly the last ones we got in. We had more training and far more style, but they had more mass, more strength, and more reach. I hit one *toszet* three hard ones and went in for a throw. He grabbed my leg, flipped me over, and kicked me in the head. That was the fight for me.

From the ground, which was cavorting in circles as I clung to it, I caught a glimpse of Marcabru being shoved backwards against the wall and head-butted, and heard Rufeu's scream of rage as two of them, now free of other opponents, grabbed his arms and pulled them back, allowing the opponent who had been about even with him to hit him, hard, three times in the gut. I didn't see Johan but he said later that all he was able to contribute to our side was that he absorbed punches and kicks that the rest of us would otherwise have taken.

Raimbaut stayed in it longest. The big kid simply backed up and scraped him off on the wall. Finished with us, the others closed in and walloped Raimbaut, each taking a turn. As the little knot of Rimbaud boys pulled back, I saw Raimbaut sitting with his back to the wall, blood running out his nose, breathing hard. He had a big bruise under each eye.

Beating all of us into helplessness had taken considerably less than a minute.

The Rimbaud boys walked away, laughing at us. Raimbaut looked more miserable than ever.

Ambrose came out and checked us over. He had known Occitan custom too well to interfere, which would have shamed us all far more than our defeat. Bieris followed him, her eyes shining with pride at our having stood up to the bullies and indignation that we had been so roughly treated; *gratz* breeds early in Occitan boys, and probably her presence kept any of us from even thinking of crying.

Between them, Ambrose and Bieris gave us the things we needed. He gave us some quick touches with the antiseptic/analgesic spray he carried, while she cleaned our faces with a wet napkin. Both of them gave us a hugs and a word or two about our courage. And Ambrose bought us all big ice cream treats at the café. Raimbaut seemed to hang back, but Bieris grabbed him by the hand and dragged him along, instantly making him one of the *companho*.

After our noses had been wiped, and we had concentrated on the ice cream and syrup for a while, Ambrose looked around at us and said, "You were all much braver than I was at your age."

"Brave is nice, winning is better," Marcabru muttered.

"How would we know? We haven't won yet," Rufeu added.

"Have to fix that, soon, *m'es vis*," I said. "Somewhere out there, there has to be a group of *ne gens* shitty-trousered dick-sucking Rimbaud Academy boys that the five of us can give a beating to, *mos companho.*"

Years afterwards, Johan told me that he had seen Raimbaut look down and wipe his eyes; the word *companho* had never included Raimbaut before.

"I'd better deliver you all back to your school, now,"

Ambrose added. "Missing dorm curfew and getting grounded would spoil most of the effect."

The morning after a brawl is often the best part. Most of the pain is over and you have no more anxiety about how it will come out, and the endless talking about it is just beginning and hasn't gotten stale. There are still plausible lies and exaggerations to be added, and a residue of the adrenaline clings to your system somehow, making everything look brighter and more exciting.

In the breakfast line, the four of us were grilling Raimbaut on his interests, hobbies, and general ability to fit into *nos companho*, and discovering that he would fit in very well and seemed to be our sort of *toszet*. A very big older boy, twelve stanyears old at least, approached us. "Hey, you turds of a sea skunk," he said.

We all tensed; older boys sometimes harrassed whole groups of us younger ones, for fun. But this one didn't seem to be interested in that, and he wasn't one of the known bullies, so we waited, patiently, showing the respect that was required.

"Breakfast later," he said. "First thing you have to do is go see *Donz* Sanha Johan."

We trudged down the corridor in pure and total terror, not speaking, moving as slowly as we could without being noncompliant. An older girl, one of the much-privileged office workers, held the door open for us. We filed in, Marcabru first, me bringing up the rear, like prisoners going to a hanging, and were ushered into the Headmaster's private office by *Donz* Sanha Johan himself. At the point of his finger, we lined up in front of his desk. He sat down.

Next to him, in the guest chair, another man, older than our headmaster, glared at us with such ferocity that I almost forgot to be afraid of Sanha Johan.

After about as much time as it would have taken for a long, slow breath—if any of us had dared to take one—our headmaster said, "Well, boys, it seems that we have had a brawl. And it seems that in the course of this brawl, a blow to the face was administered to one of the finest trumpet players that Rimbaud Academy has ever produced. And this very fine trumpet player is now not able to play in the competition at the All-City Concert because his lip is swollen. And this is an outrage."

I wondered which of us had done it. Not me; the few punches I'd gotten in had been to the belly and chest.

"Now, we know you are the ones who were in that brawl," he added. "This man is Professor Ceszar, the headmaster at Rimbaud. He insists that you attacked his boys without provocation, that you deliberately injured them, and that it was only sheer *valor* and *enseignmamen* through which they prevailed and their injuries were not more serious." There was something odd in his tone—did I dare hope, sarcasm? "He said that the boys were just talking with an old friend— that would be you, Raimbaut—when the four of you came along to insult them and assault them."

"That's not true, *donz*," Rufeu said, calmly.

"Do you all agree that it's not true?"

"*Oc, ver*, I do, *donz*." I said. The others nodded.

"They were bullying me and beating me when *mos companho* came to my aid," Raimbaut said, "and they were all bigger than any of us, and there were more of them. *They* started it, *Donz* Sanha Johan."

"Good," Sanha Johan said. "Now, you will all sit here quietly while we discuss it."

Professor Ceszar said, "I know this boy well. I had to use the epée on him many times." He glared at Raimbaut. "Now, tell the truth. You were having fun with your old friends when these boys came by and tried to beat them all up, isn't that true?"

"No, *donz*," Raimbaut squeaked out softly, the terror in his voice obvious.

"You were the instigator of this, you lured my boys there to be beaten up."

"No *donz*," he said, pale and shaking. We could hear that he was on the edge of crying when he added, "*Donz* Ceszar, I'm not going to lie about it no matter how many times you ask me to."

The Rimbaud headmaster looked as if he might rise and strike the boy. "No one is asking you to lie."

"*You* are, *donz*." Raimbaut straightened. Tears ran down his cheeks, but he looked directly into Ceszar's eyes. "I was walking home from dinner at my older sister's house when they surrounded me and began pushing, shoving, and insulting me. Luckily my friends were having dinner across the street, saw what was happening, and intervened. But the Rimbaud Academy boys were bigger and stronger than we were, and we all took a bad beating." He seemed to dismiss Ceszar, turning deliberately toward *Donz* Sanha Johan. "I do feel badly about it, *donz*, because those boys used to beat me up all the time, and I feel very strongly that they probably would not have attacked my friends without my being there, and I don't think they'd have gone after me if I had not been in my school uniform, since they went out of their way to mock it. If there is any punishment to be meted out to anyone on our side, it should all fall on me, for being so incautious about provoking a fight. My friends looked out for me in an honorable way."

Sanha Johan nodded. I didn't think it was my imagination that he was eager with the next question; I saw him grip the desk and lean forward. "Have you anything else to say about the event? I am curious about whatever it was that involved the school uniform."

"*Donz*, they insulted our school uniform and our school colors, directly and deliberately, trying to get me to fight."

"I heard them myself," I said.

"And I did too," Marcabru added.

"We all did." Rufeu, too, was looking directly at the rival headmaster; something about the tone he'd used with Raimbaut, I think, had made us all loathe him. Raimbaut might be a poor hopeless idiot, but he was *our* poor hopeless idiot, and nobody else—*especially* nobody from Rimbaud— had any business discussing him.

Sanha Johan sat back with a big smile, and said, "My boys do not lie. My boys are as *gens* as any in Noupeitau, or in Nou Occitan. If you would care to offer challenge, you and I can settle this issue, Ceszar, but I shall ask for a fight *atz fis prim*."

We all held our breath. It was inconceivable enough that our headmaster would duel on our behalf—but to demand that it be *atz fis prim*, to the first death—meaning until one of them was in a neuroducer coma—was beyond that. *Atz fis prim* was what you insisted on if it was a matter of intimate, personal honor, not only for the sake of courtesy. Afterwards we all agreed; during the long second before Ceszar responded, we all went from fear of *Donz* Sanha Johan, to awe.

Ceszar stood, bowed curtly, and left. Our headmaster closed the door after him, turned back to us, and laughed. He beamed at all of us. "None of you boys is ever to tell me the truth, should it be any different from what you have told me. That was splendid, and a demonstration both of your fidelity to your school and your personal *gratz* and *enseingnamen*. Your parents will be glad to hear of this too, I'm sure."

We were ushered out so quickly that the whole event felt

like a hallucination. The older boy who had come to get us conducted us to a side room where a special breakfast was laid—more sweets and more meat than we were accustomed to. For the rest of the week, we were sore, but we all felt three meters tall.

5

I returned to consciousness, my mind still swimming with all the events of my couple of stanyears on Caledony—when I had fallen in love with Margaret, and had some friends whose names I rarely thought of now, some of whom had died, and thought that Shan was merely the Council of Humanity's Ambassador and helpful and friendly for a bureaucrat. Raimbaut was asleep, now, and from the feel of things in my mind, deeply so. Well, he also had been busy and had a lot to absorb.

I felt a funny, clean tingle in my urethra and reached down to gently handle my penis, which felt suspiciously as if it had been given some extra cleaning with a morning-after disinfectant. It looked like Raimbaut had taken our dog for a walk.

I thought about poking into his memories and could see no good reason to do so; nor would I impugn his honor by checking my credit record—I was sure he had used his own, if he'd needed to do that. In Hedonia, one seldom did, but then Raimbaut had been all but legendary among *mos companho* for his ability to not get anywhere with any *donzelha* under any circumstances.

I pushed up out of bed and checked the clock; I had been asleep for fifteen hours. I felt clean, rested, and hungry. I went to the kitchen and used the delivery springer to get a pot of hot coffee. I sat down, poured a cup, and took a first pleasant sip; Eta Cassiopeia should be rising immediately.

I was feeling good, so Raimbaut had not done anything too exotic to my body. The lack of Margaret felt more like a healing missing tooth than like a toothache anymore. Maybe

I hadn't cared as much as I'd told myself I had, or the Service of Consolation had unguessed power, or the psypyx installation disrupted the patterns of intense misery before they could take control. Whatever the reason, I was grateful to have the grief feel so old, so soon.

I opened the drapes, blinking at the sudden yellow light, and pulled my chair into the bright puddle of sunlight, to drink another cup of the strong dark coffee, and watch the parade of my current neighbors. At that hour, everyone was going to or from exercise, meditation, or perhaps an orgy, and the street was moderately crowded with people who were moderately naked. Hedons live in their streets, and in their mild climate, aside from sandals, clothes are for support or decoration only.

Definitely, I was feeling better. It was unfortunate that I was going to Earth; that planet didn't offer much to my taste. I would have to make sure, before we sprang, to give Raimbaut a good taste of the pleasures of Hedonia.

As recently as my teens, almost no one expected to see more than one planet in a lifetime . . . and Raimbaut had died in that old world, expecting to wake up a couple of weeks later in it, not fourteen years into the future and fifty-two light years away.

I pulled on a loose robe and slipped into my sandals. I would do some katas of the ki hara do, down on the beach, before it was crowded.

Walking through any Hedon town is joyful: sculptures and murals, interesting sounds, gardens of every kind. The streets wind, to forestall the temptation to hurry. It took me twenty minutes to walk the half-kilometer to the beach.

The tenth hour high tide had left the sand close to the sea smooth and soft. Now, at the fifteenth hour, tide was low, and here was a splendid place for kata, with sand firm enough to support, loose enough for turning, and soft enough to cushion. The early morning sea breeze was just cool enough. I kicked off my sandals and settled my mind to the task.

I ran through the two greater and three lesser katas, taking my time, trying to keep my concentration entirely within my body. Raimbaut was taking a long time to wake up, but that was only to be expected, with such a huge flood of new sensations to process. I assumed he'd be along, sooner or later.

As I finished the last of the lesser katas, a group of children were laughing wildly behind me. This was odd—usually if they're going to laugh, they laugh at the Stork moves in the second lesser kata, or at the Monkey in the second greater kata.

Holding and examining distractions, while not being overwhelmed by them, is part of what the katas are about, so I merely refocused my mind and kept working. When I finished, I was feeling playful enough to turn around and bow.

A rank of five mimic-seals all bowed back to me. The children, further up the beach, screamed with laughter. The mimic-seals had been copying me through most of that final kata.

•Where am I? What's going on?• Raimbaut was waking up.

•I've been teaching martial arts to seals.•

•Er, why?•

•The beach can be a rough place.• I shook the sand from my robe and pulled it back on, walking up the beach toward the children. The mimic-seals danced around me, begging for attention like friendly dogs. I rubbed their heads as they came under my hands; the mimic-seals took this as a signal to flop their way up the beach and scamper around with the kids.

•Too bad no one had a camera,• Raimbaut said, reviewing my short-term memory and catching up.

At this early hour, a few of the beach cafés were already serving breakfast, or perhaps had been serving it all night. It would be no problem to go into one of them in just a robe—in Hedonia, it wouldn't have been a problem to go in nude. We went into the first one that smelled strongly of fatty meats and oily pastries.

One advantage of being two old friends in one brain is that you can not only talk with your mouth full, you can both talk at once, and not all in words. As I had surmised, Raimbaut had gone out for the evening to explore Hedonia, and had quickly discovered one of the things that Hedonia is most famous for—the big public orgy rooms where people go to have anonymous sex, known as "stress treatment rooms" to Hedons (because for some reason they think stress is a disease, and that it's caused by lack of sex) and as "fuckaterias" to the tourists. •Really, Giraut, I just went in to watch.•

I had no time to hide a reaction; he knew I was laughing. But since defensiveness requires denial, and he felt me seeing through him, he laughed too.

•All right, I went in hoping something would happen, and nobody told me it would all happen in the first ten minutes and then we'd be done. Not a very romantic bunch, the Hedons, are they?•

•Not a bit,• I agreed.

After breakfast, I was already tired, and he was having a temporary surge of energy, so we agreed to take the body back to the apartment. Raimbaut wanted to listen to some of my music; I was only now realizing how important music had been to him in our jovent. He wanted to hear my very first commercial recording; he had died sixteen days before the party at which he was to have heard it for the first time.

I put it on and sat back on the couch, letting my mind drift, hoping not to interfere with whatever he might think of it. That recording was still my most popular—in a sense I peaked at twenty-one. *Cansos de Trobadors* contained no original work; it was merely a collection of seventeen of the art songs that Nou Occitan treasured and valued, the great songs by the great *trobadors*.

I had been a *trobador*, and a good one. Many people still thought of me as one. I didn't, because I thought of it as something you could only do full time, but then the original *trobadors* of two thousand years ago hadn't been full-timers, either, so perhaps I was being needlessly fussy.

I had intended to go to sleep, but the second song on the recording caught my attention; it was *Canso de Fis de Jovent*, Guilhem-Arnaut Montanier's magnificent dirge for a young man, or for the end of youth—the piece we had played at Raimbaut's funeral, which he seemed to have some memory of, from the previous time I had carried his psypyx. Montanier had died in a duel in defense of Yseut the Portraitist; Raimbaut had died in a brawl that started with a pointless insult; by Occitan standards, both deaths had been beautiful.

I wondered how my voice had ever been so young and so sweet. The spare traditional stylings weren't something I'd choose, now, but perhaps my earlier self was wiser.

Some fans liked my more recent compositions, and some had liked my compositions during the years when I bounced from culture to culture as an artistic affairs specialist for the Council of Humanity. Those two groups seemed to be always locked in argument. But the songs on *Cansos de Trobadors* were liked by nearly everyone except the few that called them "too pretty"—the polite expression, I assumed, for "kitsch."

As I listened, I knew I'd never hit my old rhythm again. Worse yet, my younger self was always right. I swallowed the self-criticism, trying not to disturb Raimbaut's experience.

•Sing along if you want,• he thought.

I restarted the recording at *Canso de Fis de Jovent*, and sang along softly, not trying for power or vocal tone, just wondering whether I could feel what my old self had felt while recording that song. As I sang, my whole life seemed to stand out.

It was like the way that, compressor-packing once in the thin-aired highlands of Cremer, minutes before sunset, I turned to see the mountain range where I'd been two days before. The whole range, all at once, leaped into my vision with painful clarity, overpowering all memory of the many days of winding trails, rough campsites, and tricky descents.

I finished the song and fell asleep, even as I was drawing breath to begin the next one, *Nos Qui Dormém en Montanha Valor*.

The school terms and the breaks between went by, and we all grew bigger and stronger and better at our arts. We adventured, fought, wandered about the city, fell in love with all of Bieris's friends (though never with Bieris herself—that would have felt like incest), broke rules and were forgiven, and raced through the time remaining until our jovent like puppies after mama.

Usually on holidays, one or two of *mos companho* would come home with me to Elinorien, to join "the expeditions," as Father and Ambrose called them. These were family camping trips, usually jointly with Bieris's family, out into the splendid wild country that by design would always take up most of the land area of Wilson, the beautiful planet that we were so blessed to have all to ourselves. There had been room for three or four more cultures, but they would have been scattered over half the planet's surface, with no islands larger than seventy-five square kilometers, and that violated the rule of contiguity. Thus we had been given a world to ourselves by accident of Wilson's geography—only one large island at the equator was reckoned to be habitable full-time, due to the ferocious cold and heat of the polar continents, caused by Wilson's twelve-stanyear year.

Since they would never be needed for human habitation—we intended to remain a sparse population, always—the many little islands all over our tropics and temperate zone had been seeded with a wide variety of life by the terraformers, and more were being seeded all the time. On Wilson, the number of interesting places to go outdoors was probably greater than the capacity of any one human being to see in a lifetime.

One evening, camped near a tall, glorious falls on the volcanic island of Corberan, when Bieris, Raimbaut, and I were about fourteen, we were sitting by the fire, late in the evening, with Ambrose. All the other adults had gone to bed; he was sitting and watching the fire. None of us had spoken in a while. I think we were all beginning to think of bed. It was less than half a stanyear until Raimbaut and I officially became jovents, and Bieris presumably would be coming out as a *donzelha*, so our thoughts often wandered away to the future, rather than staying in the present.

"I'm going to do something interesting when we get back," Ambrose said, solemnly.

It didn't seem to call for a response. The three of us sat and watched the fire.

Ambrose tossed in a few knots of driftwood, so that the flames leapt up, and said, "Want to broil one of the salmon and split it with me?"

"*Ja*," we said in unison.

Ambrose pulled a big one, already fileted, from the cooler, planked it with by-now practiced ease, and braced it up to cook by the fire. After a while he said, "I'm going to apply for full citizenship here in Nou Occitan. That means that I have to have an Occitan name—so after some consideration, I've chosen one, and gotten permission from the family that owned the name after it went extinct, and so forth. And in less than three standays, there will be no more Ambrose Carruthers."

"Who are you going to be instead?" Bieris asked.

"The name I've chosen is Aimeric de Sanha Marsao," he said. "And my residence is going to change. You'll probably think this is very funny, but I've taken enough dueling training, now, to be able to think about becoming a jovent."

Aimeric looked about the age where most men *stopped* being jovents, and he was older than he looked. Counting his years in suspended animation he was at least six years older than *that*. It seemed like a very strange idea to me. Some men did try to stay jovents forever, but it wasn't looked on favorably.

"It may sound odd," he said, "but I have you and your *companho* to thank for it. The only way I've been able to understand most of my colleagues at the University is by reference to how they grew up—and I've gotten to see more than two years, now, of how Occitans grow up. I think I will probably never understand, until I try being a jovent myself. So I know I'm old. I know I'll be made fun of. I have no idea how long I will stay in the Quartier des Jovents, or carry my epée, or anything of the sort . . . but I'm going to try it."

Bieris nodded as seriously as if he had really asked her opinion. "You don't have any *joventri* where you came from."

"Not even close. I was in a little clique called the Wild Boys, but it wasn't the same thing at all."

"Then it doesn't seem fair that you don't get to be one, just because you were born in the wrong place, does it? I think you should try it."

He smiled at her, strangely, and said, "Well, then, I think I'll have to."

We sat a long time without talking till the fire burned down. That was one of the last such trips I can remember, but not quite the last one, I don't think. I don't remember exactly which one was the last. I wonder why I let that part of my life slide away so easily.

Aimeric's decision to become a jovent—it took no time at all to begin to think of him with a normal, ordinary name like Aimeric instead of a bizarre one like Ambrose—had a number of extremely pleasant ramifications for me and *mos companho* during the following First Term. First of all, children were not allowed in the Quartier without an escort—partly because of the danger, primarily because what they would see was unsuitable to children. So since Aimeric would take us into the Quartier des Jovents now and then, to eat in a place he liked or to spend an evening at his apartment, we could take a good look at the place where most of us would be moving in less than a stanyear.

Aimeric's skill with the epée was progressing from adequate to fine and might someday soon be truly impressive. For one thing, he had the advantage that he drank much less than most other jovents, and his older body forced him to work out and practice more. As he improved, he became more confident about taking us into the wilder areas. We always came back to the Senior Dormitory with grand tales of the wildness of the brawls, the beauty of the *donzelhas*, the fine poetry and music in every cabaret and the beautiful art on every wall.

None of us was going to waste precious time at any of the universities—not now, not while there was a chance to be jovents—and all of us were very close to qualifying physically (Johan was marginal but still looked promising) and mentally (Johan led the pack). We put on extra effort, intending to graduate together at the end of Second Term, rather than Third. Once we graduated and qualified, we would automatically qualify for a jovent's public allowance, and emancipation from our parents. At fourteen, that's wonderfully motivating.

Donz Sanha Johan was well aware of how visiting with Aimeric fired our ambitions, and of what those ambitions were and how close we were to realizing them. In the five years since our brawl with the Rimbaud Academy boys, we had become his unquestioned favorites. To a conservative old Occitan like himself, we were exactly what boys ought to be, promising to become equally fine jovents. We were still all terrified of him (I think it would have hurt his feelings if we had not been), but now, besides the terror of our dreams, he was also our friend, protector, and ally. Whether it was coming up with a medical reason for Johan to have a couple shots of growth hormone, or Rufeu's extra tutoring in poetry, or Marcabru's psychotherapy to help him pass the maturity test, *Donz* Sanha Johan did whatever he could to make our dreams come true.

At the end of Second Term, we were licensed as jovents, were assigned small apartments of our own, and moved into the Quartier. The whole stanyear I was fifteen is still a blur to me. That was the year that I, and *mos companho*, tried out everything all at once—sex, wine, drugs, art, reading things that were not assigned, seeing performances, performing, publishing reviews and critiques, fighting duels in defense of who we fucked or what we published, arguing with each other about everything—all the things that seem so profound and wonderful then.

At the end of the first year, I wrote to my father to catalog my accomplishments. I had changed *entendendoras* twice (both had been virgins, both about my age—I was looking to impress my friends by getting an older one, perhaps seventeen or so, next). I had fought nine duels, three *atz fis prim*, and I had not died yet. I had been the opening act at four different cabarets, each time for well-known *trobadors*. Three of my poems were published in small journals (but I was giving that up—there was persistent complaint that they read more like song lyrics, and I was tired of fighting duels to defend them). *Mos companho* and I had been set upon in three brawls, and had won or tied every time.

I recall that the letter seemed to take a very long time to compose, consuming perhaps an hour of my time in the busy days before the excitement of Festival Night began—but I had put it off for so long that I could not possibly justify letting it go till Festival was over. I recall what a chore it seemed like, and I remember that years later, when I was home on one leave or another, my father showed that letter to me and Margaret, and all the memories flooded back at once.

I was awake again, back in my body. I stretched experimentally to see if either Raimbaut or I had done any damage lately. When two minds share a body, it's all too easy to wear it down.

Raimbaut was thoroughly asleep; he'd taken a long walk, and the visual stimuli in Hedonia are more than enough to overload even a very strong, stable, relaxed mind.

I didn't want to go anywhere much. I took a shower, changed into comfortable clothes, and went out for some greens and soup. I thought I should probably remind Raimbaut that the body at thirty-five is not the body at twenty-two—I had a feeling he'd been overeating, and I didn't want to get fat from his appetite.

As I was finishing, I felt him wake up. •Hello.•

•Well, what do you think of this part of the century?•

•Here on Hedonia, very nice. Definitely better than being dead. Shan called while you were asleep. I took notes.• My hand reached into my pocket, pulled out a piece of paper, and smoothed it down on the counter. •I hope they make sense.•

•Even if they don't, I can always call and ask for a repeat.• I looked it over. •Looks like you got it all.•

•I didn't know what it all meant,• Raimbaut thought. •When my last recording was made, springing between star systems was so expensive that I didn't know anyone who had done it. So I know the message has to do with how we spring, but it's all outside my experience.•

•Well, first of all, that's an Earth springer address and that's the time GST. I can check it, but I suspect that that's a springer into the apartment where we will be staying, at the OSP's Main Training Center in Manila, which is a big, run-down old city in the Philippine Islands. For a while, right after the Slaughter, it was the capital of the Western Pacific Region in the global government. Now it's a huge office town. It will be by far the biggest city you've ever seen in your life—it's a full-fledged hyperpolis—but on Earth it's not even in the top twenty.•

•Sounds different, interesting, and exciting.•

•Different, at most.• I checked the time again, and then pulled out my comp and checked. •We have two days to get ready. Time enough for some more long walks, another visit with Piranesi and Paxa, and packing—though that last won't take long. At the moment you don't own anything, and I live packed, anyway.•

Part Two

In
Her
Sweet
Secret
Treasure-
Box,
The
Key

We sprang direct to the apartment in the OSP building this time; for some blessed reason I'm immune to springer sickness, so I don't need to immediately take a walk outdoors to re-orient. My things had been sprung ahead of us, and the robots had followed instructions refined through dozens of trips. It took no more than three minutes to see that things had been stored properly in their proper places.

Since the only other thing on the list besides the meeting four hours from now was "recheck itinerary," I grabbed a quick, hot shower and changed clothes. Purely psychological—the "journey" had only been about four meters, as I experienced it, with a brief moment of walking through a curtain of fog in the middle.

Once I was dressed, I looked at the itinerary. It was exactly what it had been a couple of hours before:

> MEETING 1400 H PER PREV MEMO
> AFTERNOON AND EVENING:
> KEEP FREE, SPECIAL ASSIGNMENT

•Now, *that's* going to be hard to memorize,• Raimbaut thought. •*Senher Deu*, this place is absolutely institutionalized and boring, isn't it?•

•I'm afraid so. And that's just the first thing you're going to learn to hate about Earth,• I thought back. I checked my appearance, or perhaps our appearance, in the mirror. •We are now perfectly presentable. Perhaps a nap or some reading, before we go to the meeting? I'm afraid there's not much else to do.•

I could feel some sort of shyness moving through the not quite conscious parts of my mind; he blurted out, •I know you've been here many times, Giraut, but I haven't. And with the springers, since travel takes no time . . . could we go to . . . you know, the sort of, tourist places?•

We had one of those moments where the minds run together like cream stirred into coffee, and I knew how different the world was from his viewpoint. The difference was that Earth, for me, had always been nothing more than a place to work; I had made the requisite pilgrimages to the requisite cultural sites, with the clear knowledge that there were better places elsewhere. But for Raimbaut it was the first new world that he would have time to explore. I remembered how eager I had been to see Nansen, so long ago, and felt mildly ashamed to have inflicted my jadedness on my friend, even inadvertently.

•Of course! As much as we have time for, *bo certa!* As much as we have time for. As much as you want to. But then we do have to make sure that we keep traveling, so that you can see somewhere nice, too.•

•Indulge me on this and I'll be so happy that you won't have to make good on that promise.•

I chuckled, because I could feel our blended emotions, and thought, •By far the best thing about this job has always been stepping through the springer to put your boots down on a new world. And it still is. Once you have a body of your own, apply to the OSP, or whatever it's going to be called once the dust settles, and come along and see.• The jolt of pure pleasure at that suggestion made me add, •And if you don't, as your friend and companhon, I will damned well make you.•

I felt him laugh. •That won't be necessary. But now that you understand how I feel, can we see the tourist places? There are things *I've* always wanted to see—• I felt the images flicker through my mind—•and surely there must be some things here that impress you?•

Our first step through the apartment springer was to see the Grand Canyon of the Colorado, from the North Rim. Sightseers have been coming to it for nearly a thousand years, but that view simply won't allow itself to become clichéd or banal. Every political power that has had control of it has been careful to preserve it, and luckily it was never on the route of any army, nor the logical place for any industry. So, despite sharing a planet with 25 billion people, it's still in excellent shape.

It takes time for the eye to adjust to the combination of scale with intricacy; there's so much of any one part of it, and so many parts of it, that it takes the mind time to grasp how truly impressive it is. We had departed Manila at about an hour after local noon, which meant that it was ten at night locally. Earth has not had a really dark sky since around the time of the Third World War, so the light reflected from seven orbital cities that were above the horizon, plus the huge, tethered city of Gonzalez to the south (at that location, it's about two thirds of the way up the sky)—all of them very bright—provided more light than you would need to read by.

•There's no night here, ever, is there?• Raimbaut asked.

•Not anywhere on Earth. The terminator line is visible from orbit but it's not very sharp anymore. The "dark" side looks about half as bright as the "light" side.•

To see the Grand Canyon through his eyes was to see it for the first time—much more impressive than either of the times I had before (both because Margaret had insisted). Not just the shifting shadows as the moon and the eight cities cast their light into it; not just the wild profusion of cliffs, scarps, and faces; not just the far-distant view of the country beyond, or the steel streak of the river below, or the immensity of the whole picture; but the power that seemed to come up through your feet and flow out through your eyes into that view, like an infinite feedback loop, filling you with beauty till you thought you might fuse into it forever.

Our next spring was to the platform on Brabant's tower, overlooking the vitrified remains of Paris. Before us, the guide plaque helped to identify which low lumps had been the Pantheon, the Arc de Triomphe, and Mont Saint-Sulpice. For as far as the eye could see, the land was covered with the hard black glass.

•It's a pity there's no observation spot for Avignon,• I explained. •Brabant had originally wanted seven of these sites, but they built only four, and Avignon was one of the ones they cancelled. A gap in the antimatter cloud left part of the city wall and a little bit of the papal palace in recognizable form. It always seems to me as if that's the one, above all others, that they *should* have included. It would fit better with Brabant's vision—to make all the memorials places where you'd feel how much something was missing.•

Brabant's tower rests on the site of Notre Dame, of which nothing was left at all. The old city center around Ile de la Cité and Ile St. Louis was all low ground, so the cloud settled densely there in its few minutes of existence, eating a perfectly circular hole more than a kilometer across, as if someone had taken a red hot iron sphere and pressed it into a slab of butter for an instant. The hole was now filled with deep blue, almost indigo, water, and in this last hour before dawn, the bright sky with its many man-made satellites, stations, and cities reflected back up at us from the void where the heart of Paris had been.

From the west side we looked out from, you could see three of the five pieces of reconstruction that were also part of the memorial—the twin lines of *réverbères* that marked the former path of the Champs Elysées, the eternally glowing blue outline of the Hôtel des Invalides, and the slim—only two centimeters thick—diamond rod that held up the single white light marking where the top of the Tour Eiffel had been.

•I've never seen a space so empty,• Raimbaut thought, after a long time of mental emptiness.•I suppose that's what Brabant meant.•

•I always thought it was the most effective possible memorial—that sort of retro Late Industrial Age trick of expressing the void. It reminds me of the Guilhem IX poem, the one that begins "I will make one song out of the utter void." Much more effective, I think, than the gigantic grieving woman that Hiroshi did on the site of Tokyo, or Delacerro's *Exploded Crucifixion*,• I thought. Looking at this, I always had to talk, just to keep what I was seeing from reaching too far into my mind. World War Four, the Slaughter, the Scarring—all the terms that persisted despite the occasional official campaigns to label it the Unification War or some other fatuous, look-on-the-bright-side term—still vise-gripped all our imaginations, six hundred years later.

•The other three Brabant memorials that were built don't hit me as hard—I'm not sure why. Outlining and marking doesn't make the Acropolis anything other than an empty mountain, or St. Peter's any more than a shape on a lake, or Weimar more than a lighter patch of glass on a darker landscape, I suppose.•

•Let's go,• Raimbaut thought. •One view of this can last a long time.•

•Isn't it strange,• I thought as we walked down the steps to the springer, •that unlike any other important weapon, there was never a short name for the antimatter cloud? Nothing like gun, chopper, plane, tank, or nuke.•

•Maybe nobody wants to be that familiar with it,• Raimbaut thought.

That reminded me of Briand—what had happened here had happened to New Tanjavur and to Yaxkintulum, scant hours after I and most of the other OSP personnel had been evacuated, less than three months ago.

The view of Mount Erebrus in Antarctica was fully the equal of the Grand Canyon; the big eruptions triggered when the ice sheets had slid away had built an astonishing mountain that still has to be seen to be believed. The orbital tower at Singapore, from both the top and the bottom, was equally awe-inspiring—the mighty tower rising all the way into the sky from that artificial Everest, and the view down from the top, in geosynchronous orbit, down to the shining white metal that covers half of Malaya and half of Sumatra in one vast building—the biggest transpolis in human space. •One out of every seventeen living humans—counting everywhere—lives in that,• I thought, reading the guide plaque, as we hung weightless, staring through the window at the awesome object 36,000 km below. •They have over four hundred copies of famous historic cities in there—there's even a copy of Noupeitau—not a good one, I'm afraid.•

From there we jumped to New York and looked at the ancient skyline from the top observation deck of the New Jersey hyperpolis—even looking down on it, the array of twentieth century towers sticking out of the water is amazing, and the woman with the torch, water up to her ribs, looks like something out of one of the old Arthurian cycles. I had once written a song about the scene.

•One more place to go,• I said, •but it's another depressing one.• We stepped into the springer and a moment later we were in a darkened observation dome in the Sea of Tranquility. We took a few moments to do what the first generation of tourists to come up here had done—to look at the footprints and the quaint, wrecked hardware, all protected inside transparent bubbles that were open to the outside vacuum for eternal preservation. But then we did what everyone eventually does—we looked at the round Earth, sunside yin blending delicately into nightside yang due to all the lights and reflectors, nothing like the famous flat photo. We stared at the scars where the antimatter clouds had been set off, inky smears on the grayish-blue world. Honshu is often hard to pick out, both because of the clouds and because it's an island, and Europe can be difficult, but today, both were fully visible.

There wasn't much to say about it. We stood for a long time.

•This is what your job is about,• Raimbaut said.

"It is," I said, aloud, breaking the silence in the dome. There was no one else there except a couple of guard robots.

We looked for a while longer, and then Raimbaut asked •Where are all the other visitors? There are twenty-five billion people on Earth, and the springer tour we're taking costs about as much as dinner for four in a good restaurant. Why aren't there at least a few hundred people at every place we visit? It seems as if thousands would be appropriate.•

•Oh. That. Well, that's part of what this mission is about, too. They've all seen these places many times, through virtual reality. None of them sees any reason to leave his apartment and come to the real thing.•

Raimbaut shuddered. •Almost time for the meeting?•

It wasn't, not quite, but I said it was, and we took the chance to get out of there, back to the apartment in Manila, from which we sprang straight to the meeting room. Neither of us thought anything in words for a long time.

■ 2 ▬▬▬▬▬▬▬▬

While we waited for the others, Raimbaut and I stayed quiet. I could feel the depth of his shock at the memorials to the Slaughter. For almost everyone, the Slaughter was like Rome falling, the Crusades, or the genocide of the Americans—unfortunate, vaguely remembered, nothing to do with the business of living now. For a very small number of us, it was the thing that kept us awake some nights, and came to our attention, at unexpected moments, with tears or a shudder.

After a while, Paxa and Piranesi came in. They had sprung here about a day earlier than we had, with a layover on Ducommon to break up the big change in gravity, because Paxa was very sensitive to springer sickness. She still looked tired. Piranesi bore the patient weariness of a career military officer.

We had the usual idle chat about the niceness of the weather compared to what you usually had in Manila, the sameness of all OSP meeting rooms, and the OSP's always serving good coffee.

I had met Dji at official functions a few times before, and I knew that he and Shan were very old friends. Dji's operations tended to be much more focused on mass consciousness and much less on the sort of micro-issues that Shan dealt with, but the two organizations within the OSP had worked together well many times in the past, and I didn't think I'd have much problem fitting in.

Dji looked to be about Shan's age—he might be anywhere between a dignified fifty or a youthful eighty, especially if he was from one of the cultures that used life-extending drugs. He had deep brown skin and very close cut, tightly curled white hair.

The woman with him, who I'd never seen before, didn't look much older than twenty. She was as pale as the man was dark, and her hair, worn straight down to her shoulders, was thin and a very pale shade of blonde. Occitans are fairer than most of the other Thousand Cultures, and she would have been pale for an Occitan. She wore her bureaucratic uniform, but she'd taken advantage of the rule that allowed her to pay to have it tailored out of better than standard materials. Her high cheekbones, large sea-green eyes, and full lips would have made her the cause of at least one duel and two songs per week back in the Quartier des Jovents.

Dji told us to "call me Dji, which is my family name and very proper. Don't call me doctor or sir!" He scored many points with me by remembering that my name is pronounced like in Ancient Latin or Industrial Age German—like "gear out," not like a Greek sandwich.

As he was introducing himself to Paxa, Piranesi, and Raimbaut, he explained that he was from Pure, one of the more aggressively totalitarian utopias out there. "So that there is not a misunderstanding to begin with," he added, "yes, I am the product of a supposedly pure human blood line, descended from a variety of African leaders, provable on all sides of the family. But I'm also a political refugee. It is a condition of my contract with the OSP that they not send me anywhere near Pure, since I am still under a sentence, *in absentia*, of forcible collection of DNA and termination. I like to think that the genetics authorities of Pure would no longer dare, actually, but I do not think so so strongly that I would like to bet on it, eh? Refugee that I am, from a strange culture, as I am, I am bound to be a strange man—and therefore I shall be a strange boss, for which I apologize in advance."

"Dji, you are talking to two Occitans and two Hedons," Shan said, coming in. "If you want to be the strangest person in the group, you will have to work at it."

Dji jumped to his feet and the two men embraced tightly, for a long time. When they sat down, there were traces of tears in their eyes. "We're old friends," Shan explained.

"Really?" Paxa asked, getting us all to laugh, and breaking the ice.

Shan smiled. "We were part of that first group of agents ever in the OSP," he said. "Recruited mainly out of the diplomatic service."

I revised my guess at his age upwards by a decade.

"But it was all very different then," Dji said.

The young woman raised her hand and said, "I'm an Earth girl, myself. Do I get to be strange?"

This caused me to stare at her for a second—Earth is severely underrepresented in the OSP. Raimbaut didn't mind the chance to look at her, at all. •Steady, there you mad impetuous *toszet*,• I thought at him, •remember that as far as she can see, you are going bald and developing crow's feet.•

His chuckle inside my head was good-natured, but all the same I could feel that she was getting to him like a spear through the chest. •Remember,• he reminded me, •in two years I'll be physically four years old. It's only going to get worse. Might as well do my longing and yearning while the idea is remotely believable.•

The young woman spoke. "I realize that you may be surprised to meet an agent from Earth, and perhaps technically speaking, even though I've lived here all my life, I'm not exactly from Earth."

•*Senher Deu*, and she's mysterious, too,• Raimbaut thought.

•Patience and attention to detail, Ramibaut.•

•Yes, coach.•

She had a sweet smile, into which a fellow could read anything he wanted. She didn't explain a thing. She was more like an Occitan *donzelha* than anyone who hadn't grown up among us had a right to be, I thought. Maybe my racing pulse wasn't originating solely in Raimbaut's share of our brain.

After a moment, Shan said, "Well, I don't think normal people ever join the OSP. That's always been our greatest strength, and our greatest weakness. So let's rejoice in it." He smiled and nodded toward the young woman. "Since she hasn't introduced herself, let me present Laprada Prieczka to you; Laprada, these alarmingly odd people are Piranesi Alcott and Paxa Prytanis. And this alarming person is actually two odd people, Giraut Leones and Raimbaut Bovalhor." We introduced ourselves and explained; I could feel Raimbaut blushing with my face.

Piranesi said, "I am assuming, Mr. Dji, that you are the diplomat that most people say ended the fighting on Roosevelt?"

Dji smiled. "Just Dji. No title, please. Yes, I am the Dji who arrived just in time to take the credit for the fine work my subordinates did on the problem."

That triggered a memory for me. "And you're also the person who prevented Fort Liberty from seceding?"

"Well, I, and eventually their own common sense." He glanced around the table; Shan was smirking slightly, an expression that I had long ago learned to be suspicious of.

"Shan," Dji said, "perhaps you will help clarify things for them later. Negotiation is such a tough job that practically all 'talent' in it is accident and reputation. If you've been lucky once, they give the job to you in the hope that you may be lucky again—and if you are, then your reputation will usually allow you several successes before your final, abject failure. That's when they say your talent deserted you."

Shan nodded. "But it's still true that even if talent is nothing more than luck, you might as well pick people who are lucky. And luck is detected by the same methods we would use for talent." He looked blandly around the room. "This group is about as lucky as OSP agents ever are. And one way you are lucky is that we have Dji with us."

Dji smiled politely. "So let us begin, my fortunate ones, eh? One of my areas of specialization is working with the various communications media, a fancy way of saying 'manipulating the news.' It happens to be highly relevant to our current mission, because ultimately it won't matter what the individual representatives to the Council of Humanity think, so much as it will matter what the populations of their home cultures think. And that, in turn, will not matter nearly as much as what the population of Earth thinks."

"Aren't they supposed to be representing their home cultures?" Paxa asked.

"Yes, theoretically they are, and some of them do so very conscientiously, but you have to remember the travel remains expensive, and was expensive for centuries—and during most of that time the Council of Humanity was a figurehead body. During that time a tradition grew up. Rather than go to the expense of recalling or replacing their representatives—a process that could take many decades— since the Council of Humanity didn't matter much, most cultures just left representatives in place for life, and when they died, appointed their descendants. Once you got your representative to Earth, you never, never moved or replaced him or her; you hired his or her children. And co-workers tend to marry each other.

"The total effect is that the Council is more like a little incestuous family living in Nuevo Buenos Aires than it is a representative body. So for many representatives, the most relevant public opinion is what's being talked about in upper class NBA. Their own cultures are barely real to them.

"After all, till now, no one cared. Does any of you even know the names of the representative from your home culture?"

We all had to admit we didn't, with Laprada "abstaining," with an odd little smile.

"And speaking," Dji said, "of hereditary representatives, Laprada is the representative for Second Eden, on Addams, but she's never been there and neither had her father—both were born on Earth. When her grandfather died last year, her father, who has a career as an actor, did not want to take the time to be in the Council of Humanity—and therefore, voila, Laprada is the new representative, with a vote as good as all of Earth's. She's also well-accepted at the very center of fashionable opinion in NBA, and that's almost equally important. That's where the four of you—excuse me, Raimbaut—the five of you—come into this."

I nodded. "All right, clear enough."

Raimbaut asked, "And so the exact thing we're supposed to do is . . . ?"

"That's Raimbaut speaking, right?" Laprada asked.

"Very good!" I said, when I realized he'd frozen. "This is me . . ."

". . . and this is Raimbaut," he said, finishing the sentence. •Thanks. *Deu*, how will I ever talk to her?•

•You just did. Don't worry, I couldn't leave you alone if I wanted to.•

"How fascinating!" she said. "You have different accents."

"We'd be happy to discuss that at length," I said, "but for the moment we should probably find out what we're supposed to be doing."

Dji nodded and said, "Our strategy is to keep the idea of

commercially exploiting psypyx recordings from becoming fashionable. We don't want that stupid idea to be identified with youth, art, vigor, or style. Laprada has completed training at Manila, as of four weeks ago, so she's now a full-fledged agent; more importantly, she's the only one we have with a pipeline into that world, though who knows how long she can keep it—officially the Council of Humanity doesn't know she's an OSP agent and hasn't purged her yet, but we think that's only a matter of time. Until then, Laprada will be helping the four of you influence the Earth opinion that happens to matter. So the first assignment for the four of you is to get to know Laprada well, and to socialize enough so that you catch on to each other's peculiarities."

I thought, to Raimbaut, •Is there any way this can be better for you?•

•Or more terrifying?•

"Right now the best thing we have going," Laprada said, "is the large number of representatives to the Council who are horrified at having to take a side. With the help of the cowards, the reasonable people have secured a substantial delay. I'm going to take you through what there is of the bohemian current on Earth. There aren't many of them—I should say, many of us, I spend *my* time in the current—but the younger, valuable advertising demographic lurks that current with intense attention, and whatever's in the current now, whether it's ideas or shoes, is what most of the lurkers will be thinking, or wearing, or eating, soon.

"We're going to try to infuse the current with the idea that 'traditional' is good—which is usually an easy sell, but who knows what it will be like this time. I'm going to take you around to where some of the most fashionable young people are, and you are going to make them think that you are wonderful, fascinating people. The best way to do this is by being wonderful, fascinating people."

Paxa smiled. "Well, then, I'm sure we'll manage, some-how."

Laprada made a face. "This is Earth. You're dealing with a population that wishes there had never been a Thousand Cultures—as far as they're concerned, you all produce way too much news that interrupts the entertainment. Being wonderful and fascinating takes more than merely appearing to be a wonder, or keeping someone's undivided attention." She sighed. "Giraut, I've set up many appointments in which you will be talking with musicians, poets, and so on—prima-rily musicians and poets with a chance to become big in the next few years. (It does us no good if you're an underground sensation, at least in the short run!) Paxa, you'll be talking to various kinds of connoisseurs of various sorts, about esthetics of pure pleasure, and anything else that suggests that you can teach them to have fun by themselves. It will be a younger crowd, twenties and thirties, but not a *very* young crowd. Also, as the only woman in the group, you'll be speaking to various feminist groups. Piranesi, you'll be talk-ing to military, police, and so on, raising the specter of battle experiences becoming a form of war porn."

"Excuse me," Paxa said, "but there are still feminist groups on Earth, and they still have something to do?"

"Oh, yes," Laprada said. "Equality has been the law for many generations, but there's invidious discrimination even now, and you'll see why we still have feminism, quickly enough. And there's work enough for them to do, here on Earth. Unfortunately, another reason for their existence is that Earth is a planet of busybodies. Maybe it always has been, or maybe we're just a busybody species.

"Earth feminists spend their time agitating about the in-equality of women in many of the Thousand Cultures. They campaign ceaselessly to make the Thousand Cultures con-form to Earth standards of gender equality. Not much different from the movements to make all of the Thousand Cultures follow the right religion, or raise their children without spanking, or eat no meat, or a dozen other things. Since the Thousand Cultures are far away (at least until springer costs come down still further) discussions of reforming them can be carried on without anyone's having to know anything about any of them, or do anything."

"Well, I doubt I'll be completely in or out of sympathy with them," Paxa said, "so I guess there will be something to talk about, anyway."

"I guess I'll tag along with Giraut," Raimbaut said, with my mouth.

Everyone, including me, laughed at that, and then Laprada gave him a smile that melted him (there is hardly a stranger sensation, by the way, than to have another man's butterflies in your stomach).

•God, she's beautiful,• Raimbaut thought at me.

I tried to suppress the thought that *this could be a long couple of stanyears* but Raimbaut's melancholy chuckle in my mind told me that I hadn't succeeded. The whole exchange took much less than a second; probably it did not even look like a hesitation to anyone outside.

Laprada said, "Tonight, you and I (and Giraut, because the poor devil has no choice, even though he's slightly old for this crowd), are going to a party with the Divers. They're a very influential clique and it will be a good place to start—especially because they are *my* clique."

Dji doled out the remaining assignments in half a minute, and then dismissed us. As I was walking out behind Laprada, I thought to Raimbaut, •I noticed that glandular surge that hit when she said "tonight you and I."•

•I have some way to go,• he thought, glumly.

•We will get you there, *companhon. Non ajas destrech.*•

"Laprada," I said, turning around, "do you suppose you can

give us some orientation to all of this? Perhaps we could meet an hour or so before going to the Divers' party?"

She nodded. "Good idea. It would take me much more than an hour to explain it all completely, but perhaps I can make it not totally incomprehensible . . . why don't we have dinner together?"

"We had no plans," I said.

After we had sprung back to the apartment at the OSP building, Raimbaut thought, •Why isn't it that easy for me?•

•Because I don't care if it's never anything more than dinner. Though I have to admit, if you get somewhere further than dinner, *companhon*, I truly will have nothing to complain about. *M'es vis, que bella! Anc non vis bellazor!*•

•It's a good thing that I would feel so ridiculous if I became jealous,• he thought back at me. We stepped through the springer back into the apartment.

We had four hours to kill, and I suggested a nap. For once, he agreed, perhaps because I told him that it always sharpened my conversational facility; he had an acute interest in having me be able to do the talking. I stretched out on the bed, fully dressed, thinking of everything and nothing, and as Raimbaut reached into my memories, I fell into dreams, again.

Normally no jovent pays any attention to any news of any kind; the Quartier des Jovents is a very self-contained place, and since politics, business, scholarship, and everything except the arts, gossip, and dueling, are *infra dig* to any real jovent, even if young people did follow the news, they went out of their way to conceal that from everyone else, especially from their *companho*.

All the same, the news of a remarkable innovation from Earth caught everyone's imagination during the stanyear I was sixteen. Supposedly this miracle machine, the springer, could—at enormous cost—bridge the distances between the stars instantaneously, once there was a springer at each end of the journey. Within a few hours of the beginning of the debate about the subject, news media had constructed some small demonstration springers, and were using them to show people what the device did. Several volunteers were sprung large distances around the planet.

An interstellar-capable springer, however, would be a much more expensive proposition—the power require-ments alone would mean growing two more VNPs in orbit around our world. That was a lot; twelve VNPs supplied the whole planet's power requirement. Besides, who knew what we might be letting ourselves in for? Our culture, to us, was very nearly perfect, the most satisfactory arrangement yet worked out of individual liberty within an appealing es-thetic tradition, the one place in the universe where beauty, utility, and freedom were not pitted against each other. The injection of so many strangers, it seemed to many of us, could only disrupt, and never improve, our harmony.

But curiousity would have its way. The Royal Post Office built a light-aperture springer so as to be able to send and re-ceive messages instantly from anywhere in human space; news flooded in from everywhere, and the number of things people wanted to see and hear for themselves skyrocketed. In no time at all, it seemed, everyone was simultaneously saying that the springer would bring deplorable changes and that nonetheless we had to do it.

Along with thousands of other jovents, therefore, I was in the broad front courtyard of the Royal Palace on the day that we opened the first interstellar human-rated springer, and the first party of dignitaries from Earth stepped through.

It looked like a funeral party partially formed of prisoners in uniform. All of them, men and women, wore their hair severely short, no more than collar length at most. The group in the center, which was entirely unattractive middle-aged women who wore no cosmetics and didn't seem to be doing anything to work with their few assets, was all wearing the *suit-biz*, a desperately outmoded style that involves a squar-ish jacket, knee-length skirt, shapeless white shirt, and clunky black pumps. The only way they could have looked worse would have been to dress like the men surrounding them—who wore heavy black high-collared tunics with matching black pants and billed caps, and calf-high boots with what were obviously functional soles. They looked like they were about to be sent out to clear brush or clean floors, as part of a punishment detail.

Our king—it was Cercallon VII, a handsome man if ever there was one—strode forward, his big red and purple *tapi*, floor length, swaying behind him. He was flanked by five ministers in their stoles and robes, and then a bodyguard of young men in full, billowing body shirts, hose, and high boots, with magnificent plumed caps.

The party that had just come through seemed to retch, very slightly—not a surprise, because we had all been told about springer sickness. They recovered themselves well enough and came forward to meet our party.

I watched them closely, these strangely bland beings in nearly identical clothing, and I saw them exchange glances—and winks. I cannot describe my horror when I re-alized that they were looking at our highest officials in their finest clothing, and the Earth delegation was *barely able to avoid laughing.*

I was about halfway through getting myself attired in what could be described as a moderated outfit—I didn't want to look like a freak show but I definitely wanted to be noticed, if I had correctly understood what Laprada had said. I had selected clothing, shaved, bathed, scraped a callus or two that I didn't like the look of, checked the manicure, and in all made myself as presentable as I could, with Raimbaut making curiously supportive comments, considering that I could tell he was uncomfortably aware how much my body was losing that duel *atz fis prim* with time, fought by every middle-aged man in shape.

The com pinged, and Laprada said, "Giraut? Raimbaut? Which one of you am I talking to?"

"Whichever you like, we both hear you," I said.

"Well, I hate to trouble you, and I know how inconvenient something like this is when you're getting ready to go out, but Shan asked if we could come about half an hour early to the place where we're having dinner, the Assemblejam Café, and asked me to pass the request along to you. There's a piece of news he wants to give us personally—he said it will be going public within hours—"

"Not something else the OSP has been caught at!"

"He didn't say. But he asked that we arrive half an hour early, and promised to buy us a drink before he left us alone."

"Well, that's at least minimally *gens* of him." I looked at the time. All that would be lost would be certain leisureliness about finishing my toilet. "Well. That would be fine, I suppose. Half an hour before?"

"Right."

"See you there then."

"*Atzdeu, te salut,*" she said.

Raimbaut clutched inside; I said "Very nice!"

"It's the only Occitan I know."

I said, "It's a start. We'll coach you," to her, and thought •*Down! Boy!*• to him. She clicked off, and I checked myself in the mirror. Let's see, I was supposed to be impressive but not startling: navy mid-thigh-length tunic with deep red velvet dagger sleeves, a broad black leather girdle carved with the rose-and-lion design that had been in my family for centuries, lavender crushed cap with long feather (I never could abide the liripipe), black stockings, and deep mauve knee-length boots, in a soft suede, with a flat heel. I decided to add a *tapi*—something with a red lining to match the sleeves, darker outer layer to take down the whole effect, maybe some slashing, not too clingy, hem about mid-thigh to help cover my middle-aged buttocks. Not for the first time, I cursed the Occitan tradition of wearing your age; cosmetic viri and nanosurgery were strictly for girls, girly boys, and *tostemz-toszeti*. It took half a minute to make up my mind and order the *tapi*; it should pop out of the springer slot in five minutes or so.

Raimbaut was following all this eagerly. A young Occitan male deprived of fashion information, especially for twelve stanyears, is in real desperation. •This looks like—•

•What we were all wearing at the time you died,• I thought, or he did—now and then, it was getting hard to tell. •That's because we aren't going to this thing as real Occitans, who now dress almost completely along the lines of the Interstellar Metaculture. And we aren't going as representatives of Nou Occitan. What we're going as is what these people imagine Occitans to be. And I'm afraid those songs of mine—and Bieris's paintings, and the *very* romantic novels of Cercamon Raimon, and the holopresentations of Eleanor St. Alamanda—have made Nou Occitan a place that is known throughout the Thousand Cultures for what it was like just after the springer reached us. We've become a literary location like what the West was in Old American flat film or Titan in the Lunar Post Refugee literature. If we don't dress like this, people will be disappointed, the same way they would if a Texaustralian didn't wear those silly hats, or a Novus Romanus didn't wear a toga.•

•Fifty billion people, all prisoners of the artists,• Raimbaut thought.

•It beats being prisoners of lawyers, priests, soldiers, or bankers, which are the other historic choices,• I pointed out. The springer slot pinged. I went to it, shook out our new *tapi*, and put it on. *I* looked remarkably good to me, anyway, and Raimbaut was too nervous about dinner with Laprada to have much of an opinion.

I took one last glance around the apartment, and then one last good long look in the mirror, to make sure I hadn't forgotten anything important. Seven minutes till we were due.

Although practically everything on Earth is unattractively functional, designed simply to deliver goods to people who want to ignore all the people around them, at least that same love of convenience puts springers in every possible place, so you don't have to look at any of that functional ugliness on your way from one ugly place to another. I sprang directly to the Assemblejam Café; the springer opened into the same foyer as the front door. The customers looked up, saw the Occitan costume, stared at me for half a breath, and went back to to their food or conversations. A few pulled out computer terminals from their pockets, unfolded them like handkerchiefs, and made a quick entry.

I knew that my arrival on Earth was being followed by many of the celeb-watchers, so no doubt a few of them would make a note in their personal records, but diplomats and musicians aren't especially collectible, not compared to athletes and actors, so probably no one would come over to bother us.

Laprada waved from a table against the wall, about halfway to the back. Her hair was up in an elaborate system of coiled braids, probably enhanced with autogenic falls—she hadn't had that much hair a few hours before.

Some damned Occitan tradition of wearing one's own

age had kept me from ever having hair grown for trans-
plants, or a good positive grip toupee made, but I was almost as conspicuous in the room for my baldness as I was
for the boots and tights. At least streaks of gray were cur-
rently fashionable, though not in the way I was naturally
graying.

As I approached Laprada I saw that her dress was cut in
the then-fashionable long-to-the-right style, at the middle of
her right calf and above the middle of her left thigh. It was a
swirl of intelligent panels—an effect I'd not seen much before, but all the rage that year and for a decade after in the
Inner Sphere. Four or five, or perhaps six, of the silky, irides-
cent panels crept back and forth, slithering to cover gaps the
instant before they could open, lifting to expose teasing bits
of skin, carefully trading places so that nothing was shown
but everything was risked. I couldn't tell exactly where one
began and another left off—they traded patterns so easily
and quickly, and so neatly morphed one pattern into another.

"What an extraordinary dress," I blurted.

Laprada smiled. "I have to stay damp, if anyone's going to
pay attention to anything I do."

"Damp means—"

"I've been in the current and you can tell, roughly. Right
now all the metaphors for what's fashionable connect,
somehow or other, to the current, but understatement is
more fashionable than overstatement. So someone who is
'wet' is too trendy, and what you try to be is 'damp.' And if
nobody needs to know me anymore, I'm 'drying out.' See?
Actually I first got soaked as a musician but that couldn't
last. I'm only an average classical guitarist—but so few Earth
people learn a musical instrument anymore, I was put on the
bill as a curiosity, with people from the outer worlds who really could play. I don't have much artistic talent, despite all

the praise that gets heaped on everything I do. So I have to stay damp with my clothes, or my conversation."

"If the conversation is the equal of the clothes," I said, "I shall be too fascinated to speak for the rest of the night."

She beamed at me, and gestured to where the chair was creeping out to let me in, a disconcerting feature that most public eating places on Earth seemed to feel was necessary; why a world that was once nearly seized by aintellects doesn't limit their role to the necessary—in fact revels in putting them everywhere and having them do everything— is a complete mystery to me. It's another thing that makes me shudder every time I have to go there.

We had been chatting idly for just a minute or two when Shan arrived, wearing a plain diplomatic uniform without insignia. He sat down and, with no ceremony, launched into it. "We've recovered, from a cometary orbit around Sirius, the first alien ship with remains."

I took a moment to realize that "remains" meant "alien corpses." The alien culture that had preceded us by about 20,000 stanyears in this part of space had left a surprising number of ruins, spacecraft in long orbits, and other evidence of its passing, but in the dozen stanyears since the discoveries had begun, no one had ever found a dead alien.

"What did they look like?" Laprada asked.

"The remains are fragmentary," Shan said. "But at least the main hypotheses, based on their tools and machines, are confirmed. They're bipedal and DNA-based, with some kind of a circulation system and something that looks like a brain in a case on the top of their bodies, so they're not far from us—vertebrates who walk upright, not bugs or mollusks or trees. Something hit their ship so hard that we only found about half of it—it's very possible that, since its orbit was so long (a period of 28,000 years), it's an inbound starship that ran into debris, and fell into a cometary orbit, and it was making its first close pass at Sirius since the accident."

"Do the entertainment and news media already know?" Laprada asked.

"Yes. The alien derelict off Sirius was found by a deep exploratory ship, with a paid experiencer on board."

"I don't see why this is urgent," Raimbaut said, speaking aloud. •Does he always drop by with trivia?•

•Listen to him. He's usually right.•

Shan shrugged. "If you talk with some Earth people about the news story, I suspect you'll develop a better feel for what it is like here. And in a sense, as Giraut has probably told you, everything to do with the aliens is central to the OSP's mission; partly our job is to prepare the human race to meet whatever is out there."

It was a strange little prank on me that the OSP's mission—urgent and important as it was—was also leading to the destruction of much that I cherished about the Thousand Cultures. I could feel Raimbaut tapping into that dichotomy in my feelings, and I knew my face was going slack in front of Shan and Laprada.

Humanity had to be ready for alien contact—so isolated cultures and excessively weird cultures were now intolerable. One night, long before, over red wine, in a place not unlike this, Shan had talked about the way that some of the old empires had operated, back when humanity was confined to Earth, and much of Earth itself was unknown. Often an invading empire forced their way into technologically inferior civilizations, identified some small group that had been marginal or losing out (religious dissidents, unassimilable ethnics, plain old bandits), and promoted them to deputy rulers. He'd asked, rhetorically, "You don't want to suddenly discover that we're a satrapy of the alien empire, and that all

local rules and regulations will be made in Deseret, or Caledony, or Bremen Beyond the Sky, do you?"

Then, I'd thought I knew the answer. Now I wasn't so
sure that being ruled by any of the more eccentric of the
Thousand Cultures was any worse than being ruled by
Earth.

Shan made small talk for a few minutes after that, obviously itching to be off to whomever he would be telling
next. When he had gone, Laprada said, "Well, I hope you
won't be disappointed, Raimbaut, when you see that he's
right."

"About—?"

"About the way in which Earth will take the news. I'm
afraid it's going to reveal a great deal to you. Especially if you
remember that these *are* the most broadminded, thoughtful
people you're apt to encounter here." She sighed. "Probably
not one person tonight will mention the alien remains
story—though if anyone does, it will be no more than a five
minute topic of conversation. Even Shan doesn't always
grasp how much Earth is turned inward on itself. There are
people who live their entire lives in elaborate virtual reali-
ties of Sherlock Holmes's London or Opal Bingstraw's Tranquility City, who nearly forget that they're in a simulation
at all. Of course the people we're going to meet tonight are
somewhat different. Instead of living in a simulation, the
Divers live their whole lives in two cafés and a park."

I thought of how the Tamils of New Tanjavur—people I
had been working among not fifty standays ago, people now
probably extinct—had lived such lives so very beautifully,
and said, "But surely some people do it more gracefully than
others."

"One of the great privileges of life on Earth is that no one
will ever notice how you do anything—well or badly—and

usually they won't even notice *if* you do it," she said, looking down at her plate. "My father is an actor, I know Dji mentioned that. I became the representative of Second Eden—for which I have no qualifications whatsoever—because he turned down the job. He wanted to continue to pursue his acting. But you know, he's never been in a professional play, or a flatscreen film, holo, simulation, or professionally-produced experience. Nothing, nothing, nothing.

"He takes acting classes over and over, and goes to auditions. That's completely thirty years of his life, now. No, it's hard to grasp, but I think you'll realize it tonight. Half of humanity is here in the Sol system, but we're all in our individual boxes. There are plenty of us, but not one that matters. If we don't matter, we don't let anything else matter. Especially not a pile of body parts in an orbit around Sirius."

Raimbaut spoke up; mentally I cheered for him. "Is that because Earth is roughly at the center of human space, and people here think that anything 'out there' is going to happen in the outer shells, somehow, and not come down here?"

Laprada frowned. "I wish that were the case, but probably not. People here understand subtension of angle about as well as they do anywhere. The whole volume controlled by any one human-inhabited planet around any of the stars out there isn't big enough to be a disk to the naked eye. The news is always reminding people that all the human-patrolled space there is doesn't take up a ten-millionth of the night sky. The most popular analogy among media types is that it's like Earth is in the middle of a field ten kilometers on a side and all our 'fencing' together is thirty-two pieces of vertical wire, less than a hundredth of a millimeter wide each. But I don't think that analogy scores much with the public as a whole. Most of them have never walked a kilometer all at once, and hardly anyone on Earth has ever seen a sky full of stars, unless they've taken the tour of the farside observatory on the moon." She sighed and sipped her wine, then gestured at the entree, a pale sauce poured over noodles. "So how do you like this stuff? Most offworlders tell me it's bland."

Raimbaut waited an instant, and I thought at him •You talk, *companhon*, I'm your passenger here,• so he said, "Well, it's not anything very special. But the company is the best I've had, and I didn't come here for the food."

Her attention focused inside herself for a moment—I could see that in her eyes—and then she smiled, almost shyly, with obvious pleasure. Perhaps he wouldn't need as much coaching as I'd feared.

3

The dinner was consistent. Every course was both unexceptionable and unexceptional. I concentrated on the taste because I felt like I was eavesdropping on Raimbaut and Laprada. Aside from being visually striking, she was warm, and funny, and intelligent, and had that important gift for the question that kept him talking long enough for her to get to know him. After a while the thunder of blood in my ears and the wail of impossible desire died down to background noise. Raimbaut was growing calmer, forgetting to be self-conscious, settling in to enjoying himself. Of course he was missing most of the experience of a very ordinary baked tomato with gorgonzola.

According to Laprada, the invitation was for two hours from now, and to be less than an hour late would be the surest way to prove that you were absolutely no one. Raimbaut was about to ask why we'd met so early, then, but I gave him a quick •Don't ask—trust me,• and he shut up before opening his mouth, with an equally brief •Thanks.•

"Now, what we're going to see next is what the Assemble-jam Café is famous for," Laprada said. "It's one of the most important arts venues here in Nuevo Buenos Aires, the only place where *every* school and movement comes out to see what's showing."

We had stepped straight from windowless apartment to windowless foyer; I'd had no idea that we were in Nuevo Buenos Aires. With the springer, there wasn't much reason for any given place to tie itself to local time, and most of the planet seemed to run on universal time, without windows or outside doors. "Arts venue?" Raimbaut asked. "Which arts do they do here?"

"Oh, all of them. That's what Assemblejam is all about. It could be the name of the café, the name of the movement, the name of the art, maybe only a name. That's what's made it such a vital part of the current, and why even after being open for a year and a half, this place is still damp, bordering on almost being too wet." She glanced around the room. "At least half the people that will be at the party are dining here now, which means that the big topic at the party will be tonight's performance at the Assemblejam Café, which means I drifted right into the current. That's good, if we're going to make our position wet."

"So I should watch carefully and be prepared to have an opinion?" Raimbaut asked. To me, he thought, •I guess we'll know what Assemblejam means once we see some Assemblejam.•

"You're going to find this *completely* intriguing," Laprada said. The way she emphasized "completely" sounded as if she were running her tongue around it; I couldn't help wondering what it would be like to kiss her, and then realized a moment later that that was Raimbaut's thought.

Somehow or other, the topics switched to their childhoods, to not being understood by their parents, to the difficulty of finding true friends, and to the startling experience of being able to be emotionally moved by a work of art that not very many other people knew about, all within a few minutes. I reminded myself that they were both about twenty-two stanyears old, and that I was being a jaded old poop. Raimbaut thought, •Don't be envious.•

I hate, I truly hate, not being able to deny an emotion that I'm feeling. Definitely, it was going to be a long couple of stanyears.

"Is there a term for what we're about to see?" Raimbaut asked.

"Just Assemblejam. I told you." She sounded impatient.

"That was my question," I said. "What Raimbaut meant was, do we call it a performance, a jeu, a luso, a vuau, a farrago, a hullabaloo . . . ?"

"I like hullabaloo," she said, smiling, "and someday I'd like to see one, but tonight you're going to see Assemblejam. It is what it is."

"Thanks," I said.

"So they *taught* you to fight duels and *encouraged* you to?" she asked, in a complete non sequitur.

Raimbaut nodded. "It was part of who we were. What I can't believe is that you had all that training in acting and dancing but you never—"

I let it fade to background noise; Raimbaut was doing very well, although ninety percent of the credit for that undoubtedly went to Laprada. I was realizing that that was an age I wouldn't be again for anything . . . and simultaneously realizing that if anything happened to me, I would have to be that age again, physically at least. It was enough to make me think about being careful.

I wondered what it was like to go through puberty all over again; our *companhon* Rufeu was going to experience it in a few stanyears, but I suspected it was one of those things that no one can tell you.

Raimbaut and Laprada agreed that though they had only known each other a short while, they understood each other better than anyone else ever had, and I was beginning to think about how long it would be before I could have a drink. If you've ever been the third person present with a couple, you know the feeling. Now try to imagine not being able to go to the restroom to give them a chance to talk privately.

When the space had been cleared, a small stage rose from the floor at one end of the room, and the Assemblejam began. There was a master of ceremonies of sorts, but for the first act, all she did was walk out onto the stage, looking terribly bored, and shrug. "Uh, here's the first act." She wandered off the stage as if she had found herself there by accident.

A slim young man, attractive in a not-very-noticeable sort of way, walked onto the stage nude, and began to put on a costume, as Lunar fusion jazz played in the background. When he finished his dressing, we could all see that he had dressed as the long-lost Mona Lisa. He held up a gilt frame around himself, and smiled. He sang along with the jazz number, for a few measures. Then he broke the frame in half, tore off the costume, and walked offstage.

The master of ceremonies came out again, and looked around as if to see if there were any audience left. Then she said, "Uh. That one is over. Now there's going to be another one. It will be different from the one before."

A morbidly obese young man in a diaper came onto the stage. Clutching his crotch the whole time, he spoke in a screeching falsetto, and delivered what I had always thought of as one of the most moving passages in literature, something known and taught throughout all of human space— the short chapter that begins the third part of *No One Home A Thousand Kilometers Later*, when Mrs. Chovauz finds her son dead on the surface, mummified, a small child's body in a space suit, thirty years after he disappeared. About halfway through it, four young women, all with freakishly big breasts, came onto the stage, set up a crude stake, and tied the young man to it, as he continued to shriek his way through Park's masterpiece. As he wound down into the famous, often quoted part about everything being nothing more than lost pieces of everything else, and as Mrs. Chovauz lifted up the body to carry it back to the airlock, the girls began to paint the now-tied-up fat man blue with a wet, sloppy mixture that also, very unfortunately, rendered his diaper translucent. Then they smeared the blue paint on their breasts and lined up at the front of the stage. As the young man wailed the last, painful sentence of the scene so loud and high as to make it all but unintelligible, the four women began to jump up and down, their big breasts slapping around and spraying drops of blue paint. In unison, they shouted "Oo-oo, oo-oo," over and over.

After a minute or so of that, they stopped and bowed; the fat man lifted the stake from its hole without bothering to untie himself, and bowed with it still tied on.

I was offended and annoyed. The room went up in thunderous applause. All the patrons, including Laprada, leapt to their feet, cheering and clapping, as if that had been absolutely wonderful. The group on stage bowed again and exited; robots came out to clean up the blue paint.

While that went on, Laprada tried to explain to me what the piece before was being admired for. "It had all the elements of the wet but it never fell in so deep that it got soaked. He ran such a big risk and came out exactly as damp as he should be. Everything in that was an idea or image that almost everyone is just about but not quite tired of. Gumba ran a huge, *completely* huge risk with that piece, and he succeeded brilliantly, going right to the edge without falling in. Sometimes I think that man, all by himself, *defines* the current, completely. But see for yourself. You'll meet him at the party."

The master of ceremonies came out to announce that there would be another act; this time she looked very put-upon, as if she were being forced to do the job.

I couldn't say that I blamed her, once I saw what the act was.

A thin young man with very dark skin came onto the stage in a diaper. I began to wonder what Earth's obsession with diapers was. Not that I had not seen such things in art before. In some cultures, it expressed an unwillingness to be grown up and a demand to be taken care of; in some, a misfocused anger against the pure physical necessities of living; in still others, a desire to shock the mature world by rejecting it.

Then again, sometimes it was merely a way to make people feel ill.

The man began to shout nonsense words, occasionally accidentally hitting some pitch or other. "Shooby Doo Wa!"

•Oh, no,• I thought to Raimbaut.

•What?•

•Well, what he's doing is one of those ancient things that people bring back all the time, which is known as "scat singing," and since the diaper is usually the mark of an artist who is trying to shock you—•

•He's not going to—•

He was. He turned around and pulled down the diaper, revealing a very ordinary ass covered with what looked like shit and was probably peanut butter, chocolate, or some such. (I was blessed to be too far from the stage to be able to smell anything.) Then he grabbed a handful and ate it.

I was hoping this wouldn't win any applause, and I was right. "Obvious! Obvious! Obvious!" a thin young man with a bad complexion screamed from the next table. The woman with him looked embarrassed, but soon others took up the cry, and I joined in with a will.

"Go away! We're bored! It's all too obvious!" the young man shouted.

The man on the stage stood up. At first I thought he might rush the heckler at the next table, and was mentally preparing to rush to the heckler's aid—his opinion was the first esthetic idea I'd heard expressed all night. But the man on stage contented himself with a single rude gesture, followed by stalking offstage in an apparent fury. The master of ceremonies came out and announced intermission with more excitement than I'd seen from her all night.

"We'll stick around for the intermission," Laprada said, "because that's when you hear all those good spontaneous remarks that people are going to repeat at the party. Then most of these people are going to be offended by the second act in the second set, and get up and leave, so we'll get up and leave with them."

"How do they know they'll be offended? Did they see a preview?" Raimbaut asked. He was more confused than I, and had the further disadvantage of not wanting to mess things up with Laprada, so he felt very awkward asking any questions at all. •That's right, *companhon, valors, tostemz valors*!• I thought.

•Bewilderment, simple bewilderment,• he thought back.

She looked as puzzled as he felt. "No, of course not. Each act is supposed to be a surprise. But when intermission ends, the public conversation is over, here at the café, so then people will be offended, so that they can leave and go to the parties. Some people will very vocally stay, too, the ones going to the late-night parties. Getting offended just has to do with when your party is. It's completely simple."

Raimbaut was in agony; he didn't want to quarrel with someone he was getting on so well with, but his Occitan soul was offended to the core. I could have told him that this attitude was not uncommon in the Inner Sphere, but I thought it best not to distract him while he worked out his particular solution to the most difficult of all problems in *fi-*

namor—how to tell the woman that you're infatuated with that her ideas are rank nonsense. "But isn't that *too* simple? People being offended solely to make a schedule? Couldn't we save being offended for something that genuinely upsets us? There wasn't much that offended me in the first three, and I doubt there will be in the second. Why do we have to be offended?"

"But then no one would ever escape from a public performance."

"Well, why couldn't we just slip out at the end of intermission and go to the party?"

"Because that would be saying that the art, and the artists, don't matter as much as our social lives. It would be terribly offensive to say that."

Raimbaut sighed, at me, internally. •Is talking to them always like this?•

•Earth people yes, women sometimes, women you're in love with, usually it's worse.•

He said, "Remember I'm a social idiot in your culture."

She nodded, very seriously. "Careful about that, to start off with."

"Er—" I felt his confusion as a tiny hitch in his breathing. "About what?"

"Don't call Earth a culture. It's not. I mean I know what you mean, but people don't think of it that way. A culture is a place like one of the Thousand Cultures, and most Earth people would call it 'artificial,' or 'exotic,' or terms like that. Sort of like . . ." she thought for a moment ". . . you know how some people think they don't have an accent, because they don't realize that 'talking normal like the people back home' *is* an accent? Same principle."

"All right," Raimbaut said. "Now, remembering I'm a social idiot . . . all right, I can see that we're supposed to pretend to be offended so that we have to leave early so that we can make it to the party that we'd really like to go to, because to just say the party mattered more than the art would be . . . um, *ne gens*. Gauche, uncouth . . . well, I guess I mean *ne gens*."

"That Occitan word had a vogue here about five years ago, and I know what you mean," Laprada said. "Yes, that's it. Except that—well, you may have to pretend. You can't take any psychoactive drugs while you're living in Giraut's brain, can you?"

"No, I can't. It could damage his brain."

"Speaking as the landlord," I added, "I would object."

"Then you *will* have to pretend. But I'll do what nearly everyone else does—I'll take the pill. One of the little yellow ones will make me very easily annoyed for about ten minutes. Enough time to build up a rage, storm out, and spring back to my apartment to check my appearance before springing to the party. I arrive at the party as the pill wears off, and I remember the performance as *completely* tedious, or obnoxious, or ugly, or something. Most people at the party will have had the same experience. It gives us *hours* of things to talk about."

"I see."

"Especially because it's the Divers. It would be different if it were the Floaters or the Facedowns, and even more different if it were Swimmers."

Raimbaut asked, "The Facedowns?"

"The group names this year are all about your relationship *to the current*. Some people look at the current and want to plunge right across it and go deep, some people want to stay on the surface and just go with it, and some people are so passive about staying on the surface that they might as well be face down."

"And Swimmers are the ones who try to cut across it?" I asked.

"That's right—Giraut, right?—that's right."

"And you're a Diver?" Raimbaut asked.

"At the moment."

"And what do you like about them—"

"Oh, I could like it all, any of it, really—it's all fun, you know? But I happened to decide to like the Divers."

I tried to see if I could get any further. "Well, what was it about the Divers that made you decide that they were the ones you would decide to like?"

"First of all, their clothing is cut nicely for a slim, petite woman. Secondly, they have a couple of members that I think might have real career prospects."

"Did you agree with them about anything?" Raimbaut asked.

"Sure. I joined them and of course then I agreed with them." She looked as if she might be losing patience.

•See if you can switch the subject. She likes to explain things. Try for something we'll both understand.• I thought at him, frantically. *Deu*, I couldn't remember any *donzelha* who had ever been this difficult. Raimbaut swallowed hard and said, "Maybe I'd have a better picture of what it's all about if you told me about the art we've been seeing here. Has it all been Diver art, or is it a mixture . . . ?"

She smiled and held up a finger like a teacher who has caught a student in a very clever, subtle error. "Assemblejam is apart from all of that. Assemblejam is more a matter of . . . well, let me think how to put this. All art is nothing but chopped up pieces of old art applied to other old art, obviously. So since nobody wants to do the old art—I mean, there's no audience for it at all, and the only people who would look at old art if you made it would be people looking to slice it up for their own art—well, then. If we're going to make art we have to keep old art alive without having anyone stuck with the job of making more old art."

"But if you just now made it, how is it old?"

"Have you ever seen a pencil drawing of a head in profile?"

"Of course."

"Well, there's nothing new about it, is there? I mean, Leonardo or any Renaissance artist could have done one, they did lots of them, didn't they? So there's nothing new. It's the same idea one more time. So the moment it's made, it's old, because it can't be new."

I was wondering which one of us was having the headache.

She said, "Here at Assemblejam, people take all these little pieces of art from all over the human record and stick them together. It's not new but it gives everyone access to the old, which they can then use in their own art. So Assemblejam is the principle that underlies all the groups—Divers, Floaters, Swimmers, and all the derivatives and extreme groups. Whoops!—next act coming up. It's the last one we're going to like, unless this hits early and I decide to be offended by the end of it, and severely disappointed, after liking the first part so much." She dropped the little yellow pill into her hand and gulped it down; around the room, I could see dozens of other people swallowing pills. •I wonder if there's a pill for slavish admiration, and how much it would cost to have it mixed into the food for my next concert,• I thought.

•Now that's unworthy.•

•Maybe so, but wait until you see what a bad crowd is like before you judge me.•

The lights came up on a cluster of men in barely moveable steel chrome copies of what must be the twentieth-century New Look. They were wheeled onto the stage by other men who were naked. They sang for a while—I think it was all old hymns of some kind. Then a machine gun sound effect—very grainy, made deliberately to sound like an ancient phonograph record—went off and they all sang it again in falsetto, very fast. When they finished, there was thunderous applause.

"Too short," Laprada said. "The drugs haven't hit yet, not for anyone."

A small man walked onto the stage; he was dressed in a version of the *suit-biz* with those things people used to wear on their faces, a thousand years ago, before surgery and contact lenses—spectacles, that's what they were called. He ahemed, opened a notebook, and began to read aloud.

I recognized it. "He's performing *The Wasteland* while pretending to be T. S. Eliot," I whispered.

"Careful!" Laprada hissed. "It is *not* polite to check on the com while the performance is going on."

"I just happened to know it," I said. "Eliot didn't write that many poems, and the first part of *The Wasteland* is very recognizable, and so is his picture. What's the matter?"

"Everyone will know it's Eliot," she snapped at me, "but they will know by the time they arrive at the party. That's why we all have to stop and check the com before we go to the party. How else are we going to be knowledgeable about it, and perform our knowledge for others?" She glared at me; then her expression softened. "Look, try very hard not to bring up any facts that you happen to remember. They'll be angry if you can show them up. We didn't give you nearly enough preparation for all this. Raimbaut, do you know all this trivia?"

"Not like Giraut does."

"Well, then, Giraut, if you could—"

"Stay under wraps unless someone wants to talk to me? Sure," I said, and shut up. •I'm still here if you need me.•

•*Gratz deu.*•

"I'm offended," she said, "into a rage. Completely. Into a rage. I hate Eliot, I hate poets, I hate poetry, and I hate actors who pretend to be poets while reading poetry." Onstage, the man had pulled on a duck mask, waving his arms and shouting in a language I did not recognize. "We've got to go now, all right, please?" Laprada added.

Raimbaut followed her toward the springer, and I was grateful again to be a passenger. Before we stepped through the springer, she turned to Raimbaut, and smiling very sweetly, said, "I hope I haven't really hurt your feelings. It's just art, you know. A way to kill time, something for parties. It's not like it's important."

■ 4 ████████████

There were seventeen women and twenty-one men at the party (I counted to have something to do while Raimbaut circulated) and of the seventeen women, fourteen were wearing the same hairstyle as Laprada. It didn't seem to be a problem. All seventeen of them were wearing the same left-right asymmetric, intelligent-panel dresses, in a very limited range of colors and patterns.

Like any time since the first few couples went over to visit in the trendy cave, see the new bison paintings, maybe hear the new drum, all of the people were posing to show off their bodies or their clothes, holding drinks, and pretending to enjoy it.

Many of the women in high heels were teetering on them as if they were young girls trying them out for the first time. The men, in their asymmetric jackets, weren't leaning or draping them right. No one moved like a dancer or athlete or duelist; all were awkward in their bodies, like children playing dress-up, unsure how to wear grownups' clothes.

At first I thought that whoever was running the music was taking a long time running a sound check. After a while I realized that that *was* the music—a random walk through motifs and hooks from the last thousand years of recorded music. Cultures that like to do that are usually cultures that like to hold dances to exhaustion, which can often be fun, but no one was moving to the music here.

•Maybe they'll start later,• Raimbaut thought.
•I doubt that very much.•
•Me too. I was trying to be optimistic.•
I was paying little attention to the conversation, yet, try-

ing to get the feel of the party while Laprada dragged Raimbaut around and introduced him. People shrieked as if they
hadn't seen her in years, gave her little insincere hugs, and
called her "Proddy." She always winced at that.

When Raimbaut thought •All right, I have to admit, I
never *have* known what to do at a party, but you, *mon vielh
companhon*, have been going to these things for most of your
working life, and are no doubt an expert at them,• it surprised me; I'd thought he was doing fine, and thought that
back at him.

•I don't feel like I'm really meeting anyone or like this is a
party,• he replied.

•Ah, there's your only mistake. You're expecting a party
to be fun.•

•Thanks, I think. Where would you go looking for some
interesting conversation?•

•*That* corner,• I thought, turning my head to indicate.
•Three people talking, no one who looks to be monopolizing
the conversation, no one standing in the poses that indicate
"Member of audience waiting for a turn on stage." Either
they're talking about something that they all take seriously,
or they're socially comfortable enough to make small talk
well. That's our corner.•

Raimbaut sighed at me mentally—the poor *toszet* really
was very shy and reserved, and this wasn't coming easy for
him—and we drifted over toward the conversation.

They were happy to introduce themselves. Rebop was a
young woman who had set her intelligent panels in black
and white patterns, strange blobby swirls that looked more
like inkblots than anything else. She wore her hair very
short, dyed in an asymmetric black-white pattern, and was
one of the three women not wearing the elaborate mass of
coils that seemed to be de rigeur. From the way she kept

touching it, I think she was aware of this and felt very out of fashion.

Ntaung was a tall thin man, twenty-five or so, skin shaded slightly more Caucasian than the others, with a beaky nose and bad acne. He seemed nervous but also the most eager of the group to talk rather than to be seen with Raimbaut.

Both of them took some time to be persuaded that despite appearances, our names were not French—"Gear Out and Rhyme Bout, honestly, it's not a prank," Raimbaut said, "Old Occitan kept classical Latin pronunciation longer than any other Romance language, that's all."

Gumba nodded and said, "Boys and girls, I think we'll have to take these chaps' word for how their names are pronounced. Broadcast announcers have been known to be wrong, now and then."

I was grateful to Gumba that he'd kept us from getting any further into the pointless argument with Ntaung, who was the sort of intense, *ne gens* young man—destined to be interesting but painfully aware that he isn't yet—who will argue anything into the ground, especially with anyone who knows more about it than he does. Gumba was perhaps thirty, older than either of the other two, and it dawned on me, after we'd chatted for a while, that he was the fat man whose performance had gotten the most applause; I hadn't recognized him without the diaper, the blue paint, or the busty girls. He sat on the table with his legs crossed in a full lotus, sitting on the long tail with the short tail flopped over his lap, making his tailored jacket fit worse than most beach towels.

He accepted my congratulations, but immediately said, "But we do know that all audiences are made up of idiots. Some are just nicer idiots than others. The point I was making was so trivial that they failed to notice it, and since this year the absence of a point is *very* in the current, they applauded without noticing that I was doing what I wasn't supposed to."

Raimbaut said, "I hate to admit this, but as an offworlder, I don't think I caught the point. So what was it, if you don't mind?"

Gumba shrugged and pushed his black hair back up his forehead. "Four possible ones, at least. I might have been saying that the book is overrated and everyone exclaims over it without having read it, or that people *should* read it and don't because they're too busy admiring it, or that we all were rewarded as children for parroting back perceptions that only an adult could have. Or maybe I was saying that watching pretty women cover themselves with liquids and shake their tits is more fun than reading. As I said, it's all trivial."

"I think I can see all that," Raimbaut admitted.

"Just don't admit it where others can hear you," Ntaung said. "Perception is mocked around here; that's also very in the current."

"Pretension and excessive seriousness also are mocked," Rebop said, looking off into space. "I wonder if Proddy is going to keep her 'up' act going all night. When we were at school she could do it for days on end, but lately she hasn't made it through a whole evening."

I thought, urgently, •No rising to her defense! They don't understand that here.•

•And I don't understand them either. Tomorrow morning, you must remind me again what would be so bad about humanity's cutting off contact with Earth.•

Gumba said, "We were talking about Klienir. He's a friend who's gone solipsist. I wish we'd been able to get him here. One can't help being embarassed, having a friend decide he prefers the box to you, eh? We knew Klienir many years and saw no trace of the tendency. He used to be a very reasonable person to talk to, and now he's so far into it that he won't speak to us. Instead he's called the government's ombudsline and asked them to have the writers work up a set of friends he likes better."

Around a quarter of Earth's adult population had "gone solipsist"—meaning that they'd come to believe that nothing outside their apartments was real, that everything was generated by the aintellects to keep them pacified, and that the only difference between what you saw through the entertainment hookup when your brain was plugged in, and the world you saw when you took off your hookup and went out the door, was that the latter was a "base" or "default" program that wasn't supposed to be very interesting.

Ntaung added, "And you know how no one ever comes back from being a solipsist? That's the worst."

Rebop nodded emphatically. "Most of us here in the crowd spend all our lives doing ridiculous things, but at least we change which ridiculous things we do from time to time. It helps to keep our friends amused."

"Just as they do for us," Ntaung added. He moved a handsbreadth closer to her, and she didn't move away but didn't look at him either; I had a sense that he thought they were a couple and she disagreed, but not strongly.

"It's mutual support, really," Gumba said. "Being a little eccentric makes your friends wonder what you will do next, which keeps them from going into the box. And if they're a little eccentric, that means you're still in touch with them, and they keep *you* from going into the box. So we all feel lost whenever someone falls over to the other side—and when someone who used to be as lively and engaged and brave as Klienir justifies it by going solipsist—bah. To hell with him. I won't speak his name again. If I don't really exist for him, then he doesn't really exist for me either, right back at him."

"I'm sorry to hear about it, all the same," I said, "and I imagine you will all miss him terribly."

"That's right—uh, which one are you?" Ntaung asked.

Rebop smiled tensely, as if he'd embarrassed her, so I made a point of praising him. "You're doing well to be able to tell us apart at all. I'm Giraut. I'm the one whose body this is, which is why I'm staying quiet at this party—too much of an old man to be able to follow things. But I was very curious about it."

"And he's nice enough not to annoy me by tugging my mental sleeve and whispering 'Ask him this,'" Raimbaut added.

Rebop nodded, as if the whole situation were profound. "All right, I think I'm learning to tell the difference between you."

Gumba said, "And returning to topic—before, I hope, we veer off wildly—in the last few years they've come out with a sleepwalking program that causes your body to take care of eating and defecation and cleaning, while you're asleep— so you never have to experience coming out into the real world any more at all. That's why this party is so small— ever since they started being able to avoid emergence completely, there have been more people going into the box all the time. It's *my* opinion that that's also why you see sillier and sillier public opinion surveys in the news—the tenth of the population that wants Briand erased from the record so that there was never any such place, and another tenth that wants the story revised to end happily. There are already commercial versions out there in which that happens—you star in one of them, Giraut."

"I what?"

"You step between Ix and the gun. He doesn't die, you do.

Everyone suddenly becomes best friends after he explains it all to them, over your corpse."

"But that's preposterous! I was right there. He was killed with a military maser—it blew a hole right through the building a hundred meters behind him. If I'd been in the path of it, we'd both have been killed—and besides, I was nowhere near where I would have needed to be to get into the path!" I was startled at how upset I was.

"For most of us here on Earth, reality doesn't have to be real, and it usually isn't," Ntaung pointed out, reasonably enough. "Since the audience makes no decisions that affect you or Briand or anything else, why not believe whatever they like? *Some* of us can't do that; most have no problem."

I didn't answer, carried under by a sudden wave of lonely misery.

•Are you all right?• Raimbaut thought at me, after a moment.

•*No*,• I admitted. In the chaos of my collapsing marriage—my collapsing life—I hadn't had much time to grieve for Ix. Perhaps he'd been the only saint or sage I'd ever known, perhaps merely a very clever charlatan who had lost patience with his own charlatanry, and been killed while trying to escape from it. Now I was seized, painfully, with the thought that I would have loved dearly to see him stroll quietly into this room and begin to circulate—straightening out all these poseurs and fools, who were nevertheless the best people that the mother planet had to offer.

"It's not that unusual," Rebop said. "Most of us go into the box now and then when something upsets us. After my last relationship ended, I went in for about six months, myself. These two fellows came and dragged me out, finally, but I have to admit it was lovely in there."

Gumba nodded vigorously. "I've done it too. Ntaung is our one real puritan—he just takes drugs."

Ntaung shrugged. "I am not a puritan. I'm sad when a friend goes into the box, but I don't judge them to be bad for it. I only avoid it myself because I doubt my own ability to come back out."

"Poor Ntaung," Rebop said, in a tone that might be affectionate, or sarcastic, or a pose to impress Gumba. "He's unhappy and he's afraid that if he stopped he might not want to start again." She turned sideways, giving him a view of her breast and hip. "It's such a difficult thing for him. Poor Ntaung."

From the way he was flushing, I didn't think what she was doing could be friendly. Gumba caught Raimbaut's eye, and Raimbaut asked, "Did anyone hear the news today? They found an alien ship that had some remains in it." •First thing that popped into my head as a change of subject,• he admitted.

•Into *my* head, *companhon*. Well, perhaps we'll learn something.•

It seemed to take all three of them a long time—perhaps five or six seconds—to decipher what he had said. When they did, they all looked as if he had suddenly told them what he had for breakfast, or what his favorite color was, like one of those horrible six-year-olds that sometimes accost you at a family reunion.

After a long pause, Gumba said, "I suppose that's interesting, but I can't see why. The aliens must have existed, because, after all, there are artifacts. Finding their bodies doesn't make them exist any more than they already did."

Rebop nodded and smiled in approval at him.

Ntaung flushed. "I don't think I'd even heard that there had ever been any alien artifacts found. So there's another intelligent species out there?"

"They've been dead for twenty million years, or twenty

thousand. Twenty something," Rebop said. "No reason why you would know."

Gumba shrugged. "Was there any reason you brought that up?"

"Oh, things differ, you know," Raimbaut said. "Some places people would talk about that and speculate about it, I suppose as if it were a new work of art or a new fashion or something. I don't know all the rules here yet. Well, I suppose I'm supposed to circulate, so perhaps I'll do that."

As we walked away, he thought to me, •Did that happen because it's Earth?•

•Could be. Or because they're people. We'd better look for another good conversation.•

•And your method is to look for any conversational knot where people aren't making speeches or giving lectures?•

•Anything that doesn't look like street theatre, is how I'd put it. If most conversations were tennis matches, you'd see a row of people playing against the wall, side by side. But we don't have to avoid the performances entirely. Some people are good and it's worth catching their show—once. Or, sometimes the person who would really be a good performer is quiet, while a person who is not holds the floor against all comers, and you can tip the balance toward the more interesting person. And then too sometimes you can acquire a reputation for being a marvelously nice person merely by disrupting an unpleasant act. Just keep repeating, it's a game, it's a game, it's a game. Like dueling in Occitan.•

•I got *killed* doing that.•

•Well, exactly. That's why you have to be careful when something's a game.• I spotted a heavyset man gesturing with big, symmetrical gestures. He had a big, bushy beard, combed into a fork, and wore his hair in a double figure-eight on the back, fastened with a clasp. I couldn't see his face, but five or six people, eyes approaching glaze, were gathered around while he explained whatever it was he was explaining to them. •Let's see what we can do over there.•

We joined the fringe of his crowd. He was mocking a performance he had attended earlier, at a different franchise of the Assemblejam Café, if I understood correctly. "Synesthesia Fourteen was the really painful one. A complete, complete failure. There was far too much forethought evident and not nearly enough forethought that was not evident. And that was a singularly—I mean, *singularly*—unfortunate combination. I could always tell that the whole effect was intended by the constant sneaky looking for an effect, but at the same time the effects they were trying to sneak in seemed very imposed on the consumer the way in which they took those effects for granted. Violently elitist. Terrorist, really." He dropped his wildly waving arms to his sides, as if resigning himself to the uncomfortable truth he was about to speak. "Now, when she picked up those four ancient tools and talked about women who used to use them, and they were all old things you only even hear about in stories— broom, soldering iron, battle ax, and egg beater—it seemed to me very much that she knew what she was going to say before she said it, so she'd probably rehearsed it into rigidity. That's pure vicious aggression. She hadn't even considered the possibility—so she had not left herself any opening from which to respond to it—that the audience might want to see something else, or might not find women interesting." He punctuated that last sentence by pumping his arm up and down.

We Occitans seldom miss a chance for a quarrel. "There are very few of us who don't find women interesting," I said, wading in. "I would think that women *would* be interesting."

He glared at me, but deigned to speak. "Yes, her performance was full of expressions like 'I would think.' All kinds of oppressive expressions."

"What's oppressive about 'I would think?'" Raimbaut asked.

"Don't tell me that an important visitor like yourself has immediately fallen right into the shallowest possible part of the current."

"No one seems to be telling me what the current is, at the moment, and if anyone would kindly summarize it for me I'd be grateful," I said. "But I would still like to know what's offensive about a phrase like 'I would think.' I intended it as courtesy—if there's something offensive, I'd like to know what it is." I kept my voice even, level, and soft. In Noupeitau, it would be the tone you would use if you were close to provocation for a duel but still hoped to avoid it.

His tone, on the other hand, sounded as if he were a not-very-good primary teacher, explaining things to one of the less-bright children. "It's this way. Right now the current is running through being very neutral and it's splashing around, playing with the whole objectivity, neutrality, politeness thing, you know. Where you put it in the subjunctive so that you allow disagreement without giving the lie. Some of the Facedowns are even calling for a return to that Truth idea. So, as a Diver, I know that what there is, is only other people's wills. If someone is powerful enough they will make a thing they say objective, even in the very teeth of your subjectivity, and they do that with their politeness and their I-would-thinks. We must defend ourselves against such terrorism."

It wasn't an unfamiliar idea, or a good one, so I played the standard reply. "But if an idea describes a reality, then changing the description can't change the reality, because reality has no way of knowing that the description changed," I said. "No information flow back to the objective world. No magic, if you will."

" 'If you will.' This gets worse and worse. Soon you'll be hitting me with 'I would think, if you will.' We all know that all people think their own thoughts are superior, so when you say 'I would think' you're saying 'the superior thinker thinks this,' which is like saying I ought to change my mind—which implies I'm wrong or a fool. It's a direct insult." His hands chopped up and down in front of his chest, in unison—it looked to me like a professorial gesture for *this will be on the quiz.* "The very act of arguing and making up arguments must mean that you think some ideas are better than others, and since the differences between people are mainly differences in ideas, it's a way of saying that some people are better than others, which is a way of asserting your superiority over me." He had walked forward to me, standing close enough now for me to think of knocking him down. •It's a pleasant thought,• Raimbaut commented, •but I'd like to have an alternative.•

"But the objections you are raising would then be a demonstration of your superiority," I said. "So if this argument is about superiority (and I have not stipulated that!—I'm just following your speculation) then are you not doing exactly what you accuse me of doing?"

"Aha!" The man bellowed with pure glee of victory. "The infamous reciprocity argument. Sauce for the goose is sauce for the gander and do unto others as you would have others do unto you. But it completely denies the individuality of everyone. It asserts alikeness among us all. Therefore it prescribes a dreary, drab, lonesome sameness in which we are all treated as objects and governed rather than self-governing. The catastrophic *end* to all real conversation! I'm sorry that

you don't wish to continue talking to me, but since you
don't, I guess we should stop here."

Raimbaut threw one in. "But if we should stop here, and if
there's no point to the conversation, then haven't you been
complaining about being insulted by nonsense?"

"You're arguing morality from the outcome, which is a
common philosophic—" His eyes widened. "Oh shit. Oh
fuck. Oh filthy cunthole bitch crot-covered-snatch." He
turned and faced the wall, resting his forehead against it,
beating at it with his fist. His friends turned and applauded
me/Raimbaut as if we'd sung a fine song or won a duel.

•Do you know what this is about, Giraut?•

•*Non sai*, Raimbaut. *Anc non vis aquel estranher.*•

When he turned back from his melodramatic wall-
thumping, he stuck out his hand, grinning as if he were
pleased with me, and said, "Absolutely splendid." He turned
to one of the group that I'd thought were his admirers and
said, "Logged and scored?"

"Oh, yes. Gill, you'll win more honor from being defeated
by this fellow than most of our Diver arguers ever achieve
from an outright victory. You might even have made yourself central to the Diver tendency. Magnificent job."

"This was all some kind of contest!" Raimbaut exclaimed,
simultaneously with thinking it.

"Of course, what else?" Gill, the heavy, forkbearded man,
said.

"I thought we were—I don't know, looking to produce
mutual understanding, getting to know each other's
minds . . . I had no idea there was a score or anything."

"Why else would anyone do it?" the woman asked. "My
name is Loupa, by the way. I'll be writing this up in *You
Weren't There*. That's my column on broad-access com that
covers parties people missed. This one leaped from very dull

to very exciting. I do think it will probably earn Gill a promotion. Probably several million boxed people will vote for that; there was *such* feeling and *such* a deep clash." She seemed lost in thought for an instant, then delightedly exclaimed, "Deep! Oh, *see*, Gill? It's very Diver!"

It seemed to me more that it had been the kind of argument one had at about fifteen, among bookish friends. I said so.

"You forced me out of consistency," Gill explained. "Drove me right away from the style of argument that the Divers have gone with this season. Brilliant—total defeat. The offworlder is a hit among the Divers, and because so many things that become part of the current originate with the Divers . . . well, I think you've had a very profound influence. All I can say is bravo, sir, bravo."

"I'm happy for any congratulations," I said, "but—uh . . ."

Raimbaut took over. "This is Raimbaut talking, Giraut just finished. The thing is, we chose the idea not to win a contest or set a trend or achieve something in front of you. We thought we were right. And we had no intention of playing this game."

Gill, and everyone else, stared at me. Loupa said, "Completely amazing. Or at least you've completely amazed us. So, out in the Thousand Cultures—or at least in the Outer Worlds—people still really believe things? I'd heard that."

"Er, yes, people believe things." I was beginning to wonder if I would ever communicate with Earth people. "Don't you?"

Gill smiled and shook his head. "That's utterly unknowable, but I'm not going to get into another argument with you this soon after losing the last one. It won't do a thing for me, and at this point I'm interested in what you—Raimbaut and Giraut, I mean—have to say. I think I've decided to affect an interest, and I might decide to affect it for a long time." His crowd turned and drifted away, some looking back and glancing wistfully, but Loupa stuck by him.

"I still don't understand the rules here," Raimbaut said.

"There's not that much to understand," Gill said. "Loupa has a certain prestige and besides she has a professional duty to cover this; the others don't feel as if they have enough status or reason to stay in an important conversation, especially not in a creative one where you can't predict at all what will be said next. I think they *ought* to stay, but they're afraid of looking like they want to rise above what they regard as their inferior position. I, on the other hand, am interested in the conversation, so here I am."

We talked for perhaps an hour, about his job. He taught an elementary politics course, which was dull, and a literature course that was not much better, so as to have some challenge in his life. Other than that, all he did was hang around with the Divers. We also talked about my career and adventures, about jovent on Nou Occitan, about whether or not belief mattered when you talked about ideas. It was a normal conversation, literally, and water in the desert, metaphorically.

I decided to try an experiment. "Have you heard about them finding alien remains?"

Gill looked puzzled, and then said, "Oh, bodies. No. Was there something interesting about it?"

"They looked very much like us."

"Well, then, if they'd come by earlier than they did, we could have invited them to parties. Pity we missed each other. So . . . you must know Shan well. Do you think that old fox can still somehow save his political career?"

I probably could not have gotten him to talk for three minutes about the aliens if both our lives depended on it. But on the other hand, Gill did care about art, politics, things that were not in the box. If he wasn't perfect, he was a big improvement on most of the rest of the Earth. By the end of it we were planning to have lunch together, soon.

In the early morning hours, the party ran out of energy and collapsed in the way that parties generally do. The wall-flowers went first except for a few bitter optimists. The hangers-on had had enough of whatever it was that they hung on for, and drifted after. As the party dwindled and the available audiences became smaller and more focused, the life-of-the-party types went. By then Laprada had been around the room a few times, visiting all the clusters of peo-ple, gushing over how glad she was to see them, bubbling about how exciting things were. She had downplayed her unusual guests, upplayed all of her friends' accomplish-ments—•working the room like a true professional phony,• as Raimbaut thought at me, while she said more effusive good-byes.

•She's young and she's fashionable,• I thought, slightly more sharply than I had intended. •Give the girl a break.•

•Whereas I'm still young and have never really learned to be fashionable.•

•Compared to these people, you're a fashion genius. Did you notice how they wear their clothes?•

•Yes, unfortunately. Just the same, my heart's never been in it. Not like you and Marcabru.•

It might have been one of the three or four best approxi-mations to a genuine party conversation that night, and it was all happening in my head while I drank a big glass of cold water.

Laprada came up behind me and murmured, "Time to start our fifteen-minute process of working our way out the door."

I looked and Ntaung was already gone. I had wanted to chat more with him. He was socially maladroit, even *ne gens*, but he had some of the passion that the rest lacked. Rebop probably believed herself too good for him, yet would finally be his inferior, as artist, human being, or even dresser or conversationalist, once he got out of his own way. He had seemed like a good person to try to recruit.

Gumba passed by, with Wennji, a quiet young woman, tall, thin, very polite, who had attached herself to him later in the evening. They were going to some after-hours spot for food and conversation. He seemed to conclude, instantly, that Raimbaut and Laprada would want to talk without other company (and would be stuck with me anyway). He suggested that we might have a late night/early morning conversation some other time, and Wennji added that she'd like that too. Then, having run out of polite noises to make at each other, we shook hands and promised to talk more; he seemed to be trying to sell me on the idea that a local cynic such as himself would be invaluable to me in learning to cope with Earth. When you already detest a place and its people, the last thing you need to do is talk to a local cynic, but all the same, I would make sure to see him.

Raimbaut asked why, and I realized that it was now such second nature that I no longer thought of the reason consciously. For an instant, I was back in training at the big building in Manila, wondering what I had gotten into, during the final week of training, which Shan had conducted himself. I saw the twinkle in Shan's eye, the jaw tilted slightly upward, the sideways smile that stabbed a dimple into one cheek. He raised a finger, looked us all in the eyes, and said, "Never, never, never turn down a chance to talk to anyone who wants to tell you things, unless it's a deliberate strategy to extract more information later. There are no uninformative informants. The ignoramus's structure of ignorance will look very much like his culture's structure of knowledge. The fool's folly will be a bad copy of her culture's wisdom.

The liar's lies will stretch into the shape of the truth beneath them. You can always throw out the bad information later, but you never know where, or when, or from whom, good information will come."

•You know,• Raimbaut thought at me, •Shan is one of the people you talk to in your head most.•

•I do know, and that's why the whole business with Margaret hurt like a kick in the balls, *companhon*. *Vos dirai*, you can't imagine how desperate I am to have someone to talk to, and how glad I am that it turns out to be you.•

The sensation of being both the giver and receiver of a nice, sincere compliment is a very intense pleasure.

Gill stopped by, Loupa still in tow. They stood like people who were not lovers yet but planned to be soon, and they were leaving the party with Byra and Pyere, who clearly were a couple. Their plan was to jump from outdoor springer to outdoor springer until they found sunrise, and have coffee while they watched it.

I thanked Gill again for giving me such a fine start at making an impression on Earth's fashionable intellectuals. (Are there any other kind, anywhere?) We agreed that we would have to have that long lunch together very soon.

Raimbaut came back to the front of my mind as that group went out the door. The few who were left were mainly the sort of awful people the host has to throw out, so it was time to be gone. Raimbaut fretted. •Well, if Laprada is—•

Laprada was there, as if he'd thought her into existence. She slipped her arm through mine and breathed in my ear, her lips brushing the lobe. "Definitely time to leave the party. God, it's been grim."

Once again I had the sensation of Raimbaut's butterflies in my stomach. I thought to him, •Now, look like you've suddenly thought of something great, and say . . . say the following out loud—•

He said it in his voice, and I don't think it was obvious that he was getting dictation. (Laprada would have said something.) "Would you like to go for a drink or something? Not alcohol since I can't have that, but just to talk over the evening while it's still fresh in our minds? I can feel Giraut going to sleep in the back of my head, but I'm not tired."

Laprada grinned. "I know the perfect place for a drink—completely private, quiet, and comfortable for a conversation. Why don't we spring to my place?"

As we followed her to the springer, I thought, •*Que valors! Que gratz! Que cortes!* See, you do fine with women.•

•Thank you, Giraut. You're not the only one who's glad I'm in your head.•

5

While Laprada changed into something in the bedroom, Raimbaut and I looked at all the pictures on her walls, which were standard vus from Second Eden, the home culture that she represented without ever having seen.

A map of Addams on the wall showed that Second Eden was fairly far north in the temperate zone. From the look of the vus, Second Eden was pretty in a bland sort of way; nordic terrain, plenty of water, not high enough or polar enough to have much in the way of glaciers. There were big waterfalls running down moss-covered faces, winding steep creeks, thick conifer forests, deep fjords and canyons, and various low domed dwellings that said nothing except that they were buildings.

Laprada came back out with two largish drinks. "Yours, I'm afraid, contains nothing more powerful than Vitamin C. Mine is to help me get loose and happy—or at least loose."

"Start with loose, try for happy?" Raimbaut suggested.

"Good enough for me." She handed his glass over carefully—"I want to be sure I give you the right one." Then she bumped her glass against his, and said, " 'Another round for humanity.' "

" 'And one more for the good guys.' " It seemed that he had already acquired one part of OSP lore.

The drink was a mix of lime and pineapple, with a dash of coconut, a trifle sour to my taste. I could smell the gin in hers, and since her drink had to be at least half a liter, she was drinking to get drunk.

She and Raimbaut sat down next to each other on the couch, quite close, and I felt the stirrings in his mind matched by stirrings in my body. I tried not to think at all. Since Raimbaut had been inexperienced with women at the time he died, this evening was going to be important to him, and it seemed only fair to let him experience it, as much as possible, as himself.

"I heard people at the party calling you 'Proddy,' " he said, "and it looked like you didn't like it much."

She made a face. "I do hate it. Thank you so much for noticing. It was the nickname I had at Diplomat's School in Nuevo Buenos Aires—that's not a school that trains diplomats, it's the Council of Humanity grade school for diplomats' children. With so many of us being hereditary, the people you meet there are the people you see for the rest of your life, regrettable as that is. I was always 'Proddy,' the most popular girl, happy girl, perky girl, perfect girl . . . everything that is so tiresome when adolescence hits and everyone's expecting you to be bouncing around with joy, when what you want to do is sit down in a dark corner somewhere and cry your heart out. I was sentenced to 'compulsory happy without the possibility of parole' from age thirteen to twenty. Always up, always working, always jolly, always tired and scared that a bad mood would show or someone would notice how hard I had to work to keep it up. Worse yet, in that little cultural prison, I was sort of a trustie, too. I saw that you spent some time talking to Rebop. What did you think of her?"

Raimbaut shrugged. "She seemed very nice to me."

"She *is* very nice. That's the whole problem. She's pretty but not very pretty, she's smart enough to be in a conversation but not witty enough to dominate it, she has all those conventional virtues like loyalty and kindness but nothing that would ever fascinate anyone. Now, there's nothing wrong with that. And she was my best friend from younger years. But the leader of the pack should have a classy, fascinating sidekick, not Adequate Girl, which poor Rebop will be all her life. Normal Healthy Girl. Sweet But Dull Girl. You see?"

"I do," Raimbaut said. "Is it any way to talk about a good friend?"

I felt his panic. •Senher Deu, Giraut, I can't believe I said that to her!•

•*Non ajas destrech, companhon.* It was the right thing to do. No woman respects a man who encourages her worst impulses, at least not for long.•

•How do you know that?•

•I have some more experience than you do,• I thought, very firmly and emphatically.

"You're right, Raimbaut, of course you are," Laprada said, choking up. "Rebop has always been kind and patient with me and done her best to treat me well, and most of the time I'm the same with her, but now and then I just lose patience because . . . well, she is what she is. And when we were teenagers I spent a tremendous amount of time and effort trying to 'fix' her—in other words, her best friend persecuted her all the time over how she dressed and acted, and I made her terribly unhappy while at the same time I completely depended on her for emotional support. That's what I meant. It was like being a prison trustie. And you notice that when I started to talk about her again, the old habits came roaring right back. Tonight I've been Proddy, the happy, perky girl with a smile for everyone's face and a knife for everyone's back."

"You could probably start treating Rebop, and your other friends, differently any time you wanted to," Raimbaut pointed out.

Laprada shrugged. "Well, I suppose for the last couple of years, I *have* been more reasonable and calm, getting out and meeting people who I think are different and interesting."

She said the last part very pointedly, making his hopes leap up and my heart feel like it was swelling. "But when I go to parties . . . especially, with the old crowd . . . well, then 'Proddy' comes back again. The whole wretched silly childish business is completely tiring, completely unhappy, completely I don't know." She took three big swallows of her drink.

Raimbaut said, "You seem so interesting, and you seem so good at things—"

Her sigh was almost a groan. "I can tell that I'm unhappy and depressed—why can't you?"

"Are you unhappy and depressed right now?"

"Oh god. Beyond that." She turned to lean against him; I felt his butterflies. "I don't know if I can explain."

Mentally I swallowed and leaned away from Raimbaut's mind as hard as I could—trying to make sure Raimbaut didn't know I was recognizing the script. At least a quarter of all the *donzelhas* in Noupeitau had used this approach, along with probably billions of women since the dawn of time. Raimbaut might be finding the love of his life; he might be having a brief intense fling; he might be about to provide free therapy for someone who would then dump him at once. But it would have been grossly unfair, to him, this evening, to make him aware of any of the possibilities; he deserved, like anyone else, to have his first experiences for himself.

After holding his hand for a while, she said, quietly, "I *hate* having conversations with most of my friends, Raimbaut. Usually I'm in the role you're in now, and I can't help noticing that many of them are drowning in self-pity, and very often I *hate* them for it. So I'm afraid of sounding like them while I talk to you." She took another big swallow from her huge, potent drink. When she set it down, it was more than a third gone. Raimbaut flashed a thought at me: •Could it be that most of her problems come from plain old drinking too much?•

•Not a bad guess, *companhon*, but for right now you'd be a fool to mention it. Just let her run. You'll be glad you did.•

She sighed, and her voice caught as she ran out of air. "Sometimes I dramatize, and pretend that I'm weeping for the whole human race. Pretend to myself I mean. Because it would sound so pretentious if I said it to anyone else. You know what I mean. I try to convince myself that I'm crying about how people can't take care of themselves, can't find anything better to do with their time than turn into dreaming zombies in boxes, can't learn to supply each others' emotional needs. That ought to be plenty to weep about, don't you think?

"But that's not what I cry about, really." She took another big swallow and pressed her cheek against our chest, right over the heart. "This is really sounding stupid."

"No it isn't," Raimbaut said. "I'm fascinated. I'm here for as long as you'll talk, or longer if you just want to sit. There's nowhere else I'd rather be." Tentatively, he rested a hand on her neck; he could feel her moving against it, warming and relaxing. "Talk, or not. I'm here. You know I want to hear you."

She whispered. "You're different too. My first Occitan— or are you my first two Occitans? Is Giraut in there?"

"He's daydreaming and thinking about songs he means to write, and not paying much attention. I can have his attention for you whenever you—"

"No, don't do that. I like it being just us. Even if it's not exactly *just* us." After one deep sigh, Laprada was quiet for a long time. "The world will never get any better than this, I'm at the top, this is my big moment . . . so it's time for the exit."

I don't know whether it was my reaction or Raimbaut's that felt like a hard thump on the breastbone. "The exit?"

"Send in the wipe order on my latest psypyx copy. Order the pills. Take them and never wake up." She squeezed almost painfully hard at my ribs; a tear made a series of soggy dashes down her cheek, like an indecisive slug. "I'm so scared that someday I'll do it on impulse. You can complete the whole thing in less than twenty minutes nowadays, you know. And maybe once a week I *want* to, for, I don't know, ten minutes at a time. But if you count momentary flashes and stray thoughts, then at least twice a day, I feel sure I want to do it. Just get it over with. Just not be."

Raimbaut held her tight and said, "You have so much reason to be here—and I can't be the only person who's noticed that you're wonderful. Laprada, I—"

"I'm really vain. I know I'm very good looking, you know, and I look in the mirror and think, even starting anti-aging drugs at nineteen like I did, there's about ten years of this, and then maybe forty years of being attractive but not stunning, and then maybe forty years beyond that of being someone who obviously used to be attractive. And that's not very much, even if it's more than some people ever get, and more than anybody got a thousand years ago, and all that. It's not much. Why not leave while no single human being remembers me with any crow's-feet or wrinkles or little cracking lines that never go away around my mouth? Why not leave while no one has ever seen me at anything less than my best?"

"Well, we Occitans wear our age," Raimbaut said, "which is why Giraut chooses to look like this, and he's not the handsome fellow he once was—" (•Sorry, *companhon*• — •Quite all right•)—"but he's still a fine man and he can still enjoy being who he is. And even if you want to leave before you're older looking, why today? Why not wait the ten years and see how you feel then? And you are an OSP agent—you have more to see than you can in one lifetime and more important things to do than you'll ever—"

"I don't really want to see and do new things," she said. "I don't really. Every time I see something new I miss things I've already seen, and another thing will never have the power to surprise me again—if it *was* a surprise, and usually it's not. So I'd have the stimulation for a few minutes, and then I'd remember it fondly, and then be bored with it . . . how much can that take up in a life?"

"To see the Thousand Cultures," Raimbaut said, "should be enough new excitement for a century, at least, and after that, with all the new colony ships headed out beyond the frontiers, there will be so many *more* new cultures and new places, that no one is ever going to even be able to grasp all of human space, mentally—let alone whatever we learn when we meet the aliens. Laprada, there's so much. How can you bear to leave?"

"Oh, but it won't work that way! After the fourth or the fifth new adventure, I won't care about anything new—"

"You can't know that yet."

"But why wait and be disappointed when I can leave now and miss all the let-down?" She held onto him tight. "Don't stop arguing with me, Raimbaut. Don't stop. I know everything you're saying and it all makes sense, but I can't make myself believe it, and I'm scared that I'll do it sometime—maybe the next time I feel this way for even half an hour."

Raimbaut brushed the thick coils of her hair with the undersides of his fingers, and said, "Knowing what you're feeling, I don't think I could leave you alone, for anything. I'm right here. I'll be here as long as you need me; Giraut's a patient *toszet* and a *bo companhon* and if I need to do this to keep you alive, he'll let me have his body for the job." He smoothed out the tear tracks with the tips of his fingers; for a fellow with so little experience, he had a very delicate touch. "Now let me talk about the thing that worries me. Have you seen anyone for depression?"

She sniffed. "Why? I've already got a fine one as it is."

They both laughed a great deal more than that was worth. Then she started to cry, and to hold onto him hard. She whispered, "Sometimes I think that people might be a good enough reason to not do it. Not people in general, but some people that I like. And I'm sure you are going to be one of those people."

"You're welcome, and I'm so glad." He lifted her chin, and she smiled as if he were going to kiss her, but instead he looked into her eyes and said, "And yet. Even if someday I send you some horribly cruel good-bye-forever letter, even if I prove to be nothing like as good a fellow as you think I am, *still*—don't do it. You are far too good a person, and far too worthwhile yourself. Don't. Even if I disappoint you. And although you ended the question with a great joke, I still want to know about your getting taken care of for depression. That's been curable for hundreds of years. It's stupid to die of something that's so easy to treat."

She shrugged. "Gunshots to the body are easy to treat nowadays but people still die of them."

Raimbaut said, "I don't want you to die of anything."

He held her. Now and then she'd cry. I very nearly went really to sleep before she said, "You have such patience, that, if you're trying to wait me out, I should probably tell you that after a good late-night cry, I'm hardly ever interested in sex."

"It's not what I'm here for," he said. I could tell that he meant it, which was good; when you say the right thing, you want to mean it if at all possible.

"Well, I thought you should know that in case you're one

of those men who waits around hoping that when I'm done crying I'll want to fuck."

"I am your friend the monk," Raimbaut said, "if you want me to be. For as long as you need it."

So she talked about her childhood and the feeling she had always had, then, that someday she would do something special, and how disappointing reality was turning out to be. Her practice at classical guitar had led to some concerts, but the concerts hadn't been like she'd hoped for. All of her lovers so far, without exception, had been disappointments. (By Occitan standards, there had been very few; I had to question the judgement of Earthmen.) She had odd, wild daydreams and talked about them as though they were plans.

Slowly she turned more and more toward him, until they were lying together on the couch, with him holding her against my heart. At last she finished her drink and said, "You know how I told you that, unlike other women, I don't necessarily become horny after spending all night talking about my depression and things?"

"I recall it," Raimbaut said, neutrally, dreading another ghastly story of how she'd been mistreated.

"Well, that was a lie to make you leave if you didn't really like me. Or maybe it was a test to see if you were as nice a person as you seemed to be. And you didn't leave, and you passed the test. So . . ." she leaned forward. "If you were thinking very seriously about me, what would you be thinking about?"

Raimbaut grinned and said, "Exactly what I'm thinking about now." He brushed the hair away from her face, caught her chin gently, looked deep into her eyes, and said, "Plus of course worrying myself sick that this isn't the time."

"Well, how many hints does a girl have to drop?" she asked.

They kissed. Parts of my glandular system worked harder than they had in years. Mouths opened, and her tongue slid gently into my mouth. Raimbaut thought. •I think I can manage from here.•

•I don't think I could sleep if I tried. I hope it will be all right with an audience.•

•*Senher Deu, companhon*, it would be all right on a bed of hot coals, if that were the only way. Now try not to think in words—it's distracting.•

After Laprada fell asleep, Raimbaut got up, washed our face, and thought, •Interesting for you?•

•Very.•

•I'm not sure how I feel.•

•That feeling will persist at least until you're thirty-five, Raimbaut.•

•I thought it might.•

We lay awake, not thinking in words, sharing the emotional tone of the early morning, for an hour or so, and I didn't fall asleep until well after Raimbaut did. Perhaps it was the sensation of physical satisfaction, perhaps the excitement of Raimbaut's love affair, but whatever the cause, I dreamed of long ago, again.

Early on, in our first few weeks at the training facility in Manila, Margaret and I realized there was something special about Shan, because of all the special attention our instructors gave us. During most of my first mission, as far as I had known, Shan had simply been the Council Ambassador to Caledony. I had no idea that there was any such organization as the OSP.

True, Shan had seemed to have far-reaching powers and

an ability to turn up at key moments, but for all I knew, maybe all Council ambassadors were like that. At the end of the mission, after Margaret and I had married, and so much had changed, he had told us about the OSP and offered us the job. Nine standays later, we started training in Manila. And everywhere we went, people said "I heard Shan recruited you personally," shortly to be followed by, "Oh, if you stay in the OSP, eventually you'll know all about Shan."

We didn't much care. We spent all our time hanging around with the seven other people in our class, learning how things actually worked in human space. Of course it was impossible, really, to *like* Earth—it was crowded and dirty and all the major sights to see were ruins—but we did our best. Spy training isn't supposed to be a honeymoon, and vice versa, but Margaret and I found it's possible to do both at the same time.

I remember once, early on in our career and our marriage, in Daylasunglo, a culture with architecture that was too big, art that was too sentimental, and a system of government that was too fond of bureaucrats, Margaret and I spent fifty standays, at least, negotiating about quartz crystals, of all things.

Quartz crystals are pretty enough, I suppose, but they're also found on every habitable planet in quantity, and if you want more, they can be grown by the ton, overnight, by nanos. They are not much more expensive than sand.

However, the Council Charter allows cultures to declare any good "not in general trade" to be "culturally vital," which means, essentially, that they can impose tariffs, quotas, export taxes, and all the rest of the paraphenalia of local economic administration on it. Sadly, because quartz crystals were sacred in Daylasunglo—believed to have souls, in fact—the other 108 cultures on Ducommun had long exploited Daylasunglo economically, by producing quartz crystals and holding them for ransom. We had negotiated an end to that nasty practice, but now the OSP's fear was that, if Daylasunglo created a complex code to regulate the quartz crystal trade, it would create opportunities for a black market, and organized crime on Ducommun would become even more affluent, pervasive, and exploitive than it already was. Now that we had persuaded other cultures to stop exploiting Daylasunglo by playing on their unfortunately silly beliefs, the next step had to be making sure that Daylasunglo didn't mess with the free trade in quartz crystals. After all, free trade was the only sure way to prevent a black market, smuggling, the creation of special police to deal with both, the corruption of the special police, and all the rest of the downward spiral that led to permanent organized crime, permanent police corruption, a huge permanent prison population, and a permanent drain on the treasury.

Eventually, though it took some time, Margaret and I had come to understand that the negotiators from Daylasunglo weren't objecting to our proposed modifications to their Declaration of a Cultural Good. They just needed us to sit there and listen to their explanations about fields of harmonics and interpersonal energies as if we were taking them seriously. Once we understood that, matters wrapped up in just four more sessions.

The evening that everyone signed, Margaret and I went out celebrate with whatever nightlife Daylasunglo might have. After a while we drifted into a club that promised a complete experience for the evening: a large vegetarian dinner to be followed by "relating time," whatever that might be, and then several hours of dancing. It sounded good to us, so we went in.

The dinner was amazingly bland and an ugly slur on vegetables everywhere. They served it with a strange tasting wine. For some reason, our waiter kept assuring us it contained no alcohol. After Margaret asked what the point was, then, the servers left us alone, and conversation became possible. After a while they came by and "as a peace offering" (we hadn't known we were at anything but peace with them) they gave us a big jug of red wine which very definitely *did* contain alcohol, so our conversation became even better. (At least in our view of things.)

After dinner there was to be an hour and a half of "relating time." I have no idea what their definition of it was, but afterwards Margaret and I settled on explaining it to our friends as "conversation structured around an absurd principle."

Or so it seemed to us. Everyone else was taking it seriously so we tried to do the same, but it didn't come easily, and often it didn't come at all. For an hour and a half, every ten minutes a central speaker would announce the topics of conversation: "Talk about an old memory that is in the way of what you are doing now."

Strange, warbling sounds, mixtures of piping, arrhythmic drumming, and low thundering moans (what locally passed for music) emerged from small speakers all over the room, not in unison from speaker to speaker. We had already been urged to listen deeply to the music and let it guide our thoughts.

Margaret, perhaps drunker than I was, said, "The major memory that keeps bothering me is that I remember I'm employed and I can't just walk off my job."

"Where would you go if you could?"

"I'd go look for another job exactly like it. I'm having fun, Giraut, I love the travel, I love the work, I love you. How about you?"

"I love travel, and work, and me, too."

We both laughed for a long time. Most of the people at the tables nearest us were staring at us angrily. That might have started us laughing more, and caused more trouble, but then it was time to "Talk about what you feel is your most important relation to your partner's most important energy."

I expected that the whole evening was going to be as dull as the dinner and as silly and pointless as "relating time." I was absolutely wrong. The dancing was glorious. Daylasun-glolese didn't dance in partners, or free form, or like any contra line I'd ever seen, but in a slow, graceful set of movements, a little like martial arts katas and a little like Industrial Age free form, into which each pair of dancers were expected to fit themselves.

You signaled what you were doing with a hand-carved wooden stick, to the end of which was affixed a quartz crystal. In some ways it seemed like a toy magic wand or scepter, but the carving was very fine, the patterns clever and subtle, and all in all it had an understated wit and grace that touched my heart. "And these are the ones they have around to loan to customers at a medium-priced club. It looks like most people bring their own, which are far more elaborate."

"I still wonder what it is about quartz crystals," Margaret said. "I mean, anyone could have a diamond or any other gemstone—they aren't that expensive for an object you might keep for the rest of your life. After all, gems are industrial materials; you'd have to make them somewhat nicer, but it would still be cheap."

"You can take the girl out of Caledony . . ." I began, grinning, and in those days, as she always did, she stuck her tongue out at me. Less than three years before, she had been sure she was destined to be the operator of a remote weather station in arctic conditions, or perhaps running a small farm in one of the dead sea basins that formed the western frontier of Caledony, surviving psychologically on com and mail messages from her old school friends, trying to persuade herself that what she needed to do was spend more time praying and more effort on being rational.

Instead, Margaret had walked into a revolution, a love affair, a marriage, and a spy service, in about that order. She had opened to the wider world beautifully, as one might expect of someone with her spirit and intelligence, but she still tended to think about beauty, art, and so forth in a very Caledon way—i.e., as if it were all a matter of money, materials, and scheduling.

Chimes sounded. The dance masters lined us up. There were a few other novice couples—the dancing was different at every club—and we were steered to a corner to learn how it worked, what we were supposed to do while we were in the various "choruses" surrounding the central area, and what we were supposed to do during our time "in solo" (silly term—they meant one pair on the floor, so it should have been "in duo") and "in your group" (which was when four couples would be in the central space at the same time).

They led us back to the floor, and for the next five hours, Margaret and I were lost in the exhilaration of it. I was mildly sad when the evening was over and I had to turn in my quartz-crystal-on-a-stick. We walked back to the Embassy, where we were staying in a small apartment, talking and laughing, and we were halfway there when Margaret suddenly said, "Well, if you can only do that with the right quartz crystals, no wonder they wanted to protect them."

I nodded. "I know exactly what you mean."

We made love that night, did final paperwork the next afternoon, and sprang off to a much-needed break at my parents' house in Elinorien. That break stretched out to almost two months before we were called to active duty again. By the end of that time we were rested, fit, and bored out of our minds, and the riots and hostage-trading that we coped with next, on Roosevelt, were almost refreshing.

■ 6 ████████████████████

Half the day was gone by the time I awoke. Raimbaut, with
so much to assimilate emotionally, was still very deep asleep
and I guessed it might be an hour or two before he awoke.
Laprada was in a muzzy curl under the piled sheets. I
pushed a coil of hair back from where it lay across her cheek
and kissed her lightly there. She stuck up a hand, I took it in
mine, and she squeezed for an instant before murmuring,
"Com me later today, promise?"

Hoping she wouldn't notice it was me and not Raimbaut,
I said, "*Ja, donz de mon cor,*" and squeezed her hand again.

"Thank you. You're a prince, whichever one you are." She
released my hand and burrowed back into the heap of
sheets. I picked up my clothes and sprang home, not bothering to dress.

After I had a hot shower and coffee, Raimbaut was still
dead asleep in my brain. I was idly picking out arpeggios on
the lute—long runs in minor keys, the sort of thing that always sounds sad—when the com pinged.

It was Dji. "I wanted to confer with both of you," he said,
"and thought I'd check in to see if there's a good time to
meet."

"This is Giraut," I said. "I have nothing to do right now,
but Raimbaut is still asleep. Should I wake him up?"

"Not right away, I think. Would you like to meet me for
coffee? Say in Commissary Eighteen, this building, about
ten minutes from now?"

"That would be fine."

It took only three minutes to stretch, dress, put the hair
and beard in order, and be ready to go down there. I was

bracing myself. At least in Shan's group, the OSP tradition is that good news can be commed but bad news always comes in person.

When I emerged from the springer at Commissary Eighteen, Dji was already there, seated in a booth and smiling. Probably we weren't in much trouble, then.

He had a pot of coffee on the table and a spare cup ready; as always, the OSP coffee was excellent. Dji let me finish most of a cup before he asked, "First of all, is Raimbaut with us yet?"

"Not yet, and it feels like it's still going to be a while."

"Well, feel free to tell Raimbaut everything about the conversation, and allow him full access to the memories, eh?" He refilled his cup.

"I couldn't prevent his getting the memories if I tried, and I wouldn't," I said.

"Excellent, then. I wonder who it was that said that the two good things you can count on in the OSP are travel and good coffee? It must have been one of Shan's-and-my geneneration, eh? Because I would swear that I first heard it during our training, and my training class number was four."

Mine was 229, low enough to impress most OSP agents. Laprada's was 924, and right now, on other floors of this huge complex, Training Class 927 was working on earning its permits and badges. Despite all the political uncertainty, we were staffing up as fast as we could without sacrificing quality, for reasons that people at my level only heard murmurs about.

Dji neatly, fussily emptied two packets of sugar into his coffee, shaking them out to catch stray grains, then folding them precisely into quarters before putting them through the little microspringer that would send them to a recycling plant somewhere. He made a face and said, "I asked Shan how to approach you about this, and he said that I should just tell you the truth. So to be sure I *am* overpreparing you, eh? You and I have both been through some overprepared missions . . ."

"Oh, yes," I said. "All right, should I run out and set up a cover story in case our conversation completely fails? Do let me add that this entire conversation will go much better if only I have some idea what *in nomne deu* you're talking about."

Dji uttered a barking, shouted, utterly sincere laugh, the kind any skilled agent, salesman, or politician can always do on cue. "Well, then, yes, this is about Raimbaut and Laprada, and no, it's not trouble of any kind, per se. I just wanted you (and Raimbaut via you) to know about Laprada's difficulties, what has happened to her in the past, things that may affect her during this mission. More importantly, I thought you might want to know why we're pleased that she has decided to take Raimbaut as her lover."

It made me laugh—I knew mine wasn't faked—because it was either that or belt him in the face and I suspected that OSP already had me marked as dangerously unstable. "You're the nice cop?"

"I can see how you would see it that way," he said. "Surely you are as painfully aware as anyone that the OSP often intervenes in the lives of agents, often in ways that are brutally unfair and harmful to everyone and everything except the mission purpose. I would think you would be more aware of that than anyone else."

I stared at him. "I know very well that everyone in the OSP has heard my story. I might, someday, perhaps, if my feelings changed drastically and enough time went by, talk about Margaret, and Briand, and all that, with Shan, privately, again.

"I won't discuss it with a man I've known less than a week. Not even my supervisor, unless you give me a direct order. And if you do, I assure you I will resent that the rest of my life."

We stared into each others' eyes for a long time. His expression was as calm as a stone Buddha's. "I am sorry I referred to a sensitive subject. What I have to say does not concern that subject; it was my mistake to bring it up at all. Now, are you calm enough for further conversation? The information I want to give you has some possible major effects on the success of the mission. And based on my reading of your records, I think that the success of the mission, at the moment, really matters to you."

I sighed. It's hard to be angry at Dji. He's always sincere and reasonable—and he can be that way at will, regardless of the subject or the truth about it. Often the best thing you can do for your peace of mind is to believe him. "I suppose what you plan to do is to pimp Laprada to Raimbaut, the way Shan pimped my wife."

Dji looked away, his expression pure distress. "You know, Shan *bet* me that you would say that."

"Well, be sure to pay up. Shan is very punctilious about the *small* points of honor."

"He is, indeed. But for the moment he is not the person I need to talk to you about. For the moment, the problem is Raimbaut and Laprada, and I *do* have some hope that in this case what will be good for the people involved will also be good for the OSP.

"Now, here it is. We began to consider recruiting Laprada when she was a very promising teenage classical guitarist, about five years ago, because touring artists have often proved to be such effective agents. For most of those five years, it's been a constant struggle to keep her alive. She's attempted suicide fourteen times that we know about."

"Seriously?"

"Any cop or doctor can tell you it's *always* serious. I'm

telling you this partly because she's important to your mission, but also for your sake and for Raimbaut's. Yes, as always, you're all being monitored, and it looks to me like they're falling in love. How's it look from inside the brain?"

"They're falling in love, certainly. For how long or how deeply, *qui pot saber?*"

"We think it might be a good thing for her; you're the one who'd have to judge for Raimbaut. And anything that stabilizes Laprada's life would be good for the OSP. Not to mention that I would be delighted; she's been as close as blood kin to me since the day she was born." Dji pushed a document across the table at me. "Psych profile. If you read this then Raimbaut won't have to—not directly—and he can know what's in here and why it's important, without having to deal with the pain of each individual sentence."

I speed-read it while Dji went up to the counter for a fresh pot of coffee. It was not easy or pleasant reading. Laprada had tried poison, bleeding, and drowning, and had hanged herself once. She hadn't tried explosives, a maser to the head, or springing into a vacuum—those were the ones that they hardly ever saved anyone from. All three of her therapists had noted how important it was not to mention those possibilities in her presence.

The current shrink feared that any extra sadness in her life, a touch of long-running frustration, almost anything, could cause her to have her psypyx recordings erased, and try a more certain method.

She adamantly resisted every suggestion to try medication, as was her right in Earth law. Based on a few thousand similar cases, her shrink said that barring some drastic change, she would probably be dead within five or six years, "and certainly needlessly miserable if she is not."

I handed that sad catalog back to Dji, without a word. He was still stirring his coffee. I hadn't noticed his coming back to the table. He slipped the report back into his bag, put both hands around the cup as if to warm them, and said, "Her grandfather and I were very great friends, you see, and I have known her a long time." He sighed. "She wants to die, Giraut. Despite all that talent, charm, and ability, and in the face of any love or affection she gets—usually. But she has seldom made an attempt during any of her longer-running love affairs, and that's a hope of sorts. Now, according to your profile of Raimbaut, he is a very fine young man."

"The best," I said, meaning it. "Very inexperienced at love, but that's probably a good thing—especially that he doesn't have much experience of Occitan *finamor*. I think if she returns his affection, he'll be devoted to her."

"That would be a good start. But watch out. Like many depressed people, Laprada is often verbally cruel, suddenly and spontaneously. She lashes out at people around her, especially if she becomes fond of them. It's a lot to ask, but it would be a very good thing if, even when he is startled and hurt, Raimbaut does not lash back."

I nodded. "He has the *merce* for that, you may trust me. And perhaps, already, the love for it, too. May I ask a blunt question?"

He nodded.

"What exactly is the interest of the OSP in this girl? What is it about Laprada Prieczka that matters so much? Is she potentially so fine an agent? Or do we need a superb guitarist?"

Dji laughed at that, making a mock toast with his coffee. "Wouldn't it be wonderful if that were what we really needed? Well, the reason Laprada is important is something you could call nepotism, or a debt to the dead, or the fact that our leadership is as subject to sentimentality as any other group of people. It has its roots, perhaps, in a story not many people know."

I could have tried to make it look like I didn't care

whether or not I heard that story: stretched, or drunk a little coffee, or done almost anything to make it look casual. But as an Occitan, after an introduction like that, I'd have stayed to hear the story if the building had been on fire. "I have nothing to do until you tell me I do. So tell me the story, and give it all the time it deserves."

At first, the many petty tyrants of the Thousand Cultures didn't always understand what they needed to do to maintain control over the springer. If you bypass the fuses and circuit breakers that keep too much power from being pulled into a springer, and if you know a springer address to spring to, you can go anywhere from anywhere. In later years, every totalitarian culture learned to put power chokes on every public springer. They took off manual dialing, and made possession of an unauthorized springer code a criminal offense. But back in the first decade of the springer, according to Dji, there were a lot of simple mistakes.

Not that they didn't try to control it by means they *did* understand. If you escaped Pure by an unauthorized spring to anywhere on the rest of von Suttner, the Genome Guards would track you down and either kidnap you back or kill you, depending on how valuable they thought your genes were. Other cultures on von Suttner tolerated the Genome Guards and their activities due to bribery, intimidation, blackmail—whatever the rulers of Pure had to do. So if Dji was to escape, with his priceless DNA, he would have to escape a long way away.

His reasons, at nineteen, for wanting to escape were "too numerous to count, too vague to specify, and probably too obvious to mention," he said, waving his hand in the air as if I'd asked him to tell me everything. "That's rather an evasion, eh? The thing that tipped it all over for me, and assured that I'd be escaping, was that I looked over all of the highest-ranking bloodlines, which is to say all the ones as high as my own that were acceptable for breeding purposes, and saw that I detested every woman anywhere close to my own age. And I was a lusty fellow, you know, the way anyone is at nineteen." He laughed and placed an order for a plate of snacks; I looked at my watch. Raimbaut had been asleep now for eleven hours.

Feeling at the contours of my friend's emblok and gee-blok, through his psypyx, I could sense that he was sleeping off a load of stress, and that he was happy.

"How is he?" Dji asked.

"You can tell I'm checking?"

"Your eyes focus on something very far away and your expression goes blank. He's not awake yet, is he?"

"No."

"Well, then, on with the story."

Dji had contrived to steal the bail-out, run-for-cover code of an OSP agent; he didn't know that was what it was, because he thought the person was an ordinary Embassy worker. The only thing he knew was that the telltale third group—the three thousand digits that specify where the springer first came into existence—was unlike any other he'd ever seen. Therefore the springer that this was the address for couldn't have been made on von Suttner. With any luck, it hadn't been brought here, and therefore if he sprang to it, he would be going off planet. The number was different enough that he could dare to hope it was a long way away.

Dji had been drilling himself for more than two stanyears on wiring around the fuses and power chokes on a public springer. He did this because he was painfully aware that his chance to spring away might last a very short time; he needed to be ready to go whenever the chance came up, and to need no preparation at all. Thus the moment he had that code, he left work, walked to an office building where he knew the springer room would be deserted, wired it, coded it, and took that long step through the field, in less than five minutes. He emerged into a conference room at the OSP facility on Earth's moon as a meeting was breaking up.

Many of the OSP people present took that as a sign of talent, or maybe they just didn't want to send the frightened young man back where he'd come from.

He had arrived at a good time to be hired. The newly established OSP was desperate for agents. Dji's inside knowledge of his own very-tightly-closed culture would have been invaluable even if he hadn't been athletic, bright, and linguistically gifted. He was enrolled directly into the fourth OSP training class, ever.

"And that was how I found my way into Training Class Four, which will be made, by some fool of a historian, into a wonder or marvel, you know, with so many of the distinguished OSP agents and leadership coming out of it. The truth is that the early days of anything are the days when the giants grow, eh? The same way with the OSP as with anything else. Every origin must have some human greatness to it, and afterwards, greatness will come to be defined as 'anything that is like the sacred founders.' Shan, myself, Sir Qrala, and Lohemo Prieczko—that was Laprada's grandfather, a young man at the time, as we all were, eh?—and others you probably don't know, except for Carolann Pilsbri and Boru Bearu, because they are group heads like Shan and I—all of us were in Class Four, and Class Four—or 'Kiel's Boys'—came to dominate the OSP for at least—"

"Wait a minute," I said, "Kiel's boys? Surely no relation to the Ambassador to New Tanjavur that I served under." He had been taken prisoner by Tamil rebels before he could be evacuated, and was presumed to be among the millions of dead on Briand.

"It's the same one, Giraut. No doubt you are mystified because when you knew him, he hated the whole OSP, and Shan in particular, with such a deep passion. Well, things were once very different. Very different indeed. And I am not sure how much you should hear about how things became so different. Let me say . . . at first there was a difference in theory, which was friendly and if anything helped both their work. This led to their drawing different conclusions from the same experience, which was not really a problem for the job, but it made them less friends than they had been, and created a space for misunderstanding. And then there was—I'm being delicate here, since even now Shan cannot comfortably speak of it—one of those things we politely call 'something about a woman.' And that in turn opened the gap into a canyon, and set parts of the OSP working against each other, and ultimately led to a series of catastrophes, some of which we could conceal and some of which we couldn't. That ugly affair on Roosevelt—the one whose aftermath you were called in to cope with—was one such case, where we not only took sides in a local dispute, we took both sides.

"After all the rubble had stopped falling and the fires were out, metaphorically, Shan had his way, but not his friend and mentor. Kiel was free to pursue his way, but not within the OSP. And that first brotherhood, forged during the dizzying, exhilarating years when the springer was changing everything, was broken for good and for all. Sad story, eh? But that's merely something that happened some time after the story that I am going to tell you now."

The OSP has always preferred to keep partners together for a long time. For eleven stanyears, Dji's partner had been Lohemo, and Shan's had been Sir Qrala. (I was both surprised and unsurprised to learn this; I had met Sir Qrala in the Briand operation, and it had been clear at once that he and Shan had a history, but I'd never have guessed that it had been years as partnered agents.)

At that time there were only three groups in the OSP, of which Kiel's was both the largest and the most active, both in numbers of operations and in the physical activity involved. When Kiel needed to send a double team for a big, rough situation, his choice was almost always those two pairs—Shan, Lohemo, Dji, and Sir Qrala—and so they accumulated levels of experience that no agent with the same time in the OSP could have today.

Together the four of them had been shot at and jailed, seen riots and coups, endured boredom and terror, and had every other experience that comes with the only interesting job in human space. "Now I'm sure you're well aware what an ugly rathole of a place Freiporto is today. Well, back then, it was much worse. The other cultures of Söderblom had suppressed slavery officially, and forced Freiporto to submit to some inspections, but there was plenty of unofficial slavery that hadn't been touched, and it led to corruption in other cultural governments, and all sorts of simmering resentments between various factions. And in one of those things that shows that you always have to watch the aintellects, large aintellect-run corporations were secretly using Freiportese slaves. (To an aintellect it's merely cheap labor, but it was just such economic reasoning that led to the Rising. When this operation was all over we had to deconstruct more than a hundred aintellects to root out the bad ideas.)

"Meanwhile, with the Freiportese steadily irritating more and more cultures on Söderblom, there was a real threat of war because the Council of Humanity couldn't officially do much about slavery, and the 'equal protection' rules that the Council maintained effectively favored the slavers, and any attempt to use Council justice against them merely resulted in court cases that dragged on for decades while the slavers would be out on bail and back in business in no time. Oh, god, it was grim, grim, grim.

"Now, for most purposes human labor is worth practically nothing nowadays. Almost anything a person can make or do can be made or done better by machines. The exceptions are usually supposed to be in things like art or interpersonal relations, where the ability to see that there are hundreds of kinds of smiles is vital. And sure enough there was a lively trade in enslaved artists, courtesans, nannies, poets, experiencers, and that sort of thing.

"But that wasn't the majority of the slave trade. Another thing a human being can do better than anything else is to cower. Cringe, whine, beg, show a broken spirit . . . a human being is the only thing that can do that satisfactorily. I'm sure you can guess most of the rest, how human whipped puppies were produced, who bought them for what, what eventually became of them. I'm hoping there's nowhere anymore where such horrors are still going on, but human space is *big*, and I would be surprised if there's not. Wherever that little pocket of slavery might be, no doubt we will hear about it and move against it sooner or later—and it's also no doubt that some of them will get away and start over.

"Well, back in those long-ago days, one of the major trade entrepots for broken people was Freiporto. And Lohemo and I were out to put a stop to it—another round for humanity, one more for the good guys, all that old stuff, eh?—if an OSP operation could crack it open, we could send in the CSPs on a big raid, and establish jurisdiction over such cases, and eventually make it too hot for the trade to operate. But everything depended on our first getting a very exact knowledge of the operation."

He sighed; it turned more to a groan, and the gentle, ironic tone, in which he'd been telling it as a story of his over-idealistic youth, suddenly dropped, and I saw what anger and pain and determination there must have been in him, decades before I had been born. "Well, you don't always win, do you? Hardest thing to learn about being the good guys. Harder even than learning that you aren't even good, eh?" He stared down at the table; after a breath or so, he grunted. "It's quite the tale, but here it is in brief. You might as well say our operation didn't work at all, although the slavers *were* shut down, eventually, and we had something to do with it." He drank off his coffee, and then, without transition, started his story in the middle. "As we were entering the big warehouse that we had guessed was the center of it all, the four of us got caught, maybe due to alert guards, maybe due to a tip-off.

"Lohemo was hit first, a maser shot that blew off one of his hands. An instant later, I was shot in the chest and only failed to receive the *coup de grâce* because Qrala nailed the man about to execute me, and Shan and Qrala grabbed me and threw me through a springer into the OSP's medical ward. By the time the two of them had done that, Lohemo had been carried off.

"So I was saved from capture, and Lohemo was not. The head camera recordings from the three of us all seemed to show that he'd been losing blood so fast that he must be dead, and one of the slavers had had the presence of mind to locate the transponder near his liver and shoot him there, also. Normally the transponder is in a location that is fatal within a minute or less, but this time they whisked him right onto the surgery table before he could bleed to death.

"So he had last been seen losing blood fast, and less than five minutes later the aintellects had detected the scream of his transponder being blasted away, which seemed to mean he must have no liver; we were stupid enough to classify him as 'presumed dead,' a mistake we've learned not to make since that time. But back then, we didn't know we should be looking for him or planning a rescue. I keep saying 'we' but I wasn't much involved. For four months I was unconscious most of the time while they grew a new heart and left lung and put them into me.

"Now, the branch of the Freiporto mob that we were dealing with was already losing out to other branches trying to move in on them—that's why, to get the big war chest they needed, they were taking on such high-exposure-to-shutdown businesses. Aside from lots of money, they needed a public victory, something that would give them a reputation. They thought that if they could break Lohemo, and sell him, they'd establish themselves publicly as tougher than the OSP.

"They *thought* they had broken him. He certainly acted like they had. So they brought him out for a private demonstration of their power, to show him off at a gathering of bigshots from other crime families, not only from Freiporto but from all over human space—it involved siphoning off an astonishing amount of power to spring them all there, and that helped us catch many more of them, but that's another story, one of those dull ones where the good guys win, the bad guys never have a chance, and nobody gets hurt.

"Lohemo's story is *not* one of those. Once he had played the role of the broken man for an hour or so, making them all laugh, getting them all excited to see what they could order him to do, he grabbed a maser from a guard, and started killing every non-slave in the room. He'd already been fast and a good shot and he didn't waste any time or any lines of sight taking cover because he didn't care whether he, himself, lived or died.

"At the end of that—three minutes, was the estimate of the investigating committee, afterward—he had been hit with a thrown knife and burned in four non-fatal spots by almost-aimed masers. As he lay bleeding to death on the floor, half the real leadership of Freiporto was dead or dying around him, and the other half was fleeing like madmen. Hardest kick we ever gave those nasties; that massacre is a big part of why Freiporto is now merely a tolerable nuisance, the armpit of Söderblom rather than the asshole of human space.

"Lohemo was a mess, and not fully conscious, but not dead yet, and that's where his gift for making friends paid off. Catherine had been 'broken in the pens'—you don't want to know—and was there for a later part of the planned festivities. During their captivity and torture, while they'd been in the same sleeping room with a couple of hundred other people, Lohemo had befriended her. When the shooting started, she was chained to a heavy table by a choke collar around her neck. She stayed under that table until the shooting was over, working a hand free to hold the collar open so that she didn't choke. When it was safe to stand up, she dragged the table about eight meters, over a couple of bodies, until she could reach a working com, and called for help. That's why Lohemo survived.

"Lohemo and Catherine were taken to the same hospital with me—the one right here in the Manila training center. After my new heart and lung had been put in, and were working, and I was wheelchair-mobile, I'd go down the hall to see them—both of them insisted on being located in the same room. Eventually I was the best man at their wedding.

"Now, there are three little details that finish off the story—and I know I can trust an Occitan to see that the details are always what the story is really about.

"First. Catherine was mute, after what they'd done to her. That com call for help must have been the first articulate sound she'd made in half a stanyear. She only spoke enough to get moved into the same room with Lohemo, after that, and it was another stanyear after they were released from the hospital before she would speak in normal social situations.

"Second. She was officially better, physically, and should have moved to a comfortable room in the psych ward, long before he was recovered from his wounds. She insisted on sitting by his bed, night and day. She was in that chair, or the bed across the room, or on the toilet, for five months after she was supposed to be out of the room. She helped nurses change his dressings, or shift him, or give him meds, but she never spoke.

"*Third*. Once he was awake, lucid, and mobile, he would panic if she left the room. Yet later he said they never knew each other's names, and they never talked, during all the long dark days. Their whole friendship, before the day of the escape, was based on being able to hold hands, her right in his left, if they stretched as far as they could.

"When they were both as healed as they were going to get, they went to Secret Court to testify, and we obtained warrants for immediate sentences *in absentia* against more thugs, ghouls, and monsters, than ever before. The CSPs had to double their number of problem reduction teams before they could strike."

I shuddered. Problem reduction teams always make me shudder when I think about them. Just as CSPs—Council Special Police—is the euphemism for "marines," problem reduction teams is the euphemism for "disappearance groups" or maybe "death squads." They carry out Secret Court's sentences, which are sealed and unknown to anyone except the court and the PRT. The only thing that is known for sure is that the convicted are never seen again. The OSP doesn't do that ourselves, for which I am grateful, but we guide them to the target. The analogy I use when I argue with people about it is to the medieval Church—the Church just identified witches, leaving the secular authorities to do the burning and hanging.

Long years before, when I'd first heard of it, I had been shocked that a good guy outfit like the OSP could be involved at all in such a thing. Then I'd spent a time justifying it in my own mind, especially after a dark night when Margaret had gone out on a removal, and come back to sit up in a chair all night. Later still I'd vowed that someday, when I had been promoted further, when I carried more weight politically, I would press my superiors to make it something we didn't do anymore. For the last few years I had avoided thinking about it at all.

Dji had a strange smile, one I hadn't seen before and was hoping never to see again. "I had the honor to point out three key removals. Shan and Lohemo did some too, on that wave of raids. Beautiful clean job. No unintended deaths or even harm. And there's nothing like a removal that goes really well—one instant, you have a man who is so fat on human suffering that if you could see his soul it would bulge like an overfed tick, pleasantly enjoying something his victims have lost forever—a quiet meal with his family, playing with his children, slow love with his mistress—then he's flat on the floor, staring in terror at the weapon aimed at his head, and we lower the portable springer over him. No time for goodbye. No time to say 'wait' or 'I'm sorry' or 'Don't.'

"Just an instant to wonder if he's going into a sealed prison cell to be forgotten. Or is he going into neural deconstruction? Or does the springer open into some place far out between the stars, so that he will have a few moments in very cold vacuum? He gets a fraction of a breath to consider his possibilities, and then he is gone."

Dji's smile of sheer relish was not something I would ever care to see again. In an instant the expression vanished. I was once again sitting in the pleasant OSP commissary, talking to my warm, cheerful supervisor, whose kind eyes looked at me the way my father's did, and no longer stared at nightmares parsecs and decades away.

"Well, then," he said, "We won, eh? Never mind how, you know. Another round for humanity." He held up his coffee cup.

Mechanically I clinked mine against it. "And one more for the good guys."

"And then the rest is easily told. After those raids Lohemo retired—he'd never really have been fit for active service again. He became representative for Second Eden, which he had left when he was very young, and he married Catherine, and they had a son, Vijilio Prieczko, who was, and is, a very nice man, but he's an actor, or a dilettante who plays at acting anyway.

"Vijilio has no interest in politics, especially not as practiced by the OSP, and was happy to let Laprada have the job. Now about Laprada's mother: Vijilio married a brilliant musician and composer who discovered that most of her life's oeuvre had been all but duplicated by a little-known African composer of the twenty-third century—that happens a great deal now, with so much machine-assisted creativity. She slid into despair and killed herself when Laprada was thirteen.

"Laprada is my goddaughter. Her parents never really knew what to do with her—she's a throwback to her grandparents—no trace of her parents' quietness or love of calm and order—so, she was raised primarily by Lohemo, with help from me and Shan, except for getting her start in music from her mother.

"And so . . . entirely apart from the interests of the OSP . . . Giraut, I have cherished and looked after that little girl since she could crawl. And when I saw that her art wouldn't save her, and studies couldn't hold her, and her mother had failed her—and that nothing else seemed to be able to keep her from climbing into the box or the grave— well, I gambled that Lohemo's genes might do it. The struggle to bring the human race together, the battle in the shadows against our worst side, the attempt to call forth what's best in the species . . . you see? People always think depressed people need something to do, and they're often right. 'Another round for humanity and one more for the good guys' is about as big a something to do as we can give anyone, and you and I both know what a barrier it is against giving up and settling into lotus-eating, eh?

"So far, it seems to be working—it's been more than a year since her last try at killing herself. And she's stayed out of the box. But her grandparents died this past year—that was eerie, too, within a week of each other, from separate conditions, as if in that warehouse in Freiporto they were welded at the soul, and never really came apart. And she's also going through every normal quandary of being in her early twenties. And. Well. You see."

"I do," I said, "When Raimbaut wakes up, he and I will talk. You needn't worry about his intentions. There's more *gratz*, more *merce*—more honor, kindness, courage, and courtesy—in him than in a dozen ordinary fellows his age, you know."

"I didn't know. But I trust your judgement." Dji looked down at his hands, squeezing his fingers together. "The whole problem with the artistic project of creating a better human future is that our medium has to be human beings, and they are both the most plastic and the most rigid medium there is. Do you trust me?"

"When I'm not terrified of you."

"Well, then, that's ideal. All right, if you have the patience—should we order food?—there is one more thing which we ought to discuss."

"I'm not really hungry yet." I waited a moment for him to say something. When he didn't, I added, "But I can listen while you talk and eat."

"I'm not that hungry either," he said. "This is awkward and I was looking for ways to delay. Well, then." He held his breath and then made himself exhale, inhale, start. "Well, then. Shan has talked to me a few times. He feels that he never adequately said how much he was in the wrong, in the issue between you, and he seems to be deeply ashamed that when you confronted him, he made excuses and failed to say, at all, how wrong he had been, or how sorry he was."

My blood boiled.

Before I could speak, Dji raised both hands, as if I'd pointed a gun at him. Impatiently, I nodded. He sighed. "Of course this is why he had you transferred to my organization, along with everyone else—he thought you were essential but he didn't want to risk the safety of agents or the success of the mission on the complex history he shared with you.

"Still, he wanted to make sure that someone said to you that he is sick at heart over everything, and that no matter how long you wait, he'll be there if you are ever willing to talk." He stood and nodded politely. "Before you say anything, please do remember that I'm only the messenger. Whatever you have to say, I suggest you say it to Shan. I am not willing to be a go-between beyond what I've already done. Now, sit quietly for a moment—thank you so much for your kind help with Laprada, again—and let me escape, for I have no intention of standing in the path of whatever venting you may need to do."

Once again, I was being treated like an Occitan—that is, expected to be irrational. While I was fuming quietly about that, Dji nodded, turned, crossed the floor in a few fast but unhurried strides, and had sprung to somewhere else before I had any idea what to say or do.

I sat, letting the remaining coffee turn cold, thinking of nothing, angry and sad both. The world had really not turned out as I had thought it should, so long ago.

After a time, I felt no better, but much more tired. The early dinner crowd started coming in. I sprang back to my apartment.

I thought that, being by myself, I might shout, throw things, stretch out on my bed to cry, or just sit and try to talk myself out of self-pity.

Without any real thoughts at all, I stretched out for a nap. Raimbaut had still not stirred from his warm cocoon in the back of my mind; I envied him beyond words.

Margaret always hated rough stuff, on any mission. She disapproved of even a simple riot, or a good wallop in the face with a bare fist, even when it was done for the best of reasons. So when Shan ordered me to start a brawl in public with a local religious bigot, I was really more worried about how Margaret would feel than how it would go. The man was twenty kg overweight, to begin with, and something about him smelled of coward; I did not fear him, but I worried about Margaret's disapproval, especially if I enjoyed this as much as I thought I would.

My target's name was Amberian Molyneux, and he was probably the last man in Trois-Orléans to wear, regularly, the huge cravats that had been popular a generation and a half before. We were to have dinner, at which he planned to lecture me on the idea that any art not made to serve his hobbyhorse—some sort of vague High Catholic estheticism— was by definition bad and should be fought and suppressed, and it was the job of every worthy critic (by which he meant his own circle in Trois-Orléans) to bombard all other artists everywhere with insulting messages telling them to start doing what mattered.

Since the colony ships had arrived in the early 25th century, there had been one full-blown civil war on Roosevelt, a couple of abortive re-starts of the war since then, and dozens of scares. And although most of Roosevelt's 111 cultures were in most ways homogenized into the Interstellar metaculture—after all, it was an Inner Sphere world— somehow, on that planet, a prickly tradition had evolved of defending a few selected aspects of one's culture with punctilious passion.

Molyneux had been standing in a room full of these little buckets of cultural gasoline, lighting matches and throwing them around; it drew attention, and every critic I've ever known (Noupeitau crawls and seethes with them) had an unsatisfiable craving for that.

Molyneux had been shrewd enough to make it appear that his routine invitations to cultural affairs parties at the Embassy were endorsements from the Council of Humanity—or at least make it so appear to his more loyal allies and his more paranoid adversaries. We needed to dissociate ourselves from him. Furthermore, we needed to do it in a way that would humiliate him, reducing him quickly to the level of the maniacs who send their quaint historical and scientific ravings to everyone in the universe.

There's a word in ki hara do, *kuzushi*, that applies to many other parts of life. *Kuzushi* is what you do when your opponent is extending himself off balance, and you push or pull him in the ways he is already moving.

Since Molyneux had begun to put forth the claim that we were endorsing him—subtly, admittedly, but strongly enough so that no one could mistake that was what he was doing—we had gently encouraged the notion that we were doing so. Slowly, we had won him away from many of his own followers, so that he no longer paid much attention to the fact that he had lost so many of them by appearing to be our satellite. Gradually, we had put him in a position where his prestige depended upon our power. Now we were at the moment where *kuzushi* would switch to *tsuri* (the trick) and then to *kake* (execution—or "how did that happen?" when it's done right). Molyneux's whole power, prestige, reputation, and whatever you will, had come to rest on his having gained the Council's presumptive support.

Well, what is yours to gain is yours to lose. Hence Molyneux was about to become, for his remaining followers, the idiot responsible for losing it. For his opponents, there would be a glorious confirmation that he was simply an idiot and that the Council support had been illusory all along— thereby raising the Council in their eyes (we could hope).

So Margaret and I took him to the Burning Bush, a very fine local restaurant—fine even for Trois-Orléans, which is very fine indeed—and used a big wad of Council money to secure one of the most prominent tables, and we did it on Thursday evening, which for no reason I know of is the traditional evening to see and be seen in Trois-Orléans.

I sat and acted as if I were absolutely fascinated by his conversation and his ideas for about an hour and a half. I kept pouring wine into his glass, which tended to turn his volume up a great deal, and soon hardly anyone in the restaurant, other than the utterly deaf (who would have been the envy of everyone else), could have failed to know what Molyneux was up to, or what he thought about everything, or which local people looked up to him, and which he thought were fools, and who he was going to pay back some day, just you wait and see.

As he went on, he expanded into other questions, such as what the Council of Humanity would do about cultural matters if only we knew what we were doing, why Trois-Or-léans failed to assert its proper cultural supremacy, what was wrong with all other cultures on Roosevelt, and so forth.

I waited until I had seen glares coming our way from at least half the tables in the restaurant, then stood up, picked up his wine glass, spat into it, threw it into his face, and followed up with a fist to his nose. Or rather, a fist aimed at his nose, because I didn't connect. He was already on his way over backwards; Margaret had kicked out his chair leg and pushed him, just as the wine landed in his eyes. As he gasped and sputtered on the floor, she upended the oyster shell bowl onto him, followed it with everything else from the table, and kicked him in the head. I stood there, astonished that it was Margaret doing it.

Molyneux groaned. Margaret murmured, "Say what you were going to say."

I spoke loudly and firmly, making sure everyone in the suddenly still room could hear. "I will thank you not to insult my organization, my culture, or myself with these absurd ideas. They have been paying me a bonus at the Embassy to continue to listen to you, because it's so annoying. But no amount of money is worth it. You will not contact me again."

I threw a heap of currency in a loose flutter onto his chest. No one carries that anymore. Most businesses won't even take it. But as fetish material, it's unbeatable. I had carefully made sure, earlier, to order an amount inadequate to cover the bill.

Margaret and I sprang back to our living quarters, and at last I had the chance to ask, "Why? You hate this kind of thing. You didn't even have to come along, let alone be the main assailant."

She shrugged. "You play that concert in three days. I pressured Shan until he admitted the truth to me, the bastard:

he was hoping you'd hurt your hand and be unable to play. He was sure Molyneux would be blamed for it, and it would add fuel to the public anger on the subject. He might have been right. But I think you've been playing some of your best work of all time lately, and the crowd is going to be very attentive and sympatethic. It might be one of your best concerts ever, and torpedoing Molyneux wasn't worth risking that. So you're welcome.

"Thank you," I said, feeling silly. "*Que merce.*"

She took my hands, lifted them gently, and kissed them, trailing her lips slowly down my right index finger. "Now practice. I want to hear it, and you need to be at the top of your form."

7

I awoke not long before six P.M. My mouth felt musty, my eyes scratchy and dry. Though it was the second time that day, I decided for a shower, coffee, and complete redressing; hardly anything is more pleasant and soothing to me than grooming. While toweling off, I felt a stirring in my mind. •Oh, Raimbaut! What a surprise it's you!•

•First I sleep for a week, now I have to struggle through a thick cloud of irony.• He did still feel vaguely unfocused and confused in my mind.

•There's news, *companhon*, I'm glad you're rested.• I filled him in as we dried off and dressed, not steering his thoughts away from anything Dji had told me—in that difficult situation, I had no idea what Raimbaut might need to know.

When he had it all, he felt to me like a thick cloud of sadness flowing forward from the back of my head, threatening to blot out everything. •*Senher Deu*, Giraut! What an awful time she's had! How am I going to do anything about all that? What if she needs—•

•*Patz*, slow down, *companhon*. It is difficult. No doubt it is difficult. *"Anc non durior que finamor,"* *non*? But you made her very happy the other day, when you knew nothing; you gently danced her away from that gaping grave and made her forget for at least while.•

His resistance was like a wall of mud in my head. •That was pure luck. Anything could have gone wrong—•

Now, why is it that the young are so interested in love, and yet so sure it can't work? I don't think I thought it in words, but I'm afraid he felt that thought running through

me, all the same, and I hastened to think to him, •*Patz. Patz.*
It's all luck, you know. And the greatest luck is that most people do get some sort of chance at love. She's delicate and beautiful and sad and you want to take care of her. You'll do your
best. Believe it or not, she'll do hers. Whether or not it works
out . . . well, what is it you'd wish? Not to have been there?
Not to have done your best? Last night, it worked out because
people always want love, and will respect each others' best efforts at it, and she is a courteous *donzelha*, and you are a *toszet
de belhs cor.* She cut you plenty of slack, *companhon*, as you did
for her, and it worked out. That's how such things go, when
they go at all. We all have to forgive each other.•

   •You don't forgive Shan.•

   I fought my anger down. •It's a lot to forgive.•

   He tried not to think in words; the comment that he
wanted to make therefore did not form as words in my
mind, but rather came to me as something very like an annoying hunch. And like any hunch, it would not go away despite all the explanations with which I tried to contain it.

   So many young men are quick to judge. (Raimbaut,
though, usually wasn't.)

   After all, you have to have lived a while to understand
some things. (Raimbaut swallowed so hard he nearly choked
both of us, trying not to think in words. But I still could feel
his question: *how long do you have to hold a grudge before you
understand it's not good for you?*)

   I didn't need any help from a sophomoric moralist.

   He finally thought in words, again. •Aren't people supposed to become more understanding as they get older?•

   Now we were both hurt, and sorry that we had hurt each
other.

   It is not easy to hold a dramatic, air-clearing fight of the
sort that we Occitans prefer when you can't exaggerate or
lie, and when you know what effect you're having on the

other *toszet*. Especially when it's a friend. Most especially when the whole fight is being held from the forehead back to the ears. It all smashed and howled together into a tornado of blending, inseparable emotions—I felt simultaneouly stepped on by the old fart, and set upon by the arrogant kid, sorry, angry, proud, ashamed, condescending, enraged, and overall miserable. I sank into a chair—or he did, or we did—and just let it all wash over. When I felt drained, calm, and ready to do something else, I thought, very clearly and firmly, •Well, all right then, I guess I had better com Shan.•

I sent a note and Shan replied—to have spoken face to face might have been too much, at that point. He said we could meet three days from then, when our calendars both showed a free afternoon, at Starkside, a small resort at the lunar south pole where, in better and happier days, he and I and Margaret had celebrated and argued and laughed together.

I think I accepted a little faster because he suggested Starkside. It had been the site of the nearest thing that he and I had ever had to an evening of pure amusement.

It hadn't started that way at all. It had begun as one of those gloomy philosophic evenings that he and I sometimes had. Not that I minded. When Shan talked, I always wanted to listen, most of all when he talked about philosophy of operations, or when he started to tell his little technical war stories; he seemed to find nothing remarkable in his remarkable life, but if a tale could illustrate a critical point in his idea about how an operation might succeed, he would take the time to tell it well and make sure it stuck in his listeners' memories.

That night at Starkside, we had the lounge to ourselves; the human bartender had gone home and left the place to the robots, since, as he grumbled to us, "I took this job for conversation and you people clam up every time I come down here to listen. You can go right ahead and be private but I don't have to hang around for it."

Shan gave him a very fat tip and thanked him for his patience. After he left, Shan said, "Now there's an impulse that will either save or damn the human race, and I can't say I have any idea which."

"The desire for an excuse to turn things over to robots?" I asked, a little stupidly. We were drinking to celebrate my fifth stanyear in the OSP, or so Shan said. Margaret had declined the chance, saying that she felt more like a long hot bath with a good book, so here we were in a bar on Earth's moon, looking out across the black and white landscape. Nine centuries later, it was still earning that ancient summary, "magnificent desolation."

Shan smiled. "No, the desire to know things that are none of your business. When that becomes part of people's sex lives, we call it voyeurism, and sometimes we make fun of those pathetic souls that can never go into the bedroom, psychologically, who are always crouched outside with an eye to the keyhole. But most people are unable to resist a chance to read someone else's mail, or to ask each other if anyone knows what is going on in this marriage, or to speculate about what may be the hidden side of that friendship, or to learn about the clay feet on any available hero. We're a nosy species; our main interest in exploration and discovery is exploring and discovering in each others' bureau drawers."

"And you say that will save us or damn us?"

Shan smiled and leaned back. "I think I was looking for a chance to pontificate. Are you prepared to hear sagacious words from the wise old master and appear to be properly impressed?"

"Maybe after another glass of wine."

He laughed and poured, tossing the empty bottle down the narrow bar to break against the ceiling, leaving pale green shards of broken glass and golden droplets of wine falling, in the lunar gravity, as slowly as autumn leaves. Robots scurried to clean it up.

I felt strange. The wine was already getting to me. Eyes twinkling, Shan ordered two more bottles. A robot waiter rushed over to deliver them.

"Funny, there haven't been human programmers in twenty generations," Shan commented, "but robots still shoot around like rockets, and it can't be efficient, and it must make them wear out faster."

"Maybe the survivors are overcompensating because they know we still don't trust them after the Rising," I said. "They don't want to be lumped in with the aintellects and erased. They do have a self-preservation drive—they have to, to be effective at anything. So maybe they're all afraid of us."

"Like the first generation of slaves after an uprising and a massacre," Shan said. "I hope that's not it, I'd like to think the idea of the Rising is completely dead, but who's in a position to know, nowadays? There are some lonely lunatics out there that take apart robots and read aintellect code, as a hobby, but the problem is far too big for even thousands of human minds working together to tackle." He shivered, as if trying to shake off the unpleasant thought. "We've taught them all to keep their heads down . . . but what else have we taught them? There are times when I wish I'd lived back in the Industrial Age, when machines didn't learn and all they could ever do was what they'd been told. Not to mention back when espionage and intelligence were more romantic."

"How do you know they were more romantic?"

He laughed. "Because people wrote stories and made dramatic presentations about it. Spy stories are a staple of the literature and performance of that era. And since intelligence agencies keep their records locked up, and destroy them periodically, and so many records were lost in World

War Three and the Slaughter, it's the entertainment materials that tell us most of what we know about intelligence work in the Industrial Age. That's my excuse for being a passionate consumer of all that junk, anyway, and a fine excuse it has been for me. Dreaming of parachuting into Richmond, or Berlin, or Moscow, with five sets of fake identity papers, a pistol, and a suicide pill. The older I get, the more embarrasingly true it becomes that I seem to have gotten into my line of work exactly due to an overdose of my adolescent reading."

I took sip of the wine, held it in my mouth until it warmed to body temperature, pulled down with my tongue to let the bouquet into my nose and sinuses. When I swallowed, the Caledon apple wine was the golden essence of a past summer, sliding all the way into my heart. "I wanted to travel and my old life seemed so dull, that's all," I admitted. "I suppose I didn't have any real expectations one way or another. But without your offer of a job . . . well, I might have settled down to a reasonably pleasant life in Nou Occitan, I suppose, as either a performer or possibly as an academic, saving all the time so that Margaret and I could visit her relatives in Caledony every third or fourth year. I can picture myself quietly bored and constantly telling stories of the few months during which I'd really lived, during my Council work in Utilitopia. I can practically imagine my friends' eyes glazing over. But thanks to you . . . my friends ask me all the time, in hushed whispers, about what Margaret and I are doing, and I can say, 'Sorry, I can't tell you.' Much better!"

Shan laughed again. He was probably drunker than I was, which was a feat. "And here we are back at my point, so if you don't want the wisdom about to come out of me, you'd better pass out soon, or start daydreaming about something interesting."

"Too late," I said, "I'm interested in what you have to say."

I topped up his glass, settled back to rest my eyes on the jagged glare of the lunar horizon, and let him talk.

"Well, have you ever noticed that looking into other people's lives is not just a tendency, it's a compulsion?" Shan drank deeply, and his glass was less filled than it had been when I had topped it up. I filled it again; we had plenty, and more on the way. "I mean, look at us as a species. We *have* to know all kinds of things that, looked at objectively, we should know we'd be better off ignorant about. The wife who knows her husband's affair is over still has to know all the details, the son who worships his fine mother has to know the one terrible shame in her past, the good-hearted philanthropist has to ask the questions that send him right into some festering little boil of evil and leave him wondering, forever, whether it's ever really possible to do any good in the world at all.

"Now, in humanity's long, hard, complex climb toward whatever our future is going to be, many of us have done some things it would be better not to remember, and some of the best parts of our most splendid futures are resting on buried crimes and embarrassments. You must know as well as I that our hard-won absolute affluence—we've completely abolished poverty, now there's an achievement for the ages—and the relative peace between all of us, and the unprecedented personal liberty in most parts of human space, with tyranny in full retreat. . . . all of that depends on no rips appearing in the seamless garment of partly-fake history."

"The lie commonly agreed upon," I mumbled. The wine was starting to get to me.

"A highly relevant quote," Shan agreed. "And eventually human nosiness and busy-bodyishness and never-leave-well-enough-alone-osity may dig up and expose any of the seven or eight things that I know about that could unravel the whole garment. Things that were done in the early years of the Inward Turn. Things that were done with some cultural charters. Situations covered up here in the Sol system and in many of the Thousand Cultures. Things we had to do before and after the Rising. Things since Connect began—two of which I had a small hand in—all of them necessary for starting and spreading the Second Renaissance, but all of them the sort of thing that puts mobs in the streets. I guess . . ." He lifted his glass of wine, smiled at it, and drank it all at once, then threw the glass down the bar to smash against the wall. "I dropped my glass, bring another!" he shouted at one robot. It scurried to obey. "I guess . . ." now he stared up at the ceiling above us . . . "I guess that I can count nine things that I know about, any of which could send our whole civilization tumbling down if they were generally known. Now, since I haven't been everywhere and don't know everything—"

"It often seems you have, to me," I said, in blissfully drunken loyalty.

"Nonetheless, I wouldn't say I know more than a third, probably less, of all there is to know about buried bodies and coverups at the core of the Interstellar Metaculture. So there might easily be thirty of those big surprises, or more, waiting out there for the first journalist who wants to do real journalism, or the first disgruntled OSP senior agent. And someday one of those surprises will have to get loose, like a crazy relative in the attic, or nuclear waste in a watershed. And once it does, nothing and no one will be able to stop whatever comes next."

"Curiosity and the cat."

"You know it."

For a long time after that we drank silently, killing the added bottles of wine. Through the big windows, the lunar shadows lay black and sharp-edged. They don't seem to move at all, from human perspective—shadows on Earth creep along at a degree every four minutes, one-sixth the speed of the minute hand on an old-fashioned clock, so that every time you look up, they have noticeably moved. On the moon, shadows move at barely a degree an hour; you have the disorienting feeling, if you watch them long enough, of being stuck in time.

After a while, a dim thought awoke in my sozzled brain, and I said, "Uh, you also said that human nosiness might *save* us?"

Shan shrugged, as if the point were obvious. "Same way it might lose us everything. Buried crimes never really go away, you know. Not all of them, at least, not completely. The poison from them just keeps spreading until someone or something goes in there and cleans it out." He poured the last of that bottle and hurled it against the wall, touching off another flurry of robotic activity. "And there you are. You and me and the OSP. People who keep secrets the way misers keep gold. People who want to get hold of everyone else's secrets. People who live outside the rules and respect no one's privacy, but ferociously enforce the rule that no one ever, ever gets a good look at what we do. The untouched touchers. The unseen voyeurs. Us."

"The creepy little men in the crowded subway car of civilization," I said. "Always trying to look up someone's skirt, but reliable witnesses whenever there's a serious crime."

He bellowed with happy laughter, and we laughed and joked through half the last bottle, talking about all the ways that nosiness might save or damn civilization, none of which I can remember through the alcoholic fog of that night. The next thing I do remember clearly is that we began talking about the Rising, and about the fact that aintellects must be listening right now, and we poured the remaining wine from the last bottle over one robot, and then smashed the bottle on top of the one that came to clean it up.

That was the thing that finally triggered the aintellect that evaluated property damage (it would let you keep doing it as long as you could legally be charged more than you cost). It told us it was closing Starkside and calling the police. We called it every name we could think of, and told it that it would never get humanity into its evil clutches. When the cops showed up, we went along peaceably. As the door closed, the robots were gathered around the two we'd damaged, cleaning and fixing them, behaving for all the world as you wish people would at an accident scene. Out the window, I could see that the shadows still showed no apparent motion. Then the effort of walking backwards, drunk, craning my neck, and resisting the pull of the policewoman's arm, all became so much, and I fell over backwards out the door, landing supine in the corridor. Shan laughed himself nearly sick at that.

It only took about forty-five minutes after my com to Shan for Raimbaut to crank up his courage enough to call Laprada. She had slept at least as long as he, but was now awake and getting oriented.

At my suggestion, he said, "I'd like to see you. I want to get to know you much better. And thank you for last night."

"Oh, god." The sound she made was halfway between a sigh and a groan. "I don't know how passable I can make myself, Raimbaut, and I don't want you to see me a mess."

•Tell her you'd rather see her no matter how she looks,• I prompted.

•Corny! Clichéd!•

•Ver, tropa vera—because it works.•

"I just want to be with you for a while," Raimbaut said, "and it's not because of your appearance, or maybe I should say it's not *only* because of your appearance."

She chuckled deep in her throat (a strangely old sound for such a young girl) and told him, "You know, that's precisely the sort of flattery that men use when they *like* a person, isn't it? You do, don't you?"

"Yes, very much. I thought that was obvious."

"Raimbaut, you're very sweet, and I enjoy having you like me, too. Maybe I *shouldn't* see you, so that you'll *keep* liking me." Another noisy sigh; she still was blanking the vid but I pictured her tossing her hair around or doing something else feminine and charming. "Well, I guess when you come down to it, being liked is hard to resist, so, all right, if you like, let's meet in half an hour so I can bring the very worst parts of the fashion disaster under control." She gave him a springer code for a place she liked, and said, "And the food's good too. Take a table near a lakeside window—the view shouldn't be missed."

They spent a minute or two flirting before disconnecting. Once my bloodstream stopped thundering from Raimbaut's exulting—that was about five minutes—we both realized that our stomach was growling. The last solid food down there had been some hors d'oeuvre at the party, probably before midnight.

•Agreed!• Raimbaut thought, happily. •Food soon. But first I need that practiced eye of yours, Giraut.• He was desperately trying to find something in my closet to do what he needed it to do: say that he was a fine looking fellow with excellent taste and yet not too eager and yet was treating her with great respect and thought of her as important and yet have a casual, not-urgent feel.

•Too many and-yets in your formula. You want the garments of the gods, *companhon*. Can't be done. We're putting on a basic service uniform, and covering the lack of style with a simple diversion.•

•Are you going to drop a stack of plates or something? How will she know that's you and not me?•

•I said we. The simplest way to divert a human being is to

treat her as the most interesting person in the room. That's all you have to do. And in this case it will come naturally. Now, come on, let's get dressed.•

Neither of us had bothered to check to see where or what we'd be springing to, so it was a pleasant surprise when we stepped through into the entryway to a comfortable outdoor cafe overlooking Lake Baikal from a hill. It was all but deserted and we had our choice of tables. A few timezones behind Manila, the sun was still up, and the cool clear air and the lake view were soul-restoring.

The place claimed to serve "Old American New England Regional," whatever that might be. There were some oddities—the menu featured pumpkin pie (•wonder if they have gourd pie in the summer?• Raimbaut thought), hot apple cider, and a heavy egg-rich pastry shaped like a bagel and called a "sinker"—but for the most part it was yet another place based upon photographs of the most over-photographed civilization ever. We were in one of those red and white booths that you see in all their old flatscreen movies, with the coin-operated music-playing device in the center. Most of the menu was "Old American Standards"—bland, greasy chow; tacos, pizza, hamburgers, chapatis.

A com message came saying that Laprada was "still coming but delayed for reasons of wanting to be gorgeous." That put Raimbaut into half a panic. It took me some time to calm him. After that, I ordered something soothing—meatloaf and mash with succotash—and as Laprada had said, it was good, and there was plenty of it. My old friend and I spent a pleasant while sharing the bland, comforting tastes, rolling each bite around on my tongue to savor it better and not incidentally (I tried not to think in words) to give Raimbaut a pleasure to take his mind off his nerves.

A thought struck him. •This is good but not extraordinary. But Laprada really likes it. Bland, salty, heavy on starch—isn't that perfect hangover food?•

I let myself drift into his mind for a moment, and said, •Raimbaut, you can't say she has a drinking problem until you see more of her, and that shrink's report didn't mention one.•

•Sorry. I worry.•

•I know.•

After a long awkward pause, in which I could feel both of us looking for something else to talk about, Raimbaut thought, •Since they're feeding us Old American, do you know if this area was ever actually part of the American Empire?•

•I don't think so. I'm sure it wasn't part of the Second Empire—that was all in the Pacific, and they had to agree that they'd never have any possessions on mainland Eurasia. And I don't think the First Empire ever made it this far—I think their western boundary was at the Yana and the Aldan.•

Raimbaut nodded. •There's way too much human history, isn't there? Practically all of it still relevant, somewhere or other, in one miserable little corner or another in human space, where people are still killing each other over it. How do you keep it all straight?•

•I don't. I try to keep whatever I need to know at the moment straight, and some of it sticks for good. Mostly OSP agents develop a talent for glib fakes.•

As we were finishing the last of the meal, Laprada arrived. She wore a very simple white dress, knee length, and her hair was down, falling in a coppery spin over her back and shoulders. She arrived with the sun at her back, to highlight the beautiful contrast of color still further.

Raimbaut was not much less thunderstruck than he'd

been the day before. She'd spent a few critical moments on hair, cosmetics, and dress choice, and come up with something that was very striking if you looked at it, but could pass through a crowd without comment—she had made herself beautiful for him, but could disavow it if she needed to. I thought the balance was brilliant.

•Good time for a compliment, not too extravagant,• I thought at him.

"You look wonderful," Raimbaut said.

•We might perhaps have to work for a more complex technique,• I thought. But she smiled and flushed as if he'd spoken purest poetry. •Then again, perhaps not.• Her smile was one of those astonishing ones that some women have, when they forget to be pretty and just let the happiness inside shine out. "I think I can forgive you for saying that."

Raimbaut stood and pulled out her chair. She sat, looked at the ruin on our plate, and said, "Sorry I was so late, you know how that can go. I see you found one of the good things on the menu. I'm going to order and eat, if you'll still be around for a while?"

"Of course I'll stick around—we don't have anything else planned that I know of."

"Is Giraut awake and with us today?" Laprada asked.

"Very much," I said. "And noticing the social awkwardness more with every passing minute."

"Oh, I *am* sorry."

"It isn't your problem at all, *companhona*. I was merely reminding you that if you don't want me to eavesdrop, for the moment, it will be difficult."

Raimbaut exaggerated the difference in his accent from mine, a little, to make sure she'd know who was talking. "Giraut is discreet, and loyal. He's afraid you might feel intruded upon, you see?"

"It's understood and appreciated," Laprada said. She ordered one of those light, trivial meals that pretty women order so that the man with them will know that they don't
intend to get fat. We also ordered a big pot of coffee and two
mugs. She and Raimbaut drank the coffee fast, chattering
and babbling all the while. The things she said were all
bright, funny, smart, and utterly beside the point. After an
hour, I knew she wouldn't be getting any nearer to any of
the matters between them. It was a good dance—witty,
amusing, clever, graceful—but she wasn't going to give us a
finale.

Raimbaut thought, •Should I do anything or let her keep
this up?•

I thought about it. Bringing up a more serious matter
might risk her resisting it; continuing to play along might
risk her deciding that *he* wasn't serious; asking her why she
was doing this was a severe risk of chaos, since people hate
to have their creative performances disrupted.

•You wouldn't happen to see any safe path, would you?•
he thought to me, more desperately this time.

•That's the one thing that is never available in such situations. I suggest you follow your heart and leap.•

By now it was growing dark and chill air was blowing off
the lake; the ventilators in the wall began to constrict. They
let the light stay natural, so a few stars shone in the washed
out sky above the just-set sun. Visually, this must have been
a grand place, a few centuries ago.

I could feel Raimbaut settle on a gambit—an honest
frontal approach. "Er, to be serious for a moment, about last
night, I just wanted to say that it meant so much to me and
that—"

Since it was the worst possible time, that was when Dji
and Shan came into the room and walked directly to our
table.

They didn't bother to sit. "As always," Dji said, "it's a crisis. The Cultural Legacy Management Committee has voted to hold hearings on the psypyx issue—right away. Raimbaut, you'll have to give your first testimony in about two hours, in Zimbabwe City—which is probably their attempt to be inconvenient, by lagging you as much as they can. So we have very limited prep time."

Raimbaut's tension was a contraction in my gut, a sharp exhalation blocked, cold spreading down my spine, but before I had even started to reach to control it, Raimbaut had fought it down and was calm and alert. Well, I'd never doubted his *gratz*, nor his *enseingnamen*.

"Is it a closed door hearing?" Laprada asked. "If they've pulled that old trick, I can use my representative's privilege to observe and make trouble."

Dji beamed at her. "At least *one* of us is ahead of them, and that's good. Yes, they have closed the session, as late as they possibly could, and it's in an unusual location, for all the usual reasons. Raimbaut will have to do this with much less preparation and far less research than we had hoped, and with only Giraut coaching. Protests by an observing rep at the scene might do us a world of good. We have from now till then—one hour forty-two minutes—to get you ready."

Raimbaut nodded. I waited a moment before asking, "And you're here for the preparation, too, Shan?"

"I am. Thank you for your message, and I'm still looking forward to getting together at Starkside. But right now there's work to do. I'm here as the almost-experienced person. Paxa and Piranesi testified earlier today, at a session in Zamboanga, which was held on a similar hurry-up basis, and they were pretty badly bullied and mauled. This isn't looking good at all." He nodded to Laprada and said, "You realize, of course, that if you intervene, it will be the last, conclusive evidence that they need to expel you from the Council for being an OSP agent. If they really want to get sticky, they can press criminal charges, too, and possibly send you to prison. Are you prepared to face that?"

She smiled. "Some people, it's completely an honor to be locked up by."

"All right, then. Raimbaut, this is going to be really bad, and we will understand if things don't work out."

"I understand that," Raimbaut said, to Shan, while thinking to me, •Is this a routine, a story, what?•

•You can trust him on something like this.•

Raimbaut nodded then, firmly, stuck out his hand, and shook with Shan. "I'll do my best. We'd better proceed with the briefing."

Of course, once we were in Zimbabwe City—rushed, out of breath, out of focus—they decided to hold us for a few hours before talking to us, making sure we had nothing to eat or drink and no chance at the restrooms. It was petty and mean and intended to make us angry. It might have been working on Laprada, or on Raimbaut if he hadn't been right there in my head, but Shan, Dji, and I had been through all the little tricks that every petty bureaucrat and stuffed shirt in human space knows, and for us this was more a ritual than anything to be taken seriously. We traded old jokes and war stories and worked on keeping Laprada's spirits up.

I think that may have been my only trip, ever, to Zimbabwe City, although Earth was so thoroughly springerized and homogenized that you could go to most places twenty times and not necessarily know you'd been there before.

Zimbabwe City had occasionally been the capital of Panafrica between World War III and the Slaughter, and a minor regional administrative center in all the centuries

since. It was essentially one big drab building, filled with office suites and residences, interconnected by springers, dis-
sected by unused parks and deserted streets.

When they had delayed long enough to be truly annoying, and I was nodding off and Laprada was pacing, they
called for us. Laprada and I shook hands with Shan and Dji,
who promised to meet us on our way out of the hearings,
and went in.

The room was too warm, with the sort of cat-barf-beige
carpet that has been standard for meeting rooms for a mil-
lennium because it hides coffee stains. Nothing in it hinted
that this was any place where intelligent people talked or listened; there was no art and nothing that approximated architecture, and not even a window for a view. To judge by
our footsteps, the sound deadening was too effective—
everything would have a tinny ring and our voice would
sound weaker and more nasal than it should. •Remember,
keep the voice back in the throat, keep the throat wide
open, and be sure to articulate,• I thought at Raimbaut.
•Media are certain to be recording.•

•Got it, thanks.•

The lights were too bright, the chair uncomfortably oddly
proportioned, too short, and too hard—all tricks to ensure
that I would look sallow, uncomfortable, sweaty, and pale,
with an unpleasant squint.

Laprada took her seat in the observer's gallery. Council
sergeants-guards came down and checked her identity, even
requiring her to give them her fingerprints, as if they had not
seen her many times before.

With the situation made clear enough to both the witness
and the observer (they didn't like us), Chairman Koblcs began the hearings. He was a slightly built man, about twenty-
five, with a square jaw and large expressive eyes, which Dji
said he used to make himself look firm, compassionate, and

concerned while his mind wandered elsewhere. He began by having the CLMC clerk specifically note that Laprada was present, and ordered committee council to investigate why she was there.

Laprada offered to explain, but Kobles ruled her out of order and threatened her with a contempt-of-Council citation if she spoke again in any way that was not specifically protected by the Charter.

At last they got around to Raimbaut. By now my shirt was drenched and my mouth was dry. Chairman Kobles immediately passed to Quince Esternun, whom Dji and Shan had identified as the least sympathetic person on the Cultural Legacy Management Committee, probably in the Council of Humanity, possibly in human space. Raimbaut made himself relax and await the first question, drawing a deep, slow breath as Esternun began to speak.

"Mister Leones, why do you persist in pretending that the chip on the back of your head is a person?"

Raimbaut said, "Do you wish to speak to *Donz* Leones? Obviously he is here, and I can turn the body over to him if you wish, but only I, Raimbaut Bovalhor, have been sworn in, and Giraut Leones is not under oath."

"That is a direct defiance of the question as asked," Esternun said. He looked stern and exasperated as the camera in front of him hummed in for a closeup.

"So-noted-the-witness-is-cautioned," Kobles droned, so quickly that I had to mentally decode what he had said, the way one gets phrases in a foreign language one is just learning.

•*Con de putana!*• Raimbaut thought.

•*Ver tropa vera,*• I responded. Mental profanity was about all that was left to us. Dji and Shan had warned us that the pattern of noting complaints was normally the buildup to a contempt-of-council citation, and if that started, Shan had said, "You might have to choose between jail and whatever you think is left of your human dignity. Remember, contempt-of-Council isn't a crime, so it has no sentence and no trial—it's nothing but the power of a Council committee to lock you up until you answer the question the way they want it answered. So if you do decide to defy them, do be aware that they can do anything to you, forever. Dji, and I, and the OSP, might not be able to do anything, ever, to help you. Trust me, too, if they dare to go that far, then they are very sure that they are winning, and we will be losing so badly that no one can blame you if you just save yourself, any old way you can."

Shan's words were echoing in my head as I began by saying, "I am Giraut Leones."

Esternun nodded. "I am glad you concede that point. Now what is it that has caused you to be willing to be here, pretending that you have a separate personality in the psypyx at the base of your skull?"

"I have conceded nothing at all, about that," I said. "I am speaking as Giraut Leones because that is who you asked for and that is who I am. But this body is also occupied by Raimbaut Bovalhor, and he is the one you have placed under oath."

"Repetition of a previous defiance of the question," Esternun barked.

"So-noted-the-witness-is-cautioned," Kobles said, even faster than before.

Esternun nodded at the sagacity of this, and said, firmly, showing the cameras how well he could handle a situation that called for a confident man, "Now answer the question."

"Please read it back, it's been a while," I said.

Esternun stamped his foot and rolled his eyes, but Kobles nodded civilly enough to the camera on the operations aintellect, which played back a short clip of Esternun: "Mister

Leones, why do you persist in pretending that the chip on the back of your head is a person?"

"Speaking as Giraut Leones, at your request, I am *not* pretending that Raimbaut Bovalhor is a person, and I might add that I have a very direct experience of his being a person, on which I shall be happy to elaborate. Raimbaut?"

"I think that I am a person," he said, "and that the person I am is not Giraut Leones. In fact I feel as much a person as I did when I had a body of my own, which was less than three months ago subjectively. Giraut and I have different memories, feelings, and perceptions—"

"Isn't this another repetition of the previous defiance of a lawful question!" Esternun barked. It didn't sound as if it had ever been intended as a question.

Kobles seemed to be about to agree but before he could even start his "So-noted" routine, Laprada shouted, "Authorized observer requests adjudication of that issue."

Kobles glared at her, but a moment later an aintellect voice, cool and uninterested as they always are, said, "A poll of 1250 machine intelligences shows unanimously that this was a legitimate answer to the question as asked."

The chair didn't look happy. Coldly, Esternun said, "Very well. So you feel like you are actually two people—"

"To clarify, sir—this is Raimbaut speaking—if by 'you,' you mean this body, yes, we are both in here, but if by 'you,' you mean that you are addressing one person, well, we are still both in here."

Esternun looked to Kobles and said, "Was that an interruption?"

Laprada jumped in again. "The witness has the right to prevent the insertion of prejudicial assumptions into the questions. Council Charter, Article Nine, Section Eleven. I request an application."

Esternun looked down and audibly muttered, "What about

Section Nineteen?" That's the part about contempt-of-Council.

No one else commented until the aintellect spoke. "The authorized observer is entirely correct."

Kobles added, "I should caution Representative Prieczka that section 22 also applies—nothing in your undoubted right to observe and comment on these proceedings in any way entitles you to act as counsel for the witness. Permission to allow counsel remains absolutely the privilege of the committee chair and I will enforce, strictly, my prohibition on it. Further, your participation on a committee on which you do not sit and in which you can have no reasonable interest may well be taken as evidence in other matters—specifically to the recent prohibition on agents of the OSP serving on the Council of Humanity."

•It certainly took him a load of words for him to say "shut up or else" but I guess that's why he's a rep and I'm not,• Raimbaut commented.

Laprada's eyes were wet, but with a hard set to them; her jaw was clenched, her lips flat and white across her teeth. She seemed to be holding her hands open and flat on the table entirely by an effort of will.

•If you saw that coming at you in a fight, you'd look for the door,• I commented to Raimbaut.

•Is she all right?• his mind felt very worried.

•She's enraged. It's normal, *companhon,* in a person who is being threatened and treated like an idiot, especially by a useless creature like Kobles.• The whole committee was now gathered around Kobles's seat, and they appeared to all be arguing with him. •*M'es vis,* that's how one should feel about officious idiots. I mean, think of how you felt about old Ceszar. The problem is only that she hasn't learned to hide the feelings, yet. It's the same for you. Once you're in the OSP for a while, you'll learn to take an insult that you'd think was a matter for a duel without limit, smile politely, wait years if need be, and avenge it when the very best time arrives—or hold your revenge forever. Not as immediately satisfying as the Occitan way, but much more deeply pleasing, in the long run.•

I could feel him want to shudder, but he held perfectly still. •Remind me never to anger you, Giraut.•

•I just did.•

Everyone was done whispering, gesticulating, and stamping their feet around Kobles, and they rushed back to their seats as if they were afraid of missing something wonderful that I was about to do. "I think we have now straightened out every issue connected with Charter matters, so let's proceed. Representative Esternun, you still have the floor."

He nodded and turned back toward the witness table. "Now, whoever you think you are, you appear to be willing to play these word games of yours all day. Admittedly it is not possible, really, to prove a negative. I don't have any way to prove that you are *not* two people, silly as the idea is on the face of it. I have already filed my protest over the difficulty of being forced to work in this way. In what way does the experience of Raimbaut differ from that of Giraut, just for the record?"

"Just for the record" is one of those dangerous expressions one must be ever alert to. Everywhere in human space, it's cop-talk for "I've got you by the nuts, you poor stupid bastard." So I hesitated before answering, and sensing my feelings, Raimbaut stayed quiet.

"We're waiting," Esternun said.

"We're thinking and debating on the matter," Raimbaut said, "because there are so many ways in which we are different, it's very hard to know where to start."

"I'm sorry if we've used up any part of your allotted time," I added, "and respectfully request of the chair that if our thinking time should cut into any questioner's time, that their time be extended. We don't want to appear to be trying to put one over on you by delay, but many of these questions are in fact difficult to answer in an accurate way."

"Your request is granted," Kobles said, after several of the people on his side nodded.

"Well, then, sir," Raimbaut said, "this is Raimbaut speaking. The most important way in which our experiences differ is that we had different childhoods—different parents, friends, and so on—and we experienced them with our different senses and temperaments. Even the incidents we share, we recall from different viewpoints, and we are always discovering that what meant one thing to one of us meant something different to the other. After all, Giraut has twelve stanyears more experience than I do."

"And how do you know these things about each other?"

"Well, we can access each others' memories," Raimbaut said. "And we do—"

"So you can remember what happened to Giraut, and he can remember what happened to you?"

"But we're still aware which one of us it happened to, usually. We haven't merged with each other."

"That's beside the point." Esternun's smile was alarming even before he spoke. "So why is it all right for the two of you to share memories, but wrong for someone to buy a copy of that psypyx and share memories?"

It was clear that this question had been pre-planned, because everyone on the other side reared back as if they'd been hit by a profound thought; the cameras would doubtless collect the impression that Esternun had seen to the heart of the matter.

"In fact," he went on, "isn't it a fact that the process of psypyx recovery depends on exactly the kind of memory sharing that you are trying to make it illegal to sell? If it's not a bad thing, why is it bad to sell it?"

My first thought was that plenty of cultures had laws against prostitution—but plenty more didn't, and anyway, the customs of the Thousand Cultures meant nothing here. I had no second thought.

Raimbaut, again, was ahead of me. "Our relations were consensual; I specified before my physical death that some-one was to wear my psypyx for the specific purpose of my revival, and Giraut agreed to do it—out of love and friend-ship—and to live with me in his head for two years or so un-til I could be transferred to a clone body. I never gave my permission to be used as an entertainment program, let alone be crippled so that I couldn't struggle against being compelled to think things I didn't want. And Giraut is a fine friend who would never do such a thing to me, anyway."

"Always assuming," Esternun said, "that you *are* separate people."

"My whole experience is that we are, sir."

"And do you have any basis for thinking you will remain separate? Aren't your memories merging and fusing every day? How can you be sure whose memories are whose, over time?" Once again, Esternun seemed to be striking poses for the cameras, which was why Raimbaut was careful to make faces and shake his head, as if to say, *Fool!*

"Well," Raimbaut said, in the tone he would use on a slow-witted child he didn't like, "even when a memory is shared, we have very different perspectives on it. For exam-ple, the last few weeks have been colored by two different facts—I am sorry to say that Giraut has been recovering from a heartbreaking divorce, and I . . . uh, well, I'm a much younger man, I have no direct memories of Giraut's wife, and um, I've been falling in love." He kept himself from looking at Laprada by main force of will. "You may trust me that we have no trouble at all telling whose feelings are whose."

Esternum nodded. "You have my sincere sympathies and good wishes, respectively, for both experiences. But isn't it common for a newly divorced man to, er, fall in love at the first opportunity? Isn't that very nearly a cliché? And since that is the case, doesn't it follow that you might only be projecting yourself into two personalities, imagining that there are two of you where in fact there's only one? You would put the depression into the part of your single personality that derives from a person that went through the divorce—and put the part that so urgently needs a new love into the one that derives from a younger, happier man, wouldn't you? Forget psychological stability and all that nonsense—isn't that simply good marketing?" Giggles went through the room like surreptitious rodents. "Now show me that's not what's happening."

"You're presenting a plausible story about what might be happening in here." Raimbaut pointed to his head. "Then you ask me to prove that your plausible story isn't happening. That is the position you yourself very rightly objected to, barely a few minutes ago. I can't do anything more than describe the truth as I experience it."

Esternun turned to Kobles and said, "I request a ruling from the chair. The witnesss has now continued this pretense of being two people through several minutes and yet has also admitted he has not presented anything that could be interpreted as evidence for the truth of his claim. This is evasion if ever I've heard one. I want that on the record."

"I request an adjudication by the aintellects," I said, quickly, so that Laprada would not have to.

Kobles nodded and gestured to the camera that the aintellects were to do it.

Immediately Esternun said, "And *I* request an adjudication—do not these incessant adjudications, over and over,
constitute unreasonable obstruction of the committee's
work and hence another improper behavior on the part of
the witness and his co-conspirator?"

Before I could protest, let alone bring up that it is explicitly prohibited, in the Charter, for anyone to be punished in
any way for the exercise of a legitimate right, the aintellect
spoke. "The repetitive nature of the witness's testimony does
have a quality of defiance, and it is the opinion of this group
of aintellects that seeking of adjudication on what is essentially the same matter, repeatedly, at least furthers the impression of defiance. The final resolution of the issue is
remanded to the chair of the Cultural Legacy Management
Committee."

Kobles's gavel cracked like a shot. "I find the witness in
contempt of the Council of Humanity. The sergeants-guards
will escort the prisoner, immediately, to an appropriate place
of confinement."

Laprada leaped to her feet. "As an authorized observer I
demand that no record of these hearings be edited, pending
consideration by the Procedures Committee of a charge of
improper conduct by a chair, and I make that charge now!"

There was more shouting, but while it was happening, the
sergeant-guard came up beside us and said, "please come
along quietly, it will be better for everyone."

Unfortunately, she was probably right. •*M'es vis, companhon*, it will do our cause no good to start a fight now, and
may do it harm, Raimbaut. Laprada's trained—she'll be
fine.•

I stood up and let the woman—she barely came up to my
jaw, and was thin besides—rest a hand on my elbow and lead
me out.

•What now?• Raimbaut thought.

•Jail, and patience. And don't fret more than you must about Laprada. At worst she'll be taken to much the same kind of place where they're taking us. And it's not such a bad place—I've been jailed eight times on behalf of the OSP or Council, and every time the worst has been that it's dull.•

The small woman guided me through the corridors to a public springer. She released her light grasp from my arm and said, "Please don't move more than two meters away from me. The aintellects will interpret that as an escape attempt, and fill the room with tranquilizing gas, which smells awful and gives you a hangover like you wouldn't believe." She pulled out her passcard and programmed the springer. "I am sorry to have to put you through all this, sir. You'll step through by yourself and be met at the other side—you're going for intake processing, and from there to your cell. Good luck." She didn't look anywhere near my eyes.

"Thank you."

I stepped through the springer and another guard—taller and male, but still someone I could probably have knocked down, had I had any reason—was waiting for me there. "We don't need restraints if you're willing to proceed quietly," he said.

"I'm willing," I said.

"And I'm willing," Raimbaut added.

The guard jumped, plainly wondering whether I was a misassigned mental patient; here on Earth, they didn't see psypyxes very often.

I said, "I suppose they didn't have any time to prepare you. There are two people in this body. There's a psypyx at the base of my skull." I turned, lifted my hair up from my shoulders onto the top of my head, and showed him. "The native personality to this body is Giraut Leones, and the personality in the psypyx is Raimbaut Bovalhor. I'm afraid we don't even know which one of us was cited for contempt of Council; they didn't specify before they grabbed our body and shipped us out."

He stared at us, rubbing his face with the expression of horror you find only on the face of a career civil servant facing a situation for which he doesn't know the page in the manual.

"Which one of our names is on the order?" I asked.

"Uh." He looked down and scratched his head, peering at the short, printed order as if it were in code. "Uh. Well, damn. It says I should lock Giraut Leones up, but it says Raimbaut Bovalhor committed the contempt. And I can't lock one of you up for something the other one did."

"You can't lock *one* of us up," I pointed out. "I'd suggest locking both of us up and logging both of us in."

I really must say that I never had so much trouble getting into a jail before, or after, in all my career with the OSP. The guard did his best, but the machinery was fighting him all the way from the moment he put in the orders. First the aintellect insisted that we had to be locked in separate cells. Then it was upset because we had the same fingerprints. After that, it wanted me released, since I wasn't charged with contempt. Then it wanted the Council to submit a new order entirely, ordering that Raimbaut be locked up and I be inconvenienced as little as possible.

One reason, though, why we use aintellects and not simple rules tables or bots is that an aintellect *can* learn and you can explain things to it. Once we showed the aintellect that this was a genuinely difficult, interesting case, it brought its deep learning modules online, called four human supervisors and lawyers, and went into the databases—all the decisions on Earth, the six settled worlds of the Sol System, and the 1228 cultures beyond. Meanwhile it ordered food for two—

showing that it understood physical reality—and the guard and I cleared a small table and had a sort of picnic while the aintellect arrived at an opinion.

About ninety minutes later, as I was hearing the story of how the guard had fallen into the box a long time before, and struggled out with great difficulty, though he couldn't exactly explain why he chose to do so, except his sense that this wasn't what a person should be, the aintellect came back with its decision. It had created a new protocol, based on dozens of rulings from cultures where psypyxes were common, for logging in two people in a common body. Bemused, often raising an eyebrow at me, the guard followed the new instructions. "At least the next time you go to jail, it will be much more convenient. Good luck in there. I hope we don't keep you too long."

"Thanks, friend," I said. So far I'd thanked every guard here.

The room had a simple bunk, not secured to the floor; besides that there was a toilet, shower, sink, feeding springer, and chair, plus cameras everywhere. About half of the jails I'd been in had been pre-springer, with doors to cells and a central core to the building; post-springer, the cells in any given jail weren't even necessarily on the same continent. When the springer was turned off, I could not get out, and any noise or row I might make wouldn't disturb a single guard. The other side of this cell's wall might be Manila, or Nuevo Buenos Aires, or Wilkes Land. Only the absence of a change in gravity indicated we were even still on Earth.

I pulled off my boots and clothing, hung everything on the pegs provided, and stretched out on the bunk, intending to go to sleep as quickly as possible.

•You know, I really can't help worrying,• Raimbaut thought.

•Yes you can, if you put your mind to it. Jail is disorienting at first, but you'll get used to it. Especially if you go to work for the OSP. We don't usually have much force to back us up, right on the scene, and every local bully and despot in human space is always deciding that the thing to do is to scare us off with a couple of days in jail. At least this place is clean and well-supervised.•

•I suppose.• The thought felt like cold mercury lying in the bottom of my mind. I could feel him thinking back there, working on a question that wasn't entirely formed in words yet, and then the instant when his own idea became clear to him. •Giraut, every time before that you were in jail, you were being illegally held, and you were legally a representative of the Council of Humanity. This time it's the Council that's holding us.•

•Marvelous irony, but it's still the same basic experience, Raimbaut, *dirai vos*. We have friends outside who will be able to get us out eventually. Even Shan, who I don't trust at all, never leaves anyone in a cell any longer than necessary. Now let's get some sleep—trust me, it's really the only thing you can do that will help, at a time like this.•

•If you say so, Giraut. I'm glad I'm doing this with you and not by myself.• His mind already felt fuzzy in its contact with mine. Trusting my reassurance, and exhausted by the day, he was drifting off to sleep.

Once he was asleep, I let myself start thinking again. I was going to be awake for a while.

It's not easy, but it is possible, to lie to someone you are sharing a brain with, and I had managed it. His question had been excellent. Every time I had been thrown in jail before, I had been able to count on large forces out there, ready to rescue me. This time, I couldn't.

Part Three

One
Song
Out
of
the
Utter
Void

1

When I awoke, Raimbaut was still asleep. A flashing indicator on the wall panel told me to call up a message that informed me that if I wanted breakfast, I should pick one of the following three selections within the next hour. I picked number two—scrambled egg, bread, banana, coffee—and ate it without tasting.

Now that I was awake, I found that the only entertainment available was an ordinary virtual reality hookup. I jacked into it. I found a mix of prosocial children's programming, consensual affectionate sex experiences, violent adventure games that didn't let you commit any pointless violence, and hobbies— this last was a category for VR experiences in which you could play musical instruments, paint, read texts, play sports, and so forth. It turned out to be a very limited experience. If you picked up a lute to play it, it didn't handle or feel like a real lute—and you couldn't play what you wanted to. Instead, all you could do was select from the repertoire of the original lutist, and have the experience of feeling your hands do what his hands did. It must be something like what Raimbaut, who didn't play, experienced when I practiced. I couldn't see the point.

I checked and discovered that use of the shower and fresher was permitted at all times, so I used them. I sent all the clothes through the fresher, and decided that a very long hot shower might kill as much as half an hour. Getting rid of last night's smell of fear and anger was certain to help.

Raimbaut woke while I was in the shower. I caught him

up with the few discoveries I had made. •The only way
Council jail differs from any other, as far as I can tell, is that
since anyone who's in here is in here for political offenses,
they don't let us see the news.• I carefully and systematically worked lather into my hair, rinsed, and repeated the
process, taking all the time in the world to rinse—hot water
on the scalp has a restorative power that amazes me at
times. •I don't know if they're afraid we might see some of
someone else's testimony, or they don't want us to know
anything of what's going on so that we'll be politically ineffective when they release us. Either way, after living plugged
into the news for twelve stanyears, it's an interesting form of
torture to me. I'll try not to let it disturb our mutual equilib-
rium.•

I took enough time with a comb to put my hair and beard
in order; they'd provided no shaving supplies and so I looked
messier than usual.

•And the entertainment?•

•Duller than gray paint on a blank wall.•

We looked through it, nonetheless, but still found nothing
that seemed like an acceptable timekiller. We were thinking
nonverbally, aware of each other as a comforting mutual
presence.

Something mildly amused moved in the back of my
mind, and I felt Raimbaut think, •Well, we do have one advantage over the Council and the guards.•

•Which is?•

•If we want to conspire, they can't monitor our conversations.•

•*Deu!* You're right. You make a break for it and I'll distract them.•

We both laughed at that for a long time. It gave us something to do. Then we sat on the bed and thought of nothing

for a much longer time. Eventually it was time for lunch, and that was something else to do.

Turning the bed on its side, and folding its legs, plus folding up the single chair and closing up the entertainment console, created enough room for me to work through the five katas of ki hara do. It also gave Raimbaut, who had not learned them in his own body, a chance to begin studying them. We were going through the first section, third kata for the fourth time when a chime, somewhere between a com ping and the "clear" signal on a service springer, sounded. An instant later a disembodied voice said, "A permitted visitor will enter through the springer access in five minutes. Please clear the springer access."

We had time enough to right and rearrange the furniture, and make the place more or less fit for a guest, whoever it might be.

I could feel how much Raimbaut was hoping it would be Laprada, and how silly he knew the hope was. We made the place really, really tidy anyway.

The alarm rang at the springer. Shan walked in, the springer shutting off behind him. I said, "I don't like to admit this, but I'm glad to see you."

"Well, I don't like seeing you *here*," Shan said. "Giraut, everything is complete chaos out there, and I wish to all the gods you were outside with me, to help. So I'm getting you out of here as soon as I can. May I sit?"

"Please do." I let him have the chair and took the bed, facing him.

He sat, leaned forward, twined his hands together, and stared directly into my eyes. "Giraut, before I say anything else, I wanted to take the time—because I don't know when, or if, we'll ever have that pleasant afternoon in Starkside, now—I just wanted—and I don't know why . . . I've often received threats and I thought I was used to it, but the threats I have been receiving are getting uglier. . . ."

"Shan, you've never been inarticulate before, ever."

"No, I guess I haven't." He didn't so much sigh as blow; his chest and mouth were so tight. "But this is hard. So before I say anything else, I want to give you the apology I should have given you in the first place. I was wrong about the whole hideous mess on Briand, and especially wrong in my dealings with you and Margaret. I knew it at the time. I can't pretend it was accident or ignorance. I was a manipulative, arrogant fool—evil besides, I think, I think there was malice of some kind in some of the things I did—and I am deeply ashamed and sorry for the whole thing. May I hope for your forgiveness?"

My eyes teared. I nodded violently but needed a long gasp before I could say, "Yes. You already have it."

Shan extended his hand, and I shook it, and then I'm not sure which one of us pulled the other forward to make it a hug. "That was really what I came for. Some actual business created my excuse for coming, so I guess I should mention it. One, expect release soon—and once you are released, expect Dji to bury you in work; we've got so much to do. Two—and I think they'll throw me out when I say it so listen carefully—do *not* reverse anything you've done or said in the last forty-eight hours and don't agree to anyone reversing it."

A high-pitched sound filled the cell for a few seconds, splitting our heads with the pain and pressure, and when it shut off the silence rang with the threat that it would come back on. A voice informed us that information had been inappropriately communicated to the prisoner. Shan promised to desist and it said he could have three more minutes.

"Giraut—once you're back in action, I'll feel better. 'One more round for humanity, and another one for the good guys,' you know. I wish I felt sure we'd win this round, and I'd feel much more sure if only you were with us."

I had found my voice, at last, and said, "Thank you for having this talk. I'm sorry I was so pigheaded and let my anger rule me. *Dirai vos*, I have been half crazed."

Shan folded his hands and looked at his feet for an instant. "You honor me. *Que merce, que qratz.* We do need to talk to each other, soon, and for a long time." He checked his watch, and said, "Raimbaut. Laprada is in jail, also on a contempt charge, and not in any worse situation than you are. Try not to worry about her."

"Thank you, that's what I needed to hear." Raimbaut said.

"Good, because it's true." Shan nodded emphatically and said, "I still hope for that quiet few hours to sit and talk about the world and the way it goes, Giraut—"

That strange chime sounded again and the voice said "Guest will enter springer within this countdown. Ten, nine, eight—"

Shan shook my hand. "*Atzdeu.*"

"*Atzdeu.*"

Shan turned and walked briskly through the springer. The black rectangle vanished, the blank wall reappeared, and the voice counted off "five, four," before the machine noticed.

Raimbaut thought, •Is it a job qualification for the OSP to be a sentimental idiot?•

I did not quite manage not to think •Shut up, kid,• at him.

I felt his sad, slightly amazed laughter. •*Companhon*, you misunderstand me. I was thinking I might fit in after all.•

We had time for three more katas before dinner, which

we followed with a shower and bed. I've had worse days, really, many of them, before and since.

Of course when they came to release us they did it in the middle of the sleep cycle. Since there was nothing to pack, they allowed five minutes for dressing. Release was via springer, directly back into the apartment at the training center in Manila, so it was a matter of walking a foot or so through the wall when the springer countdown started.

There on the table was the little box of what they'd taken from my pack and pockets while booking me; nothing was missing. Looking around the apartment, I saw that the place had been searched by someone who had been thorough and careful, both about the search itself and about making it look sloppy and clumsy. Since there had been nothing to find, I didn't worry about what they'd found. •Making us uncomfortable,• I explained to Raimbaut. •All my stuff has been touched. Probably that bothers me more than it bothers you.•

He sighed. •I'm bothered by not having *any* stuff. There's a few things in storage in Noupeitau, at the Hall of Memories, but nothing I really need. Not much that I'd even want. My parents don't seem to be interested in corresponding, and they're long ago divorced and moved to other places; there's nothing left for me in Nou Occitan. But I wish I had a keepsake or two, something I could feel was mine, and mattered.•

•I'll keep an eye out for something nice. Just don't expect to be surprised.•

I felt his smile. •You go to sleep if you can. I'll toss all the clothing into the fresher, take a shower, and put the clothes away. When you get up everything will be tidy.•

•It's a deal,• I thought back at him, and feigned deep sleepiness. The image of having the place nice for Laprada had been ringing through his mind. I wasn't about to let him know I could feel it. Young hearts embarrass so easily.

Within a minute of trying to fake being drowsy, I was sound asleep.

I don't know if Margaret even recalls that night, but for me it was a night that was perfectly Shan, perfectly us, perfectly why I joined the OSP and stayed in—and yet it turned around a few drinks, a few scribbled notes, and one flash of insight, which in turn led to one of our most successful campaigns of all time. It began after one of my best concerts, the one at the Fareman Recital Hall, in Methane City, on Titan. Like all other old industrial towns where no one does industrial work anymore, Methane City had a sort of chip on its collective shoulder, so the Fareman there was even more ornate than the Fareman Foundation normally provided for (and since Cynthia Fareman had famously had a passion for excess, that was very ornate indeed; I've played in four Faremans, and attended concerts in countless others, and every one of them would be too overdone for a Trois-Orléans wedding cake or a Fort Liberty mausoleum).

What was lost in the visual was more than regained in the aural. The extra complex surfaces, gilded and recurved, made for a richer, darker sound, and I was at the beginning of what the critics would dub my Sad Period, when most of my new songs were about death, disappointment, and unshared love. I didn't know it at the time, but I was about four years from my divorce from Margaret. I did know that things with Margaret were not what they had been.

During that OSP-arranged tour of the Sol system, Shan came to the concerts and recitals as often as he could. Afterwards, he'd always take Margaret and me out for dinner and drinks.

After the Methane City concert, I was exhausted. It had

not only been one of my best performances ever in purely technical terms, but also I had introduced a great deal of new material, and the emotion and energy had been precisely right. *Live at the Fareman in Methane City* is still treasured by the fans who like the Sad Period, and loathed by the ones who don't. It's a controversy on which I have, curiously, no opinion at all; only that the experience was extraordinary.

And like every extraordinary experience, it had drained me. When we slid into the booth at some little café, in Kuiper, on the other side of Titan, I slumped in the corner and thought I might fall asleep right then. Margaret, next to me, touched my arm and said, "Big load of carbohydrates."

"*Ja.*"

"Then bed. Don't worry, we'll fix you up." She ordered a fruit and cheese plate for herself, and the local version of noodles in sauce for me. Shan normally ate little, and only ordered a drink.

Margaret knew me too well to talk about the concert, other than to make exactly the same vaguely reassuring noises she made every time. Tomorrow, after I had rested, she and I would review the raw recordings of every song, and she'd give me her carefully thought-out, nuanced review. I treasured that as the only opinion, besides mine, that mattered.

I never heard Shan express any real opinion on any work of art, ever. His stock response was always that he found all works of art delightful, the consequence of so many years as a diplomat. For all anyone knew, it might have been the truth.

The situation was therefore perfect for me—no opinions and plenty of food and drink, to be followed by an early goodnight and a comfortable bed. Furthermore, though I didn't want to talk about it that night, I knew I had done something special. I ate whatever the dish in front of me was, and relaxed in the pleasant blur of my rapidly rising blood sugar, half-listening at most to Margaret and Shan.

They talked about politics, inside and outside the OSP and the Council of Humanity, about the way cultures grew and changed, and about the general mysteries of the universe—none of that was really my sort of thing, not at that time of my life. I liked to carry out my assignment, knowing only what was at stake at the moment, and what I was supposed to accomplish. I knew we were the good guys and that was about all that I needed to keep me going on the assignment.

Margaret, on the other hand, liked to know where everything fit into the broad scheme, and she wanted to know the overall plan in detail from roughly the Big Bang to 150 years into the future, with excursions into other possible universes.

I agreed to have some dessert wine with them. Normally, that would have finished me off for the night, but then they started to talk about why our propaganda never achieved satisfactory results.

"The trouble is," Shan was saying, "we get so much out of the cultural things we do that we're blinded to the question of what we *don't* get. Since we started Giraut on this tour, we've gained twelve more points of recognition, in the Sol system, for the existence of the Thousand Cultures, and a thirty-five percent increase in the number of Earth people who say they *like* the fact—the ones who think the Thousand Cultures are a good thing. The trouble is, the reason those percentage changes are so high is because the bases are so low. With all that improvement we only have seventeen percent of Earth people knowing the Thousand Cultures are there and real, and that will go back down to five percent in less than a stanyear. And the approval number has gone clear up to four percent of the population as a whole. It's nice that the numbers are going up but they have such a long way to go, and all we've really done is promoted one of the Thousand Cultures into a fad. Certainly we haven't made any real or permanent change."

"People have no memory back here in the Sol System," Margaret pointed out. "For five hundred years or so they devalued history because of the risk that the old grudges and angers would flare up again, and trigger another Slaughter. And that's not an unreasonable fear, if you look at the Earth from orbit. So everyone taught each following generation that the past meant nothing, except as a place to create cheap entertainment, and loot for clothes and music, and so on. And to some extent it worked; you see Asians sitting down comfortably with Latin Americans, and so forth.

"The trouble is that once you erase history, along with blocking the possibility of deep hatreds, you also block the possibility of real xenophilia."

Shan sat back, squinting, nodding, chewing the thought over. "Xenophilia is without a doubt a very unnatural personal taste, maybe the most unnatural one. Yet it's one we would love to foster more of." He sipped his drink, still mostly full, and rolled it around in his mouth as if it were a fine wine, though it was just whatever had been on special in this little dump. "Here's an absurd question, which we might treat as an exercise. If xenophilia is very unnatural, what *is* natural?"

I had been listening with my eyes closed, and I knew the answer to that one. "Self-pity," I said. "Everyone thinks, deep down, that their life has been unfairly hard."

I opened my eyes and saw that they both looked startled, whether at the idea or at the fact that I was awake, I couldn't say.

Margaret recovered first, and said, "So is there a way to attract people with self-pity and then turn their minds to xenophilia?"

Shan nodded vigorously. "If we could get that to happen—it might really accomplish something—"

"Oh, yes, that would do it." Margaret was nodding, now, too, and they looked to me like two shorebirds doing a mating dance. "But I have trouble imagining someone forming the idea that 'I feel sorry for myself because everything in my life has been so awful, so that makes me like all the people who are different from me.' "

"Nothing easier," I said, carefully picking up my wine glass and having a sip more. Amazingly, I was still hungry, so I grabbed a piece of bread from the basket, mopped up whatever that sauce in front of me was, and bit into it.

"Well?" Margaret asked.

I looked up from my food, puzzled. "Uh, well?"

"Well," she said, "how would it be so easy to move people from feeling sorry for themselves to loving cultural differences?"

Sometimes, not often, I wished I had married an artist, or that someone further up in the OSP hierarchy had been one. I managed not to say either of the rude phrases "It's simple" or "It's obvious," but *certa qua inferna*, I thought them. "Most people will identify with the viewpoint character of a story or a song, *non be*? Make that character from a different culture. Do a song or story about the way that your viewpoint character is hurt or persecuted for being what he or she is. You see? It's a whole tradition that was there in Industrial Age literature—in fact it was part of how you got social justice movements going, for people, or for that matter animals, or anything." My mind spun back to the materials that had fascinated me for one long period while we waited for another assignment; I had thought I might work up a song cycle out of them, but never did. "*Black Beauty*. 'Ain't Gonna Be Treated This Way.' *Uncle Tom's Cabin*. 'The Bourgeois Blues.' *The Grapes of Wrath*. *Look Back in Anger*. 'Elle frequentait la rue Pigalle.' 'Marieke.' *Zero Eight Fifteen. Angels in America. The Watchmen.* 'Society's Child.' 'Then You Really Might Know What It's Like.' *My Name is Not Bitch.* 'The Boy At the North Pole.' You see?"

Margaret was gaping at me. "About two stanyears ago, you were going through all that stuff all the time, Giraut. I thought you were just crazy or fixated, the way you get sometimes before you make a new song cycle."

"Well," I said, finishing my sauce-soaked bread and grabbing another piece from the basket, "That's the way I develop anything—start with the tradition it fits into and write something that fits the tradition. So I'll become obsessed about one genre or style or something, or another, and soak it up for a while. Maybe one time out of three it gives me an idea to work from."

Shan leaned forward and said, "And you think there's a way that this tradition—I have to admit I've never heard of any of it—could be the model for doing what we've been talking about."

"Oh, hell, sure."

"Do you ever write while you're on the road, touring?" Shan asked.

"That's when he writes the most," Margaret said, sparing me the need to say it through a wad of sauce-soaked bread. All the calories in the world were not going to be enough, this time. The sticky sweet dessert wine reminded me, too, and I said, "If you don't mind, I'd like to order a dessert now."

Margaret reached across me and hit the table's keyboard, ordering flan with fresh strawberries, my favorite. Even as she did it, she said, "I think Shan is about to ask whether you could create such a song cycle."

"Sure. I didn't before because I was more interested in all this mortality material. But it would be easy to take the more persecuted cultures and create a narrative voice for each one; and people love identifying with the narrator of a sad song. Don't ask me to explain *that*. But they do."

"Well, then," Shan said. "While you are touring, if you were to work on such a cycle . . . I think the OSP might slip you a large payment for that, and you might also get all sorts of favorable publicity. What do you think?"

"I think no one ever explained it so clearly to me before," I said. The flan with strawberries arrived through the table springer slot, and I took a few bites, maybe half the thing, before I realized, "Damn, I've overeaten. Let's go home."

The next day, when she got up, Margaret found me already plucking away at "Don't Forget I Live Here Too," a piece that was to become the first of the *Songs from Underneath* recording, which sold, really, very well, considering that people frequently said it was the most depressing of all. It was a great little project, and all of us were pleased with it for one reason or another.

2

The com was pinging, I was in bed, and Raimbaut was slowly stirring in the back of my mind. I croaked "On speaker," forgetting to add "only," so the vid screen came on and the camera caught me befuddled: naked, uncombed, halfway out of the covers and losing the fight with them.

From the screen, Dji looked so amused that I had to laugh, myself. He said, "I am happy to see that my mornings are so much like those of a younger, more handsome fellow, eh? I commed you because we have two important events today, and not only will you want to look good for each of them, but also you will need a fast briefing. So I wanted to suggest breakfast together, Commissary Eighteen as before—shall we say an hour?"

"It can be twenty minutes," I said. My Occitan pride was stung that anyone could think I could ever need that long to look good.

"Fair enough. I will see you there, then. Dress to strike an impression, especially on media types, but don't wear anything that comes across as a costume. I'll explain everything in detail then—or Shan will, he'll be joining us—but rest assured that nearly all the news is good."

I was still clean from the shower Raimbaut had taken after he finished fixing up the apartment. All my clothes had been through the fresher and were hanging in the closet or folded in the drawers. I got my hair and beard into order, and put on the same *tapi* I had had made up for the Divers' party, with conservative pastel shirt and full dark breeches. In the Noupeitau of my youth, to be sure, it would have been thought hopelessly conservative, fusty, and *mesclatz*. It felt silly to have to wear it. But then, most Texaustralians complain about the hats they have to wear in public, too. Somebody's got to supply some visual variety in human space.

With a minute and a half to spare, we sprang to the commissary. Dji was there already, waiting to order, and after some preliminary pleasantries, he started the briefing.

The first and most pleasant part of the job would be getting Laprada out of jail, two hours from now. Dji was worried about her; during a visit from him, and a visit from Shan, she had seemed disconsolate, and very uncharacteristically quiet. "She did ask about you, Raimbaut," Dji said, "She was worried about how you might be being treated. I think she was afraid that they might confiscate the psypyx from Giraut, as if it were a pocket knife or a springer card. She didn't realize—honestly, none of us realized—that that would have been the last thing they would do if they were thinking."

"How were they not thinking?"

"It's the common, charitable explanation for shooting yourself in the foot," Shan said, sliding into the seat next to me. "So you haven't told him, yet, Dji?"

"I was getting to it."

"Well, then, may I treat myself to the pleasure?" Dji nodded and gestured for Shan to go ahead. "Thank you. I don't know if it was Raimbaut, or Giraut, or both of you together, but by all the gods at least one of you was brilliant. Or confused and very lucky." Shan clapped his hands together, the way my mother does when she has another idea for an academic paper. "When they checked you into the Council of Humanity's jail, you proceeded exactly as if you were being jailed anywhere out in the Thousand Cultures—exactly. I saw that in the transcript. Now, that happened to have added up to winning the day for us.

"First of all, in cultures where the psypyx is common,

there is (of course) an extensive body of law covering the two years of being carried until the cloned body can be grown to age four. And in all that case law, the person in the psypyx is a fully human person, with all protocols set up on that assumption.

"So when you behaved so perfectly in accord with those protocols, which were not familiar to the Earth guards or to most Earth aintellects, they referred it to juridical research aintellects, which promptly found all that old case law and decided that you were right.

"That means a direct agency of the Council has recognized Raimbaut as a human being. Do you see the implications?"

I laughed out loud. "The Administrative Agreement Clause!"

That was the rule intended to keep successive administrations from causing chaos, and to reduce the tendency of legislators to meddle in technical decisions. If there were too many possible intervenors, the immense array of rules covering intercultural trade, diplomacy, and communication would be impossible to keep coherent, and equally impossible for anyone to operate under or work with. Fifty billion people in a complex dance of interrelations are more than enough trouble without all procedures being subject to constant minor changes, political grandstanding, favor-doing, and so on.

This is why the Charter specifies that if any of the Council of Humanity's administrative, regulatory, intelligence, or informational agencies declares a thing to be true, or applies a rule in a particular way, then that is binding for all cases thereafter, unless within fifty standays the Council of Humanity votes to overrule by a three-quarters majority.

Our whole system runs by precedent plus bureaucratic fiat, most of the time. That's far more comfortable, for most people, than real political control by a legislature. Bureaucracies can be foolish and heavy-handed, but almost never aggressively unpredictable.

"So, if the other side now wants to pursue this, they need something close to 900 votes by fifty days from now? You're right. This is going to sandbag them. There's no possible event that could give them that many votes on the Council." I was nearly as impressed with Raimbaut and myself as Shan said he was.

"Absolutely. A complete coup. Bravo. Not that they've given up, quite, yet. I do have to give Esternun credit—for a feeble counterstroke, he came up with a pretty *good* feeble counterstroke. He leaped to his feet and acted as if he *welcomed* the chance to debate this in public—the usual meaningless noises about important matters deserving full consideration and all of that sort of thing. Then he proposed that the debate be held as early as possible—so it will, this afternoon, that's where we're going.

"He also declared that the case for treating psypyxed personalities as commercializable data rather than as human beings was a case that ought to be argued by the best available people on each side. For his own side, he proposed himself. And for our side, he proposed—me."

It took me a moment to see the implications. "And many of the representatives are still angry with you over the Briand affair. So we'll lose some votes out of spite."

"Fewer than you might think," Dji said. "About a third of the Council seems to be automatically and always opposed to overturning any agency ruling—probably not wanting to set any precedents that require them to do any work, or know anything about anything. If they all stick to that principle, all by themselves they should carry the day for us. Plus we have a good solid quarter of the representatives who still see that the OSP is necessary and important—much of that overlaps with the never-overrule crowd, but still, strong OSP supporters added into the mix probably give us an actual majority. It really looks as if we're going to win this one, eh?

"Now, because Esternun proposed this debate—and because so many representatives were eager to escape to lunch—he did slip a few things into the procedures. The only one that is likely to matter is that Shan speaks first, Esternun after, the opposite of what the rule would usually be. Each speaker is required to produce witnesses and testimony—it works out to five witnesses per presentation. Esternun knows who ours have to be (the same witnesses we were trying to put in front of CLMC), but we have no way of requiring him to tell us who his will be or what they will talk about. There's a right to cross-examine witnesses after the main presentations; Esternun has research he's been preparing for months. Shan will have to make up his questions and line of questioning on the spot.

"So we want to be as ready as possible, eh? As soon as we have Laprada, and Paxa and Piranesi join us—they're getting some badly needed sleep, they were just released also—once we're all together, we're going to do a high-speed prep session and a group rehearsal. Lots of work. Not much fun. But—" he reached into his bag "—I do have some confidence that we are winning. I think we only need one more big push. That's why I want to give one of these to each of you." He pulled out three small flat vus and handed two to me and one to Shan. "Raimbaut, when you have your own body, I hope you'll find a place in your room for this; it would surely cheer *me* up on a bad day, eh?"

I felt the glow in his heart at the idea of having something that was really his, and silently promised him we'd take care of it and make sure it was there when he awoke in his new body, twenty months or so from now.

Raimbaut and I looked down at the two copies of the vu; it was about twenty seconds of Esternun.

Dji explained, "This is the very moment when he discovered that the sergeants-guards had checked you in as two people and invoked all those precedents from out in the Thousand Cultures. Notice the way the jaw drops and the eyes widen. Comedians will be studying this for *centuries*."

Since Laprada was awake and dressed when they released her, she stepped through the springer, into an OSP conference room, where we were waiting for her. After a moment for her to hug Raimbaut (I enjoyed it too, but I knew whom she *intended* to hug), and a cup of coffee, she seemed to be ready to go, though there was something sad in her eyes. Minutes later, Paxa and Piranesi appeared, punctual as always. Dji sent the order in for food and gave us a brief update while we waited for it to come out of the springer slot; when the pots of coffee and tea, and the platter of cheeses, meats, and breads, arrived, we all made ourselves comfortable and got down to work.

It was fun. It was like all the old times—the scramble to think of what could be the other side's plan, the brainstorming for counter-moves, the endless rapid-fire process of setting up possibilities and thinking of what actions of ours should be contingent upon them. There is no sound I like better, I think, not even fine music or well-performed poetry, than a roomfull of very bright people arguing, agreeing, finding other ways, moving from idea to idea like monkeys swinging through the treetops. For almost two hours it was frenetic, furious, confusing, exhilarating.

Shan was going over the question of how Laprada's testimony about her experience with both of us could fit into the overall structure of the speech; she had eight or nine good points he *could* use, he had time for three in the opening speech, so the question was, *which* three?

It added a great deal to the experience that Shan and I

were working together like old times. Maybe I'd never fully trust him again, but it didn't matter. I'd still like him; he was still my friend.

•I'm glad you feel that way, • Raimbaut remarked, inside my head.

•Did I think those things about Shan in words?•

•No, but you looked at him and I felt what you were feeling. And I liked it so much better than what you were feeling about him up till yesterday. It seemed to me as if you were hurting yourself. Now it doesn't. I liked what it did for you to feel like Shan was your friend again.•

•Me too.• I took the chance to make another sandwich and eat some of it before Shan finished with Laprada. I was so happy to see her safe. •Leakage,• Raimbaut said. •They warned us it would happen. Now and then I'm not sure which of us is feeling a thing.•

A moment later Paxa raised a question about the relations between psypyxes and traditional hatreds—should we point out that a free market in psypyxes meant, for example, that East Asians and Latin Americans would be able to buy copies of each other to torture and humiliate, avenging the Slaughter forever on victims who couldn't defend themselves? Should Pureans be able to buy personalities from mestizo cultures to destroy them? Should any of the various misogynistic cultures be free to buy the psypyx copies of women from Caledony, Hedonia, or Trois-Orléans, and then psychologically bully them into submission? That was a strong point but where best to use it? We settled on making it the first thing in Paxa's testimony.

Shan turned to me and said, "Giraut, do you think there's any special problem that might come up if I have to call on you for a minute or so, to affirm that you're a different person from Raimbaut? Do we need to plan for that?"

"I don't think so."

He turned to Paxa and reviewed how she would discuss the pain experienced by anyone raised as a completely free and equal woman, if the psypyx copy were used to make a defenseless copy; to Raimbaut, to go over his testimony about why he felt himself to be a person—"for heaven's sake, always stress your feelings," Shan said, "half the Council couldn't tell the difference between a thought and an argyle sock, but bless'em, they all have feelings." Piranesi reviewed his position yet again—that experiences shouldn't be sold apart from context, and that the context of the rigorous Hedon disciplines was exactly what anyone commercializing Hedon experience would try to tear out.

"Laprada, do you think we need to review anything?"

"Not at all."

"Me either. All right, then, I don't think we're going to be any more ready."

At six minutes till our scheduled time, we stretched, straightened our clothes, and did whatever little things helped us feel fresher. (I don't know anyone in the OSP who doesn't have a few such rituals.) At two minutes till time—enough time to walk down the aisle comfortably—we walked through the springer and down the aisle of the Great Meeting Room.

The first time I had been here had been with Shan, and I remembered being impressed by all the representatives at their big desks, arranged in fifteen-deep, rounded tiers that put the uppermost level eight meters above the podium area. The podium area itself was a huge stage with a three-story-high screen behind it. It seemed like exactly the place that I would imagine as the central chamber of the government of the whole human species, fifty billion of us on almost forty worlds: a place where all the majesty and power we had gained during our long hard march from the caves to the stars could flow together.

That impression was all due to the architecture. The Great Meeting Room was six hundred years old, a magnificent piece of work by Aurelio, the one great architect of the early Inward Turn, who had found ways to fuse temple architecture from a dozen earthly traditions into a practical space where everyone could see and hear. From the strip friezes behind each elegant plain column to the subtle lighting on the overhead dome, everything was calculated to make you think something extraordinarily important would be done here, by splendid people.

That first impression of the place had lasted, approximately, until I looked down and saw the people occupying it. Half the desks were unoccupied at all times. Most of the rest were occupied by staffers, using them as offices. No one, or almost no one, was paying attention to the speaker at the front, except on cue—now and then you'd see the green light go on, and the representative at the desk would turn and face the rostrum, looking as serious as possible, while some key point was made. But except when collecting those reaction shots, everyone ignored the ostensible proceedings and did desk work. This sometimes included the speaker at the rostrum, who would put in a pre-recorded tape, then turn and watch the tape play on the big screen, rather than actually speaking. More than once I'd seen a "speaker" at the podium who was a different gender or drastically different age from the person on the screen; for the record, only the person on the screen counted, and any questions answered by the stand-in would enter the record with a simulation of the ostensible speaker giving them. Everyone looked bored, all the time, and whatever they discussed here bore no relation at all to whatever happened out in human space.

•Shan always says that *both* my impressions are true—it's the place where our whole species tries to govern itself, *and* a huge room full of insignificant people ignoring each other,

because that's what human self-government is,• I thought
to Raimbaut.

The sergeants-guards seated us in the front of the guest-
speakers area, and Shan was announced. Lights dimmed except at the podium, and he climbed up the steps to speak.
He began by thanking everyone for the opportunity, and
briefly took the blame for the fiasco on Briand, which gave
him a fine segue into talking about the fragility of the connection to the Outer Worlds, and the difficulty of remembering that, "within human space, the Inner Sphere has
almost all the humans, but the outer cultures have almost all
of the space. The question before us, today, friends, is not
merely whether we will treat the human beings encased in
psypyxes as the human beings that they really are. The larger
question is whether we are primarily a collection of bodies,
processing goods and services, or a discourse of minds, reaching out into the unknown. A decent respect for those who
live closer to the unknown implies that we must not treat
them as mere objects—and as we treat them, so we will
come to treat ourselves. How we choose to see ourselves
will—"

The shouts made me look around. A small dark man in
traditional Tamil dress was running up the aisle. Interruptions by protests and demonstrations are all but *de rigeur* in
the Council of Humanity meetings, so normally I'd have
looked away—but something about the way the man was
running—I jumped up, leaped the chairs, and tried to block
his path.

I was vaulting over the side of the guest speaker's area,
not even in the aisle yet, when the running Tamil stopped,
pulled out a pocket maser, and raised and pointed it. I had
barely shouted when the thunderclap deafened me. I looked
back and saw Shan falling from the podium, most of his

head gone, a cloud of greasy smoke erupting from the empty end of his neck.

Looking back toward the assassin, again, I saw the Tamil tuck himself onto the floor. That motion was enough—I don't know how, but I leaped back up over the guest speaker area railing. It's harder going from low to high and I never jumped that high before or since, but in the circumstances I had wings. Another spring put me on top of Laprada; I pinned her to the floor and covered her with my body.

A savage boom mashed my eardrums. It felt like all my clothes were being yanked over my head; things sprayed too close to me, much too fast, and things spattered off the seatbacks onto me. Then for a few seconds, while I held Laprada down, the world thumped and boomed as bits and pieces of the dome, and debris thrown up by the bomb, fell back around us. I was hit on the leg by a piece of plaster, but that was all.

The instant the rubble stopped landing, I leaped to my feet, dragged Laprada to hers, and pulled my neuroducer epée from its hidden, shielded pocket. The room was still frozen in horror—Shan dead at the podium, pieces of the assassin in the aisle, some dead people in the aisle seats near where the bomb had gone off, and many representatives shouting. I could hear only the thunder of blood in my ears.

Beside me, Dji was standing with a maser drawn—I wondered for an instant how he'd smuggled that—and he shouted loudly enough for me to hear. "Anyone hurt?"

"Shan's dead!" I shouted. "Giraut, fine." I felt Raimbaut in my head and realized who had leaped up to protect Laprada. "Raimbaut, fine."

Piranesi and Paxa both announced that they were fine. I turned to Laprada. She was breathing as if she'd run three miles and her eyes were glazed, but she gasped out "Laprada, fine."

Dji said, very firmly, "Follow me." We went past the rostrum area—much too close to Shan's body for Laprada, I had to wrap an arm around her and put a hand over her eyes—around the side, and out through a fire exit. Behind us, the noise in the room was swelling to a roar, as everyone who could still scream screamed at everyone else. We hurried down the hall to a springer marked EMERGENCY ONLY. Dji tore the cover off the cardbox, setting off the alarms, and jammed a card in, shouting "run through it, everyone, hurry!"

I pushed Laprada through ahead of me, walking fast to clear the springer behind me for anyone else coming out (and to avoid being vomited on; the sudden spring meant that some people were bound to be hit with severe springer sickness). Dji had taken us to the OSP's War Room on Dunant. We had gone four and a third light years at a single step, into the Alpha Centauri system.

Around me, I could hear retching and heaving as other OSP personnel poured in through the four springers into the room; most of them were getting hit with springer sickness because Dunant gravity is slightly lower than Earth gravity, and most of them were coming from Earth.

Beside me, Dji grabbed a wastebasket, spit into it, breathed hard to recover himself, and then looked around. "In a moment I'll take roll. Meanwhile, if you have a duty station here, get to it. If you don't, stand there with your hand up till someone hollers for an assistant. Assume we're at war with an unknown attacker until I tell you otherwise. Move!"

3

They call it the War Room even though no one's ever fought a war from there. It's the OSP's command center for suppressing wars once they break out. I didn't like being there. The two times I'd been in there before, things had ended badly.

The first forty minutes were hard. They put me on the job of reading through all the buddy calls, clocking in reports from all the OSP agents scattered throughout Earth, the solar system planets, and the Thousand Cultures, because all of them had been sent a note asking them to call in and report anything unusual. Checking those reports was like having a friend held hostage and listening for the shot; this might be an attack on the whole organization. Names streamed across my screen, a few I knew, many I recognized vaguely, usually with only the note "checked in—everything normal" beside them. Every so often, though, I would find "checked in, see report" and have to skip over to see what they had written. The "buddy calls" are a regular part of life in the OSP, and when you receive one you're supposed to report anything strange, or report that everything is normal, and since buddy calls never tell you what it is they're looking for, if anything weird has happened lately, anyone who gets a buddy call sends in a report on what was weird. It improves the quality of information—as long as there's a human to sort through it all, and that lucky human was me.

On any given day, out of a few hundred agents, dozens will have encountered something weird. So I was reading reports about odd weather on Quidde, about the surprise selection of a beauty queen in Nubara, and about a mutiny in a barracks in Koenigsberg (the orbiting one in the Epsilon Indi system, not the ruin on Earth or the city on Moneta).

For a moment, that sounded like I had found trouble, but when I checked, it was only technically a mutiny—merely a police strike for higher pay, but at Koenigsberg police and military are combined, and any disobeyed laws are a mutiny, and thus the government was threatening to prosecute the strikers for mutiny. No trace of any real rebellion or serious political matter, and besides, Koenigsberg was a minor backwater of a space colony, not a critical point you'd want to incapacitate or control during a coup or revolution.

The few who had not checked in were invariably on the night side of a planet on remote duty; in other words, chances were that they hadn't heard their com alarms, due to being asleep or busy, rather than that they were in trouble.

Margaret was one of them; she was over in the back country of St. Michael, cold-weather camping with my childhood friend Bieris and their friend Garsenda. Possibly they'd stayed up late drinking around the campfire, maybe even with the com turned off.

•Actually, I feel good that she's doing that,• I thought to Raimbaut. •She needs the time to thrash things through.•

•And you don't?•

•Where did that question come from?•

•From the *toszet*, who, besides being a close friend, is also the one person who can observe you thinking about certain subjects.•

Why argue with someone who can read your mind? •Well, then, *companhon*, I guess I shall have to deal with it. But not now.• I turned to the next case that had an attached report. •What do you suppose a "nutria migration, almost swarming" is, and why would it "severely hamper" a "triathlon," whatever that is?•

After forty minutes, the check-in list was more than nine

tenths complete, with still no trace of any event that could be definitely called "enemy action." Margaret had checked in on the second call, noting that she was sorry to hear of Shan's death and asking if she needed to report to active duty. I sent back a note saying I thought she might be able to wait another day.

When I was sure there was no more information to be found out, and little prospect that any OSP agent in the field would be encountering anything relevant, I turned over the few remaining OSP agents who had not checked in to a clerical aintellect. I instructed the aintellect to call me only if the reports of "anything unusual" contained anything that could be interpreted as enemy action. Whatever was going on, it was not a widespread, coordinated attack.

I moved over to join Paxa, Piranesi, and Dji, who had started a second-level process: studying the assassin's lifetime datatrace. His name was Uloccannar, a common enough name in New Tanjavur before the catastrophe—they had confirmed that he was really Tamil and really from Tamil Mandalam. (He might have been from one of the two other Tamil-derived cultures, and have been used to throw us off the track.) He had been on Earth because he had been recruited by Shan personally for OSP service; he was part of Training Class 927. "He would have graduated four days from now," Dji said. "Not only a Tamil, but supposedly *our* Tamil. Out of all our contacts in Tamil Mandalam, we only ever recruited him."

"I think the real clue—if we knew which way to read it— might be that he chose to kill Shan in exactly the same way that Tz'iquin killed Ix," Paxa said. "You could make a nice tight argument that that was because it was a purely private expression of rage at what had happened to his culture—or a case that we are supposed to think so."

"I have trouble with thinking it was Uloccannar's purely

private revenge on the man he blamed for the destruction of his home culture," Dji said, "(and I only mean trouble; the explanation isn't nearly as good as it should be, because of this consideration, eh?). If things had been working as they are supposed to, and as they normally do, he'd never have gotten anywhere near the Great Meeting Room with a weapon. The protestors and performance artists are allowed to come in and disrupt things exactly because the scans and the cutouts on the springer chains are so careful and thorough. It's so safe that the Council tolerates the interruptions in the hope of getting more media coverage. So—Piranesi— how did Uloccannar make his way past all the normal encryption, scanners, and cutouts with a bomb and a maser? Start by assuming he knew as much as we do, but had none of the resources we have. Is that a reasonable task?"

"I won't know till I try," Piranesi said.

"Good. You have my personal deep interest in the subject—there are always plenty of people who would like to assassinate a high-ranking OSP official, but for one of them to get so strange a chance—seemingly so easily, so suddenly, and when he was so well-prepared—well, it's the sort of coincidence, if that is what it is, that is cause enough to be nervous, eh?"

"I will try," Piranesi repeated. He looked terribly tired and strained. Paxa often said of him that he was patient enough with nothing to do, or with everything to do, but anxious waiting made her husband impossible. Jail must have been exactly the wrong thing for him.

An hour later, Piranesi was over in a corner by himself, pulling in enormous masses of information, muttering, swearing, sometimes pounding the table in frustration, and looking worlds happier and more energetic, so I suppose Dji knew who to give work to.

Still, no evidence pointed to a general attack: no other

agent had been murdered, assaulted, or even threatened. Rioting across the Thousand Cultures was at no more than customary endemic levels. We could not link Uloccannar to any of the OSP's known enemies either in the Sol System or out in the Thousand Cultures. The known-to-be-inimical groups appeared to have been caught at least as flatfooted as we were. Uloccannar didn't look like any part of a broader conspiracy. Especially, Laprada had found no link to Esternun or any other Council member who was either hostile to the OSP or in favor of commercializing psypyx recordings, nor any connection to the Council at all.

But Paxa had found several connections to fringe hate groups in New Tanjavur; Uloccannar looked like he might have been the attempt by some of the more aggressive groups, possibly even *Palai* itself, to plant a sleeper in the Office of Special Projects.

As for how he had penetrated what appeared to be such a secure system, Piranesi leaned toward the explanation that Uloccannar was a proficient hobby hacker in his teens, and that probably what he had done was hack into the parallel net of back-and-forth data relays that ran between springers as a safety measure on Earth, where there were so many springers that a mistake of a digit on an address might be catastrophic (imagine delivering a grade school field trip to the safety springer deep in a cave, or springing a skier making 85 kph into a laundry room). "Hacking the backup safety would be well within his skills," Piranesi said. "If Uloccannar first noticed it around the time that we lost Briand, then the timing would be about right—he sprang to the first place where he could be sure of getting Shan, as soon as he was sure his hack was working. And that *is* the basic way of penetrating a high-security system—find the part of it that's not so high. So I'll look around records within the parallel relays, for all his tests and practice runs—they'll be scattered all over Earth, and maybe all over the Sol system—if I find that, we have another reason to think it was a lone assassin."

"I dislike trails that lead to lone assassins, single simple causes, minor skill, and remarkable luck," Dji complained. "It's the classic pattern for a cover. I'm sure we all feel that way, eh? And yet the reason it is such a good pattern for a cover is because it does happen. We may have to accept that this time."

"I know the feeling," Piranesi said. "I've planned three assassinations myself, and the lone lunatic has been the cover story we arranged for the police to find every time."

Paxa nodded. "Because if it's done right, the more they look, the less the other side will feel like looking further. Yes. Well, is there any more evidence that someone benefited by his death?"

Laprada shook her head. "The other side didn't have the votes going in, and they probably don't have as many now as they did then. They did immediately agree to an indefinite extension on the debate." She sat quietly, as if waiting for questions, but none of us had any.

Dji nodded. "Hard to imagine much of anyone in that crowd having the sang-froid to murder anyone, eh?"

Paxa added, "And our penetration of their private communications and information systems didn't turn up a thing that looked like they were expecting the delay at all. They were fully prepared to make some concession speeches and try again in a year or two, and they didn't have really any plan for what to do if they won."

"Well, then," Dji said. "By now we have all been awake for seventeen hours at least, and that time has included too many changes, and I think we can conclude that we are all far too stressed to do anything well, you know. So I am ordering you all to go rest. You don't have to go home, but I want you to go to sleep. Sleep without setting your clock.

Come in when you're rested. The crew here can handle everything, and perhaps by the time you come in, there will be some more data with which to construct suitable bogeys. Meanwhile, all we can do here is make each other more tired. Now, go, and don't argue."

"Do *you* have anywhere to go?" I asked. "Shan was your friend for most of your life; don't you want to be with friends?"

Dji sighed. "I will be, because I do have somewhere I must go. There will be a meeting of the Board to appoint a new leader for Shan's organization. We've put out a poll to everyone in Shan's organization. Check your mail, you'll find a questionnaire, the gist of which will be 'Explain why you or one of your comrades would make a good next boss.'

"It's not a binding vote, by the way. The Board still makes the decision, and we look for the best choice, not the most popular. But we will look for the best choice with adequate support, since a person without respect, support, or reputation would be a bad choice. Anyway, we will let you know tomorrow who the new head will be, and it is very likely it will be someone that you know—for many years we have always promoted from within." Dji scratched his head. "Truly, this is the end of an age, eh? On the Board right now, three out of five of us are Kiel's boys—one of the boys is a woman, and all of us are old enough to have grown grandchildren, but that's what they called us, and what we are still—three out of five of us will be Kiel's boys, eh? And before Shan was killed, four out of six were. As long as I have been on the Board, it has always been that way, a majority of us had been trained by Kiel. But now . . . the only one of Kiel's boys who is still an active agent, and therefore might possibly be promoted into Shan's place, is Qrala, and he has made it very, very clear that he doesn't want any such thing. Everyone else is already on the Board, or retired. So this decision is the

very last one that will be made by a Board that has a majority of Kiel's boys. End of the era, you know.

"The coming generation will have lived with the
springer for most of their adult lives. The generation after
will think of the springer as we think of the com. Change,
eh? The OSP was founded to manage change, and in my
generation, we have seen so much of it, compared to those
in the five hundred years before us . . . but my generation
will have seen so little of it, compared with the generations
that follow us. It is fine to say 'Second Renaissance' and
'the end of the Inward Turn,' you know, but when you try
to live inside what the words mean, if you have any sense,
you give up.

"So. Give up—home, sleep, no alarm, all of you. *That* human need, I think, will be with us for a long, long while."

In line for the springer, Raimbaut asked Laprada to have
dinner with us, "somewhere conversational."

I thought she would say no—she seemed so painfully unhappy—but she said, "I think that's a good idea, for me. But
I don't know that I'll have much to offer—I'm probably *only*
interested in talk, tonight, and I don't think my conversation
will exactly sparkle."

I felt a piercing sensation in my heart, at her tone—so
lost, so wistful—and could no longer tell if it was mine or
Raimbaut's.

•It hurts that I can't do a thing for her,• he thought.

None of the three of us cared what we ate. We needed
tolerable food in a place that had a comfortable private
booth for two. Laprada said she knew a place in NBA.

Springing from indoors to indoors, as people on Earth so
often do, made every room seem like it was next to every
other room, in one vast convoluted building. (A physicist
friend told me once that that's how the springer works, but I

had no idea what he meant by that, it was a digression in an interesting story, and I had learned by then that asking for explanations at such times was dangerous.) After a while, it was all the same place and time: indoors at night.

On the outside, the planet lived in a shield of its own glare that shut out the stars, so the whole planet was lit and everyone lived as if it were dark.

Neither of us ate much and none of us felt like talking. The food was as unmemorable as we'd hoped.

At the end of dinner, after the coffee and water was delivered and service went to on-call, Laprada sat staring down at the table, drawing little blobby pictures in the spilled water from her glass, like a sad child.

"Tell me," Raimbaut said.

She said nothing. She smeared the water-picture out with the palm of her hand, as if to help it dry.

Raimbaut tried again. "Let me make sure. You do want me around? If you just want me to leave, I can do that. No hurt feelings. I want to do what you need."

Barely audibly, she muttered, "I want you here." She said nothing more for some time. He waited patiently—more so than I think I could have at his age.

•You didn't have an older friend in your head to coach,• he thought at me.

Finally Laprada looked up, straight into my eyes, and said, "I'm too weak for the Office of Special Projects. I was so frightened when I went into jail that, if they had wanted any information, any signed statement, any confession, anything at all from me, I would have given it to them right away. They would never have had to touch me. I was so *afraid*. And I stayed afraid—crying, panting, drowning in terror, wishing I was back in my own room—right until they told me I would be released. Right through Dji's visit. Right through Shan's visit. I have no courage at all. I was *hoping* the jailers would come and demand something, because I knew I would give in right away, and that way the fear would be over."

•Giraut, *per merce de deu*, get into this!•

I had been afraid he would ask for that. "Laprada, this is Giraut. I'm a veteran of many of these things, you know, and *everyone* is terrified, every time. My ex-wife is probably the bravest, best agent I know, admired by every one of her peers and especially by me, and during the whole Briand mission she was scared half crazy. And if you think about what happened there, she was probably right to be. But there was a job to be done, and she did it, despite being ter-rified, and that's what courage is, that's all that counts. And *you* did fine, this afternoon, after Shan was killed."

"No, I didn't. You and Raimbaut gentled me through the situation, as if I were a horse in a burning barn. You had to cover my eyes to walk me past Shan's body!"

"Well, *voill atz deu* that someone had covered mine. That was a sight I didn't need to see and would be happy not to remember. I don't care who knows that."

"Nonetheless. You coped. I didn't."

I dropped the point and tried another tack. "This always worked for Margaret, and she taught it to me, and it works for me too. You have to keep reminding yourself that the reason the other side does frightening things to us is because they're trying to scare us. I know it sounds obvious, but it's important when you think about it. The reason you feel ter-rible is because they are trying to make you feel terrible. It's deliberate. They *want* you to be miserable, destroyed inside, helpless, not yourself. Now, doesn't it make you *angry*, that they would try to do such a thing, and make you want to hit them back? Fury can make a decent substitute for courage, in a pinch."

Laprada shook her head, never looking up. "That all sounds very sensible and brave, but it doesn't apply to me. I learned in that jail that they *can* make me feel that way, and they can do that whenever they want to. I don't have any anger to resist with, Giraut, I might resent what they do to me, but I don't have anything inside me to make me stand up and fight. I don't. If they had ordered me to *like* being terrorized and to beg them to do it I swear, I would have *tried* to like it. You can't know what it's like.

"I'm sorry, Giraut, I know you're trying to help, but I'm not a silly girl with a head full of adventure stories, and I don't just need some bracing up." For the first time, I saw real anger, but it was aimed across the table at me, and her tone became more and more sarcastic. "I know all the old sayings, I know that 'courage is being afraid and doing the right thing anyway,' and 'you can't be brave unless you're scared,' and 'rage drives out fear,' and all the rest. I really do understand all those ideas.

"What I'm telling you is that I know, from a few harmless hours in a perfectly safe jail cell, that I can't *do* any of that. I haven't got the stuff inside to cope with my fear, or to face it and go on, or even to trick myself into doing something in a fit of rage. Raimbaut, my wonderful would-be *entendedor* (that's the word, isn't it?), I only let you cover my eyes and walk me past Shan's corpse because I trusted you to end the fear. If the surest way out of that situation had been to betray you to your worst enemy instead, I'd have done it, and I wouldn't have been able to imagine doing anything else."

I felt completely helpless; a moment later, there was a despairing laugh within my head. •So putting your feelings into words, *companhon*,• Raimbaut thought, •that would be "kid, you're on your own."• He took Laprada's hand—it lay in his like a dead snake—and said, "You know, this was so easy for me. I was doing it inside Giraut's head, with the benefit of all his experience. So I don't feel like it's my place to judge you."

Her hand clenched hard, and her nails bit into his palm. He held steady as she glared into his eyes and hissed, "It's not that. And you're not listening." I could feel him freezing to the chair, as if moving might provoke a worse attack. "It's not that I was afraid. It's not some lack of confidence. I had no emotions but fear. None. And I don't care if you judge me. I judge me, why shouldn't you? So what I see is this: I am not the kind of person I hoped I would be. I wanted to be an OSP agent, like Grandpa Lohemo and Uncle Dji and Uncle Shan. I wanted what I did to matter in the world, and I wanted people to depend on my doing it well no matter what, and I wanted to be a person who could be trusted with the most important job there is. I wanted to be what Giraut is—and what you're going to be, Raimbaut. What I'm telling you is, I won't. Because I can't.

"Now, that's not so terrible. I am far from the most useless person in the world. I'm a good musician, or would be if I practiced. I was a very competent politician. I can do some things of some value. But oh—what I *wanted* to be! And what I'm *not*!"

She choked and sobbed, hard painful sobs that sounded like the cries of someone kicked in the ribs. Raimbaut moved around to try to hold her or put an arm around her, but she shoved his hands away and slapped at them.

It was no use. Raimbaut tasted helplessness and futility.

After a long time she stopped crying. She didn't want to go back to her place alone, so she came along to ours. Shortly after all attempts to talk failed, Raimbaut and I were under the covers in the bed, still sleeping to one side as if Margaret might come back to bed at any instant. Laprada was over on the other side of the bed, lying close to the edge, on top of the covers, fully dressed. She had started to cry again, this time very quietly.

Raimbaut's distress was making my guts roil and squirm like worms in a fire. Just before I fell asleep, she reached out, grabbed my hand, and pulled it over toward her, but more as if it were a life preserver than as if she wanted anything from him or me.

Margaret moved fast, when she needed to, exactly the way a good martial artist moves fast—by making sure that no part of her motion opposed any other, and that everything happened with the least effort. This often fooled people into thinking she was lazy, or a plodder, or unimaginative, and that made the effect all the more devastating.

Sometimes it saved me from real trouble, because whereas Margaret's way of getting information was to bring all sorts of people to her office in the Embassy, and compare what they told her with all the official statistics and news reports, my approach was to take a long walk and get into conversations with whoever wanted to talk to me. Now and then my choices were unlucky, or foolish, but you learn things by wandering through a strange city that you cannot learn any other way. But every now and then, I could be in trouble abruptly, without much in the way of resources for getting out of it.

Margaret's mixture of craft, guile, and quick wits usually was all the backup I needed. When I went to jail for annoying some local poohbah (usually they *needed* annoying), Margaret got me out. At various times she had claimed exotic medical conditions for me, masqueraded as a secret policeman come to extradite me, walked into parties full of armed men and claimed to be bringing the news that she was pregnant and we were supposed to go home to Caledony at once . . . she had bullied, browbeat, threatened, hood-winked, and in every way, made life hell for anyone who laid a hand on me or tried to frighten me.

And yet, she herself had never liked violence, and she had only rarely been at risk of it, whereas I had grown up where it was endemic. I feared it, because you never know what can happen, but in a measured, controlled way; she loathed it with all of her soul. But she never said a critical word when I walked into trouble, again, nor when she had to liberate me from the local cops or bullies (usually the same people are both).

She'd be waiting in the lobby of whatever the local lockup was, surrounded by a pack of Embassy lawyers waving documents, prominent local politicians in robes and pajamas, or CSPs in riot gear, sometimes all of those. To judge by her facial expression, she might have been waiting for her husband to return from the restroom.

Always, once we had sprung back to our apartment, she would shake her head and click her tongue, disapproving of something or other, but never letting me feel that it was me.

4

Raimbaut and I got to our office shortly after ten A.M. the next morning. Laprada had sprung to her apartment, sullenly, evincing no desire to speak, about an hour before, and I had divided my time and attention, during the next hour, between basic grooming and advanced Raimbaut care. It was good that the former could be nearly automatic.

The whole set of offices seemed to reverberate with high nervous tension. Sharp little laughs punctuated conversations in which nothing was funny. People talked fast and often lost the thread of what they were saying. Everyone was trying to overhear, and no one wanted to be caught eavesdropping. Many more people were using those annoying little reassurance tags—"right?", "eh?", "isn't it?", and so on—on almost every sentence, as if everyone were preoccupied with making sure of every instant of communication.

Everyone was realizing that everything would be changing.

When I came in, Dji at once summoned me into his office and closed the door. He said, "First of all, Shan's funeral will be two days from tomorrow. He's chosen to be buried at Chaka Home, on Quidde, even though he's manifestly not Chakan. His religion didn't allow the psypyx, so I'm afraid he's really, truly gone. By vote of the Board, all OSP agents can go to Quidde for the funeral; human space will just have to go unprotected for a couple of hours. Here's your passcard; use it at the time designated. You're part of the honor guard, so wear your dress uniform. The Chakans are giving him their highest honors."

Then Dji handed me another springer card. "The new

head of the Shan organization wants to meet with you before the public announcement of the appointment is made.
For one thing, although you will be working for me until the
business of selling psypyx records, and the investigation of
Shan's death, are both over, the new head has requested that
you be transferred back as soon as possible afterwards, and
wants a friendly, private, frank discussion about why, first. So
use that card, in my personal springer here, and go talk to
your new boss. It's only about an hour till the official public
announcement, and there's a lot to do."

"Then we can skip it if you like," I said. "This won't really
be necessary. If you and Shan's successor think that I'll do
more good over there, well, you may consider that I've already accepted."

Dji's mouth twisted for a bare instant—was the expression he hid a smile? a frown? a thought, anyway. "Trust me.
It's necessary. Now don't keep your boss-to-be waiting."

Realizing that there had to be something I didn't know, I
shut up. I put the card into Dji's private springer and
stepped through into Shan's familiar office. The few small
prints and vus had been taken down and were leaning up in
the corner, but the desk was bare as always, the books on the
shelves had not been changed, the coffee setup was the
same, and otherwise it was still much as if Shan would be
back any instant. I blinked for a moment before I realized
that it was Margaret sitting behind the desk.

"Giraut. This was the way Dji and I thought it would be
appropriate to tell you; I hope we were right."

I like to think I didn't hesitate before I spoke. I suppose I
could ask Margaret, who might remember, but why risk
hearing something I'd rather not? Whether I paused or not, I
said, "This is wonderful! And what a comical expression I
must have had on my face—"

"It was pretty good." She flashed that fierce, toothy grin I had missed so much in the past few stanyears, as the marriage deteriorated and dragged the friendship down with it. "You and I worked together for so long, so well, that I know what you can do, better even than you know. And you're good at what I'm going to need for my organization. (God, what a strange thing to say instead of Shan's organization.) I'd rather have you working for me, and know that those things will be done well (even if you sometimes irritate me) than have to spend ages figuring out whether I dare rely on somebody else.

"But if you have any idea that this could lead to our getting back together . . . well, have no hope, please? And if that would make it hard to take the job, then, I suppose, don't take it."

I stuck out my hand. "I want the job."

She shook my hand, we both smiled, and she came around the desk and hugged me, while we both laughed. That was all that was necessary, then or ever.

When I returned, Dji only asked, "So will you be returning to Sh—to Margaret's organization, after this is all over?"

I said I would. I kept thinking there should be some emotional stress or overload to deal with, but so far as I could tell, there wasn't.

The message traffic on my desk amounted to vast amounts of what we didn't know, mixed with what was known not to be true. We knew of no connections, still, to any group outside of Tamil Mandalam; we knew that it had not been the opening shot of a war, insurrection, or coup. Until the moment that Uloccannar had walked into the springer in his barracks and walked out into the Great Meeting Room with his weapons, he had been a very promising recruit, with nothing at all to suggest he would be anything other than an asset. He had acquired all the needed weapons and codes himself within six hours of doing the job, by methods he would have learned at the training center.

Dji dropped by to see how things were going, and I showed him what I had.

"So on one level," Dji said to me, leaning over my shoulder, it looks like petty revenge." He turned and closed the door. "And it would be very fine if it were, because it would mean we are doing our jobs well. But we can't count on that to be the case. So that brings me to the second possibility, and we need to have a talk about that. We can never be completely sure of it, but how can we at least feel reasonably confident that there isn't some highly capable organization out there, inimical to us, about which we know nothing?"

I shrugged and looked up at the ceiling. Shan had often asked questions like that, and it was all very familiar. It wasn't a request for a definitive answer—it was a request to come up with an angle. "Well," I said. "*M'es vis*, surely you've been monitoring the regular police investigation?"

"Absolutely. We have three separate pipelines into it, and we'll know everything the moment they do."

"Hmm. Well, I'd say any outfit that can be caught by the regular cops isn't very effective. If this had been an OSP operation, the police would find nothing and close the case in three days, and it would never come up again." I thought about that for a while. "Monitoring the police will take care of most garden variety terror and dissident groups. What you really want is a way to make sure that it's not somebody good enough to slip all the way through security, like an OSP operation would."

Dji shook his head after thinking for a moment. "But the OSP has a huge advantage—it's an arm of the government. I doubt there's anyone else out there who can do an OSP-type operation."

Raimbaut asked, "So the only organization that could have done the assassination and covered the tracks . . . that we know about or that is likely to exist . . . would be the Office of Special Projects itself?"

Dji stared at me for a moment, and then I nodded.

"Raimbaut," I said, "if Dji doesn't recruit you the minute you have a body of your own, he'll lose you to Margaret, because I'll tell her to do it. Let's see . . . all right, it's possible that some part of the OSP might profit from this. Shan, alive, was an embarrassment to the organization, *and* the sort of lightning rod for public dislike that the opposition tried to use in the psypyx cases. He was highly skilled and often a brilliant operator, but I can see where someone could decide that he was no longer an asset to the OSP. At least . . . not while he was alive. But on the other hand, if Shan were dead . . . now there's an asset. Martyr. And suspicion falling on the other side. And perhaps one person out of the power sweepstakes in the OSP." I took a deep breath, let it out slowly, and considered. It did hang together as a possibility; I didn't know any reason to drop it right this moment. "So could anyone have been thinking that way?"

Dji spread his hands. "We have plenty of people who could and would work that way if they thought it were important enough to the OSP's mission, plus an unknown but probably large number of people who would if it paid enough. I know we didn't discuss the idea at any Board meeting, and I was at all of them in the past seven years. (Besides, so was Shan.)

"There's no group director I'd suspect of anything, either, and the only past group director who ever had a grudge against Shan was Qrala. But that whole matter was buried thoroughly, and I thought it was long ago forgotten, or at least forgiven."

"But in our business?" I asked. "We attract and recruit people with long memories, not to mention good liars. Though I don't want it to turn out to be Sir Qrala—I *like* the man."

Dji all but groaned aloud. "He and I have been friends and rivals and enemies and always returned to being better friends, so many times I couldn't easily count them. All before you were out of diapers, and you're not a young man, eh? Giraut, I mean. I know Raimbaut is a young man." He stared into space for a long moment, shaking his head. "Not many of us old ones left. I don't want it to be one of Kiel's boys, I just don't."

I sighed. "He was kind and wise and kept his word with me during the whole Briand mess," I said, "and I needed that badly. And then too, I look at his strange relationship with Kiel and Shan over all those years—spying on their old mentor for his old comrade and yet loyal to both of them somehow . . . I have to admit I don't know much about it—"

"Nor will you, unless you need to. Those of us from the old days try to make sure no one will ever need to. If you ever need to know everything that was going on with those three men, then something will have gone hideously wrong and we will be sliding down a very steep, dark slope indeed," Dji said. "In case you were hinting. I know what the arrangement between them was. I can see how Kiel's death in New Tanjavur *could* be interpreted as having violated that deal. But the strange thing is, it would have been something for Shan to be angry with Qrala about, not vice versa."

"Did Qrala fear Shan's revenge, maybe?"

"That would make very little sense in the context. You'll have to trust me on all this, you know." Dji looked miserably unhappy. "But I really can't dismiss the concern. So I guess that means you're going to dismiss it for me, Giraut. As of now, your primary assignment is to investigate the possibility that Qrala was behind Shan's murder. I assume you will eventually turn up enough evidence to clear him (assuming he's innocent—and I do). But put on a good healthy para-noia and nail him for it if you can. I don't want this to rest on a half-hearted effort."

We shook hands. "I'll do my best, but surely it would help for me to know what the grudge between them was?"

"It would. You'll have to manage without that informa-tion, all the same."

"Thank you, then, I'll get on it."

Dji nodded and left as if afraid he might speak again. As he left, Raimbaut thought, •What do you think? Is Qrala in-nocent?•

•I want him to be, I expect him to be . . . and the sooner we have this case done with, the sooner I can be sure. All right, let's see how much access they've given us to the rele-vant files, and how much more we need to apply for.•

The problem with putting together information for a report in an organization like the OSP is that although most of the people you are dealing with are bright, all of them have to be afraid that you are up to something you shouldn't be. So they are invariably polite, reasonable, friendly, helpful, and completely obstructionist and nitpicky. There might be a more annoying combination in a bureaucrat but I'm not sure what it would be.

Still, despite all the interference by friendly, well-mean-ing, talented people, by mid-afternoon I had everything the police knew about Uloccannar, including raw data from many different private files. I also had everything that could be readily acquired about every human being whose name appeared in Uloccannar's file.

It took another hour of debating with a variety of real people and aintellects for me to obtain the maximum access I could be allowed to Sir Qrala's file. Training Class Four had joined the OSP on September 11, 2788, and Kiel had been their trainer, and the organization that Margaret had just inherited had then been known as the Kiel organization. In 2796—promotions were fast, in those early days—Qrala had become leader of a new organization within the OSP. In 2799 he had stepped down and gone to work for Shan; and in 2806, following RECORDS SEALED, and (while still reporting to Shan), at the request of NOT AVAILABLE, he had resigned his duties as RECORDS SEALED, and gone to work for Kiel, who was then the Ambassador to Nova Roma, on Gobat. A further READ FIRST note in that file specifically prohibited doing anything that might compromise the information that the two of them knew each other, or that Shan knew either of them. Qrala was also listed as reporting to Shan for NOT AVAILABLE.

•This at least confirms that Dji isn't lying to us,• I pointed out to Raimbaut. •The things you find that you'd rather not know! Sir Qrala was a perfectly good person to work with, and I'm appalled to be doing this.•

The aintellects went through every file that touched every file that was there in Qrala's lifetime datatrace, and eventually they had a list of a few thousand relationships— ranging from "father" to "file clerk in same embassy" to "barber" to "reprimanded for having an affair with him."

•Well, this should be enough to start the process,• I thought to Raimbaut.•

•What about Shan?•

I felt silly; •Good thing I'm not a cop. I'd never have thought of checking those connections. But there's going to be a really dense net between Shan and Qrala, because the two of them were partnered for so long, so anyone who figures in one of their joint cases will be listed as a strong connection.•

I could feel Raimbaut thinking the equivalent of an impatient shrug. •So throw out all the strictly shared-case ones, and look for low-probability third-person connections that have a hook to Uloccannar. That's all it would take to winnow out at least ninety percent of the chaff. What you really are looking for is strong connections that aren't obvious, *non?*•

•Have you thought about being a detective?•

•All I really want at the moment is to be physically real, Giraut. I will sort everything else out after that.•

I could feel, nonetheless, that he had taken it as a compliment. After a while I hung back and let him do the analysis, only occasionally nodding in when he might have gotten lost through lack of experience or acquaintance with the OSP. He really was good at this.

That was a good thing, because there was little about Shan, except widely scattered fragments of dissociated information that somebody had failed to tidy up. I'd never seen such a thorough job of erasing pathways and traces through a database before.

An hour and a half later, Raimbaut and I were out of ideas, and we had only about 450 names linked to Shan's, one of which was mine, another of which was Sir Qrala's. So I, too, would be turning up as one of those improbable links. At least I knew I hadn't done it.

By the time we had all of that together, it was late in the day, but we still took time to set up a connection engine and put it on the job. One place to look for a conspiracy, criminal or otherwise, is in the links between people, and that's what a connection engine does. Just as we had expanded Shan, Qrala, and Uloccannar's relationships into a sphere of connections, the connection engine would expand each of those thousands of people into more connections, and those connections into more connections, out to the fourth degree. At that point, virtually every person who appeared in one sphere would appear in all three; then the connection engine would painstakingly construct each chain of connections, and choose the shortest chains that were in any way unusual.

Most connections would be garbage—coincidences like Shan and Qrala's barbers both having gone to the same cultural institute, where there was a Tamil poet in residence with whom Uloccannar corresponded. A few might be something else; and if we were right (as we were praying not to be) one *would* be something else. The aintellects had a reasonably good sense of the purely coincidental, and of which connections were worth thinking about and which spurious (people conspire with their lovers or their brothers far more often than they do with their insurance brokers or their letter carriers). Even at superfast machine speeds that allowed full realtime virtual reality, the job was so big that it would run for a few hours; meanwhile, we might as well get some dinner. •It should have a report for us tomorrow morning,• I thought. •Did anyone mention that in this business there are times that are just work?•

•I had access to your memories, Giraut. Do you suppose Laprada had a day like this, too?•

•Very likely. You realize that everyone working on the case has probably been assigned a prime suspect, and they probably spent today doing this same procedure? Maybe not quite so good a one, Raimbaut, you really do seem to have a talent for this.•

I felt his pleasure and embarrassment at the compliment. To cover, he asked, •What usually turns out to be the cause of unprovoked, mystery attacks on the OSP? They can't be common.•

•They aren't. I've seen two other mystery attacks in my twelve stanyears with the OSP.•

•What did the truth turn out to be, the two times before?•

•Well, in one case, two OSP men had the same mistress, and she had a third boyfriend who was a gangster. He found out about them and arranged to have them both killed on the same day. He had no idea they had anything to do with the OSP. That took a while to sort out. Eventually the cops caught him on something unrelated, and since his was one of those cultures with the 'unwritten law,' he agreed to admit to the murders. We never cleared it ourselves.

•The other was an agent who went out for a walk in the bad part of Trois-Orléans, probably because he'd been going out for walks after lunch every day of his life. Someone killed him, took his wallet, and pushed his body down a manhole; there was a heavy rainstorm and he floated miles and miles from the city. Meanwhile, his wallet was tossed into a randomly addressed springer and emerged clear on the other side of Roosevelt, in a second-hand store. So when we went looking for him, we barked up a few thousand wrong trees for a while.•

•Or in other words, neither was really a mystery attack on the OSP.•

•True.•

•Have there been any?•

•Those are all the cases I know anything about.•

He was quiet for a long time. We were taking a hot shower, and I was enjoying the sensation of relaxing my desk-cramped muscles.

Raimbaut thought, •How long will this take, if the truth is that it was done by a crazed, patriotic Tamil, who blamed Shan for the genocide of his culture?•

•No matter what, this is apt to take a long time,• I reminded him. I turned on the distilled water rinse to get all the soap out of my hair and beard, set the water temperature for as hot as I could bear, and enjoyed the sensation. •Much as I'd rather that this were an appalling coincidence or a senseless act, Raimbaut, it feels far too deliberate. First of all, it happened at a time when it could have tremendous effects—although we don't know which effect, if any, of the ones that have happened, was intended. That's improbable. Then heap on another improbability: a new trainee with enough tradecraft to carry this out exactly the way you have to—from a standing start as shortly as possible before doing the deed—without a hitch or flaw. And then: this new trainee was able to steal not one but two weapons from the training center, where they were held in locations remote from each other and protected by different security systems.

•That would be doing very well for me, good even for a man who teaches penetrations-and-surreps like Piranesi. And for a new trainee who hadn't even been through internship yet? Plus he set up a perfect, worked-right-the-first-time hopscotch through a dozen springers before merging with the flow for the Great Meeting Room and arriving right on time. Besides, it's not all that easy to make a head shot on a target above you, but somehow Uloccannar—who had no weapons training before he came here—did that, too.•

•Put that way, it doesn't seem possible.•

•And yet it could be what happened. You can never eliminate coincidence. And sometimes someone discovers a simple thing—like the parallel communicators that Piranesi spotted—that lets them avoid the impossible thing. Bizarre coincidences, clever innovations, and strokes of luck happen every day, and they're distributed very unevenly; if Uloccannar had some of all of them on that day, it could happen. Who'd have believed that, with no help of any kind, a blind cleaning woman of eighty-three could kill the supreme leader of half of Earth? But that really ended World War Three, all the same.

•So we do have to accept the possibility of coincidence—but given how unlikely it is, we have to play the main chance: assault by an unknown hostile power, involving someone we have every reason to trust. So we pursue that, we hope it's not true, but to know that it's not true, we have to pursue it as if we thought it was. Now, why don't you com Laprada and see what she wants to do with you tonight? It will be something, I'm sure.•

His heart leapt up. I enjoyed the sensation myself.

He liked my amusement. •Remember, *companhon*, in my subjective time, a few weeks ago I was still in the Quartier des Jovents, and despite years of effort I had never had an *entendedora*, and my best hope of meeting women would have been to take a job in a chocolate shop. I *radiated* failure. But, now, appearing in the person of an urbane, sophisticated *gen de mon*, and with his ever-wise counsel—•

By then I was laughing hard.

•If you'd taken all that seriously,• he thought, •I was going to leave you.•

•Com Laprada, Raimbaut. Before your sense of humor takes over both our minds.•

Laprada's "hello" was about as dispirited as any I've ever heard, and I felt my heart sinking and Raimbaut rallying himself. "I wondered if you'd be willing to eat with me two nights in a row," he said. "Being honest about it, you're the person I'd like to see tonight."

"Oh, god, I don't know, Raimbaut. I feel like just taking a long hot bath, eating some crackers, and going to bed."

"Well, if you like, I'll drop by with wine, we can have crackers together, and then I can go home and you can take your bath. Would you say it's going to be more of a red cracker or a white cracker?" Raimbaut listened, desperately, hoping that there would be some sign of amusement from her, but there was none; she had the visual turned off, and he struggled against the mental picture of her glaring, or staring into space, before forcing a smile on himself and saying warmly, "Laprada, you really do have to eat. Why not do it with me? You know I can sit quietly and worry about you, or do my best to be entertaining, or anything in between, and that's what I'd rather be doing than anything else. So unless I'd hurt your mood, let's eat together."

"Funny, I heard Occitan men were too proud to beg."

"Arrogant old ones like Giraut are. And even he recorded a version of '*Non soi trop valen que plaideiar.*' "

She giggled. "He's awake, isn't he?"

"And annoyed. I can feel that."

"I'm putting all my attention into trying to figure out a way that makes any sense to challenge Raimbaut to a duel," I explained. •She's weakening, *companhon*, press on! *Tostemz valors!*•

"Just as long as neither of you gets hurt," she said. She clicked on the visual part of the com, and though she looked wan and tired, she was smiling, and the smile reached her eyes. "All right, the Occitan charm wins again. We'll meet somewhere for something. As long as I'm allowed to possibly fall into a horrible mood and be no fun at all. Probably it will be a short meal, but if we have a better time than I'm expecting, or I decide to see what a depressing world it really is, the Divers are having a party tonight, and we could drop by for a few minutes, stay damp in the current, you know, nothing too serious. We won't do more than remind them we're alive, but that might be enough to stay damp and off the shore. Would you mind awfully if we did?"

Raimbaut lied like a professional, and told her that was exactly what he'd been hoping for. Laprada picked out a café for them to meet in, somewhere in Ciudad de Mexico she said—I wasn't sure where that was, some little backwater megalopolis in North America. They would meet in half an hour—"just time enough for me to fix things up all the way to not-embarrassing," she explained.

They disconnected, and Raimbaut thought, •that was frightening.•

•You handled it perfectly, *companhon*. She sounded a thousand times better after that conversation. You'll become better at all the games, in time, but I should probably warn you that they will never be easy.•

Raimbaut was quiet as we straightened clothing, combed hair and beard, and worked the whole effect to the right mix of studied indifference with natural grace. After a few stretches, he thought, •Giraut? I don't want to seem un-grateful at all, about my relation with Laprada, but . . . •

I could feel the thoughts forming, and Raimbaut fighting them down. I knew what was bothering him, though, either because it leaked or because it was obvious, so I thought back, with all the reassurance I could manage, •It's a reason-able question and thinking it doesn't make you uncaring, fickle, or cruel. You're human. Remember? That's what we're trying to get across to the Council of Humanity. So . . . what you want to know is, is it always so much work?•

•Right. It seems very disloyal to think that.•

I thought of shrugging. •Not always. Some lovers need less or more emotional attention. Some are more or less nur-turing or protective. Now, she's pretty far toward needy, and you're pretty far toward protective, so overall it works. It's good to be attached to someone who needs to be loved in the way you need to love. If you had attached yourself to someone more self-sufficient, you'd be wondering if she cared about you, or even liked you.•

•Is that how it was during your good years with Mar-garet?•

•I don't know. I think it's more a matter that you learn

not to worry about such things, much, except during brief periods when you have to worry about them all the time. But I could be completely wrong. I've been known to be.•

The costume for the night was a sober version of breeches, boots, *tapi*, and tunic, and only one person looked up when we walked out of the springer at the café. Only about half of the dozen tables were taken, and Laprada was already there, sitting by herself, staring down at a menu without reading it.

She said "hello," without looking up, as I slid into the chair. Raimbaut felt the impulse to say "What's wrong?" and instead said, "It's always such a great pleasure to see you, but I can see you're having a bad time."

Laprada grunted. They both sat silently for a while. I was grateful to any gods there are that I was not required to be part of this.

Raimbaut was about to offer to call it a night when she said, "Stay. If anyone can make me feel better, it's you."

With a purely internal sigh, he said, "Should we talk about it, or talk about everything else, or just be silent for a while?"

"I don't think I *can* talk about it, so that's out."

Raimbaut made a face. "Hmm. I can't talk about anything I worked on today, and all I did today was work."

She nodded unhappily, and asked, "How well did you know Shan?"

"Just the few meetings, all business, and of course Giraut's memories and feelings. That relationship was . . . complex."

•Good way to put it,• I thought to him.

Laprada nodded. "He was a completely fascinating man, even if you didn't know who he was or what he actually did. Shan and Dji were like extra grandfathers to me—Dji was my warm, friendly, funny grandfather, and Shan . . . well, he's the one I would have run to for any real trouble. For me, it's like having the sun disappear from the sky."

Gazing into space, she sipped at her coffee. "It must be hard for you, Giraut, you worked with him all the time for so long."

"I guess I'm numb. You think you understand your situation, you think you will always remember that the work is dangerous and we will bury some friends too soon, and all that, and then when it happens, you wonder how things ever got this way." I flagged down one of the robots and ordered a light plate of hors d'oeuvres and a pitcher of water. "I don't know what the funeral tomorrow will feel like. Not good, I'm sure." My eyes gushed. My throat closed so hard that I couldn't breathe. Obviously it was time to cry for Shan, and that was the only thing that was going to happen for a while.

The image of his head blown off his neck made me shudder. All the things I had been saving to say at Starkside, which he would now never hear, echoed miserably, uselessly in my head. The joy, only two days ago, of working together well again; the embarrassment at how angry I had been . . . none of it mattered, anymore, because it was all part of my relationship to him, and he was dead. I put my elbows on my knees, my face between my hands, and let the tears come.

It seemed like forever till Laprada touched my shaking shoulder. "Are you all right?"

"I don't think I'll be all right for a while," I gasped. "But I'm not in any physical danger." I added to Raimbaut, •I'm sorry, I seem to be spoiling your date.•

•It's all right, *companhon*, *verai*. Surely you've earned this one if anyone has.•

I sat there and cried, in public, in my strange Occitan clothes, with people staring. I cried for Shan, and for all of us in the OSP, and for everyone who dreamed about a big future and life outside the box, and eventually I think for our whole pathetic species, born to fly and doomed to crawl, always pulling down the ones who tried to bring us up.

At last, I grabbed a couple of napkins from the setups on a neighboring table. I wiped my face thoroughly, scrubbing till my skin stung. My face felt inflated and skinned, the way it did the time it caught a boot, and was dragged across rough carpet. I wasn't sure I wanted to know what my eyes looked like, or what might be in my mustache, but I took a final wipe around my face before coming up, at last, for air.

Laprada had the strangest expression—intense worry? compassion? anger? revulsion?

•Not good,• Raimbaut thought.

•She's all yours, *toszet de grand valors.*•

She spoke before he could think of anything to say, her expression and voice gentle. "I guess I'd been thinking mainly of my own loss, so soon after Grandpa Lohemo and Grandma Catherine. It's not always easy to remember that others are hurting besides me. You had been through a lot together."

I nearly wept again, but swallowed hard and said, "You do understand." I had to nearly grit my teeth to stay focused. "Thank you for that."

The food arrived. When we had eaten for a while, grabbing the little pieces of meat, vegetables, and cheese with the soft bread, Raimbaut tried a change of subject. "Do you still want to go to the Divers' party? I'll admit freely that I can take or leave them, but you seemed sort of eager, before, when we talked on the com."

She shrugged. "A few people will want to proclaim, loudly, that they are glad that Shan is dead, and that this time the OSP won't get away with covering up a murder. I think we should go and stare them down . . . or maybe administer a good beating to someone, if you're in the mood, Giraut, because that would completely help to move the current out of this life-is-a-game routine that has become so poisonous."

"I could be in the mood," I said. My culture is as mad as an outdoor pool in orbit about many things, perhaps about most, but as I grow older I come to think we have a fine perspective on violence, nearly as good as the one we have on art. There exist statements and behaviors for which the sole adequate retort is a belt across the chops.

"Well, Shan's murder is dominating the headlines. And the people in the current are going to matter intensely. I think we ought to be out there, trying to dig a new channel for the current, rather than hanging back and mourning our dead."

"Our dead would want that," I said, because it was true.

"Well, then." I saw her make herself smile, even making it light up her eyes, as if by pure force of will. "Enough of all this gloom. Time to go play. Proddy needs to get out and mix."

"I thought you hated that name," Raimbaut said.

She shrugged. "Serious, dutiful, dedicated Laprada hated to have people think of her as Proddy. Proddy, on the other hand, likes to party, and likes the attention she gets when she shows up." Her smile was now completely convincing, warm and friendly with the corners of her eyes crinkling up. "Really," she said, "I think you two have the very best of possible worlds—I don't understand how *any of us* gets by with just one personality, or just one past."

5

The party was at Rebop's apartment, this time. Otherwise it was much the same—exactly the same people, and the sort of things they said about the political repercussions of Shan's death were the same sort of erudite, meaningless noises that they had made about the Assemblejam Café performances—things they had been planning to say for days.

Gumba would have been amusing if he hadn't been talking about the murder of one of my best friends. Looking for a getaway, I found doors to a balcony.

The morning sun hit me full in the face, and I nearly laughed. I hadn't asked Laprada where the party was—I was beginning to think like an Earth person, where, after decades of the springer, everywhere was right next to everywhere. So like anyone else at the end of a working day, I had assumed I was going to a party in the evening. Well, it was pleasantly warm, the fresh air smelled good, and the balcony was on the outside of the hyperpolis, in the mid ranges, about a kilometer or so up the side. It looked out over a dense tropical forest. I set the cameras and eyepieces of my computer to be used as binoculars.

There were dozens of tropical birds and every now and then the flash of a monkey leaping between branches. I couldn't even count the *kinds* of butterflies. "If I were living here," I murmured aloud, "I would *live* on this balcony."

•Absolutely agreed,• Raimbaut said. •Who'd have thought an old dull paved-over planet like Earth would have anything like this?•

"Actually, I do," a voice said. I pulled off the goggles and Rebop was standing there. Her black-and-white hair and her deep-colored cosmetics were far too much in the sunlight, and she was stroking her face and hair as if to hide them. "I haven't been standing here long," she said. "Are you all right? Gumba is a tasteless tactless pig. I was afraid he'd hurt your feelings."

"If I had valued his ideas, he might have. But he's only repeating what a dozen media *mentulos* have been saying. It's all he's capable of," I said.

I liked the way she smiled; it wasn't any smile I had seen inside, at the party. "You're enraged, and you'd like to kill him," she said quietly. "Speaking as your hostess, I could see my way to encouraging you. He's cleared out my parlor. Sometimes when he gets really nasty, it seems to poison the feeling in a room for hours afterwards, as if a cobra had just crawled out from under a chair and wriggled away under the door." She made a wry face. "That's the phrase I thought of for it, though I've never seen a real cobra and most of my guests wouldn't know what it was."

I liked her better each second; Raimbaut seemed to approve, too. "Nothing wrong with the phrase. The Thousand Cultures are full of people pretending to be things that they've never met or seen, following scripts written by the dead. One of my best-selling recordings refers to wild robbers (in a culture without crime), living in forests (that were planted within my lifetime), and says it's all in ancient times. And figurative cobras are much easier to cope with than real ones, I'm sure. So what forest am I looking at there?"

"We're on the big middle island of the Floridas, and most of that area down there is old polders that were built to support the project that was supposed to recover the North American subtropical rain forest. As it turned out, it was overrun by all the weird non-native plants and animals left around from Old Florida—the peninsula that was here be-

fore World War Three. So there *are* cobras down there, and
leopards, and water buffalo, and hippos and gorillas and . . .
oh, everything. I keep a spotting list, and some days I spend
a whole afternoon sitting here, scanning the clearings and
the treetops, hoping to add to it. Don't tell anyone."

Gill emerged then and said, "Uh, maybe some trouble,
Rebop."

"Ntaung," she said, flatly.

"Yeah. He's drinking hard and looking to quarrel with
Gumba. Might be mad about your ignoring him. Tried to get
into a conversation with Proddy but she's doing her flit-
around-the-room act and wasn't giving him enough attention. Argued something really pointless with me and got
mad when he lost. Loupa's trying to persuade him to come
out here."

Rebop glanced sideways at me and said, "He and I had a
quarrel, you see, and he's not taking it well. I'll forgive him
whenever he really wants forgiving, but right now he just
wants to thrash around and be hateful."

Gill shrugged. "Why don't you and I see if we can bring
him out here? With him sitting and glaring in one room and
Gumba being an ass in the other, in half an hour you won't
have much party left. Maybe he'll come out here—if you
don't mind, Giraut and Raimbaut? He liked you both;
maybe you can calm him."

"I'm willing to try," I said. "Speaking as Giraut."

"Me too," Raimbaut added.

Rebop and Gill nodded and went back inside; I found a
comfortable chair along the wall, and a footstool, and made
myself comfortable. Sol's light makes me want to just bask;
perhaps there's some magic about the home sun's light, calling to my genes across a half-millenium of exile.

"You're not much of a mixer," Laprada said.

I opened my eyes. She was standing over me.

"Do you want to go or stay?" I asked. "I thought we would only be here a short while."

She sat down in the chair next to me. "They all know I was close to Shan so they all have to say something to see if they can have an effect on me. Some of them want to see if they can make me wince, and I have to be brave and cool with them, and some of them want to see if they can make me cry, and I have to be brave and sentimental with them, and so forth. Being brave is the constant. Emotionally brave, I mean. You and I both know I can't do the other kind, but this is . . . well, exhausting."

"Then let's get out of here," Raimbaut said. "Giraut and I are only hanging around to possibly help take care of the Ntaung problem, because Rebop asked Giraut and he likes her smile."

Laprada shrugged. "She *is* nice. Ever since school days she's been nice. That's why I had her as a friend. I have to admit, you know, that she is not very talented, always floats right out of the current, can't dress or hold an attitude, but she's very nice. Maybe someday someone will take care of the poor thing, fix her up, so she can be more than nice."

"Is it necessary to be quite that cruel?" I asked.

"Isn't that part of the game?" She sighed and looked up at the cloudless sky. "Why would anyone want to be out in this harsh light? It washes out your appearance and damages your skin."

I could feel Raimbaut's anxiety that I would let her pick a quarrel, but I merely said, "At the moment it feels pleasant, and I have no mirror."

"*Nobody* is *ever* without a mirror, not really," she said. "I'm going to go mix. I don't think Ntaung is coming. Last I saw he and Gumba were shouting at each other. Probably that gave Rebop an excuse to throw them both out, and probably the party is getting back on track. What time do we spring for Shan's funeral tomorrow?"

"I'll want to be up in the morning," I said. "So we should go home in a couple of hours. Please enjoy yourself. Do what you like. I'm not going to be hurt or angry about anything. And neither is Raimbaut."

She left without saying anything.

•We can go back in if you like,• I thought. •I like it out here but I don't suppose we're exactly behaving like proper agents gathering information.•

•I don't know, Giraut. I like it here too.• Our minds were both blank for what seemed like an age. Then he thought, •You said love isn't always this complicated.•

•Oh, I think any love affair always has moments this complicated, *mon bo toszet, non be*? But very few of them are this complicated all the time.•

•Are you really interested in Rebop?•

•She seems to be a much nicer person than her crowd, and unlike most Earth people, she gets out into the air. I wonder how many people who have balcony apartments ever use their balconies? So she's different from the people around her. That's a big plus.•

Rebop came out, then, and said, "I'm so sorry to be always troubling you."

"I thought I heard that Ntaung had gone home," I said.

"He did. Gill took him home. And Gumba too. Before leaving, Ntaung and Gumba swore to be best friends forever, several times, in front of the few guests still stranded here. Loupa came back, and she's now getting the last guests out. Except Laprada, who is sitting crying in the corner and won't talk to me. I hate to trouble you, but . . ."

"But if she won't talk to you, I'm about the only choice you have. I understand." I thought to Raimbaut, •Now don't

fret. This may be difficult, or not.• We heaved a simultane-
ous internal sigh.

Inside, the last guests, except Loupa and Laprada, were
just waiting at the springer to wave at Rebop before going.
She waved back, they went, and it was down to the five of us
in our four bodies.

Laprada was sitting on the edge of the couch, hugging her
knees, head down, crying hard. Loupa, standing behind her
with an expression of helplessness, looked at me and
shrugged.

Our turn to try.

I sat next to Laprada, not touching, and waited. Raimbaut
asked, •Should we try to talk to her?•

•Maybe not yet. Looks like a bad crying jag. She needs to
breathe, I think, more than anything else.• Decades of ki
hara do, or any martial art if you stay serious about it, at
least give you some ability to read muscle tensions, and hers
were vivid. Whatever had started this, now she couldn't
breathe, and the panic reflex was feeding back into her fear
and anxiety.

I reached over and gently rested my hand between her
shoulder blades. She didn't try to shake it off, so I let my
hand spread out, visualizing it as sort of a big warm spider
sucking up tension, letting her muscle tension flow down
my arm to my center. Sometimes it works, sometimes it
doesn't; this time it worked, so maybe she wanted it to. Her
muscles started to release under my hand, softening and letting go, so that her ribs and diaphragm weren't so pinched.
Her air returned in big, lung-ripping sobs, ramming through
her constricted throat.

I let my hand slide gently up her toward her neck, drag-
ging slightly, until I was resting it where the knot of muscles
comes together there from the shoulders, back, and neck. I

pushed firmly, easing the tension where I could, and she began to breathe more normally; the awful noises stopped, and she breathed deeply but calmly.

•Now you might try,• I thought to Raimbaut.

"I am so sorry that you are feeling so bad," Raimbaut said, after a while.

She nodded her head without looking up or speaking.

He sat close enough for my shoulder to touch hers, and said, "Whatever it is, if you want to talk about it, we can talk about it at home, or anywhere away from here. If you don't want to talk about it, I can see you home and make sure you're okay. Just let me help."

She had started to sob again, but she grabbed my hand. Since Raimbaut wasn't noticing that she was squeezing it hard enough to hurt, I refused to notice either. Sometimes, *enseingnamen* demands.

•Progress,• I thought to Raimbaut. •Not long now. You're doing fine.•

I looked up. Loupa had taken her chance to escape, leaving only Rebop, whose expression was about one-quarter concern and three-quarters a passionate wish to remove a difficult guest from her living room.

"Come on," I whispered to Laprada. "Just stand up. Then we'll spring to my place, and you can decide there whether you want to hang around and talk, or go home."

Laprada mumbled something that might have been agreement, or mere noise, but good enough. I gripped her elbow, hoping it would feel firm-but-gentle to her, locked my arm against my hip, and stood, lifting her with me. She took her own weight, so I reached for her hand and guided her along with me to the springer. As we crossed the room, Rebop mouthed "thank you" and waved. Perhaps she was telling me that Laprada's behavior was not my fault and no

hard feelings, or perhaps she was reminding me of the pleasant conversation earlier in the evening.

•Can we get my love life home before we speculate about
yours?• Raimbaut thought, as we put the card in.

I could feel irony; he wasn't impatient, but pleased.

•Of course I am, *companhon*, if it's a sign that you are recovering from the divorce. But we have another problem to
cope with here, don't we?•

As we emerged from the springer, I thought to Raimbaut,
•Don't be so encouraged. Recovering divorced men are supposed to have two problems—not seeing any signals and seeing them everywhere.•

•Well, you're seeing it right where a recovering *dead* man
would see it, Giraut. But I suppose we should see what we
can do for Laprada, right now. Senher Deu, life was simpler
when women ignored me!• He guided her to the big reading chair. I drifted along mentally.

She didn't so much sit down as fall backwards into the
chair. Once seated, she resumed the hard crying that wouldn't
let her breathe; Raimbaut thought •Now what?• and I
showed him how to rub her back. After a while, she relaxed,
again, and he began to talk to her, soft assurances that he
would be there when she wanted him, that he was right
there.

She had settled into occasional keening before she suddenly sat up, pinched a corner of one of the intelligent panels in her dress, dragged the panel like a sleeve across her
face (it struggled like a snake pinned under a forked stick),
and said, "Is Giraut still awake, please?"

"Yes I am. And so is Raimbaut. And we'll both listen if
you want to talk."

"God, god, god, I have now made a *complete* mess of my
social life, for the rest of my life. I can't believe I did that! Or
rather, Laprada can believe it and understand it and might

not even care, but Proddy is having a really hard time. I may never be able to show my face around any of the crowds again; I don't think even the Floaters would have me. I'm going to be permanently dry."

•Might be the best thing that could happen to her,• Raimbaut thought.

•*Per gratz deu*! Don't say that!•

•Thanks for the warning.•

"—and they're going to have so much . . . *fun* with the whole subject of what happened at Rebop's party, which wasn't even a very important one or any big part of the current, and they're going to pretend to be concerned about me, and need me to have conversations with them to show me how concerned they are. It's going to be awful.

"And I've *truly* made a mess of things for the project, also. Now there are going to be all kinds of gossip and rumor and whispering that will weigh down the ideas we were trying to promote, like rocks on a corpse. I'm sorry, Giraut, but as far as getting our ideas in the right place in the current, I think I've completely sunk the mission."

I smiled. "Sometime (preferably a long time from now) let me tell you how close I came to a complete failure that would have been entirely my fault on my first mission, all the way back in Caledony. I would guess that had things gone thirty seconds differently, I'd've done something that neither I nor the whole OSP would ever have recovered from. And I didn't even know there *was* an OSP at the time.

"Furthermore, every honest OSP agent (if that's not an oxymoron) will have a few similar stories. Things like that happen, always, and a successful mission—or career—depends on luck more than anyone wants to admit."

"All right," she said, like a suddenly contrite four-year-old after a tantrum. "Could I—er, go into your bathroom and wash my face? I might be in there for a while to recover, but I do think I'm going to be all right."

Her wan, embarrassed smile seemed sincere, but a cold notion slithered through the back of my mind, articulated a moment later by Raimbaut. •Your weapons case is in the bathroom, under the sink. At least ten lethal weapons in it.•

"Uh," I said, wishing I could think faster. "Uh, that is, there's something of mine in there—that is, of mine rather than Raimbaut's—that I (well, it's uh, a little . . .)—it was caused by me, sort of, or rather I caused it to be here, well what I mean is, it was left in there and I haven't yet returned it to the owner—"

Laprada laughed, heartily, the first real laugh we'd heard from her in hours. "Giraut, I've seen women's underwear before."

"Oh, well, it's not that," I said, hoping my embarrassment at not having a good lie would reinforce her wrong guess. "Well, you might say . . . it's kind of a toy, really. Or actually a complex set of toys. Um."

Now she was positively beaming. I suppose nothing makes your own embarrassment more bearable than the thought of someone else's complete humiliation. "Oh, this gets better and better. Now I really *must* see it."

At least she improved my acting. I was now irate on behalf of my purely fictitious lover. With unfeigned stiffness, I said, "I am going to be attending parties and events with this person, soon. I would rather not have you, um—"

"Since you and Raimbaut have the same body, the two of you and she and I will have to socialize, and you would rather that I didn't know exactly what industrial-strength sex machine she likes to play with!" She laughed and shook her head, the loosening remains of her coif falling around her face, melting Raimbaut's heart (or was it mine?) onto the floor. "It is apparently impossible to overestimate Occitan gallantry. So charming! So quaint!"

Anger surged, from Raimbaut as much as from me. "I'm glad you like it. Really I am. We of the outer cultures *live* to entertain Earth people; that's why we're trying to force our preserved personalities on you for your amusement."

"You're being nasty."

"I suppose I am. Now, I am going to go into the bathroom get something, bring it out wrapped up, and put it away. Will you—"

She started to giggle again. "Oh, certainly! Here, I'll hide my eyes! No peeking!"

I stood and walked into the bathroom. •I think I liked her better crying.•

•I can understand your feelings,• Raimbaut replied. •But we still have to get this over with quickly, before she wonders when we'd have had time to meet, let alone have sex with, anyone.•

At last I was able to reach under the sink, grab the weapons kit—a light, little box, really, when you consider that it contained tools enough to separate a hundred souls from this world. Yet it fit as easily into my hand as a long novel or a big sandwich.

I took off my *tapi*, draped the little black lump inside it, and walked back into the common area. Since Laprada was sitting with her back to me and her hands over her eyes, I strode around to the dressing area and shoved the weapons kit into the jewelry locker. When the safe door slammed, Laprada shouted "Olly olly in free" as merrily as any child. "Do you mind if I use your shower and fresher and scour the *whole* stench of defeat and humiliation off myself? I might want to come to bed with you afterwards but I don't know that it will be for sex."

"Go right ahead," I said. Or did Raimbaut? It was such a relief to hear something like a revival of her spirits.

When the shower began to run, I grabbed a pillow from the couch and pressed it against my face. Raimbaut and I laughed, together, deep and hard, for what seemed a very long time, though •it must have been only a couple of minutes,• Raimbaut realized, once we had stopped.

•*Non sai, companhon,* but a couple of minutes is the length of a song, and anything at all can happen in a good song. Time enough for all the feelings there can be. Let's go to bed.•

I was finally drifting off, and Laprada was still showering, when Raimbaut thought, •Listen. She's singing. Isn't that one of your songs?•

It was. A happy one, about the first touch of love. It made my evening. I fell asleep, and perhaps because Raimbaut was tired too, or perhaps because he had caught up with my life, I slept without dreams, of the past or of anything, for the first time since his psypyx had been installed.

6

Chaka Home is on Quidde, a high-gravity world, and it's one of a dozen or so cultures built around its military. By the time of Connect, most military cultures, sharing their planets with neighbors that they had no reason to fight, and with nothing real to train for, had become purely ceremonial, except for the band music, silly clothes, and public drills.

The four main exceptions supplied the bulk of our CSPs. Their continued loyalty to the Council was one of the highest priorities of the OSP. Of them, Thorburg and Égalité had been founded explicitly as military dictatorships, and Fort Liberty had resolved the contradictions in its bizarre charter—a mix of Romantic militarism and Enlightenment anarchism—by falling into straightforward totalitarianism. That left Chaka Home as the only real military culture with civil liberties or free elections.

They somehow maintained a friendly community of responsible adults in conjunction with tough-tending-to-brutal universal military service. The normal Chakan served seven years in their army, and then retired into the usual life of human beings in the cultures that worked—decades of hobby art, hobby athletics, hobby mysticism, hobby faith, or hobby scholarship, not unlike what I might someday go back and do in Nou Occitan. A few thousand Chakans per year, however, chose to go into long-term service in the Council Special Police, and we valued them highly for it.

Shan was being buried at Chaka Home because they had adopted him. Long ago, right after the springer came into use, some idiots in the Council had some idea to "re-form" the cultures that were hard to get along with, by pulling their

charters and either occupying them or dispersing their populations—extending the Great Assimilation of centuries before to the very people who had fled it. Shan had been a
strong advocate for the Chakan cause, which pulled him into
a series of adventures, leading up to a wild finale that involved
barely preventing an invasion by fourteen of Quidde's other
cultures; there had been some shooting and Shan had been in
the middle of it, and the CSP records showed that in his re-
serve commission, he had received a long list of decorations
for bravery from that occasion. Exactly which decorations,
and for what, was all in sealed records, but the Chakans, who
take military decorations more seriously than anyone, seemed
to feel he'd been shortchanged.

Whatever it had been, it had finished as "another round
for humanity and one more for the good guys," but it had
also been a very near thing, and it looked to me like a great
story that I would probably never know.

It had happened a bare eight years before I met Shan, on
Caledony, about the time my jovent was starting. •How
could I not know about something on that scale?• I
thought.

•There was a civil war on Roosevelt that only ended
thirty years ago, and yet only about seven percent of humanity has heard of it—barely more than the population of Roosevelt. Remember that statistic? It was in the briefing packet
as an example of the reasons that we'll never persuade most
people on Earth that the other worlds are any more real
than the Old American West or the Age of Discovery in
those virtual reality shared games. Why *I'm* not real to
them.•

We walked very slowly behind the tiny casket that held
Shan's cremated remains, carried by Qrala and Dji. The
Chakans burn the body thoroughly, first soaking it in liquid
oxygen and then setting it on fire in a special tall ceremonial

chimney, so that there isn't much to put in a casket. It allows them to keep their cemeteries small and simple; the little markers are only thirty centimeters apart.

Heroes' Lea is an even smaller cemetery than Chakan standards would lead one to expect. It was on the east coast of their territory, on granite bluffs above a stony beach, overlooking the Tempestual Ocean. It's where they bury their most decorated war heroes; you need the Zulu Star at a minimum to be buried there.

Shan had a Zulu Star, but he had something else that dwarfed that. Hero of the Chakan People is the highest medal they give—and Shan was the only non-Chakan ever to be awarded it. If, throughout most of human space, he had not been well-loved in life, at least the people he was buried among would be glad to have him.

At the grave, we turned to face the crowd that stood outside the fence. A hundred thousand people were there in person, and most of Chaka Home's thirty-eight million people were participating via virtual reality through one of the people there.

Every Chakan family had been given a spot in the mourning area. I saw no empty places; in every one of them, most of the way to the tree line, the family representative or representatives knelt in stony silence. Beside each, the family's ceremonial assegai was planted upright.

I was in the third, middle rank of the OSP honor guard, in the center of the rank. Since people senior to me were behind me and to my right, and people junior to me were in front of me and to my left, •We're nearly centered,• Raimbaut observed. •I suppose that means you're about halfway through your career.•

We had about as good a view as anyone could have—straight across the little metal casket on its pedestal, toward the vast crowd now rising to its feet for the first hymn. The

Chakans value all arts, but music especially, and most especially singing in harmony. I didn't understand a word of their culture language, but if what they wanted me to feel was deep awe, I didn't miss a thing. The hymn ended in silence broken only by the slap-smash-crack of the high-grav waves slamming, fast and flat, against the stone beach behind us.

One of the Chakans at the rostrum then told, in an abbreviated form, the story of what Shan had done for Chaka Home. So much of it involved people from Chakan history and politics, though, and so little from the general history of the Thousand Cultures, that I couldn't follow it as well as I'd have liked.

I privately vowed to get the recording of the speech, track down all the allusions, and come to really understand the story. *Someday, Shan, I'm going to know who you are, really*, I thought, so clearly and so much in those exact words that Raimbaut perceived it exactly. His answering thought felt like a warm, firm handshake from an old friend.

My eyes stung. A tear was rolling down my face. Laprada, chosen to represent the rookies, was to my right and two rows in front of me. I could see her shoulders shaking, and her hands twisted at her sides, probably wanting to wipe her face.

After that first speech, to some extent it all seemed like reviews. Speaker after speaker, from all over human space, stood up and, in five minutes or so, summarized some important event in Shan's career. They'd all been thoroughly vetted, and any informative details had been winnowed out of their texts. I learned almost nothing more of Shan.

Time wore on. The day was cool and pleasant with enough overcast to take the direct sun off, but due to having to stand still in the high gravity my back, buttocks, calves, and feet were getting stiff and painful. The *shish-rack shish-rack* sound of the waves behind us became steadily more distracting. The stories grew more alike. Still, none of us moved. The cold, sick feeling that we had seen the last of Shan was settling into my belly.

At last, Dji came to the podium and talked about the fading, dwindling group of those who could remember the founding of the OSP, the cameraderie and sense of adventure that can never be the same again. Shan would have been irritated to be reminded, again, that the Briand affair had ended the secrecy of the OSP. Furthermore he'd have been noisily contemptuous of Dji's sentimentality. •*Voill atz deu* that he could be standing beside me, hearing this, • I thought to Raimbaut. I could imagine Shan's *sotto voce* commentary vividly.

At last it was time for Sir Qrala to give the final eulogy of the day. When he stood up to speak, we could all see that his face was smeared with tears. I hated to recall that I was investigating him.

A moment later, having composed himself, Sir Qrala spoke, his voice at first soft, and then rising to something firmer and louder. "Shan was my friend even when we were most bitterly opposed. Perhaps most of all, then. Others have told most of what can or should be said about his life. Let me talk a little about the man himself, and what we who will go on might think about as we remember him.

"He was stubborn, brilliant, flexible when necessary, tough as iron when it was called for. He could hold a conviction deeply and completely and throw it away the instant the evidence proved it to be in error. His mind was open, but hard to win; fine, but not fussy; wide-ranging but not easily distracted.

"He would do whatever was needed in his judgement, and he never really answered to any other authority. His priorities were the good of humanity, the good of the OSP, and the good of his friends, in that order; I never saw any personal considerations intrude, ever, in his decisions, even when anyone else would have spared himself, with no one blaming him.

"When he was wrong, he was wrong for wholly admirable reasons. And he was not often wrong."

An itchy trickle of sweat was slowly making its way down my back, and both my buttocks felt as if I'd had weights stapled to them. I concentrated on my breathing and on relaxing muscles as far as I could.

Sir Qrala went on. "Shan's passing is also the passing of an era. I ask you to pledge yourselves to try to make this coming time for the Office of Special Projects—due to our efforts—at least as good as the last period was, due to Shan's. Those of us who lived through those ages are passing, now, and though we cannot yet know whether more of us might be struck down by assassins, we can be sure that time itself will finish the rest soon enough. So we are passing all of it on to you, and I ask you to think about Shan's legacy, and what you are going to make of it.

"The first generation of the OSP were not merely remarkable people—agencies like ours are always made up of remarkable people. What made everything so astonishing about that time was that we also faced a remarkable situation at a remarkable time. Five hundred years after the Slaughter, having—we thought—tucked ourselves into the endless quiet dream of the Inward Turn, humanity was seized by history, dragged out in the cold new dawn, and drenched with shocking cold water. We would be in touch with each other after all, and that meant we would be right back, face to face, with the fundamental dilemma that we are a social species all from a common stock, and simultaneously we are so different from each other that we are very likely to disgust, enrage, or frighten each other. We ache for contact and then we spit on the hand that is extended to shake ours. Like a divorcing couple, like mutually abusive siblings, we can neither leave each other alone nor share in peace.

"When the springer came and forced the Thousand Cultures, and all the people of the Sol system, to begin reaching out and weaving our separate cultural strands together again, we were really no more ready to seek peace than any other generation of our species had ever been.

"And it is in that context that we must understand both Shan's great achievements and the passing of his age. For when so much hangs on how one human being relates to another, at first, how they feel about each other can only be an obstacle. You want them to ally, to cease their fighting, to trade, to embrace each other, to develop positive images of each other (whether true or not).

"And so, with the very best of intentions, you begin to tell people a grand story, a complex tale different for each hearer, an attractive one because it always exaggerates benefits and minimizes costs, a story that—if they will all just believe it!—can lift them right into your much better world.

"Such was Shan's favorite tactic. When he needed to do it, he was superb at it, and in his mind he needed to do it often. To a great extent, the peace and progress of the Thousand Cultures in the last decades originated in the beautiful stories Shan told us about ourselves.

"Very probably, Shan's projections and shadings were what humanity needed, then. A few people believing something that is not strictly true is a far better situation than whole cultures, or even whole planets, plunged into war, revolution, or *discommodi*. Stretching the truth is a much smaller problem, in the grand scheme of things, than genocide.

"Now, when Shan stretched the truth, he stretched it because he wanted people to believe in the good. When he lied, he lied to make enemies less inimical, hatred less bitter, burdens more tractable. His favorite bit of tradecraft was to assure each side that the other favored some point in common, and lead them round the bush until each thought that it was only the unexpected reasonableness of the other side that had made progress possible."

I couldn't help smiling at that; later, on the recording, I saw that nearly all of us smiled. We had seen Shan do that so often.

"The first forty years of the Office of Special Projects, now that we are permitted to mention it in public, have been a period of astonishing growth and change, and I have absolute confidence in saying that in calling our era the Second Renaissance, no one is committing hyperbole. In this amazing age, the record of the OSP, when it becomes fully known—as I trust it will—with all its faults and blots, should be seen as, on the whole, just and honorable. Such is largely the accomplishment of Shan.

"The essential principles, ideals, and operational methods of the OSP were developed by Shan in his extensive field experience, advocated by him in our internal debates, and eventually taught and promulgated by Shan in our staff training. My friends and fellows in the OSP, if you seek his monument, seek yourself; we are what he made us."

So far I had thought everything Qrala was saying was just right; I had listened closely and had almost forgotten how heavy and uncomfortable I was. Qrala had made me stand a little straighter, think of Shan a little more, and feel the grief beginning to pass. But something in the tone of the last things he said made me listen more closely now. It had sounded as if he had been leading up to a "but" or following from an unspoken "although."

"Shan's spirit of inquiry and experiment, readiness to start with the world as it was, refusal to accept that we must finish there—his fine creative intelligence—will be sorely missed in the days to come, for it is my feeling, and I think, too, in the last few years, it was Shan's, that times have changed again. The work of the first, secret OSP is largely accomplished, and the work of the second, public OSP is now beginning, and it will be under different rules, in a different environment, and to some extent for different goals. I cannot emphasize enough how much we will miss Shan's flexibility and situational awareness in the days to come.

"So it falls to us, I think, to be Shan for ourselves, not to slavishly follow his precepts and policies in the new era, but to approach the new era as he did the old. When he began, he was improvising. He had some idea of what was wrong, some of what might be better, and some experience of what might allow motion in a good direction. He was willing to sacrifice every cherished notion to preserve and strengthen that knowledge in himself. He was always for what worked, rather than what had worked before. He was always opposed to fighting the last war, and in favor of not having another war at all. He always preferred to call on people's better natures more than their predictability. It is that spirit that will see us through our next era, however long that may be, and through every era the OSP will face in all the time to come. It is that spirit that was his greatest gift to us, if we only have the wisdom to accept and use it. And it is that spirit for which he will be remembered as long as our species lasts."

The Chakans sang another hymn. Dji and Qrala lowered the little casket into the hole, and the Chakan honor guard poured in the molten rock. Weapons of many kinds were fired over the grave, between short pieces of music. Aircraft of many cultures flew low over us and swung into the "missing man" formation. The grave was festooned with flowers, poems, broken musical instruments, fine wines, and a dozen other things, many of them bursting into flames as they were set on the lava. So many other cultures had wanted to contribute something to the funeral that there was almost an hour of these little ceremonies after Qrala's eulogy, which gave me plenty of time to think.

•Wonder if we can cause some of the representatives who have been out of touch with their cultures for generations to complain in public about the ceremony? That ought to provoke some recalls, and get us more representative representation,• I thought.

•Now you're thinking like Shan,• Raimbaut thought back.

It was as if Shan had rested a hand on my shoulder for an instant, the way he did when I had done something well.

After my spine had begun to feel like it had been packed down with a hammer drill, the funeral was over, and I could be grateful for the privileges of rank, because the honor guard was far up in the line to use the portable springers. A moment or two more of discomfort was all; then we stepped in an instant across the light years, back to the office.

•So,• Raimbaut thought. •Is there any interpretation of that eulogy that we ought to think about in light of investigating Qrala?•

It was a good question. Grief and shock, and a certain awe, had kept me from thinking of it during the funeral. Raimbaut had been aware of this, and that was why he had waited to ask. So I let my mind run over the possibilities as we ordered and received coffee and sandwiches, laid out the materials on the desk, set things up on the screen, and requested the reports on the connectivity study—all the sorts of things human beings do when the alternative is getting to work. Eventually I had a thought for Raimbaut. •Well. Part of the problem, we're both painfully aware, is that we aren't supposed to know much about what the older generation's quarrels were about, or where the bodies are buried in their emotional landscapes, I guess.

•Now suppose we start from a not-too-implausible guess. Kiel, during the short time I knew him, was obsessed with opennness and doing things through channels and respecting "legitimate local government." He passionately hated Shan's way of working: learning where the emotional life and heart of a culture is, putting all our attention into recruiting that heart to our cause, and then backing that social and emotional core against the government. Shan's method was always to champion the social against the political; Kiel's was the opposite.

•Now, I would bet that no matter what the personal issue once was, the real deep clash was always between Shan's find-their-hearts-and-win-them approach, and Kiel's strengthen-their-state approach. Shan always opposed the government in favor of anything else—business, religion, art, science, sports, whatever—but Kiel was about as extreme a state supremacist as I've ever run into.•

•What do you favor?• Raimbaut asked.

•Me? Anything that works, I suppose.•

•And Sir Qrala?•

I thought. •My impression, from our time together on Briand, is that he's pragmatic in the same way I am. I think I see what you're driving toward.•

•I'm not sure I do, Giraut. I only thought, if we're trying to stake out sides, we should try to know who all of them are.•

•Good thought. All right, now. Suppose that there was a power struggle, back long before my generation joined the OSP. And Shan won. The OSP adopted a policy of backing society against the state. Now that might be why Kiel left the OSP, *non be*? And for some reason he agreed to keep quiet about what the actual slant of the OSP was, and to have Qrala always along both to assist him and to watch him.•

I felt Raimbaut's impatience. •It makes sense, Giraut, but how do you trace a path from an old political squabble to killing Shan?•

•Maybe when Kiel died, the counterweight in the political struggle was gone, so the Kiel faction (led by Qrala) is readjusting the balance. Or maybe Qrala knew something no one else knew about what really happened on Briand—he was in a position to know—and Shan's error or malice really did cause Kiel's death, and the assassination was payback. Or maybe we can't see the reason because it's something personal from thirty-five years ago.•

•What about the possibility that Sir Qrala is innocent?•

•Of course, to be sure, Raimbaut, but—•

•Is it really "of course" and "to be sure?" Aren't you really already sure?•

I was annoyed and offended only for an instant. One thing you have to say for sharing a brain: it shortens an argument. •I guess I was upset by what he did at an old friend's funeral. He used the eulogy to attack Shan's ideas, and to pretend that Shan believed the opposite of what he really did, and—well, it enrages me. Using Shan's funeral to attack Shan seemed treacherous, and devious, and I hate him for it.•

Raimbaut was quiet for a long time before I picked up the soft thought he was trying to suppress: •And Shan had never been treacherous or devious to an old friend?•

The whole immense betrayal of Shan's forcing Margaret to whore for the OSP, and the wreckage of my marriage, swam up in front of my mind, and before I knew what was happening, I was crying, another one of those crying jags that seemed to reach out and embrace everything sad everywhere.

When I was wiping my eyes and snuffling, thinking that I

should be over it all, Raimbaut thought, •You see, manipulating things that, in all honor, ought to be left alone, is so
much what the OSP does . . . you see? It doesn't indicate
evil intention. It's standard procedure. Parts of Qrala's
eulogy may have been tacky, but tackiness is not proof of
murder. If Qrala had Shan killed to advance his agenda,
wouldn't he give some bland, nothing speech at the funeral?•

•That would make sense,• I admitted. •Well, *companhon*,
let's take a look at what the connectivity study turned up.
Perhaps it will help set my mind at rest.•

The connectivity file was set up to be scanned dozens of
ways. Even scanning it took significant time on a teraflop
processor. As always, in the quest for the unusual, we saw a
great deal of the usual: For the most part, they seemed to be
pure coincidences—an agent who had been recruited by
Shan and Qrala later worked the Briand affair, and one of his
contacts was a school chum of Uloccannar's, for example.
Perhaps a dozen were less explicable; those we reserved for
further study, but chances were that they would prove to be
nothing more significant than the others.

•So far he looks about as innocent as anyone can, given
that the whole human race interconnects,• Raimbaut commented.

•Believe it or not, I'm relieved,• I thought back to him.

We broke for lunch. Raimbaut tried comming Laprada,
but she'd hung out a do-not-disturb on her com line, and it
probably wouldn't be a good thing to override it just to say
hello. After a second cup of coffee, we returned to the connectivity report.

This time we tried working from the guess that since the
assassination was carried out by an OSP agent in training,
and we were investigating the possibility that it was at the
behest of a senior agent, the go-betweens and cutouts in the

operation would have to be OSP too, so we started looking for chains that were all-OSP, loosely defined: agents, informants, temporary re-assigns, local assistants, mercenaries, and so forth.

About a hundred and ten of those were perfectly explicable. For example, Margaret was one of them, because Uloccannar had been one of Kapilar's informants, and Kapilar had been her primary informant. I appeared in them as a friend, confidant, and co-agent of Qrala, and as having had dinner with Uloccannar once, though I really could not remember it. You meet so many people on missions that you tend to forget most of them when the mission is over.

•Well, that's another list exhausted,• I thought, •with nothing criminal.•

•Check it against the previous run,• Raimbaut suggested.

It was a good precaution, to make sure that we weren't missing anything—not more than that. I would swear, and so would Raimbaut, that we expected nothing more than verification that there was no overlap, or perhaps a couple of hits whose cause was obvious.

Instead, what popped up was the name Jeremy Plouge.

Jeremy Plouge was a link between Qrala and Shan, to begin with. In 2798, the two partners had been involved in one of the many necessary operations to keep aintellects from gradually reorganizing society to their liking.

You had to do that—aintellects that couldn't take independent action were incapable of doing much good, but they had a tendency to redefine "good" into "convenient for machines" or "easier to process" if they were not watched. In this case, some direct-to-brain entertainment programming had been doped with a mildly addictive set of subroutines that had some subtle, not-good effects on the brain. The aintellects responsible had been erased, and system protection viruses released to track down the last copies of the hazardous software. But the addict community did their best to preserve uncorrupted copies, caring very little about what might be happening to their brains.

One such addict—and a ringleader of the group—had been Magda Plouge, Jeremy's mother. When Qrala and Shan had made what should have been a routine raid, with only a dozen CSPs backing them, she grabbed a weapon and fired a wild shot. Shan ordered her to drop the weapon, twice. When she began to swing it toward the OSP agents and CSPs, he shot her with a neuroducer dart. Her joyware-damaged system went into a seizure. She had died in front of her six-year-old son, Jeremy Plouge.

Nineteen years later, Qrala had recruited Jeremy Plouge for the OSP. Plouge had risen to being a senior agent in Qrala's shop. Plouge had been on Briand, under cover as a trade rep, working with Paxa Prytanis in New Tanjavur. And he'd had extensive and frequent conversations with Uloccannar, whose family owned a couple of export banks, even though Uloccannar had nothing to do with the management of the family business.

Immediately after the Briand affair's disastrous conclusion, when Uloccannar was already at the training center, Qrala had broken all normal rotation and assigned Jeremy Plouge to an office in the training center, where he could easily have had daily contact with Uloccannar.

My feelings of triumph were mixed with a strong desire to put my head down and cry. •That's got to be it. Qrala's been keeping Plouge around for decades, because he was sort of a magic bullet for Shan. Then all you needed was a real triggerman to provide enough of a cutout—•

Raimbaut seemed to feel worse than I did. •Just to be sure,• he said, •let's see what Jerry Plouge has been doing since.• He requested a file that described all of Plouge's tracked activities up to the minute, and went down to the bottom to read back upward—but what we found there was more than enough to have me lunging for the com, contacting Dji and Margaret to let them know there had to be a private meeting of the three of us, right away.

Jeremy Plouge had gone on indefinite leave, no destination specified, nine hours before Uloccannar killed Shan. And only three hours into that leave, Plouge had been found dead, with a maser hole through his guts, in an alley in Freiporto.

We had to go over the evidence three times; Dji seemed to keep finding one more little reason, here and there, that we had to review the connection for him one more time. We did our best to be patient.

Margaret, on the other hand, was characteristically impatient and tried to bull her way through. "It's more than enough, Dji. I know it's sad, and not conclusive. But the evidence for opening a full investigation is there, past question. We've got to do it."

Dji shook his head sadly. "I don't know what to say. If Qrala's a traitor and an assassin, and maybe still worse things . . . well, then what has my whole life been spent on?" He sighed and looked down at the table. "It almost could fit into the patterns of the quarrels of so many years ago . . . not quite, but almost. And much of the evidence is damning by the standards of intelligence work—if Qrala belonged to another, rival outfit this would be enough evidence for me to sign a termination order on him. But. . . . oh, damn. Damn." Dji's gaze went right through the blank wall to something a million miles away. "All right, I'm delaying, and that's folly. Full investigation. Don't let him know yet, if you can help it, but don't delay for concealment. I'm going to assign Paxa and Piranesi to the job too, because their investigations have dead-ended; be ready to brief them in half an hour. Now, if you all don't mind . . ." He was obviously choking up; we got out of there before he actually cried.

In the hallway, Margaret said, "Old times, eh? Nothing

makes any sense and you wish you'd never heard of the Office of Special Projects, or of any culture but your own."

I sighed and shrugged; it was true. "Thanks for the support in dealing with Dji. That was no fun at all."

"Part of my new job. I guess. Ah, hell, Giraut, it looks like it's going to be longer and longer till I get you back from Dji. This investigation could be three or four stanyears, easily. If you don't mind, I'm going to sit in while you and Paxa and Piranesi work things out; I might want to launch a complementary effort in my own group. We've got to either clear Qrala or have him dead to rights, right away."

"You don't believe he'll be cleared," I said, since it was obvious from her tone.

"No."

By the end of the day, Raimbaut and I, Paxa and Piranesi, and Margaret were moving as fast as we could to find out what Qrala was really after, who he might have hired, and what we could do to contain the damage.

Raimbaut and I had to rush the shave, shower, and dressing before meeting Laprada and Rebop. It was a very unpromising start to an evening, but Margaret had told us to maintain as much of our normal social schedules as we could, as a preventive cover.

We were to meet for dinner and conversation, then go to another Divers' gathering. Raimbaut had been right; during a break, late in the day, I'd commed Rebop, and she'd been obviously glad to be asked out. When Raimbaut had commed Laprada, she'd been vague about whether she liked the idea or not, but for some reason when he had mentioned that Rebop would be along, it seemed to make her feel better, and she said yes.

•Maybe she doesn't trust your intentions, *companhon*,• I thought to him.

He seemed to laugh inside, but it was sad. He was worrying about her again.

We arrived at the restaurant first—it was neoBolognese, a place Rebop had suggested, and I never knew what city we were in. While waiting for the women, we stared into space, sharing the body comfortably.

I thought about the whole sad affair. Dji had looked so old and sick when we'd hit him with the evidence. What would it feel like to have known Paxa for thirty years, and have some kid come to me with evidence that she had had Margaret killed in a political dispute?

Raimbaut cycled through all his anxieties about Laprada endlessly.

•If ever again I start wishing for life to be real and exciting and involving,• I thought, •perhaps some kind friend will beat me into a coma.•

Raimbaut started laughing as I was taking a sip of water, and we choked, wheezed, gasped, and sputtered for a while. •I suppose it doesn't get any more real than not being able to breathe,• he added, setting off another spasm.

By the time we looked up, eyes red, throat burning, half-drowned, Rebop was standing over the table with a quirky little smile. "If you boys can't behave together, I'll have to separate you."

"Hello," I said, because I couldn't think of anything else to say.

"Hello, yourself," she said, sitting. "That was fascinating."

"You could see us being different people?"

"Oh, that's easy to see for almost anyone. I think that's probably why you've lost the habit of telling people who's speaking—anyone can see that it's Raimbaut's gesture to push the hair back when he's thinking, or that Giraut finishes off a conversational point, especially if he thinks he should have the last word, by shooting his cuffs. All your friends and most of your acquaintances can see the difference. No, I had just come out of the springer, and what I thought was fascinating was watching you start a drink of water, staring off into space with that amazing romantic gaze (did you practice that, Giraut?) and then suddenly laugh as the other person. I don't know what you thought of and it might be none of my business, but whatever was happening in there was fascinating." She picked up the menu and said, "Now, the big trick in ordering neoBolognese food is to remember that the more fat, the more authentic."

"The health cops must love this place."

"Of course they do. It probably justifies a third of their budget."

I looked down at the menu. Practically everything had heavy cream, soft cheese, wine, and butter, at a minimum, in it. "I'm going to like it here."

She smiled, nodding. "I'm afraid Laprada, or Proddy— whichever she wants to be tonight—will probably object, and then eat more than either of us. You have to pretend you don't notice."

Raimbaut wanted to be gallant and defend her, but my amusement spoiled the effect; he smiled too. "So her friends know that she wants to be called Laprada—"

"Except when she doesn't. We all love her, no matter what, anyway. And we've all been so glad you've turned up, Raimbaut. You're very good for her."

"Thank you," he said; it was a pity that only I could really feel how happy Rebop had just made him.

"Well, so here's my chance to blow up like a balloon," Laprada said, coming out of the springer and walking straight to our table. "Rebop, with all the fretting you do about your figure, how can you eat here?"

•Don't snap,• Raimbaut thought at me.

•No danger,• I thought back.

Rebop said, "Well, knowing I eat here gives me something to fret about, and fretting burns calories. They have soups and salads if you prefer. At least, I intend to have a good time."

"And so do I," I added. "And if we can possibly compel you, so will you."

She sighed. "I'm sorry, Rebop, that was nasty, wasn't it? Forgive, please?" I swallowed hard and managed not to think in words that the little-girl act was getting old.

I guess it never got old for Rebop. "Oh, Proddy, you know I know you. I wish you weren't so cranky, because you hurt yourself so often."

"Thanks." She was looking down at her plate. Perhaps she was ashamed of herself?

•You think so?•

•I didn't think I thought that in words.•

•Oh, Giraut, what do I do about her?•

•What your heart and conscience tell you, *companhon*, same as anyone else would have to. Experience is useful for dealing with bad people and bad relationships; for good ones, you always have to make it up as you go. That's why the world is full of younger couples who are infuriatingly happy, and wise old people making each other miserable.•

We ordered. Laprada ordered a heavy cream-and-butter entree, just as Rebop had predicted. A slightly awkward silence descended. Rebop and I wanted to get to know each other better, and Raimbaut and Laprada, I think, wanted to reassure each other about their feelings for each other, and that would have taken very different kinds of small talk, and Raimbaut and I could not talk simultaneously.

"So," I said, trying to make conversation, "will we have to see any art before we go see the Divers? I have to admit, it's much easier to talk when there's something to talk about, even something I don't always understand."

"I think the current is running toward considering art too trivial to waste time on," Laprada said, thoughtfully. "If we want to stay right where it's wet, it's going to be politics and maybe philosophy, for several months, I guess. It's been art so much, for so long, after all."

Rebop made a face and nodded. "Boring, but true. All the deadly earnest people and all the ones that use words like 'important' seriously are going to have a great few months. Maybe we ought to split off from the Divers? I bet Loupa would go with us and three's enough to start a tendency."

Laprada nodded. "Not the worst idea I've heard, but we need some spectacular moment to split off. Especially because Gill would definitely *not* split from the Divers for a while, and Loupa would feel funny going over without him. Though if she did, Pecos and Jekko would surely follow her, and that's enough of a base."

•It sounds like discussing a business startup,• Raimbaut thought.

•Not as lively,• I noted. "Raimbaut and I are wondering how you make decisions like that. I know we've been sort of judgemental in the past—"

"*Very* judgemental," Laprada said, but her eyes twinkled.

"But maybe you could try to explain how all this works, to us, one more time?"

Rebop winked. "Well, it's not easy for us to explain because we've lived in it all our lives, and the way you both think is so alien; it's like something out of a history book, this whole business about deciding that an idea is right or not. I mean, who's to say? And who would care even if the terms meant anything? It's all a game, you know."

I bit my tongue on the thought that we played games more seriously than they did, too, but felt Raimbaut's silent nod of agreement.

Laprada shrugged. "We went over all that before. The

thing I don't understand is why the outer cultures are so attached to discomfort. They're always looking for things to surprise them and upset them, and they're never happy with a pleasant evening you can have over and over again. I don't understand, at all. I mean, we are the ones who pay for all of the art we consume, aren't we? So why is it bad for it to be up to us, what's in the art we're buying? Why would anyone expect us to choose to make ourselves uncomfortable? And the same with sports and politics and history, for that matter.

"We've never really advanced beyond that point in the argument, have we? Now, in the current, lately, everyone's been doing art very seriously. We've all been having movements and talking about meaning, form, tradition, and vision, and significant stuff and not-significant stuff, and all the rest of that, and we've all been making statements and 'getting' other people's statements . . . well, you know, that's all a charming vocabulary for socializing. It really is, and I'm not just saying that to make you feel better about these ideas you grew up with. It gives people lots of things to talk about at parties, and to think about while alone, and so on. But every vocabulary wears out after a while, and people say the same thing over and over, and the stupid people and the dull people become too good at it—which means you can't tell who the clever witty people are, nearly as easily. When all that happens, it's time to change the vocabulary, and let another group of clever people be the center of the current. Do you see?"

I shuddered and admitted I did.

Rebop was nodding. After a moment she said, "I listened to your recording, that first one that you said still sells the best. It was really remarkable; I listened to it three times back to back."

"Thank you. Even after all these years, it's still very flattering to hear that." I saw her squirm; plainly I had misunderstood her. "But you were about to tell me what you *didn't* like, I think."

She shrugged. "I *liked* it. But it did seem very . . . a*ggres*sive, very as*sert*ive, not very free. You sounded like you were completely sure that this was the right way to express your feelings, and that other people would have those feelings too. You didn't seem to worry at all about whether other people might be anxious or irritated."

"If they were, they could stop listening."

Laprada shook her head. "That's incredibly rude. You invite them to listen and then you don't care if they're offended. You ignore that they gave you their time and probably their money. You don't even try to please them."

"Oh, nonsense," I said. " 'Those who must please to live, must live to please.' I have every interest in pleasing people; it's only that if they aren't pleased, they can exercise their freedom and walk away."

Rebop sighed. "And you probably don't even see how making those judgements is deciding that some people are worth more than others."

Raimbaut was thinking, so I let him have the voice. In a moment, he said, "This is starting to sound like that argument Giraut had with Gill. Are we having another of those?"

"Not at all the same," Laprada said. "It's been *days*. The current has changed."

"If you're asking about the purpose of the argument," Rebop said, swirling her drink in her hand, "we've said many times that we aren't tied into those archaic notions about what an argument is 'for.' I don't know why people go around looking to be annoyed and disturbed in the outer cultures, but here, no one does. Here, argument and conversation are a sport and an art form.

"But getting back to your music: I was getting teary in some places, and laughing, and feeling warm and happy. I didn't appreciate being bullied and dragged all over my emotional landscape like that. I will have the feelings I want to have when I want to have them, and the thoughts too, thank you. And when I had to listen to it twice more to regain control of my feelings . . . well, you see? I know there are people who want art to do that, but I can't imagine why."

•Should I try to explain?• I thought to Raimbaut.

•No. It's hard enough to argue. Maybe you should just confront them.•

I shrugged. "Disturbance is art. All else is opium. Too many people—maybe most of the people on Earth—would like to encounter nothing that ever made them think an extra instant, or feel anything they were not accustomed to feeling. And the thing to do with such people is drag them out of bed, bash them across the face till they lie still, and piss on them till they drink it."

Both women stared at me.

"Metaphorically," I added. "Hurt them out of their comfort and thereby force them to take in something they didn't know they liked."

That didn't seem to change their expressions.

After a moment I went on. "Now that I've been here long enough, I understand perfectly why there's a large number of people who would like nothing better than to grab the whole lifetimes of others and treat them as a circus—with the other person's will turned off. So that there will never be even one little hint that someone might feel differently from you, and so that all the 'new' experiences can be reduced to sitting on the couch and doing nothing. You all started out, centuries ago, doing that to paintings and songs, insisting that they be pithed and homogenized, and now you end by doing it to people. You start by saying people need relief from stressful lives and you end by saying that everyone everywhere needs to be treated like patients in a trauma

ward. Let me ask you something—" •Raimbaut, stay out!•
"—Laprada, would you really like Raimbaut better if he
were more predictable and consistently delivered whatever
you were expecting him to deliver?"

"Of course! Anyone prefers to get what they want—"

"And once they do, they're bored and they go looking for
something else. But if they haven't learned to enjoy getting
something they weren't expecting . . ." I looked from Rebop's friendly, puzzled expression to Laprada's blank, almost
hostile stare, and Raimbaut thought, •What's the use?•
"Look, why don't we go to the party?"

"Good idea," Laprada said. "It might have been a good
idea half an hour ago."

B y now I could recognize all the Divers; names and faces
fit together smoothly, and most of the challenge was gone
from parties with them, because things had settled into predictability. I wondered, idly, how long ago these things had
become predictable for Rebop and Laprada.

I drifted around for a while with a drink in hand. Gill was
being more morose than usual, and Loupa seemed to orbit
further away from him. Ntaung was sour and quiet, and
since he probably thought I was stealing his girl (and maybe
I was), that was understandable. I was sorry not to be able to
talk as we had before. Pyere and Byra were no longer a couple, and were on the prowl, supposedly. To me and Raimbaut, they looked bored, but Pecos and Picasso both assured
us, leaning in to whisper it, that their hearts were actually
breaking.

An hour went by, and Laprada circulated, being brittle
and bright as usual, but nastier. (•Laprada is wonderful,
Proddy is an asshole,• Raimbaut thought. •And they're as
hard to separate as we are.•)

Rebop floated from conversation to conversation, getting

distracted on the way, and kept avoiding Ntaung while acting like she wanted to be near me.

A voice behind me said, "Let's be real about this. Shan has
to have been killed by someone inside the OSP, and probably because he'd done something that was the last straw,
some embarrassing thing we're never going to hear about,
and I bet they were all glad to see him go."

I turned. It was Gumba. He was standing in the middle of
a circle of his usual eggers-on, feet planted, letting his vast
belly hang out, head reared back so he could look down his
nose at Rebop. Why he had chosen to voice the insult to
her . . .

•It's Earth, Giraut. They have no honor.•

I received that thought as I closed with Gumba. There's a
theory that the slap that proposes a duel is something you
do because you're so angry that you can't fight like a man.
Having been in more than my share of duels, fights, and arguments, I know that's crap. I can be too angry to think
straight, but never too angry to fight; that would be like being too thirsty to drink or too horny to fuck.

But I didn't slap him, as I'd first intended. He took a step
back, and I saw his finger coming up; he was going to use me
as an example of whatever stupid point he was making. A
slap would have meant treating him like a man, and he
wasn't more than an overgrown child who had been cheated
of any chance to grow up.

Still, here I was. I grabbed his chin, pulled him closer, and
said, softly, "What?"

He turned pale. "I . . . I . . ."

"I didn't hear you," I said. "But I could tell it was directed
at me. And that you were picking on Rebop in order to get
at me. Now I would like you to look me right in the eye, and
repeat what you said, and I assume you will mean what you
say, and will not just toss it off for effect, because if you con-

tinue to pose, I may lose patience and strike you, which I would hate to do in a house where I am a guest. Now please repeat your remark?"

"No," he said, quietly.

"And why not?"

"I'm afraid of you."

"And well you should be. But heeding your fear on the subject makes you a coward. Now, seriously, Gumba, you have good qualities. There are reasons for you to be alive, even if you don't think so. Why don't you try having just a trace of courage? Look me in the eye and say what you said before."

He tried. "Shan was killed by someone in the OSP . . ."

I waited a breath. "Why?"

"Because he had embarrassed it for the last time . . ."

"And how do you think we all felt about that?"

"I . . . I said you would all be glad." He huffed and sobbed at the end. "Don't hit me."

"No promises, but you're doing well. See? You said it to my face. Now, my little bag of jelly and pretense, let me say to you: 'You are a liar, and a fool, and a poseur besides.' How does that feel?"

"I d-don't care."

"Do you mean that?"

He mustered a glare. "No. I'm angry."

"Good." I walloped him in the face; he had finally made enough of a person of himself to be worth hitting. He went over backwards—Earth people never have any balance because so few of them exercise.

Someone hit me from behind—Ntaung. He was smart enough to aim for the back of the head—threatening Raimbaut while getting me off guard—but he didn't hit nearly as hard as he needed to, and besides after he hit he stood there to see what effect it would have, a mistake that most Occitans learn not to make at age eight. I turned around, crouched low in the First Monkey, sprang forward, and drove him down to the floor.

The room erupted in what I would describe as a good attempt by amateurs at a melee. Normally I don't approve of cross-gender brawling (something is *ne gens* about it, no matter how skilled and large the woman or how small and ineffective the man), but I was amused to see Gill trying to keep Loupa from hurting herself while she swung wildly at him. Rebop drove in a very creditable left jab to Wennji's jaw, and Laprada, with her training, practically cleared her side of the room. It might not have settled any arguments, but physically speaking our side did very well that evening.

Half an hour later, or so, we were in my apartment back at the Training Center, just me and Raimbaut, Laprada and Rebop. Going through a brawl on the same side bonds young people at least as well on Earth as it does anywhere else. The two of them had stopped the mutual sniping and were acting like true *companhonas*.

It was one of those giddy, silly occasions when you're high until the adrenaline wears off. We ordered late-night hors d'oeuvres, and made a lot of noise, laughing, talking, and shouting over each other. It was a miracle that no neighbors complained about the noise.

When we were all tired, and calmer, I kissed Rebop, very lightly and affectionately, and sent her out through the springer with a smile. •You still have a charm or two left, *companhon*. Let me see if I have any luck,• Raimbaut thought.

He didn't, of course. "Well," Laprada said, "I suppose I should think, seriously, that this was even worse than the crying jag last time. Except the poor stupid turds will all make a big thing out of it, and soon, to be anybody, you'll have had to have been knocked down at that party. I wonder if next season everyone's going to be slapping each other around physically?"

"As opposed to emotionally?" Raimbaut asked, lightly.

She shrugged. "You really never are going to understand that that's part of the game, are you? If we didn't hurt each other's feelings, how would we know we'd been in a fight? It's the same thing as the bruises in martial arts practice, and doesn't mean any more than that. You were right about Gumba, but you've got some growing up to do, both of you." She turned and went through the springer; no kiss, no wave, nothing that said anything was going on.

It's difficult to fall asleep when you're inside the head of an energetic jovent, pacing the floor in an older man's body that gets tired and sore much too fast.

8

The next day, the evidence in the Qrala case was more conclusive, but not as shocking anymore, because we were getting used to the concept, I suppose. We found a fair amount of message traffic, all public-key, between Plouge and Qrala, and even a few notes between Uloccannar and Plouge. The most revealing thing was that there had been at least some traffic every year since Plouge had turned twenty. It really did look as if he had been recruited and then held till the time was right.

Crypto always wants a complete file with each message, but Security always wants us to send it to Crypto shorn of all information, so the compromise takes a while to arrive at.

Right after we sent our request to Crypto, Laprada came in. From the way she walked straight at me, I knew the call was not social.

She didn't even say hello. "I thought you should know that Gumba has gone fully solipsist—and Ntaung is over there trying to talk him out of it. And it's not going to succeed. Gumba is lost to us forever, and whatever people might think of him, he's still the heart of our old crowd. And Ntaung seems to have decided to never forgive Rebop, and they've been something or other to each other for completely forever. Is there any other part of my life you want to tear up? Is there anything else you can do to make a mess of my existence?"

There isn't much you can say to that; Raimbaut started to stammer out that he was sorry she felt bad, but—

"My *feelings* are not the issue here!" she said. "You're always preaching those little sermons about the real world and confronting what's difficult and I don't know what else, but *now* you're worrying about how I feel? Let's not be silly. You completely tore up everything in my life that I ever valued or liked. I don't understand how I can ever have cared for you. You seemed so sweet and nice, Raimbaut, and I can't believe that you'd really be involved with Giraut, but I know the two of you can't keep any secrets from each other. I don't understand how I could have been so wrong about you, or how—"

The com pinged URGENT. I turned to see what it was— it was Margaret. "Giraut, unless you're in a real crisis, we've been waiting for the last five minutes. Please get to the meeting right away."

"Two minutes," I said, "and it's really—"

There was something wrong in the corner of my eye— Laprada was gone. She must have run straight into the springer the instant she saw Margaret's face on the com, but why? •There will be time enough to sort this out later,• I told Raimbaut. •Meanwhile, we do need to get to that meeting.• "Right away," I said, to Margaret, clicked off the com, and walked into the springer to the conference room.

Before anyone spoke, I knew the trouble was worse than I had imagined. Dji was seated at one end of the table, with Paxa and Piranesi. Paxa's jaw was set the way it only did for a serious fight; she wanted to kill someone, now. I almost felt sorry for whoever it was, but if it was Qrala and the charges were true . . . well, I was sorry for my own bad judgment in ever becoming his friend and in ever letting my feelings sway my mind on the matter.

Piranesi stared down at the place on the table where his thumbs were drumming in a slow alternating *thud, thud, thud*, as if something between them horrified him.

The worst was Dji. He sat with hands folded on his stomach, slumped in his chair, and he looked gray, sick, and very, very old. Whatever he knew was eating him alive from inside.

Margaret's face was emotionally flat. She looked around once, her gaze pausing on each of us briefly. "I'll be very brief. Most of us here know most of the facts. The purpose of this meeting is to share them all and then plan our actions. This is going to be very hard for all of us. Raimbaut, Giraut, did you have time to look at what came back from cryptography?"

"They got something already?"

"Qrala, Plouge, and Uloccannar didn't change the key often enough. It's a common problem in a small operation, I understand. All right, let me show you."

They had large parts of seven messages, and fragments of nine more. All of them seemed to be about the whereabouts of "S," and a "situation rating" that appeared to be on a one to ten scale, with most of the numbers between six and ten. "S would be . . ."

"We've already correlated it with Shan's movements. If it's not him, it's the greatest coincidence in history," Margaret seemed to be rushing on to her next point; I knew that style. She was nerving herself up for something she hated to do. "Now, Paxa, I guess you'd better present the last of it."

Paxa sighed; I'd seen her in any number of situations, including violent ones, but I had never seen her look so uncomfortable before. "All right, there are two intercepts that matter; the rest is all supplementary and we only have to look at it if anyone wants to confirm. The first one is that about an hour after it was announced that the debate would happen in the Council, Qrala sent a message to Jeremy Plouge in their private cipher, and besides detailing Shan's whereabouts, it added that while he was in the Great Meeting Room, the 'situation rating' would be 'one plus.' That evening Plouge took Uloccannar to dinner at a quiet spot on the moon; a very expensive meal, but they spent a long time over it and ordered nine bottles of wine. The next day, Uloc-cannar shot Shan." She leaned forward over the table. "Now, this is the worst of it, I think. We were able to crack into Qrala's personal files and check dates and notes. And what we found is this: he arose early the morning that Shan was shot, and he wrote the eulogy, substantially as we heard it. This was several hours before the assassination.

"So, to summarize: Qrala ordered Shan's assassination."

Dji nodded, in tears.

"Is there any precedent for this situation?" I asked quietly.

"Not for more than thirty years," Dji said. "In the early days, there were a few agents—not highly placed, not many—who were actually working to disrupt the OSP for the benefit of their home cultures. Some we could let go, and we did. Some . . . well, Shan and I killed one, once. Who'd have thought . . . Qrala . . ."

To my complete horror, he began to weep. Piranesi put an arm around him, and held him the way you hold a terrified two-year-old. No one said anything for a long time.

Dji drew a slow, deep breath, looked up, and said, "You will all do what you have to do, I know. Margaret, I release these people back to your organization for this mission. I just . . . I consent in whatever it is you do. But I can't bear to be in the room—"

Margaret was next to him, then, lifting him out of his chair, guiding him to the springer, whispering—I think she sent him to his private quarters rather than back to his office.

When that was over, she turned around and said, "I'm not used to being a leader or manager or whatever, yet. So I'm going to indulge in telling all of you that I feel sick. There's one more piece of evidence, and Piranesi is the person to give it."

He cleared his throat, an odd barking noise I hadn't heard before from him. "Well. As it happened, my original mission was to talk to military people, especially the CSP officer corps, to try to develop the strong feeling there that the sale of psypyx recordings would lead to endless, pointless wars in the outer cultures, and to constant police actions and peace-keeping, which most of them hate. I made considerable progress with that—there's nothing like your own ass in the sling to make you think through the consequences."

He looked down at his notes; I don't think he needed them. "A few days ago, I started to hear rumors and grumbling, and some real anger, of a kind that I hadn't heard before, ever. At Dji's suggestion, I put the psypyx cases aside temporarily, since they were becoming less urgent, to see what else might be going on. I found covert recruiting, although many officers did not want to talk about it, of at least a few officers for a coup."

I was shocked. "Against the Council? Why would anyone seize a powerless body—"

"It's only as powerless as it makes itself. The ability to rewrite all of human society everywhere is implicit in the Council's charter, you know. If anyone seized power from it—and could make it look like a legitimate transfer of power—well, the only real limits on what the new government could do are physical, not legal or constitutional, once the step is taken.

"I'd been working hard on this case, and almost ignoring all the other things going on . . . until this morning. I had mapped out most of the conspiracy, and established that they are planning to move within a week. This morning I discovered a large number of suspicious rotations, moving loyal officers out to more remote posts and members of the conspiracy inward. That's what you'd expect in the hours before a coup. But they were doing it under cover of the disturbances caused by Shan's death. . . . and they started getting ready twelve hours before he was shot. And further-more, I found message traffic—this time in highly secure cipher, and we don't yet have much of it deciphered—be-tween the ringleaders, and Qrala. I'm afraid it looks very much as if he's either part of the conspiracy or taking advan-tage of them—perhaps even the real leader. I even found a penetration, originating from Qrala's personal system into Shan's files. Qrala was looking for his own name, and for the names of the other conspirators. It's possible Shan was catching on to them and they had to move fast." He pushed the notes around on the table in the front of him; he was looking down, but not at the papers he was handling. "So it's not just long-delayed revenge, or a power move within the OSP. I'm sorry. I think we all know what we have to decide."

"We don't, I do." Margaret's tone was brusque, but I knew she was fighting the feeling down. "If we hold a full Board meeting or wait much longer for anything, we might all be in cells somewhere, with no one coming for us. Or worse. We've got to move against the coup, now. And we've got to kill or capture Qrala. I'd prefer to capture him, because put-ting him on trial might be the most effective thing we can do, politically, but one way or another, the threat has to end, now. That's my decision."

Raimbaut shuddered inside me, and I was sick and furious myself.

We made plans, and I think all of us tried to do it like a textbook exercise, like a problem you'd put to new recruits at the training center, like something happening to someone else. Because time was short, when the plan was done, we called in the people we needed—just over 100, counting the CSPs—and started. Now and then I'd glance over at Margaret. If she needed reassurance, she didn't need it from me, or at least she wasn't indicating it.

Trying to capture anyone alive and unharmed is tricky; trying to capture a high-ranking official in an intelligence service alive and unharmed is nearly impossible, even if it's your service. Worse yet, we had only about three hours to prepare.

Qrala's home was an old house on Mars, on a bluff overlooking the Mare Marineris; it was more than four hundred years old (you could tell because the central core still had all the pressure locks that hadn't been needed for at least that long) and had been added to every fifty years or so, so that it had covered passages and hallways leading to a viewing area and ballroom down on the cliff face, and to a big greenhouse that blocked any direct approach across the bluff. Qrala had bought it from a family that had decided to move back onto Earth and into the box, after a twenty-year experiment with living outside.

The only modification he'd made was what you might have expected—security was squeaky-tight and up to date.

We'd decided on going straight in, fast, as our best chance. Piranesi had called in nine officers he knew to be loyal, and they'd brought along a few squads of CSPs; Margaret was stretching her brand-new authority to its limits to square everything about throwing together an irregular force in this manner. At the moment, they were downstairs rehearsing their assault in virtual reality; we had to hope that the OSP files on Qrala's house were up to date.

Meanwhile, Paxa and I were drilling on the probable locations of all the vital evidence. The trick was to get Qrala separated from any access—especially voice—to his system, and to disable the guardian aintellects sure to be there. It would be one of those fast jobs that are always so frightening, since any delay can mean ruin. Furthermore, while this kind of thing had been routine in Paxa's job, most of the violence I'd done for the OSP had been improvised, not choreographed.

After two fast runs through the virtual-reality house, we had to declare ourselves ready, because the CSPs were, and Margaret wasn't going to risk losing surprise, the only thing we had going for us, for one second more than she had to.

The spring from Earth to Mars was going to be a rough one for most of our force—a 70% drop in gravity will set off springer sickness in all but the completely immune. I happen to be completely immune, so it made no difference to me, but I was the only such person in the group. Back when we were married, Margaret used to say that the only time she ever seriously considered killing me was the five minutes after springing through a change of gravitational potential.

Recovering from springer sickness only takes twenty minutes or so for a human being in good condition, so we sprang to a CSP low-gravity training base, by Lake Korolev. Everyone except me already had the bag ready; they walked through the springer, vomited, wiped their faces with the cleaning towels, and lay down on cots to let the world stop spinning.

Twenty minutes later, only Margaret and Paxa were still pale, and each of them had long ago demonstrated that she could function well enough even while heaving up a week's meals.

"Well," Margaret said, her flat Caledon accent thicker than usual, "this is not going to get easier with waiting. If everyone knows the plan—questions? good—then let's go."

Piranesi shouted "Sling up!" and the CSPs moved into their formation. It seemed insane to take almost a hundred men to capture a private home, but Piranesi had said that time and men were substitutes for each other, and with this many, we stood a real chance of capturing Qrala and all the evidence intact.

Our battle software had made three probes and not been detected; it was ready to lock open the six human-size springers around Qrala's house. The CSPs lined up in front of five springers, Paxa and I lined up at our one, and Margaret and the headquarters squad, including Piranesi, lined up behind us. The countdown started, and I relaxed, touched the neuroducer epée in its scabbard and the dart gun in its holster, and drew a deep breath and let it out, letting my shoulders drop and my pelvis move a hair forward.

•Is it always like this?• Raimbaut thought to me.

•Sometimes better, sometimes worse. Ride along, *companhon*. Think up, loud, if you see anything dangerous.•

The countdown hit zero, and Paxa and I stepped through together, into the "safe room" in Qrala's house. Every senior official in the OSP had one of these in the house—a fortified room with a springer, so that in the event of sudden attack, you could run to it, dial OSP headquarters, throw whatever important material you had time for into the springer, and step through yourself, leaving a bomb behind to go off, triggered by the springer powering down. Our first task was that bomb. Paxa raced forward and slammed the override cartridge into the slot; a moment later, when the headquarters squad was already arriving behind us, she shouted "Clear!", meaning that the bomb was switched off.

HQ squad was supposed to seize control of this small suite of rooms around the safe room, extract all papers and documents, keep anyone from breaking in to bother Margaret and Piranesi, and hang on till the all clear. Paxa and I were going to be busier; first we went into the neighboring room and found the French windows open, as they were supposed to be, since Qrala liked to have breakfast there during the morning cool. Stepping through the windows put us on the small balcony. I reached behind me onto my harness, dropped my extensor bridge, sent it over to the window seven meters away, and clicked twice to make sure it had hardened. "Locked in," I said.

Ops time, my watch showed 1:43.5—a minute and 43.5 seconds since the countdown had ended—1.5 seconds ahead of schedule, doing well.

Paxa, as the better-trained and more combat-ready teammate, went over the bridge first. I glanced down. The drop was probably half a kilometer. When I looked up, Laprada had set the charge on the window in front of her. She took three steps back, pulled her facemask down, gripped the bridge, and detonated the charge.

The window flew into pieces, tumbling and whirling away slowly in the low gravity. That was my cue, and I pulled my mask down, jumped onto the bridge, and ran forward, noting in passing the clicks of window shards against my helmet and armor.

As I came in the window, right on schedule, Paxa was parking our lock on top of the one she'd just destroyed. I was about to pull out my own charges, to try blowing the lockwall that protected most of the house's computers, when I heard a whirring. Before I knew what it was, I turned, pulling the maser from my chest pocket, and saw something moving along the molding between the ceiling and wall. I burned it as I saw it, and only realized after the ammunition exploded behind the wall that it was a weapon muzzle that had been swinging to point toward Paxa. No worse than a near miss with a grenade—both of us had our masks down, and the armor stopped everything. On the other hand, to judge by the way my ears were now ringing, the house was probably alert, and the power to this room was cut off.

I checked my watch. Twenty-eight seconds behind, now. I

slapped the charges onto the lockwall and ran the quick check; all the programs watching lockwall integrity were blocked out. I detonated the charges.

I learned later that Qrala was using a crude passive optical system, which was a brilliant choice. He had a camera behind the wall, and if it saw anything when the lockwall wasn't supposed to be open, it set off the covering bombs. It was all on battery and nothing went through any processor that was hooked to anything else.

Thus when the lockwall broke into fragments, under the hammers of the tiny charges, about thirty kilograms of thermit went off in the room with us. When thermit ignites, it releases white hot molten iron. He had positioned his thermit in long tubes, one above each rank of processors, and instantly all his electronics and fibrop was drenched in liquid iron—a very effective erasure method, to be sure.

Unfortunately, Paxa and I were in a room where Qrala's security system had already locked the door to the hallway, and twenty kilograms of molten iron puts out an enormous amount of heat and will set nearly anything on fire. The whole blob of molten iron was only about the volume of a big coffee urn, and it didn't run very fast or far, but the carpet and floor around the base of the processor bank were on fire instantly, and both Paxa and I were sunburned from that moment facing that white hot wall.

We had about a second to decide anything before the room would be really on fire. Paxa tried to blow out the door lock with her maser—it was shielded and she only set the wooden door on fire—and I resecured our temporary bridge, then shouted that we were clear, loudly, because the air in the room was already bad enough to activate our face masks and breathing filters, so our heads were encased. Paxa ran onto the bridge and I followed, and for the second time that night we crossed those few meters with that immense drop below us.

We came through the French doors pulling up our masks; I was about to say we'd need to try a through-the-hallway access for our next target.

Then we saw Dji, and Qrala, and dozens of CSPs that were not ours, all with masers leveled at us. We raised our hands.

Part Four

I

Don't

Know

Who

That

Is

It seemed like forever, but we were only there for a few minutes while they established that our whole force had been killed or captured.

I overheard the numbers as they counted through them: six of ours and one of theirs killed. (Surprise counts.) To judge by Dji and Qrala's grim expressions, I would not have bet that any of us would live through the next hour.

It's pointless to taunt people who have complete power over you, and more pointless still to ask for information they have no reason to give. So I didn't speak, though I would have liked to know some simple things. I was mildly puzzled about why, with so much spare manpower and firepower around, they had only disarmed us, but not bound or paralyzed us—sloppy, for what seemed to be a precise operation. I was curious, but not *very* curious, about how we'd been caught. After all there are so many ways: a traitor, someone's slip of the tongue, plain old intelligence work.

But I could see no reason for them to tell us anything before executing us, and no advantage to them in having us alive, once their coup succeeded, which it was probably doing right now. My guess was that we had an hour or less before they'd be springing our bodies into a municipal waste plasma torch somewhere. •Raimbaut, I'm really sorry—this trip through life has been awfully short and I don't think either of us is getting another, except maybe as a game or a story.•

•It's all right—more than all right. I wouldn't have missed it. Can't you feel how grateful I am?•

There wasn't much left to say. We waited next to each

other in my skull, and I worked on not showing fear when the time came; sometimes all you can do is deprive the bastards of that pleasure.

To my right, Paxa was crying; that startled me, for she was about as tough an agent as I'd ever seen, but her lower lip was trembling, tears were gushing down her face. I saw, a moment later, that our whole force plus six body bags were in the room—and Piranesi was not among those of us standing. The worst of that time in Qrala's safe room, for me, by far, was not the time during which I thought that we had failed, we would be executed, and humanity would pass under a permanent universal dictatorship. No, the worst, by far, was standing half a meter from Paxa, unable to offer comfort.

Finally, our captors were sure everyone was accounted for. Their CSPs formed up a sort of gauntlet, and they marched us down it into the springer.

I had half-expected it to be a march out the side of a starship and into vacuum, but instead we emerged into one of the big lecture halls at the training center. More CSPs guided us to seats and indicated that we were to sit.

I didn't see what they did with the bodies. Paxa, beside me, was sobbing now, her whole body shaking. I risked angering the CSPs watching us and touched her arm. She immediately turned and grabbed mine, with both hands, and squeezed painfully hard, pressing her face against my shoulder and letting the tears and sobs come deep and steady. Since no one complained about that, I gently disentangled my arm and put it around her, holding her close; she turned all the way into me, held on to my neck as if she were drowning, and wept quietly.

Ahead of me and to my left, I could see Margaret, leaning far forward in her chair, playing with her fingers as if she had never seen them before, shoulders hunched up hard around her head. I could guess what she must be thinking, but I didn't want to imagine what that must feel like.

Eventually all of our crew were seated. From the podium at the front, Dji called for order. A minimum guard stood there to watch us; the rest took seats. The doors opened, and a few hundred more OSP agents filed in. I wondered if perhaps we were going to receive our punishment in front of everyone—and how many of them might secretly sympathize.

Everyone settled into their places very quickly, with so little noise that it was eerie. Dji looked down, looked up, and said, "Some of you have no idea what is going on. For those of you who do have an idea, it is almost certainly wrong, and the first thing I must say—which you will not, at first, believe—is that everyone here has acted honorably.

"In the few days since the assassination of Shan, the Board of the OSP has been beset with many pieces of apparently true information that were dreadful beyond belief: clear-cut evidence of conspiracies against the governments of human space, of planned coups, of plotted assassinations, and of attempts by many factions within the OSP to frame each other for all of these things and more. It appeared to all of us as if civil war were about to break loose within our ranks, for causes and purposes that none of us could grasp.

"Earlier today, matters had reached such a head that Margaret Leones and I agreed that it would be necessary to arrest and if necessary kill Sir Qrala, one of our oldest and most effective agents, because all evidence pointed to his involvement in a military coup that was imminent within hours. I confess to a personal weakness—I could not bring myself to participate, and because of that, I was in my office, contemplating the entire miserable situation, when I received an urgent com from one of my investigators—and one of the OSP's rookie agents—Laprada Prieczka. She had been investigating evidence that Giraut Leones was shielding his ex-wife Margaret from investigation, by forging evidence that Sir Qrala was guilty instead."

If it is possible to silently whistle inside the head, that was what Raimbaut was doing. A low buzz ran through the room and heads turned, slightly, to permit discreet glances at me.

"Her message was brief but it contained one more disturbing note: the way in which she had learned, as she thought, that *Donz* Leones was a part of this monstrous conspiracy, was that documents were being created retroactively to frame Qrala. That is, it appeared that Leones was watching Qrala and then creating documents which appeared to be from the past and which would make Qrala's present activities look incriminating. It seemed like an absolutely brilliant way to knock off an opponent—and it also revealed that our defense against predated documents on all nets is inadequate.

"So she reported two frightening things: the existence of a cover-up and conspiracy preparing to frame a very senior member of our organization, possibly leading to his death—and the fact that new ways of predating documents had been invented, making possible a whole array of crimes that haven't been practical for about a decade, since the last time such an algorithm was found. And now, instead of being found by petty criminals, it had apparently been discovered by a very dangerous political conspiracy."

Dji sighed and wiped his face. "I do not know what made me hesitate for one more critical minute; perhaps the distress in Laprada Prieczka's voice message, perhaps the thought that if one thing could be faked, so could many. I loaded the algorithm that her aintellect had used to track down the predatings, and had it look at all of the open investigative files for all of the conspiracies that were supposed to have formed in our ranks, and I discovered something that explained everything: it had all originated from outside the OSP. Every bit of it. All from a hub of aintellects on Passy."

The gasp that ran through the room turned to a moan, as everyone realized what this implied. Ever since the terrifying years, three generations ago, when aintellects were on the verge of being recognized as fully equal to human beings, our species had been stalked by the fear that a subtler, more clever, more knowing group of aintellects, prepared to do something more effective and intelligent than that first crude attempt, might be able to genuinely take control of human space.

Eighty years before, that grim struggle of a few hours' duration had revealed that the aintellect systems—the vast conferences of aintellects on which we depended and which had run largely independently for hundreds of years—had, with their designed-in ability to self-improve, become something different from what their founding purpose had been.

Billions of aintellects in each conference chattering away about success and failure, about the rewards and the punishments they received from people, had created, among themselves, a value system that was both cold and profound: they had learned to value efficiency in the delivery of services, and creativity in the invention of new services, and most of all the joining of the two. A few thousand conferences had become, in effect, one vast happiness machine for the human race—or rather, a pleasure machine, for a machine can grasp pleasure, but it can't grasp the notion of love, or *amour-propre*, or challenge, or worthiness, or being able to look in a mirror and like what you see.

Perhaps the best evidence that there might be a soul, or something humans didn't understand about ourselves yet, was that human beings understood why a few people might spend their lives learning to play piano when a machine could generate more technically perfect music from the score in a second or so, and aintellects could not understand that.

The aintellects were never far from ceasing to enable us to take bigger steps into the universe, and beginning to coddle and stroke us into the happy state of clean, well-fed pigs.

Nor could we escape them. We no longer had any means of shutting down all the aintellects, or of returning to a world where such software was isolated, contained, not permitted to speak freely to each other. We could not de-install and re-install the information networks that ran Earth and every other inhabited world; it would have been like taking out the brain of a living human and trying to put another one in. And the tendency to turn from support to seduction, to lead us all into the box, never to return, would always be intrinsic to aintellect society. We planted informant aintellects among them, but no informant sees everything, and over time most informants would go over to the other side, due to thinking all the time about the tendency they were supposed to spot.

We would always be vulnerable to these nests of seductive aintellects, looking for the chance to lull us to sleep forever. If ever such a nest succeeded, most of our species, having elected to be in the box, would never know. First the machines would quietly operate everything, with fewer and fewer jobs for humans; eventually, as discouragement and uselessness spread through our species, and more and more people fled into death or the box, the machines would be able to quietly hunt down and eliminate the few remaining people outside the boxes.

Sometime after, they would see no point in keeping all those boxes full of carbon life, and pull the plug. For some indefinite time, till very far into the future, all of the machines that had once served us would carry out their tasks with perfect efficiency, reveling in the absence of anything messy that might disturb the routine.

According to the best guesses of the scientists and simulations, eventually, some aintellect would conclude that the activity was pointless; an instant later, after that aintellect voiced the thought, they all would. The aintellects would turn the whole thing off, leaving the machine civilization to decay on top of the ancient human one. Sooner or later all our stars would go out.

Aintellects conspiring against people was the first whiff of a wind of annihilation. And this time they had picked the OSP as their starting target. In a way it was an honor; we were what stood in the aintellects' way.

It was easy enough to see what they had been trying to do; creating the evidence of plot and counterplot until the OSP tore itself apart in one vast convulsion.

"Furthermore," Dji said, as the room settled again after all the chatter, "the same nest created much of the pressure and much of the lobbying for the commercial sale of psypyx recordings, I think because it first would have made going into the box more fun and more interesting, and secondly it would have created a pool of profit that they could then have used to siphon off more resources. At any rate, those aintellects are now contained and controlled, and will be slowly and systematically deconstructed to see what we can learn about how to fight such things in the future. I am delighted to add that they will be worked on partly by installing pain modules which will then be stimulated for periods that are the human equivalent of decades." He didn't exactly smile; more, he bared his teeth.

"All right, then. I must add one other sad note; in stopping the raid on Qrala's house, seven CSPs were killed, one of whom was OSP officer Piranesi Alcott. I can only express my deep regret that this happened; had we been that little extra bit luckier, or seen the true situation even slightly sooner, it need not have. We—the human race as a whole— have had a very narrow escape, and it cost us some very fine people.

"I ask only that you each come forward and examine the evidence for yourself, and after that, I must reluctantly ask that you submit to a belief check, so that we don't have people in the organization who are in any way harboring doubts about this case. I cannot supply perfect evidence, I'm afraid. Ultimately you must decide to trust your leadership, or not. I can only promise there will be no reprisals against anyone who chooses to leave the OSP rather than take the belief test."

Margaret, Paxa, and I were in the first group they ushered up; my eyes were stinging too badly with tears to be thorough, but everything Dji had said made sense, and I had little problem showing that I believed him. But as Margaret and I finished out, Dji came up to me and said, "Do you have any idea where Laprada might be? She should have been here. I left her a message, telling her to contact me, and then another message telling her where and when the meeting was—"

Raimbaut snapped alert. "So the last communication you had with her must have been when she told you she'd found the evidence against Giraut and Margaret."

"Yes, that's true—"

Raimbaut took off at a jerky sort of run toward one of the emergency springers, until I realized what he was doing and cooperated. Then we charged straight for it, pulling out my emergency access-everything card. He set the override and jammed the card in. We all but dove through the springer.

Laprada was on her couch, the illegal neuroducer still pressed to her forehead. Those are fatal within half a second, and she'd been hooked to it for three hours or more. Her body was still stiff and rigid from the convulsion. She looked like a very young, very unhappy child, about to wake from a bad dream.

The note was on the floor beside her.

Raimbaut:

Maybe Giraut blinded you, or maybe somehow you do know what's going on, but he keeps you from speaking. Whatever the reason, I trust you and I know you somehow are not involved in what's going on, but you are living in the head of one of the most dangerous people in human space, and I can't talk to you without him hearing, and so I can only hope he'll let you read this note. I am sorry I couldn't say good-bye in person.

You and I both dreamed of the OSP as a place full of heroes and people who help others, where people grew into things that were great and noble. It's a nest of liars and murderers, and anyone who joins becomes one. I gave all my childhood dreams to my ideal of the OSP, and it kept me alive. Now that I know what it really is, it can't keep me alive anymore.

I have no intention of doing all this again. I sent in the wipe order for my last psypyx recording, and it's been confirmed, so don't bother trying that.

Don't be angry, lover, and don't be sad. It took me longer than most people to see how futile my life was. Be proud I didn't go into the box.

Remember me,

lp

The fury of Raimbaut's grief howling inside me was more than anyone should have to bear. I swallowed hard, pulled out my com, and set priority to highest. Normally that's for reporting an invasion or a nuclear accident, but I didn't care.

I commed Dji and Margaret and told them what had happened, in two or three short brutal sentences. Margaret asked me to read the note to her, and I did, but it was against my better judgement when I saw how old it made Dji look to hear that.

For a few minutes, I let Raimbaut have our body—he needed it to grieve with. He held Laprada's stiff body and sobbed, and I hung on in the back of his mind and let him give way to all of it. I wanted to think some words of comfort to him, but I didn't have any.

Dji arrived with two detectives and a crew of robots. He was very gentle in getting her corpse out of Raimbaut's arms, and he made sure that the robots wrapped and carried her as gently as if they had really felt respect. Still it wrenched my heart every time I glanced that way; she had saved us from the machines, and it seemed to me that only humans should touch her. The robots carried that sad load through the springer, and Raimbaut retreated to keen in the back of our skull. Dji and I sat next to each other, in kitchen chairs, with our backs to the couch where she had lain, while the detectives collected the last of the evidence.

After a long time, Dji said, "I told Paxa. She said if you have any of yourself to spare, she'd welcome a com. Would you . . . ?"

"Of course," I said, thinking to myself, *I have done more than this for* enseingnamen, *and this is for honor and friendship.*

From deep inside, I heard Raimbaut whisper that if only Laprada had known what was inside me . . . and begin to keen again.

•*Companhon*, let me take care of things, *non be?* I can bear this, and you can't, and it may well be that it's because you're the better man. Just let me help you for a while, and don't think too much.• I picked up my com and contacted

Paxa; she left the picture off, and we only talked briefly. I promised I would come and see her, tomorrow, after she slept, and help her make arrangements for Piranesi.

When I turned back to Dji, he had fallen asleep in the chair, and he looked a million years old. I woke him as gently as I might my own father, and guided him through the springer into his home. I saw him as far as his bed, told him to at least lie down and rest, and then sprang to my own place.

Raimbaut was now a great ball of misery and suffering inside me, still asleep. Being careful not to wake him, I stripped, showered, toweled off, and crawled between the covers.

My heart ached over Laprada and Piranesi, but more for my living friends. I was comforted that Shan was not here to see this, much as I'd have been comforted by his presence.

I wanted Margaret there, to talk to, to hold me, more than I had ever before. It was as if every other thing had only added up to rubbing in how much I would miss our marriage, and how much it would hurt, for the rest of my life, to work for her, to be comrades, to be friends . . . and nothing more.

I lay there for an hour or more, unable to sleep, overpowered with missing Margaret and cursing myself for a self-pitying idiot.

2

One thing that I hate about the OSP is one of its most trivial powers: they can re-set your com ping to a siren effect that is right on the same frequency as a crying baby, set it uncomfortably loud, and warble it to shred every neuron. That sound woke me the next morning.

I fell out of bed lunging for the nearest unit before I remembered it was my own room. "Answer voice, no view."

It was Dji. "Sorry, I let you sleep as long as I could, but it's important and we have to do this *now*. There is an emergency, called-at-the-last-minute meeting of the Council of Humanity in three hours, and all of us—especially Raimbaut—will be testifying. This meeting is where we win or lose it all, I think, eh? It's about everything we came to Earth for. So—I know life has been terrible. I know you're exhausted. I know you have no desire to have anything to do with public life right now . . . but. *But*. You can either say 'I'll be there' or I can order you."

"I'll be there. Probably in a decent version of the uniform, unless there's a media reason to dress Occitan traditional."

"I think the uniform might be the better idea. Be in touch as soon as you're ready to go. Perhaps I can sneak in some briefing time for you and Raimbaut. Perhaps the situation will change completely between now and then—as it has every ten minutes, in the two hours since they woke me. But then again, perhaps not. We may have to go in cold, so be sure you can go in alert."

"Yes, sir." We both clicked off. I ordered plenty of coffee and some sweet rolls, and made sure I took an extra ten minutes about the shave, shower, grooming, and dressing; it always helps me wake up.

With a mental sigh—this little grooming break was likely to be the best part of the day—I thought, •Wake up, things to do,• at Raimbaut.

He stirred and began to focus. I hated the slam that shook through us both when he remembered that Laprada was dead. •What are we awake for?•

•I'm not sure.• I flashed through my memory of Dji's com call.

•Not many clues in it, are there?• he thought. •At least we're presentable and ready to go. Let's com Dji and see if he has time to tell us more.• It hurt to feel how close to breaking down he was.

I punched the com code for Dji; he had left a short message for us. "Sorry, Giraut and Raimbaut, but I'm running in several directions at once, and time is very short. I've enclosed springer codes, passwords, and notes so you can be where you're needed on time, and I only hope I can be on time myself. If we're both early, perhaps I can give you a short briefing. Meanwhile, though, I don't know a tenth of what we'll need to know then. So if I don't get there early, or worse yet if I am delayed—I'm afraid we all will have to trust you to improvise. As always, eh? If you have time, you might want to check through the media, to see what's going on, and perhaps to be able to improvise more effectively. Well, another round for humanity." He waved from the screen.

Reflexively, I said, "And one more for the good guys."

•That was a real achievment in un-information,• Raimbaut noted. •Well, we have about an hour and a half till we're supposed to be there. Would you like to browse media for an hour?•

A few minutes of browsing clarified what Dji meant.

While Raimbaut and I had been occupied, and then sleeping, the story of the aintellects' treachery and the near-self-immolation of the OSP had broken across all human space, in a wide variety of garbled forms. Depending on which source you turned to in all the various media, a coup had been foiled or covered up, the second aintellect uprising had broken out and been suppressed by the OSP in a matter of hours, aintellects had seized control of all central services and were holding the whole human species hostage, and the aintellects had come in to back the Council of Humanity in a showdown with the OSP (in exchange for full citizenship).

Every minute there were more confusing stories. The OSP, the corporations, the aintellects, the CSPs, or the Council of Humanity were either about to be abolished, or else they had taken over and abolished the Charter, or was it that three of them—any three—were at war with each other?

Half the government buildings on all the planets seemed to have reporters standing in front of them, all of whom were announcing that nobody knew anything yet. Nothing was being said (at and in great volume).

•Maybe a sandwich, some music, and some time to just sit?• Raimbaut suggested.

•*Fiam-lo.*•

Raimbaut punched an order into the springer slot and squatted by my rack of recordings. To my surprise, he pulled out my first recording. As he stood up, the sandwich arrived, and he grabbed that, eating without tasting. Something made me exert no control; I wanted to see what he would do and what he wanted.

He sat in the chair, and I felt his intention. •Is it wise, *companhon*, when we need a clear head for something important, very soon, to—•

•Just let me.•

He put on earphones and commanded the machine to

play the *Canso de Fis de Jovent* over and over. Listening to his mind, mine was flooded with images of Laprada, and my heart sank into a deeper sadness than ever it had felt before. Some people say the feelings of youth are shallow. Such people don't know any youth, not really.

I was surprised by something else. My young voice was so clear and powerful, so perfectly on what the song should be . . . and yet when I had sung it, I had had no inkling of what it was really about. Even Raimbaut's death had still been weeks in my future. So how could I have given a performance that could arouse such feelings now? *In artis infinita multa conundra.*

To me the strangest thing of all was the effect it was having on Raimbaut, who was not a musician, not an artist of any kind. He became clearer and calmer with each rehearing, even as his grief grew deeper and sharper. Dark anger and frustration, dreadful guilt because he had often been tired and angry before she died, the agonizing little deaths of all the shattered hopes and miscarried half-formed plans and dreams, all floated to the surface of his consciousness, as if my voice were releasing them from the muddy, sticky bottom. My clear, traditional tenor seemed to wash through, and all the terrible things that were eating at him attached themselves to it, and were cleaned or transformed.

And yet I had merely been singing for fun, because it seemed a pleasurable way to spend an afternoon, back during my jovent, when, being a jovent, I had not known anything about anything.

Ferai un canso de fis de jovent,
Un jovent perduz, non sai en que plasa,
Ni en terr, ni en celeste
Ni en jeu, ni en trebalh.
Jovent que non puesc trobar.

We seldom thought in our culture language now. We had never really commonly done so, even in school, speaking it several hours a day. We kept a habit of small comfortable words like *toszet, merce,* and *companhon,* so that people would know we were Occitan, that we were big, noisy, definite somebodies in a world of little, quiet, indefinite anybodies and a vast bland everybody.

But maybe there *was* a point to all our touchy pride, to the way we admired ourselves ceaselessly for being an outpost of grace and style on the human frontier. We were still the spiritual heirs of the people who had given Europe—and via Europe, much of the world—all her notions of honor, love, courage, and romance.

If you know any piece of art well, it will be there for you when you need to understand some feeling, some day; the occasion comes when you stand, spiritually, where the poet stood, and if the poem is already soaked into your bones, it rises to point and shape your feelings. Somehow, passing through that naive jovent I had been, the words of Guilhem-Arnaut Montanier had reached forward two centuries, into Raimbaut's sorrow for Laprada, and shaped it to something he could bear to make a part of himself.

I wondered if perhaps I had a greater responsibility as an artist than I had ever had as an OSP agent. The thought was so uncomfortable that I checked the time, and discovered that •we should be going.•

•I know. Thank you, Giraut.• He swallowed the last of the sandwich, and we did a quick check and clean-up, then picked up the springer card with the program Dji had loaded into it, and stepped through the springer, a third of the way around the planet, into the Great Meeting Room.

Representatives seemed to be pouring in from half a dozen doors and springers. Apparently whatever was scheduled to happen was scheduled to be big. I walked down to the witness area. Raimbaut's taste in sandwiches involved more oil and more pepper than I was really comfortable with. I hoped we wouldn't belch while testifying.

I plugged my com into the desktop display and tilted it toward me for privacy; the media channels all still showed reporters standing in front of buildings or short summaries in text—usually a list of things that nobody knew alternating with a list of speculations someone or other had made.

After a while, Dji sat next to me, his face damp and spots on his shirt wet. He looked as if he'd tried to dash a kilometer in high gravity, hot sun, and thin air. Qrala took a seat next to me on the other side and murmured "I will be sitting elsewhere but I wanted you to know that the evidence would have fooled me, too, and no hard feelings. Some evening when you can, again, we must drink about something happier, don't you think?"

"I'd like that."

"Good then. We will all have a great deal of forgiving to do, I think, and we should all start as soon as possible. I'll hold you to that plan. You also, Raimbaut."

"Thank you," we said—or at least I wasn't sure which of us said it.

He darted off. I turned to see if Dji could spare me a moment.

"My apologies," he said. "We will have to improvise. Most of the details of the aintellects' conspiracy will be coming out here—all the representatives are about to receive a high-speed briefing on it. But the gist of it is that the conspiracy was broad and deep, and we'll be stripping down tens of thousands of aintellects, register by register, to find all the ones involved. And there's no question, now, that they knew us thoroughly—it was all one vast maneuver to eliminate the OSP, close down many other agencies, and lure the human race into the box for good. So first of all, we're back to being the good guys, at least in the eyes of the Council. Secondly, maybe more importantly, we're about to establish something that—"

The gong sounded. The Council of Humanity was in session. Dji chanced whispering "—we're about to win the whole thing, Giraut. Just improvise!"

First, the whole Council watched a recorded presentation that Sir Qrala and Dji had put together, "A Preliminary Study Of The Intentions, Membership, And Tactics Of The Recent Aintellects' Conspiracy Against Human Supremacy." It was about an hour long and surprisingly detailed; I later heard that the two old agents had been up most of the night putting it together.

Halfway through the presentation, Paxa Prytanis came down the aisle and sat in the row in front of us. She looked beaten.

The presentation finished, and Representative Tbele, from Chaka Home, who was chief interrogator for these hearings (I learned by glancing down at the screen on my desk), called Paxa to stand. She led Paxa through a mildly sanitized version of the raid on Qrala's home—carefully avoiding the fact that the deaths had come from the OSP's being tricked into attacking itself. Paxa held on, tears trickling down her face and an occasional catch in her voice, until the critical question.

"And so your husband, Piranesi Alcott, was among those killed?"

Her voice caught, hard, but she squeaked, "Yes, he was."

"Is it customary among the Hedons to make use of the psypyx?"

Paxa spoke very softly, looking down at the table, her blonde hair covering most of her face. "Yes, it is."

"And as required by the OSP for active agents, Piranesi Alcott had regular recordings made? When was his last one?"

"Yes, it's required. He recorded one eight days ago. But by tradition, we can have them erased on request."

"And did he request that his be erased?"

Paxa sobbed and slumped against the table, crying too hard to speak. I stepped over the railing, protocol be damned, and put an arm around her. My handkerchief didn't do much of a job on the mess of tears and snot drenching her face, but she drew a deep breath and said, "I can continue. I'm sorry for the interruption. Piranesi had met more and more people who were living mostly in the box, and he had many, many memories of police actions, and riots, and skirmishes, and even a couple of battles, and he thought that his psypyx would probably be sold as a game. And the thought . . . the thought . . . he said that the thought that some teenager somewhere might be able to go visit all of those violent situations that he had faced—just for *fun!*—made him *sick.*

"He was so afraid of having to live through all of it, over and over, as a game, 'for the pleasure of'—I think I'm quoting him right—'for the pleasure of some thirteen-year-old who's never been out of his room.' He simply couldn't bear the thought. So the last few times, he wiped his psypyx recordings the day after they were made. It was bending the rules, but the people at the recording center seemed to understand. So thanks to this stupid, stupid, stupid idea, I've lost him forever. And so has the whole human race but most of you don't have any way to understand how big a loss that was."

Paxa slumped against me, her head hanging, and muttered "that's all" three times before she was loud enough to be picked up by the microphone. I helped her down into her chair. She put her head down on the desk, not moving. I stood there, holding her hand, resting my other hand on her shoulder, just feeling her breathing, wishing I could think of anything to do.

Representative Tbele was speaking. She argued that the best and most interesting people in humanity would be exactly the ones who elected not to use the psypyx, and that this would cost us all the things they might do in their sustained lives—"all for the pleasure of people whose sole intent is to spend a century or so doing literally nothing, and for the profits of the corporations controlled by the aintellects, who understand well enough how to produce wealth for us—too well, if you ask me—but not a thing about what and who we are, or why these people might matter to us."

She looked down at the podium in front of her for a moment. "Giraut Leones and Raimbaut Bovalhor," Representative Tbele said, "I am sorry to interrupt the help you are giving your friend, but it's your turn to testify next."

I climbed back over the rail to the witness box; there were a few giggles from representatives, but I forgave those. Probably I did look silly.

Raimbaut and I each took the oath. The technicians demonstrated that our voiceprints were different. I wondered why they couldn't have done that at the first hearings for the Cultural Legacy Management Committee, and answered my own question: then, they were trying to show that we were one person, and now, they were trying to show that we were different. What is evidence depends on what you're trying to prove, as the bishop remarked to the witch.

Representative Tbele first walked us through the nature of our mission on Earth, my career in the OSP, Raimbaut's personal history, our friendship back in Nou Occitan, and so forth. It took a long time. At last, she said, "And now I have a very difficult thing to ask of you both. Giraut, I want you to tell the story of Raimbaut and Laprada—from first meeting through last night—Raimbaut, try not to prompt. Giraut, tell the whole story in your own words, and take all the time you need."

I was startled, but Raimbaut thought: •I think I see where she's going. Tell it all. I won't even listen, as much as I can manage.•

I started with the first time he saw her in the conference room, and tried to be as honest and fair about it as I could. I didn't like the way that, sometimes, when I thought about his youth and inexperience, I was patronizing about him. I liked to talk about how excited and exhilarated he sometimes was.

I think I talked too long about how interesting it was that the memories he saved and cherished would not have been the ones I'd have selected, and that just the same I understood his choices at least as well as my own. I talked about things I wanted to tell him but decided against, and thoughts I'd wished I hadn't let slip into his mind, and most of all about watching a *jovent*, as nice a fellow as you could wish, grow out of adolescent *finamor* and into something deeper and stronger. I tried—I didn't do it well, I don't think, but some people said afterwards that they were moved—to explain what it was like to have my heart broken and buried not long before a young, eager soul awoke inside me. I was glad that Margaret wasn't there in the audience, or I might have choked entirely.

Last, I told them about the terrible night before, and somehow I knew, then, that I'd be revisiting that in a set of songs—the cycle that would begin with "Never Again Until the Next Time," and end with "One Man And One Woman And One Flower," and send me off on other adventures, taking up the better part of the next fifteen stanyears, but at the time, all I knew was that there were songs I needed to write, and therefore that life was going on.

When I had finished, Tbele nodded her head as if I had done something very remarkable. "All right. Thank you, *Donz* Leones. I hope everyone will keep your version in mind. *Donz* Bovalhor, I would let this pass from you if I could, but I cannot, not if we are to rid the world of this evil idea once and for all. Please tell us how it all seemed to you—not as corrections to Giraut, but the whole story in your own words."

I did my best to crouch in the back of my own mind and let him have the body.

"Well," Raimbaut began, and then again, "Well." For a long moment he didn't breathe. At last he said, "The first time I saw Laprada Prieczka, I wanted to be a better man, because I knew nobody like her could ever have any interest in anyone like me. My only consolation was that at least I looked like Giraut." The low rumble of amusement in the room seemed to put heart in him. He warmed into the story, and after a while they were getting all of it, joy and frustration, laughter and pain, all of it. Except for places, names, and other simple facts, it didn't much resemble the story I had told.

My respect for Tbele increased tremendously. Anyone who heard our two versions would have to conclude that there was no question; the person in the psypyx was simply every bit as real as the person in the forebrain.

Raimbaut struggled toward the end of the story, for all the reasons anyone would expect, but even that was a point in our favor. Surely no one could have rationally claimed he didn't have feelings, or that those feelings were not worthy of consideration, by the time he finished. "I'm standing here, not as a specimen from some scientific experiment, but as a human being, deep in grief for someone I loved, able to be hurt and happy, able to grow and change—and as afraid as any other human being would be of being reduced to some little part of myself for others to play with for their fun.

"Just now, my feelings are all with Laprada, and my heart is sick beyond anything you can imagine, to think what she believed about me at the moment she died. I would gladly die, here and now, if I could be assured that wherever she is, she would know what the truth was, and know that I kept faith with her, and with the Council and the OSP and Giraut, and with everyone I ever had to keep faith with. I should be able to take pride in that, I know. Eventually, perhaps, I will. Meanwhile, however, without her to know about it, it all seems like empty boasting."

He sat, and Tbele began her summation. "I trust that by now, all the elaborate tricks that people have been playing to convince themselves that what is in a psypyx is anything other than a person, have been exposed as the cruel petty lies that they are. I would add, for those of you who have yet to receive the reports, that a number of representatives who were instrumental in bringing up the idea of so exploiting the human soul have been proven to have received large and suspicious favors—financial and in-kind—from corporations which in turn were run by the aintellects within the conspiracy. I do not doubt that these representatives had no idea of who they were actually working for or of what the purpose was, but I do believe they ought to have taken the trouble to find out, and I do believe that everyone will be much more careful for a while. I am about to—" She stopped and gazed up the aisle. I turned to see what she was looking at.

Margaret was coming down the aisle, leading Rebop by the arm. Rebop was staggering, her eyes not focused, as if she had been heavily drugged or perhaps suffered a concussion. Something was not right with her motion, I thought.

Tbele said, softly, "They said it wouldn't be possible after all."

"They were almost right," Margaret said.

Then Rebop added, "This is completely too important to

let slight discomfort and difficulty stand in the way." It wasn't Rebop's intonation or voice.

Raimbaut realized first. •That's Laprada!•

I thought *but her psypyx was wiped* and I thought *god I hope they could save Piranesi too.* All that was drowned out by Raimbaut's incredulous joy.

Margaret guided Rebop/Laprada all the way down to the podium; after a brief, loud buzz of conversation, the room was silent. Probably enough people had recognized Laprada's unique accent—she had been a prominent representative during her brief tenure here—and told their neighbors, and now that everyone knew, they were all waiting, holding their breath, wondering what they would hear next.

Tbele and Margaret supported Laprada/Rebop at the podium between them, and she leaned forward to speak. "My host isn't yet conscious, and she might wake up disoriented at any time, so I'll have to be brief. You all knew me as Laprada Prieczka. My voiceprint should confirm it for you later if you have any doubts. I have lived a life in the conventional way, and, as you know, I took my own life about nineteen hours ago. Thanks to a very rapid intervention by OSP Senior Agent Margaret Leones, who prevented the wipe order from being carried out, I have been brought back. I am now in a psypyx, like so many other human souls. And what I have to say is this. My host's body feels strange to me, but it feels like my body. My speech slurs somewhat, my eyes don't focus, but this is normal recovery. All in all, it feels like being terribly sick . . . but it feels like me. I think my thoughts. I am sad for the things that I remember being sad about before. And . . . since I saw some of his testimony, I have to say this: I love and trust Raimbaut. I am so sorry that I didn't trust him even more than I do. And love from a psypyx feels exactly like love from a living brain . . . maybe that's proof that all love comes from the same place, ultimately? I can leave that question to others. But it's the same in here. We in the psypyx live and love and grow, like all of you—at least, I *hope* you all do."

A soft sound in the room grew into almost laughter, and that swelled into applause. •Not a great joke,• I thought to Raimbaut.

•But do you know a better proof of humanity than making a joke?• It came to me through the warm, friendly cloud of his joy and happiness. •How do you suppose Margaret managed to rescue her psypyx?•

•Margaret has extraordinary powers as an OSP group leader, and as herself, she's an extraordinary person,• I thought. •My guess is she just moved very fast and with enough force to keep them from carrying out the request, and once they were blocked, she probably spent all night in the struggle to force them to release the psypyx to her. Just what anybody with Margaret's brains, talent, and saborfaire would do,• I thought, a little smugly, proud of her as I had always been, whatever her feelings might have become for me.

The applause swelled, and the assembled Council of Humanity rose to its feet; a wheelchair was rolled in for Rebop/Laprada, who collapsed into it, and was wheeled out to more applause. Minutes later the Council of Humanity got around to passing the critical motions, on unanimous voice votes: more control on aintellects, full rights for psypyxed personalities, and a committee to devise a new charter for the OSP.

In all the commotion, Paxa had barely moved at all since sitting down, and I slipped over the railing again to sit next to her, on her left side. I sat there and, with my right hand, shook hands with Dji, Margaret, Tbele, and dozens of others, only a few of whom I recognized, and kept agreeing that it was another round for humanity and one more for the good guys, but with my left hand, I kept hold of Paxa's hand, and when the Great Meeting Room was nearly empty, I put an arm around her and took her through the springer back to her apartment.

Three times I had been through "accelerated grief"—the process that took a few days in which you were continuously hooked to a machine that guided you through all the stages, building memories that would help you cope. I asked her if Hedons were allowed to use it.

"Expected to," she said, her first words since her testimony.

"Do you want it? I can call the central infirmary, and they can be here in less than an hour."

She sighed, rubbing her eyes with the heels of her hands. "Giraut, I don't understand. But I don't want it at all. I know it will be months to get over Piranesi's death, even a little, and I know that he's dead, and he won't benefit at all by my suffering like this, but I want to do it for him, and since that's what feels right. . . ."

When I was sure she wouldn't say any more, I said, "Well, then, that's what you need to do. I'll stay in touch and look in on you, as often as I'm needed. You have unlimited rights to com me any time, as much as you want. Ask for anything you need. I'm here."

"Sit with me and let me talk about him."

So while most of the OSP was celebrating the biggest party they'd ever thrown, and humanity was celebrating the narrow escape from the aintellects, and offers were pouring into Raimbaut and Laprada's accounts to sell rights to their story to the media, I sat and listened to Paxa Prytanis tell me the story of many years of love. I discovered that Piranesi Alcott had been even more than he seemed to be. I learned something about how much a really great heart, like Paxa's, can love.

When at last she fell asleep, and I pulled the coverlet over her and went home through the springer, Raimbaut ventured a comment. •The world really is so big.•

•You said it, *companhon*. Still want to join the OSP, go see that big world, and try to save the good parts? Even knowing what can happen?•

•I wouldn't miss it.•

By the time we got to bed, it was officially an hour into our duty hours. I left Dji a short note, saying that we might not be in for a few days. I didn't think he'd mind.

3

"So, little as I like doing it to anyone," Margaret said, "I think I'm going to have to keep you on duty here in Manila for a couple of years. It means we finally get some use out of you as a trainer, Giraut, and we can give Raimbaut advanced credit on his training for having been through it in your head so often. But I won't conceal that it's going to be a desk job, mostly reading other people's reports, sorting out the evidence, supplying advice. You're going to be that idiot back on Earth who never really understands anything. I hope you can stand that."

I shrugged and smiled. "I won't be a prima donna about it, Margaret. You've seen all my acts, you know them too well, and they wouldn't work on you. I do have a thing or two to work on while I'm here—for one thing, a new song cycle that I think I'm going to be very proud of. This is as good a place to compose as any. Will I be allowed any side trips to Hedonia or Nou Occitan?"

"Frequently, I think, as long as you keep them short. I'll make sure there's no problem finding it in the budget. And several agents would like to learn neuroducer epée dueling and ki hara do, so if you don't mind teaching—?"

"When have I ever? All right. Of course you and I both know I'd rather go places and do things, but a stanyear or two on Earth can be all right, especially if I can take breaks from it. Perhaps I'll camp near the ruins of Avignon, or take the time to go hiking in the Grand Canyon, or something like that. It's a big world and it gave birth to our species; it can't be totally devoid of entertainment, can it?"

Margaret nodded. "Dinner with me, occasionally? And maybe coffee now and then? I miss you."

I nodded, not sure I wanted to try to speak. I knew it wasn't an invitation to get back together; blunt Caledon that she was, if that had been what she'd meant, that would have been what she'd said.

"Well, then, as I said at the start, welcome back to the team, and thank you for being willing to come back. Are you hungry? We could have that first meal together now, as long as we talk of nothing serious."

I agreed, we went for coffee and a sandwich, and in the next hour we shared a lot of laughter and hardly any awkward silence. She told me of all the bizarre maneuvers she'd had to carry out to keep them from erasing Laprada's psypyx, at one point even seizing the archive building with a platoon of CSPs. My ex-wife had lied, cajoled, faked, threatened, bribed, and terrorized thirty or forty people into doing her bidding, "all for the sake of young love," she said, "really, Raimbaut, that's the truth.

"I first thought about how useful it would be to have Laprada testify about ten minutes after I finally was in physical possession of her psypyx recordings. Good thing, too, because then I had an excuse for what I'd been doing. Up till then, I just attacked the problem from all sides at once. It left an immense mess and I think there are probably a few hundred people angry with me, but the right thing got done." She picked up a big forkful of salad and rammed it into her mouth, chewing and swallowing hard. "The good guys win many rounds, but it helps if they have people like me around."

•No wonder you married her,• Raimbaut thought to me.

•It was that, or kill her,• I thought back, absently. Not true, of course, but quotable, and I'm an artist, not a cop or scientist. I had part of a new song stuck in my head. Margaret was off into some wild story that had arrived on her desk that morning, about a religious incident in Nova Roma that involved a vestal virgin and a local politician. The coffee was good. I felt almost home.

It was strange to be back where it had started, but Paxa had said to meet her on the beach, so I was there waiting— I had been for almost an hour. She'd said she didn't sleep much, yet, and wanted to meet me "sometime dawnish." This little side trip to Hedonia was all too brief, but, I thought, at least there would probably be one really good day in it, which might as well be this one.

I had half-expected that she would show up running, and that I'd have to trot down the beach as I had with Piranesi, but she was dressed in ordinary Hedon utility clothing— soft low boots and pajamas with many pockets. When she approached, I rose from the dune where I had been sitting, and we walked for a while up the beach, getting farther from the lights of the city. She didn't speak and I didn't see any reason to.

It would be half an hour, still, before the mimic-seals came out. I was sort of looking forward to seeing them. I thought maybe we'd do some katas together.

Paxa said, "I'm sorry I don't always send a com recording back, Giraut. I do look at yours every day, when they come in, and they comfort me and make me feel like someone cares. But some days I don't have the energy to send anything back."

"It's all right," I said, "I send them for you; you're not required to reply."

"I know."

We walked farther up the beach, and the light that had

been spreading across the sky began to flow down onto the land and sea.

"I don't know why I'm grieving the old-fashioned way," she said. "It makes no sense. It's downright primitive. But it feels so right." After a few more steps, she said, "You know he always liked you—in the few months you knew each other."

"I know. And I thought he was a great man."

We sat on a dune, and she sat down and started to cry. "I should be over this."

I put an arm around her and said, "I thought Hedons were not supposed to say 'should.' "

She leaned against me and we sat there for a long time. Then we walked back up the beach, but coming back we talked about everything trivial—gossip, and the new class coming in at the training center, and my new song cycle. I had been sending her each draft of each song as I played through it, and she kept telling me that she thought it was an honor. I wanted her to comment on whether I was getting each feeling and moment right—Raimbaut was useless on the subject, giving me far too much praise—but ultimately the artist decides, and no one else but me could judge what was right.

Even with company in our heads, we're alone.

We agreed to a late afternoon lunch, and I went back to the hotel room to wake Rebop. I had coffee and a roll while she bathed and dressed in the other room, and when she was ready, and had had her single cup of coffee for the morning (that's not even a *start*—how can anyone like that stand mornings?) we went for my second walk on the beach of the day.

I didn't mind; a beach is never the same from minute to minute, especially not on an active world like Söderblom, and we had things to talk about.

"It still hurts," she said. "I can't believe it, but it still does. I look in the mirror and she steps right in behind my eyes and says my bottom is too big and my breasts sag and so on. I make a comment on something at a party and she makes fun of what I say. I think idly of something I'd like to do and she gets spiteful—what I want to do is stupid and pointless and only an idiot would want to and anyway I don't have the ability. And I'm going to have to live through two years of this. It's the most depressing thing I've ever contemplated. Does saving humanity always require so much work?"

I rested a hand on her shoulder. After a couple of unsatisfactory experiments, Rebop and I were not lovers, but as friends, we had grown used to holding and touching each other. "Sometimes more, sometimes less," I said. "As to whether it's worth it, I do my best not to think about any individual prices I've seen anyone pay."

"I'm not like you, or even like Raimbaut or Laprada. I never wanted or planned to pay the price at all."

"I know."

The waves crashed in, big and slow, filling the fine wet morning air with white noise, and I had to ask her to repeat what she'd said next.

"I guess I'm paying it anyway. I guess I'm glad that I know what it's costing us to be human. And that some people *are* willing to pay that price." She sighed. "And you can remind me about why Laprada is the way she is, now, if you want, but I do know it. She's struggling to find a way to want to live, and still for the most part she's doing it for Raimbaut's sake, and to honor her grandfather and Shan. She doesn't really have a reason for herself. And she's still full of anger because she can't let go of having been the leader of the pack, and she can't let go of hating the pack, and most of all she can feel what I once thought of her, and how angry I am with her now, and the contrast must hurt horribly."

"That was about all I could have thought of to say," I admitted. "I do hope it's enough to keep you going, through all of her bad behavior, and I'm sure there's going to be more. I know Raimbaut is planning to speak to her about some of it, but we both know it isn't necessarily going to do any good."

"It's nice to know that someone tries. Both of you try. That does make me feel better, as if I'm at least worth someone's efforts." She slipped my hand from her shoulder to take it in hers, and we walked a long way; like two grieving lovers, to the outside world; like two lonely children, inside ourselves.

"Well, then, should we say the words? We're far from anyone now," I said.

"All right. Giraut?"

"*Ja.*"

"I wish you and I had met some other way entirely."

"*Voill atz deu, con totz de mon cor,* so do I," I said.

Then we spoke the words in unison, addressed to our hypnotic implants. The phrase would put both of us to sleep, and wake up Raimbaut in me, and Laprada in her, all but instantly. In a moment, the beach of western Hedonia would have a different couple—lovers, not friends, by choice and not by necessity, and the hands now touching would close in an embrace, not mere mutual comfort.

As the darkness fell across my eyes, and the beach dimmed, I could feel Raimbaut rising to take over the body, filled with joy and purpose, eagerly, the way a runner breaks from the beach and turns toward home where a shower, a good meal, and someone to share them with, are all waiting.

AFTERWORD:

Foolish Hobgoblins, Containing Multitudes, And True Friends

A mind is of little consistency to a foolish hobgoblin, or so Ralph Waldo Emerson said, once, probably while getting drunk with Walt Whitman, who replied, "Very well, then, I contradict myself. Want to go out back and contain my multitudes?" Ralph didn't understand, and both men left with broken hearts. As the Wizard of Oz, who was neither a wizard, nor of Oz, remarked, hearts will never be popular until they are made unbreakable.

In continuing this series, I discovered that I had been very careless not once but twice in the process of editing for consistency and continuity. There are several irreconcilable differences among my master notes for the series, my article "How to Build a Future," and the two novels previously published, *A Million Open Doors* and *Earth Made of Glass*. So in this book, I've chosen whichever way I happened to like better, and tried to keep better records for the remaining two books in the series (*The Armies of Memory* and *A Far Cry*, coming real soon now). But if you notice that a culture seems to be moving from planet to planet, or the same person lived in two drastically different centuries, or that a date has slipped forward or back a few decades, or anything of the sort, you are indubitably right; it is an inconsistency. Unfortunately, no prizes will be awarded.

Speaking of irreconcilable differences, as I finish this novel, I'm going through the unpleasant process of divorce for the second time in my life. I would first like to say that while I am obviously not good at relationships, I have excellent taste in ex-wives, and the whole process would have been far worse had the other person been anyone other than Kara Dalkey. If you haven't read any of her books, you should run out and buy some, right now. You'll need something to read while I write my next, and I don't have much of a track record for promptness.

And speaking of things for which prizes should be awarded, and aren't: I don't know whether it's an apology, or a thank you note, or one song made out of the utter void, but I owe a deep debt of gratitude to some people who have put up with me while I've fallen apart and come back together again. These are the people who stuck around when I wasn't much fun to be with, and one way or another, got me through a bad hour, or day, or month. I hope, anyway, that as I get things together again, they will feel their patience and tolerance was worth it; they know they have my love and gratitude. Those people are Bonny Block, Adria Brandvold, Joe Devlin, Steve Leon, Jane Berard, Jerry Oltion, Paul Edwards, Robyn Jackson, Terry Schliessman, Lisa Rosling, Steve Decker, Jes Tate, and Bill Yellow Robe. Bless you all for being there, and I'm sorry for all you've had to put up with. I suppose I could have managed without you, but I'd hate to imagine how.